W9-CPD-707

She knew that bigotry existed, but she had never experienced it quite like this before.

Kate couldn't say anything for a moment. She was just too astonished. "Wh—what? Excuse me? What you did you say?"

The other boy with brown hair spoke, "Sorry, miss." He giggled too. "You have to excuse my friend. He's a little drunk."

"How old are you two?"

They didn't look older than eighteen, and had acne breakouts on their cheeks, but she knew better than anyone that looks could be deceiving.

"We're old enough," the rude one said.

Sam returned just as the rude one spoke again and pointed, "Hey look, it's the Jolly Giant Nigger."

Kate shot to her feet so that she was between Sam and them.

A porter was with Sam. "Is there a problem, miss?"

"Yes," she said without facing him. "We'd like to change our seat."

"Of course, Sam asked too. We have another place for you over here, if you both come with me."

Kate moved to leave. The two young men said nothing, which was a good thing. She swore she could feel her blood boiling in her veins. If they said one more thing…

Sam stood aside to let her exit and then she heard the young man. "Goodbye now, Uncle Tom." Giggling. "Enjoy your meal, Uncle Tom, so nice to see you." More giggling. "Dumb nigg—"

He didn't have a chance to finish. Kate snatched the water glass from the table, threw the water at him, slammed the empty glass down hard on the table directly in front of him, and glared into his eyes. "You disgust me! It's people like you who have turned this world into shit!"

She wants to know the truth, but some secrets might be better left alone...

Kate Thayer has a good life as a veterinarian, running the family horse farm—until she uncovers an act of unimaginable treachery by those she trusted most and learns that everything she knew about herself was a lie. Her paternal grandmother, the woman who raised her, is behind a number of devastating secrets Kate is compelled to discover. But the deeper she digs, the more betrayal she finds, changing her life in ways she never could have foreseen.

KUDOS for Shattered Lies

"Shattered Lies is a gripping story of family secrets and their destructive aftermath. The reader is drawn into Kate's courageous choice to face the challenges of racial tension and betrayal." ~ Carole Avila, Author of *Eve's Amulet-Book 1* and *Death House*

"An engrossing tale of deceit, bigotry, and betrayal, Shattered Lies grabs you by the throat and won't let go." ~ Pepper O'Neal, author of the award-winning *Black Ops Chronicles* series.

"Francis writes a poignant and moving tale of bigotry, deceit, and the ultimate betrayal, where the people who you are supposed to be able to trust are the ones who tell the most devastating lies." ~ *Taylor Jones, Reviewer*

"*Shattered Lies* is the story of the cruel, inhuman things man does to man and the tangled webs we weave trying to cover up our heinous behavior. It's a heart-warming and heart-breaking tale of a young woman who discovers that everything she believed about herself, her parents, her very life, is nothing but a lie." ~ *Regan Murphy, Reviewer*

ACKNOWLEDGEMENTS

There are so many people involved in getting a book into a reader's hands. Way too many to thank here, but there are some I wish not to forget:

First and foremost, to Mississippi: From the friendly people and the easy-going relaxed pace; from the gallons of sweet tea and tasty bar-b-que to the AC running on a classic hot, humid Mississippi day; from the Magnolia blossoms and Crepe Myrtles blooming to the wildlife that visit us daily, thank you for sharing your land with us, your home, heart and soul. Ya'll let these born and bred Yankees into your home, heart, and soul and we thank you. God Bless. Until I moved to Mississippi I had no idea where Shattered Lies was to take place, and then, I found you.

Next, I have to thank Lauri Wellington, Acquisitions Editor at Black Opal Books. If not for her, this book you are reading now would not exist. Thank you Lauri and Black Opal Books for taking a chance on me.

To my fellow New Yorkers, I have to say: Nobody does it like New York does. Ah fuhgeddaboudit! I love you! Of course I had to include the Big Apple in a book I wrote.

To Grandmothers everywhere: Thank you for your inspiration! The characters in this book were not based on one person or persons, but as a compilation of people I have encountered in my travels and relocating around this big world. It is important to realize that our parents and grandparents were all persons before we entered their lives. None are perfect. They do the best they can with what they know and have. Sometimes they're wrong. Only God knows what's really in their hearts.

There are so many wonderful people that I met while writing and learning to write. Other authors that inspired me: Leigh Michaels, romance writer extraordinaire. Heather Neff, author of so many novels I adore, and those authors who took time out of their schedule to appear on my blog. I could go on and on, but I won't. Thank you all so much! You know who you are.

And last, but not least, to an author who helped me regain my passion for writing when I thought I had lost it. She was a fantastic story teller. She was an inspiration. She had a passion for writing that was contagious and will be sorely missed by many. Thank you, Ms. Jackie Collins! Thanks for your encouragement when I needed it most! Rest in peace.

Shattered Lies

Lies

S. J. Francis

A Black Opal Books Publication

Black Opal Books

BECAUSE SOME STORIES JUST HAVE TO BE TOLD

GENRE: WOMEN'S FICTION/MAINSTREAM

This is a work of fiction. Names, places, characters and incidents are either the product of the author's imagination or are used fictitiously, and any resemblance to any actual persons, living or dead, businesses, organizations, events or locales is entirely coincidental. All trademarks, service marks, registered trademarks, and registered service marks are the property of their respective owners and are used herein for identification purposes only. The publisher does not have any control over or assume any responsibility for author or third-party websites or their contents.

SHATTERED LIES
Copyright` © 2015 by S. J. Francis
Cover Design by Jennifer Gibson
All cover art copyright © 2015
All Rights Reserved
Print ISBN: 978-1-626943-56-8

First Publication: OCTOBER 2015

All rights reserved under the International and Pan-American Copyright Conventions. No part of this book may be reproduced or transmitted in any form or by any means, electronic or mechanical, including photocopying, recording, or by any information storage and retrieval system, without permission in writing from the publisher.

WARNING: The unauthorized reproduction or distribution of this copyrighted work is illegal. Criminal copyright infringement, including infringement without monetary gain, is investigated by the FBI and is punishable by up to 5 years in federal prison and a fine of $250,000. Anyone pirating our ebooks will be prosecuted to the fullest extent of the law and may be liable for each individual download resulting therefrom.

ABOUT THE PRINT VERSION: If you purchased a print version of this book without a cover, you should be aware that the book is stolen property. It was reported as "unsold and destroyed" to the publisher, and neither the author nor the publisher has received any payment for this "stripped book."

IF YOU FIND AN EBOOK OR PRINT VERSION OF THIS BOOK BEING SOLD OR SHARED ILLEGALLY, PLEASE REPORT IT TO: lpn@blackopalbooks.com

Published by Black Opal Books **http://www.blackopalbooks.com**

DEDICATION

For my spouse, lover, and best friend whose never-ending support and encouragement kept me going even when I thought I couldn't. Thanks for your patience and understanding through all the craziness. For our pet children, Princess, Damon, Cheyenne, Myra, and Pepper. All are rescues. I couldn't imagine my life without them.

To all the budding writers out there: Keep writing! Write the best you can and push it with all you have. Never give up, even when it seems as if you should. You are going to want to quit. Don't. If you want to be a writer, just write!

To those sufferers of polycystic kidney disease, adults and children, and their families, we will one day find a cure. I will help get toward that goal by donating ten percent of this book's sales to the Polycystic Kidney Foundation in order to help this fight. For more information about this insidious disease: http://www.pkdcure.org

Quotes used in *Shattered Lies*:

"If a house becomes divided against itself, that house will not be able to stand." ~ The Bible, Mark 3:25

"I have a dream that one day little Black boys and girls will be holding hands with little White boys and girls." ~ Dr. Martin Luther King Jr.

"Most people don't grow up. Most people age." ~ Maya Angelou.

"Happiness does not depend on what you have or who you are; it solely relies on what you think." ~ Buddha.

Chapter 1

Kate awoke with a start. It was a feeling she couldn't shake and had no idea why. She didn't know it yet, but a tide was turning close to home and, with it, a treacherous page in the book of her life. It was a revelation that she could never see coming. It was an insidious act that no one could ever expect and it would forever change her life as she knew it. The beginning of a rip current was in motion and nothing could divert it or stop it now. Kate didn't know it yet, but she was caught up in the middle of it all without a life jacket of any kind. Would she swim, or would she sink deep into the bowels of it? Only time would tell.

Uncle Lincoln's words of yesterday were still fresh in her mind. Was he accurate in his supposition, or was he merely being paranoid? It didn't matter. Today she was going to do something she'd been meaning to do for ages but never had the time or inclination to do. With hands on her hips, she tried to decide where to start first. From the size of it all, she decided the best thing was just to plunge in and see where it took her. Light filled the attic from incandescent bulbs hanging from the bare ceiling fixtures. There were a few burnt-out light bulbs near two of the four dormer windows. She scurried around the maze of boxes, furniture, and trunks when, out of the corner of her eye, she saw something move. It moved again. She jumped back and then, looking closer, realized it was just a mouse. She sighed and shook her head at her reaction. Four years of veterinary school and she'd reacted so silly. It was obviously more afraid of her than she was of it.

"Go on," she said to it. "I won't hurt you. Just don't do anything and don't let Gran see you."

After shuffling through piles of aged boxes of various sizes for a few hours, Kate found one small box under larger ones. The box was completely worn out and smashed in from the weight of the others. All were covered in dust. Curious, she reached into the small box and pulled out the smashed-in pieces of cardboard. Inside the box were loose paper clippings of nothing significant. The clippings were yellow, worn, and fragile to her touch. She took them out, flipped through them, and found articles about Mississippi and Yazoo County. She placed the pile of clippings to the side. Underneath the pile, there was a little book. It was pale blue in color about the size of a small paperback. The cover was made of cloth and there were tears in the fabric on the corners. The cover was blank with nothing written along the spine.

"Miss Kate." It was Elsa's light voice mixed in with the creaking of the stairs. "Are you up here?"

"Yes, it is I, Elsa, and I'm fine," Kate said, anxious to go through the book she found. Her back was a little bit sore and she could feel the beginning of a headache coming on.

Elsa coughed and let out a sneeze as she came to the top of the stairs and glanced around. Her bright blue eyes were as wide as silver dollars. "Do you need anything?"

"No. I'm fine. Go on now."

Elsa gave it one quick go over and moved to go back downstairs. "You sure? It's a bit spooky up here." The older woman had been employed with them for two years and Kate appreciated her levelheadedness and efficiency, and her quirky sense of humor. "Don't you need some company or anything?" She wasn't from the South and found everything fascinating.

Kate laughed. "No. Go on now."

She just wanted to be alone. She heard the creaking of the stairs as Elsa disappeared out of sight. Kate should have come up here sooner. She had a sense that there was a great deal of history up here, but there were always other things that preoccupied her time. Things happened on a working horse farm. There was always something to do. There were fences to mend, crops to plant and harvest, trees to plant or trim, brush to burn, chores to do, and animals to vaccinate and tend to. She always took charge personally. Life was never boring at Magnolia Lane Farm. It was anything but that.

୧୬୧

Elsa hurried down the stairs and right into her husband. "Whoa! Who put this good looking wall here?"

Sam was a handsome man with caramel skin and eyes to match, though at this moment his eyes weren't so warm and gooey. "What are you doing up there?" he demanded.

"K—Miss Kate went up there. I went to check on her—"

"What do you mean? You let her up there? Why?" he asked.

"I didn't let her up there," Elsa said. "And why not? It's her house, too."

"I told you no one is allowed up there. No one."

"Relax, Sam. I'm sure Miss Katherine didn't mean Kate," Elsa said.

"Damn it, woman! I told you when we first came here that Miss Katherine has rules—"

"Don't you shout at me, Mr. Johnson, or curse at me! I'm not one of your soldiers!" She'd take that kind of attitude from no one and set her hands on her hips.

Sam sighed. "I'm sorry, honey, it's just…you shouldn't have let her up there. Is she still up there?" He glanced up the stairs.

"Yes…you mind telling me what the big deal is, anyway?" she asked.

"Later, help me get her down from there." His eyes pleaded. "Please."

"I beg your pardon. She's not doing anything up there. This is her house, too. You're not going to stand there and tell me she isn't supposed to be up there? Why?"

"Damn it, woman, you can be positively frustrating sometimes."

"Well, you're not exactly my prince charming everyday yourself, but I still love you, anyway."

He sighed. Sometimes there was no arguing with his wife. "I love you, but please help me get her down, now." He headed for the stairs. Up he went and entered the attic.

"Miss Kate? Are you up here?" He didn't see her—just a whole lot of junk was spread out before him. "Miss Kate, where are you?"

"I'm here." Her voice answered from behind. She stood up surrounded by old, wrinkled cardboard boxes stacked waist high.

"Miss Kate, you shouldn't be up here," he said. He hadn't been up here in years not since…it wasn't important anymore. That was a long time ago.

"I'm fine. Don't worry about me," Kate said. She didn't face them. She was focused on the boxes that surrounded her.

He didn't like this at all. "It's not too safe up here. You don't know what you may find."

"Like a mouse?" Elsa said from behind him, using his broad-shouldered body as a shield. Her eyes scanned the attic. "Looks like a place they'd hide in. He's worried you'll get hurt or get asthma."

"She's right, Miss Kate. It's pretty dusty and dirty up here. You should come down now."

"One just doesn't get asthma," Kate replied. "When I'm done. You two go on now."

"Really, Miss Kate," Elsa said. "Let us clean it up a bit and you can come up another day."

"It's fine the way it is. I'll be fine. Go on," she told them.

Sam appreciated his wife's input. Elsa always backed him up, even when he didn't tell her everything at the outset. She was his partner through and through. If only he could be honest with her. Maybe he would soon enough. "Miss Kate, we can't leave you up here on your own. What if you get hurt or something? Your grandmother wouldn't be happy."

"Sam, Elsa, I appreciate your concern, but I've survived life for thirty years on this farm, and in this house. I think I can handle a few hours up here in this attic. Now go on. I insist."

Sam went to open his mouth but shut it. Kate could be just as stubborn as her grandmother. "All right, Miss Kate. I give up. Just don't be too long and be careful. Please."

"I will," she said, moving one cardboard box off another.

When he saw that, he moved to intervene. "Maybe we should stay up here and help you. Those boxes might be heavy."

"Go on. If I need a hand, I'll send for you. Stop being a worrywart, Sam. Both of you scat. I'm too old for a babysitter."

Sam hesitated. He had to get her out of the attic. If Miss Katherine found out, there'd be hell to pay, but he couldn't physically make Kate leave. That left him without any other options.

"Let's go, Sam. She doesn't want our help," Elsa said.

He knew how much Elsa liked Kate, and he also knew she wasn't about to bother her anymore without an explanation from him, and that he couldn't do.

He hesitated. Elsa almost had to drag him down the stairs. Down on the landing, they stopped. "Why did you let her go up there?" Sam asked.

"I didn't allow her to do anything," Elsa said. "You still haven't told me what the big deal is."

"It doesn't matter now." He moved to leave but she caught his wrist.

"It matters to you and if it matters to you, my teddy bear, it matters to me."

"Later. I'll tell you later. I have to go shoe some horses." He kissed her cheek and went down the stairs to the second floor.

୧୬୧୬

Alone again, Kate finally gave the attic a closer look. The place was a mess. This was so unlike her fastidious grandmother. Boxes were strewn everywhere. Trunks lay against one wall and were visibly worn with tattered edges and rusted locks. Old pieces of furniture and antiques were everywhere. Mirrors, large and small leaned against another wall. Some items were covered with grayish sheets while others were open for view. Dust covered everything. The attic was huge! They could hold a dance up here, if need warranted it. Now she knew why no one came up here and why her grandmother kept it locked. It looked as if someone was just trying to discard portions of their life. Or someone had a yard sale when a tornado hit. There was no organization to it at all.

Kate cleared a spot on the large box and eased down, slowly at first, to test its sturdiness. When it held her weight without issue, she sat, placed the small book on her lap, and opened it. The pages were yellow and unevenly cut along the edges. Inside, the handwritten words of a long time ago came to life, revealing some things she didn't know, and raised a great deal of questions she never knew she had, until now. There was hardly anything in it, but what she did read raised feelings she had never expected.

Visiting with Uncle Linc yesterday made her think about how little she knew about her parents and just how little her grandmother discussed them. Her grandmother always spoke of her son, Jax, Kate's father with great regard. That is, when she spoke of him. Her grandmother never mentioned Kate's mother, Olivia, never. Not once. Not even to say she didn't like her daughter-in-law. Kate guessed the two women didn't get along, but she wanted to know more. Maybe, just maybe, there was something in the attic. There certainly looked as if this was the place that could hold the secrets of a city, if need be. Secrets? Why had she thought of that? She had no secrets and neither did her grandmother. Her grandmother was an open book. What you saw was what you got. She bent to no one. Kate admired her. She was one tough independent lady, way ahead of her time.

Kate never gave it any thought before why her grandmother kept the keys in her bedroom instead of downstairs in the kitchen with the other farm keys. Kate had retrieved the key ring from her grandmother's dresser draw. Her grandmother had a certain way of doing things and sometimes there was no rhyme or reason to it. It was the way Katherine Thayer wanted it, plain and simple.

After reading, Kate closed the small book, rested her hand on it, and shut her eyes. After a moment, she placed her other hand on the book, picked it up, brought it up to her chest, and held it there, as if to absorb the feelings inside. She had to know what it all meant and went to the one person she knew would know more than anyone, to the one person she could trust. Without a beat, she stood up and rushed down the stairs and to her grandmother's room. With a cursory glance out the hall window on her way downstairs, she noticed that the yellow pickup was back. Grandmother and Carol obviously returned from their trip to do the weekly shopping. Outside the door, Kate stopped, not exactly sure how to approach this delicate situation before her. She had never questioned her grandmother's actions before, but then she never had any reason to, did she? Now, she wondered, about a great many things.

After a long moment she lost track of, she knocked. She heard her grandmother's voice tell her to come in. After taking a deep slow breath, Kate grasped the brass knob and entered.

There she was, her usually larger than life self, but not as large as Kate thought of her just hours before. Katherine was seated at her antique roll-top desk with Carol seated next to her. The sun filled the room, but right now things didn't seem as bright to Kate as they usually were inside here.

"Grandmother, I'd like to speak with you," she began as she took a step forward.

"Of course, darling. Sit down," Katherine said. "You may go, Carol. Thank you."

Carol stood up and headed for the door, giving Kate a smile on the way out. Her mouth revealed a set of perfect white teeth.

Neatly cropped black hair framed her pecan-colored skin. She had wide brown eyes that were full of life.

Kate gave a perfunctory smile in return. Carol pointed to the front of Kate's shirt and waved at it, then went to the oak door and closed it behind her.

Kate looked down and brushed the light blue oxford shirt off, not realizing she had some dust on her, probably all over her. Great. So be it. Now was no time to clean up and no time to worry about it.

"I was just going over the replies for the party," Katherine boasted, not looking up from her task. "We even received some checks for donations in advance. I think we will do extremely well this year."

"I'm glad." However, that was the farthest thing from her mind right now. "Grandmother, I need to ask you something," Kate said, taking another foot forward, one at a time, until she was near her. "Why don't you just let Tessa do that? Isn't that why you have a secretary to begin with, to help you with all your charity work?" Kate sat down in the Queen Anne chair that Carol had vacated next to the matching desk.

"Because, my darling Kate, when it comes to the handling of money, there are only two persons I trust. That is you and I, and no one else. We agreed. You run the farm. I handle any finances." Katherine extended her hand to rest on Kate's. "You're the only one I trust implicitly."

"Thanks, Gran. I trust you too," Kate said. She appreciated that her grandmother truly trusted no one else.

"Darling." Katherine released her. Her right eyebrow rose momentarily. "Whatever have you been doing? You're covered in dust?" Her grandmother brushed her hands together to the side of the desk, discarding any dust into the wastebasket below.

"Cleaning up. Nothing special," Kate said. "I need to speak with you."

Katherine returned to flip through the stack of RSVP cards and checks on her desk. Her elderly fingers were quite nimble in their task. "Now go ahead, darling. I'm listening."

"It's important."

Katherine set down the paperwork and turned to face her. Her hand immediately went to Kate's forehead. "Darling, are you ill? You don't feel warm."

Kate caught her hand as her grandmother lowered it. "No, I'm not ill. Please stop fussing." At least not with a cold. "Do you know anything about this?" Kate placed the worn blue journal onto the desk before them, in front of her grandmother.

Her grandmother's perfectly trimmed eyebrows arched. "One of your recent acquisitions from the library, no doubt."

"No, Grandmother. It isn't."

Katherine turned away. "Then I really don't know, darling."

"Grandmother, why aren't there any photos of my mother in the house?" Kate asked, curiosity nipping at the bud.

"I told you, she was camera shy," Katherine said.

"This is my mother's journal," Kate said and looked for a reaction.

"Is it? I had no idea."

Katherine didn't look at her, which puzzled Kate immediately. Whenever they spoke, her grandmother always gave her utmost attention.

"Where ever did you find it?" Katherine asked.

"In the attic," Kate said.

Katherine's eyes widened then she furrowed her eyebrows. Kate noticed her grandmother's lower lip quiver or was it just her imagination?

"The attic?" Katherine asked. "What were you doing up there, darling?"

"I just felt like it. What difference does it make?"

"I don't want anyone in the attic." Katherine was abrupt. "It's dangerous. You could have been hurt."

Kate ignored her concern. She wanted answers. "Yes, she wrote this apparently just after she married my father."

"Did she now? Well, I wouldn't worry about it. There's nothing worth reading in there. You can burn it," Katherine said.

"It belonged to my mother. Why would I want to burn it?"

Katherine faced her. Her gaze was steady and unmoving. "Your mother had very little to say when alive. I doubt there is anything of value in there."

Kate shot to her feet. "How dare you, Gran?" Katherine had never mentioned Kate's mother, ever, and to hear such coldness in the words about her astonished her. "She did say that you hated her. Why did you hate her?"

Katherine raised her hand. "Now calm down, darling. That is an exaggeration."

"No, it isn't. She said you hated her. You couldn't stand her.

That you actually tried to split her and my father up—more than once, as did her parents."

Without warning, Katherine seized the journal and threw it into the nearby trashcan. "There is nothing in there for you to worry about. And that is where it belongs."

Kate reached for it unsuccessfully. "Grandmother—"

"I had nothing against your mother—personally. I just think she wasn't suited for my son, your father. Now leave it be." Katherine turned away and focused back on the papers. "I'd like to get these checks in order before the party tonight."

Kate remained for a moment but knew that once her grandmother ended a conversation it would remain that way. She sighed, walked over to the small brass trashcan, and bent down to retrieve the journal.

"Leave it," her grandmother ordered.

It was the first time Kate ever heard that tone in her voice. "It's my mother's." She took it out. "I'd like to keep it."

"I'd rather you didn't," Katherine said.

"Why?" Kate asked and met her unwavering gaze.

"There's nothing important in it. Nothing of value. Why keep such a thing?"

"I want to," Kate said. She noticed the veins in her grandmother's neck twinge and the edges of her mouth stiffen. "It's mine. I want it," Kate said.

"Fine, darling, if it'll make you happy. I see no reason for sentimentality."

Katherine turned back to the work at hand. Kate studied her. Her grandmother said nothing, which was puzzling. No lecture, nothing.

A very anxious knocking on the door interrupted them and it opened. Carol rushed in and was clearly out of breath, "Good afternoon—Miss Kate—Miss Katherine. Forgive me."

"Goodness, Carol," Katherine said. "Calm down, girl. What is it?"

"Out—at the barn. It's Mr. Carl. He—says that Delta is—about ready to foal. He's been calling you and calling you for the last ten minutes. He said it can happen anytime soon."

Katherine stood up. "Tell Carl we'll be right there."

Kate forgot she had shut off her cell phone while with Uncle Linc yesterday and never turned it back on.

"Will do, Miss Katherine. I laid out that nice blue dress you wanted for tonight, Miss Kate," Carol said as she moved toward the door. "It is sure to be a fine shindig."

"Yes, it will. Thank you, Carol," Kate said.

စာၵၵၢ

Kate headed downstairs and out the door with her grandmother leading the way. All Kate could hear on the way down was the sound of their shoes on the wooden floor and steps.

Seventy years old and her grandmother never slowed down. When she had a job to do, the older woman just did it—no complaints, nothing. The short walk would do Kate good, even if she did rush it. Besides, it looked as if the three pick-ups were in use at the time.

They arrived at the brick barn in five minutes. Carl was on his knees with Delta Darling, one of their prized Andalusian mares. Delta Darling was ten years old. Kate had raised the female from a foal. She was as beautiful as freshly fallen snow. The mare was already on her side. She was breathing rapidly but appeared fine otherwise.

"Where have you been, Miss Kate? She's about ready," Carl said. "I was worried about you. Why didn't you answer your phone?" He stopped when he saw Katherine alongside her.

"Sorry, Carl. I had it off." Not that she owed him an explanation but he deserved one. After all, he'd been with her family forever.

Kate took a canvas smock from the shelf inside the door, unfolded it, and put it on. She also took a pair of thick black rubber gloves off the shelf and put them on. She went to her knees and patted the mare on the neck. "Easy, girl." She began to speak soothingly "We're here. You're not alone. We'll get you through this just like before. Easy, girl."

The horse neighed at her, as if acknowledging her presence.

Katherine echoed Kate's words as she entered the stall, went down to her knees, and took the mare's head on her lap. "Easy girl. No need to worry. Easy. We're here like always."

Her glamorous grandmother was quite out of her element, dressed simply in faded blue jeans, an untucked long-sleeved shirt, and her long hair flowing around her shoulders, but it didn't faze her. Nothing fazed the older woman. Her naturally attractive grandmother could fit in anywhere without any effort at all.

Kate should have eaten something more substantial this morning. After a hurried shower in her private bath, she merely rushed downstairs for a quick breakfast snack—a glass of orange juice and a yogurt. The orange juice went down quickly, but when she tried to eat the yogurt, she couldn't. She just wasn't very hungry. Come to think of it, she hadn't been very hungry in a long time and especially since yesterday. She did manage to swallow a couple of finger sandwiches at lunch yesterday, but that was it. She'd have to try and eat more tonight.

Delta handled things gracefully. The birth was uneventful. The mare grunted during the process trying to expel her young as soon as possible. It took a little over fifteen minutes for the entire process to occur. The mare gave birth to a solid black foal, black as the stud, Standing Tall, its father. Already an experienced mother, Delta started licking her newborn, cleaning it of the afterbirth.

While Katherine examined the foal for any abnormalities, Kate noticed something more. It was exactly six minutes later when it happened.

"My God, Gran, its twins. She's having twins." There was another foal on the way out, this time a smaller white foal. Kate grinned as the small head and feet exited first, very slowly. Kate pulled the translucent placenta and afterbirth away from the foal as it made its way all the way out and onto the ground next to its mother and Kate. Delta lifted her head, got up on her side, and gave her attention to her new babies.

Kate took a stethoscope out of her black bag that was on the shelf. She listened to the mare's heartbeat. "Good girl. You're doing fine. Good girl. No worries." She checked on the each foal. She removed the stethoscope from her ears and nuzzled each one and their mother behind their ears.

Carl stood up. "I'll be damned," he said. "Twins. Now isn't that something? Are they all right? How's our girl?" Carl was a lanky White man. The only White man they employed. He had been with the plantation thirty years and knew everything there was to know about horses. Rumors had it that if he didn't know it, then that fact didn't exist yet. He had started work at Magnolia Lane Farm right after college just like his father before him had done. Kate appreciated his wisdom and experience.

"They're fine, Carl," she said. "All three girls are fine." She released a breath in relief. No matter how many times she witnessed their animals giving birth, the whole thing still amazed her.

She heard Carl release his breath. "I knew it'd be twins. I just knew it. I wanted to check, but your grandmother said no. Every time we check first, we lose one, or both, or all of them. When we don't, they all make it. Rare, huh, Miss Kate. Very rare."

"Odds are about 1 in 500,000 for them both to be born alive," Kate said. "Now we have to keep them that way."

"They'll be fine, Miss Kate. We'll see to it, you and me. It's nice to have you around, especially at times like these." He leaned against the stall fence. "Now we just let mama do her job and help her along."

"They're beautiful, Gran. Look," Kate said, leaning back to admire them. She turned around, but her grandmother was gone. "Where did my grandmother go?"

"Don't know. Didn't see her. I was watching the foals. Good looking animals they are too," Carl said. "Maybe she went to get ready for that fancy party of hers. You better get freshened up too. You know that Miss Katherine expects things on time."

"I should. Hate to leave these girls though," she said.

He leaned his long arms along the top of the stall fence. "You know, Miss Kate, you can tell me to mind my own business but—well I have to ask?"

"Go ahead, Carl. Ask away." She knew he would anyway.

"You don't seem much for these fancy dress parties any more than I am. Why do you go?" he asked.

"Why do you think I do?"

"Honestly? For your grandmother, Miss Katherine. I figure she'd do the same for you. You're both alike in that way. You're a lot like your grandmother, you know."

She appreciated the compliment, but...

"Me? No way, Carl. I'm nothing like her. She can do anything. She'd ride a rogue bull if she had to. She'd break a horse if necessary."

"So would you. You've proved that," he told her.

"You're being too kind and you're making me blush, so I am getting out of here." She nuzzled the two babies and patted the mare on the head. "I'll be back, girls." She got to her feet. "Take care of them for me, Carl. Call me if anything changes. Good night."

"No problem, Miss Kate. Good night."

She looked back at the small family of three. *Now we have something to celebrate aside from the regular occasion.* She couldn't help but admire the new foals. They were an awesome sight. No matter how many times she had witnessed the miracle of birth among their horses and cattle, she never tired of it.

∾∾∾

Back inside her bedroom suite, a fury was building up within Katherine. She didn't want to lose her temper in front of Kate. Now that she was alone, she could let loose. She threw the stack of papers and checks she had so meticulously put in order across the room. She snapped out of her chair so quickly that her chair slammed back onto the wooden floor.

Carol opened the door just as the chair slammed.

"Find, Sam! Get him here now!" Katherine ordered.

Carol knew better than to ask twice, even though today was his "official" day off. "Yes, ma'am," was all she said and scurried out the door, closing it gently behind.

Sam never really had a day off, when there was something he had to do.

"I'll kill him," Katherine growled. "I swear I will. Damn him! Damn them all!"

Chapter 2

Sam received the call on his cell and went up to the big house. He wasn't pleased at being beckoned back to the house on his evening off. His back was sore along with his leg. He hoped nothing was wrong. Sometimes, Miss Katherine could get quite a bit emotional and high-strung. Most of the time he could calm her down, but not always. The woman was so damn pig-headed at times. But she was his employer and he put up with it. Not to mention, he had taken an oath years before to do just that.

He hoped it wasn't about Kate being in the attic. There'd be hell to pay if she found that out. That was for sure.

He entered the front door and Carol greeted him.

"What's going on?" he asked.

"I don't know, but she is pissed. I haven't seen her so angry in a long, long time."

"Any idea what set her off?"

"Uh-uh. Can't be good, though. Her room looked like a torna-do blew in."

"Sam," Katherine stormed down the stairs, brushed past him and swung open the set of parlor doors closest to the staircase.

Sam answered the summons by following and closing the doors behind him.

"Problem, Miss Katherine? I came as soon as Carol called me."

Without a beat, she swung out at him with her hand and he fell back onto the floor onto his back. Hard.

She was over him. "You stay where you are or I'll knock you down again!"

He brought a hand to his cheek and saw blood, not a lot, but enough to tell him that it was not just her hand that hit him. He glanced at her hand, but didn't see anything, but her clenched fist.

He held up a hand to calm her. "Miss Katherine. What is wrong? What was that for?"

"As if you didn't know," she snapped.

"I don't know. I swear—"

"You're a bold-faced liar."

"Miss Katherine, I really don't know—" Sam said. He'd never seen her lose control.

"Are you going to sit there on your black ass and tell me that you didn't know Kate was in the attic today?" Katherine declared.

"Miss Katherine, Kate wanted to go up there. I tried to get her out as soon as I knew—"

"Well, you didn't try hard enough because she found a journal her mother kept."

"That's impossible. Livie never kept a journal—"

"Not impossible. I saw it." She began to pace the room, which wasn't a good sign for him. "Did you or did you not swear an oath to me? Answer me! To your parents?"

"Y—yes, I did. And I have kept it. I haven't said anything," he said. He wanted to move, but thought better of it, for now.

"And your wife?"

He shook his head. "Neither has Elsa. I swear it. She doesn't even know." He slid on his butt to sit up straight. "What was in the journal?"

Katherine was back over him again. "Does it really matter?"

"No," Sam said. "I guess not."

"Get up on your feet!" she ordered. "You swore to me not to say a word and you swore to your parents!"

He held up his hands. "I swear. I didn't."

"Your mother swore, too."

"She didn't say a word." Sam protested. "You know she didn't."

"How can you be so sure?"

"Did Kate say she knew anything? Did she? Maybe this journal she found doesn't have anything in it. Livie never liked to write."

Her green eyes glared at him and he saw daggers. "Oh, it has something in it. It just better not have in it what I think it might."

"Even if it does, don't you think it is time she knew? Maybe it's time she knew the truth. We can't keep the secret forever. One day soon she's bound to find out—"

Katherine spun on her heel and struck him again. This time he caught her hand and tried to stop her from catching his face. She was crazed. She wouldn't be deterred, began pounding on him, and kicked him in the groin. In reflex, he fell to the floor and she stepped back.

Just then, the door opened and Kate entered with Carol on her heels. "Grandmother, I want to ask—" She stopped when she saw Sam on his knees holding his stomach. She ran to him. "What the hell?"

Sam brushed her aside.

"Leave him," Katherine ordered.

"He's hurt," Kate said. "His leg—"

"Leave him!" Katherine repeated.

"Let me help you," Kate said, giving him a hand to get up.

Sam rejected her assistance. He didn't want her involved in this. Not now. "No, Miss Kate. I'm fine."

Katherine rushed to her and snatched her away from him. "Damn it, Katherine Thayer, I said leave him!" She turned to Carol. "Get him out of here! Now!"

Carol went to his side. Sam leaned on her for stability as he slowly came to his feet. "It's all right, Miss Kate." He said, waving Kate away. "I'm fine. I fell down is all," he told her as he led Carol to the door.

"Damn Black bastard! I should have killed him!" Katherine began wringing her hands across her chest as she paced. "I should have killed them all."

Kate stared, terrified of what had just occurred. Terrified of what she was hearing. Cautiously, she took a few steps toward her. "Gran—are you all right? What happened to Sam?"

Katherine paced right up to her. "Of course, darling. I'm fine." Her entire demeanor had changed in a moment right before Kate's eyes. Katherine reached out a hand and touched Kate's cheek then moved toward the window. "Nothing happened. You heard Sam. He fell. It was probably that stupid leg of his. He should have let them cut the damn thing off and put on a fake one. At least he'd have one that worked correctly."

"Grandmother! That was a horrible thing to say." Who was this woman before her? "He was hurt in Afghanistan and you know it."

"Does it matter? It's the truth, isn't it? That leg of his is useless. Why I allowed you to hire him is beyond me?"

"You gave me the farm to run. He needed a job when he retired from the Army. We needed a blacksmith. You still haven't told me what happened here—"

Katherine's eyes darkened. "Forget it! Let it be!"

Now Kate was even more concerned. "Gran, are you sure you're all right?"

"I said I was fine," she snapped. She took a deep breath. "I'm fine. You should go get ready for dinner."

"But what happened to Sam?"

Katherine turned away and stared out the large picture window. "It's nothing for you to be concerned with."

"He was on his knees, Gran—"

Katherine spun around and her eyes were ablaze. "I said—" Kate saw her grandmother take a breath and her voice softened. "It is nothing for you to be concerned with. Go get ready for dinner, darling. Please. We have the party tonight."

Kate stared at her. She didn't recognize this woman before her. Her normally white skin was red and her green eyes seemed almost red, which wasn't possible. Her grandmother was obviously upset. Perhaps too upset to talk about it right now. Kate would have to let it go for now, but not totally. "All right, Grandmother. I'll get ready for dinner."

She hesitated a moment for a reaction, but there was none. What on earth had just happened? Sam had been with her family since before Kate had been born. He had been born on the farm's grounds just like she had been. He was like family to her. She knew him for her entire life. What on earth could have happened here tonight?

જાજાજી

Meanwhile, Carol led Sam into the kitchen. His hand rested on her shoulder. "I'm all right," he said. "Stop fussing at me, Carol. I'm fine."

"What happened?" she asked.

"Nothing. I fell. That's all," he said. He wasn't about to discuss personal matters with an employee, no matter how long they worked here. "My leg's been hurting on and off."

"Miss Katherine was awful angry with you. I saw it," Carol said. "Maybe you should see a doctor. I could call Doctor Lincoln—"

"Nothing happened and you saw nothing. Nothing, Carol. You understand?" he said. "I'm going home. Keep an eye on Miss Kate for me."

She nodded.

≈≈≈

Dinner was quiet that night. Katherine wasn't her usual talkative self. She barely touched her meal, even though it was her favorite. Every Saturday night Carol prepared southern fried chicken from scratch—the best southern fried chicken in the entire South. Along with the meat, she served fried okra, mashed potatoes, brown gravy, a large green salad, and biscuits. It wasn't exactly the healthiest meal around, but it certainly was tasty. More so, it was tradition.

Kate pushed aside the plate. "Grandmother, do you want to talk about what happened with Sam?"

"No. I already did," Katherine said and took a sip a wine. "You need to eat something. You've barely touched your food."

"Neither have you," Kate pointed out. "One does not live by red wine alone. That is your third glass."

Katherine set down her wine glass and glared at Kate. "Carol, you may clear the table."

Carol was waiting by the doorway and, at her order, moved in and cleared the table, putting their dishes of uneaten food onto a tray.

"Thank you, Carol," Kate told her when the small woman removed her plate. "Would you leave us alone?"

Carol nodded and left.

"That was unnecessary," Katherine said. She reached out for the crystal wine decanter, filled her glass to the top, and sipped.

"I felt it was." Kate got up, moved down to the other end of the long table, and sat next to her grandmother. "What is it? What happened? I'd like to know."

Katherine faced her. "Kate, you mean the world to me. I love you, darling, but I am not in the habit of repeating myself over and over to anyone. Nothing happened. Stop fussing about it."

"I know that, Gran, but I saw—"

Katherine shot to her feet. Her wine glass flew out of her hand and across the room against the wall, fell to the hardwood floor, and shattered. "Enough! I will not be cross examined in my house!"

"I'm sorry, Grandmother. I'm just concerned. You are obviously very upset," Kate said.

Carol rushed in.

"Get out!" Katherine yelled and Carol disappeared as quickly as she had entered.

"I am just fine, darling," Katherine said and stormed out of the dining room before Kate could say anything more.

If she wanted to know anything, Kate would have to try another tactic altogether, one that didn't involve her grandmother, but it would have to wait.

৩৩৩

After showering and changing into the blue evening gown Carol laid out for her, Kate made her way downstairs. She placed her hand on the cool wooden banister, began her descent, and stopped at the bottom. The house was full of people tonight for the charity event of the year in Thayersville and in Yazoo County—the event that her grandmother prepared for all year long.

The chatter amongst them and the clinking of glasses, plates, cups, and flatware filled the air. As usual for people down South attending fine gatherings, the guests wore their best attire. Her grandmother's list had sent out invitations to one hundred people—friends, friends of friends, and influential persons of Mississippi—and it appeared as if every one of them showed up in addition to a few more. That should make her grandmother immensely pleased. The more the merrier and the more donations they would receive. The people of Mississippi, especially in smaller towns such as Thayersville, were a generous lot and watched out for each other, and especially for their neighbors.

After her grandmother's sudden erratic behavior with Sam and finding her mother's diary, Kate wasn't in the mood to be present longer than necessary to be the cordial hostess her grandmother expected. Plus, no matter how many times she played hostess at one of her grandmother's charity fundraisers or social events, she could never get used to making small talk. Of course, she was also concerned about the foals. Twins being born was a dangerous event for both the mother and her foals. As a veterinarian, she knew that better than anyone did. The first two weeks were the most dangerous and telling time—if they all survived that period, odds were they'd be fine. Two weeks was a long time.

It didn't take long for her to find her grandmother in the crowd of guests. Katherine had a way of being at the center of attention. It had a natural way of centering about her. Her grandmother was the typical Southern belle when it came to entertaining. She epitomized Southern hospitality, beauty, and a flirtatious, yet chaste demeanor.

"Kate is looking beautiful, tonight," Pookie Carter commented to Katherine. Pookie was married to the mayor of Hattieville, a nearby town. She was also one of Katherine's oldest friends.

"Yes, she is, as always," Katherine replied. She couldn't deny the pride she had for her granddaughter.

"It is so terrible what she had to endure—losing her parents at such a young age, and then her husband. I don't know how she does it."

"She does it because she has to, just as we all do," Katherine said.

"But for her and Adam to have such a short time together," Pookie said and shook her head. "Such a pity."

"Yes, but she is doing fine now," Katherine said, determined to change the subject. The past was the past and belonged where it was.

"Of course, she is. She is a strong woman, like her grandmother. She comes from fine stock, now, doesn't she?" Pookie said with half a grin.

"Yes, she does. I hate to break this up, Pookie, but I have to see to the others—"

"And you never told her the truth about her parents? Ever?" Pookie said over the rim of the champagne glass she slowly sipped from.

Katherine reached out a hand and placed it on Pookie's shoulder. "Now, Pookie, you know that is a closed subject." She could always rely on Pookie to say something to set her on edge.

"One day soon she is sure to ask. She'll want to know—"

"And I will deal with it then," Katherine said. "Until that time, lips are sealed, are they not?"

"Oh, darling, relax." Pookie patted her shoulder. "I won't say anything, but that kind of thing you can't keep quiet forever. You have to know that."

"Pookie." Katherine bit her tongue. "Enjoy the party."

Pookie held up a glass of champagne and waved her on. "Oh go on, honey, you know I will."

With that, Katherine moved on to her other guests, playing the perfect hostess, as always. She didn't realize her left hand was clenched until she walked away from Pookie. How dare the other woman bring up the past? How dare she? First, the attic and the journal, then Sam, and now Pookie.

❦❦❦

From the other side of the room, Kate watched her. She couldn't help but admire her grandmother. In fact, there was no other person in the world she respected more. Her grandmother was a loving woman. She was intelligent, sharp, and a force only matched by the strongest tornado. People who crossed Katherine Thayer only did it once. Kate wished she could be just a little bit more like her. Strange how Elsa wasn't working tonight? She always assisted Carol during the parties. Strange that her grandmother, a stickler for details, didn't say anything about it either. She hoped Sam was all right.

"How are you tonight, dear lady?" Lincoln Castle said from behind her. She couldn't miss that slow, deep melodious voice. He always drew out his words, more so than most Southerners did.

She faced him with a grin. "I'm fine. And you? Enjoying the party?"

He grinned. His eyes remained across the room. "As always. Your grandmother looks extremely beautiful tonight."

"Just tonight? Don't let her hear you say that," she scolded. She had to agree. Tonight, her grandmother was in her element. The older woman was stunning. As usual for her appearance, she tied her long, thick red locks up in a bun and secured it behind her head. The makeup she wore only enhanced her natural features. Dressed in a smooth fitting calf-length gown in her favorite color of red, her grandmother attracted the eye of many male guests. And why not? Her grandmother was poised, well-spoken and most of all, quite sure of herself. No wonder men of all ages found her grandmother irresistible. She wondered if her grandmother knew what power she wielded over the opposite sex.

He laughed. "True. How are you feeling tonight?"

"I'm fine. Really. Don't fuss."

"Dinah says you didn't stop by to make that appointment," he said.

"I will. I will. I had a headache. Tired," she said and fervently hoped he believed her. She knew it was a reluctant promise she made. Nevertheless, she also knew that she would keep it, eventually.

"Headache?" There was no doubting the concern in his voice or in those warm patient brown eyes—the eyes that possessed years of wisdom.

"And tired. I will make the appointment. I promise," she said. "No fussing now, Uncle Linc."

"I'll take you at your word, for now, but your grandmother will want to know if something is wrong—"

She cut him off. "But we don't know, and you promised not to say anything until we did."

He sighed and bit his lower lip. "I did and I won't, but she worries about you."

She placed a hand on his elbow. "Which is why we're not saying anything until I'm absolutely sure or not."

He nodded. "All right, Kate. Your secret is safe with me. But there'll be hell to pay when she finds out we said nothing to her."

"I'll deal with her then. I better go mingle. Enjoy yourself, Uncle Linc." She leaned over and kissed him gently on the cheek.

She made the necessary rounds, greeting guests and ensuring everyone was enjoying themselves and no one was alone or without something to eat or drink. After exchanging small talk with the bank president and his wife and other local luminaries asking how she was and hearing how well she looked, she needed a breather and stood off to the side near the stone fireplace, scanning the parlor. There was her grandmother in the middle of it all.

"Hello, beautiful."

Kate recognized right away the booming voice that came from behind. It was the only accent that was clearly out of place, and quite noticeably, too.

She turned to find her handsome father-in-law beaming at her. His right hand was rubbing his chin. "My, my, you do look more beautiful each time I see you, Kate. My son was a very lucky man."

He was a lanky man with neatly trimmed gray black hair. He kissed her on the cheek.

"Thank you, Perry. I like to think I was the lucky one. Where's Abigail?"

"I don't know. Lost her the minute we walked in the door," he teased. "Left me surrounded by all these Johnny Rebels and I don't know what to do."

"Don't worry, I'll protect you," she kidded back.

Her father-in-law was a jokester. He was always in a good mood. In fact, the only time she ever noted he wasn't was when he lost his son. Then his normally cheerful, ocean blue eyes were as dark as night.

"You guys didn't have to come way down here from Philadelphia for this," Kate said. "My grandmother would have understood."

"Nonsense. You're still our daughter-in-law. We wouldn't miss getting a chance to see you. Besides—" He leaned in closer. "Your grandmother's invite strongly suggested we'd come or she'd out me as a Yankee next visit."

She chuckled and it was a great relief. "Something tells me, everyone knows already."

"Shucks." He snapped his lean fingers. "You mean everyone here knows? Must be the East Coast accent, huh?"

She nodded. "How long will you be down here?"

"Just tonight."

"Gran will be disappointed. With all the room we have in this big house, you're always welcome."

"Our regrets, but I have to be in Little Rock tomorrow evening for a conference, and then out to California," he said, puffing out his chest in mockery. "I'm the guest speaker."

"I'm impressed. Well done, Doctor Logan. She'll still be disappointed, though," Kate said.

"Don't worry. We already cleared it with her. She understands. Some of us still work for a living," he said. "You know…when my son said he was coming down south to do his graduate work, I was strongly against it. What's wrong with our Ivy League schools up North, I asked him. Of course, his mama being a Southern girl herself backed him up. Then I met you and I was so glad he did." He took her hands into his and examined her, pursing his lips. "You do look a bit pale, or is it the lighting? How are you feeling?"

"I'm fine, Dad. No worries, please."

Then Abigail entered the scene and Kate was grateful for it.

"Whatever are you going on about, Perry?" Abigail said to him. "Hello, Kate, is this Yankee Oak tree bothering you?" She stepped on her tiptoes and gave her husband a kiss on the cheek.

She grasped Kate's hand. Kate admired the deep love they had and showed each other without shame. Obviously, that was where her husband received it. He was never embarrassed to kiss her openly either.

"She looks a bit pale to me. What do you think, Abigail?" he said.

Abigail did a quick once over. "She looks fine. Stop playing doctor." She stepped near her and greeted Kate with a kiss on each cheek and a tight hug. She faced her husband. "Why don't you run along and mingle with the men and let me spend some quality time with our daughter-in-law?"

"All right, honey." He held up his hands in surrender. "I know when I'm not wanted and outnumbered. I'm going to get something to eat, if that is all right with you," he said to his wife and winked at Kate. "Go on. Go do some girl talk. I'll just be around here—all alone with these Rebels. Don't worry about me any. And I'm not playing doctor. I happen to be a very good cardiologist, the top in the country."

He backed up into a couple he recognized and they took him into their group.

"I can't believe I've been married to that man for thirty-six years. He can be so irritating sometimes, but I still love that Yankee," Abigail said. "I wish you and Adam had that long together."

"Me, too," Kate said and tried not to think about past events. She agreed with her grandmother about the past. It belonged right where it was, back there.

Abigail placed her arm around Kate's waist. "Oh, honey," she said. "I didn't mean to upset you."

She wore an off the shoulder ivory dress with frills at the top. With dark wavy brown hair that cascaded down about her shoulders and light brown and wide eyes, she was another attractive woman who age barely touched.

"You didn't. Adam and I were happy during the time we had. I'm grateful for that."

"Of course you are. I'm grateful to you for making him happy. He was always such a serious boy, all work and no play. That is until you stole his heart. He was always smiling. Work was no longer his whole life. He relaxed more, became more like his father."

"He made me smile too, a lot."

They worked their way through some groups of guests acknowledging each other, exchanging pleasantries to make their way to the back door and out into the hall.

Abigail's hands met hers. "Now, Kate, tell me the truth. How are you feeling? You look well. I'm so glad."

"I'm doing fine, Abigail, Mom. Thank you for saying so."

"Well, you are a beautiful young woman. You stole my son's heart—hook, line, and sinker. Of course, we all know, it wasn't just your beauty that besotted him. He always said he wouldn't marry a girl unless she was smarter than he was. And then he found you. He said you were way too smart for him."

"Thank you, Mom. You always know what to say, don't you?"

"I try." Abigail took Kate's arm in hers.

"My grandmother would say it isn't that difficult to outsmart a man," Kate said. "They're all so gullible."

"Amen." Abigail laughed. "True, quite true. So where is the grand madam tonight?"

"She's about." Kate indicated across the room with a nudge of her head.

"She does know how to give a party," Abigail said. "Let's go outside and get some air, shall we? It is a bit stuffy in here. Too many..." She lowered her voice to a whisper. "Rebels."

It was a private joke. Abigail, as all the inhabitants present at the house tonight minus her husband were all die-hard, born and bred Southerners from way back when. All were proud descendants of the men and women that stood up to the attack from the Northern aggression, or the Civil War years before.

Kate was grateful for the other woman's strength and her moments of levity. Her grandmother was always so serious, almost distant, though, Kate never doubted her love. It always seemed as if her grandmother was holding something back from her. They exited through the set of French doors from the hall. They were open to let in the cool evening air. There was a cool front passing through from Canada, quite abnormal for this time of year. Early May was often the start to the long hot summer. Her grandmother preferred the fresh air to the artificial. So did Kate.

They stopped at the end of the stone patio. The smell of blossoming roses and trees revealing their greenery filled the night air. She loved the aroma of all things beautiful. Soon the scent of magnolia and crape myrtle blossoms would join the scene. She couldn't forget the words Uncle Linc had said to her just the day before. She hadn't fully comprehended all that he said for, as soon as he had said it, her mind began to wander. She found it often did that as of late. She hadn't really had any problems to think of, just some dull abdominal pains that came and went—for months at a time now. The air was still and she was grateful for the respite of spring just before the heat of summer soon to come.

"I miss him, too, Kate," Abigail remarked, her gentle words cutting through the darkness.

A new moon began tonight and if not for the outside lights, it was dark outside.

Kate did miss Adam, but she couldn't tell her mother-in-law that, for once, he was not on her mind. Other thoughts took their place—such as what had Sam done to have angered her grandmother so much this evening. She wouldn't obsess over it, but it tugged at her. She gripped her mother-in-law's arm. "I'm fine, Abigail. Don't worry about me."

Abigail stared at her under the patio strobes. "I see that. I'm glad. You're too young to sit up in your room and give up. Adam wouldn't want that. Neither would I. I love you. "

Kate's heart skipped a beat. "Thank you. I love you, too."

"Besides," Abigail said. "I know Katherine wouldn't let you do anything slightly foolish. I always admired your grandmother. She has more guts than most men in this town have sense."

Kate couldn't help but laugh. "Abigail, you're terrible."

"I know. Isn't it wonderful, though?" Abigail grasped Kate's arm. "Let's go inside. I need to pay my respects to the grand madam of this big house and get something to drink. I'm simply dying of thirst."

ԑ৩৩

Once back inside, Abigail released Kate and moved through the crowd of guests to see Katherine. Katherine heaved a sigh of relief. She didn't mind parties. After all, they centered on her. It was the idle chatter that bored her. Katherine excused herself and moved to meet Abigail, another of her dearest and oldest friends.

"Abigail, darling, so glad you came by," Katherine said, as she planted a gentle kiss on each of her guest's cheek. "How are you?"

"Fine, sweetie." Abigail returned the kiss to Katherine's cheeks in turn. "I wouldn't miss it for the world. After all, I hear you have a reason to celebrate tonight. Twin foals." She brought a hand up to her chest. "I am impressed. You're the only one I know to see a mare safely through such a birth, and not just once either."

Katherine gently poked her on the shoulder. "Now, darling, you know I had nothing to do with that. It was all Kate."

"It is nice having an animal doctor on the farm to take care of things." Abigail looked across the room. "I'm so glad she's here tonight, out and about. I worry about her."

"She's fine."

"I don't know how she does it," Abigail said. "She's amazing."

"She meets adversity head on. She doesn't give up," Katherine said.

"Just like her grandmother."

Katherine grinned broadly. "Well…yes. I guess she is."

☙❦❧

After a considerable amount of time, and after she made her apologies and said goodnight, Kate headed out to the barn to check on the foals and their mother once more. The barn was dark except for the small night light that was kept on for the middle of the night visits Kate often made to check on their animals. She reached across the doorway and flipped the switch to turn on the barn light. Once she was at the stall, she found the mother and her twin babies sleeping soundly. She leaned over the fence and patted all three on their heads. The mare looked up and nuzzled her hand. Kate leaned over and nuzzled her with her chin. "You're a good girl, aren't you? And a fine mama, too. Don't you worry. I'll take good care of you. I promise."

The mare nuzzled her again and then rested her head back over the foals. "Good night, girl. Good night, babies" She moved to turn but stopped. "I forgot to tell you, dear girl, I'm not breaking up your family. This time, they're yours." She turned off the light and made her way back up to the house.

Chapter 3

Katherine took center stage in the middle of the large parlor. She stood in front of the expansive stone fireplace. "Thank you, my dear friends, and friends of friends, for coming tonight. I hope you are enjoying the good Southern food and liquor before you."

Someone yelled, "You're welcome, Katherine. Delicious food!"

"Let her talk," said Pookie. "Go on, honey."

"In these harsh economic times we've endured the last few years while our government leaders bicker amongst themselves like little children in the big white house up North, we find that our neighbors, both in and out of Yazoo County, need a little bit more help than the government can or wants to provide. It is important that we assist the less fortunate, especially in our community. Put our money to use here, in our hometown and in the county, where it belongs. I'll be counting those checks you leave tonight so, I expect you to be generous. Think of it as your good deed for the year. Or payment for all the good food and alcohol you consume. Whichever you prefer to believe is fine with me. Thank you. Ya'll enjoy yourselves now."

She waved her hands for them to go on. She then stepped down from the makeshift podium and went back to her guests. The guests who had drinks in their hands held up their glasses to her in salute.

A few glances around and she approached Carol. "Have you seen Miss Kate?"

Carol was carrying a silver tray around with champagne glasses. "Yes, Miss Katherine. She just came back in and went upstairs to bed. I asked if she needed anything. She said she had a headache."

"Thank you, Carol. Carry on. Make sure no one runs out now."

"Yes, ma'am," Carol said and went about her way.

ᔕᓂᔕᓂ

Kate undressed and laid her evening gown on the back of the chair by her desk. A quick glance out the side window below showed her that the party was still going strong. Some guests were outside on the lawn chatting away. She stepped away from the window and lowered the venetian blind. She lifted the night-gown over her head, went to her bed, and crawled beneath the down comforter. The soft mattress beneath her was a relief to a day she would not forget. What had happened between Sam and her grandmother? That would have to wait. It was too late to confront him about it.

The knocking on the door caught her just as she slowly dozed from exhaustion. The door opened slowly and she heard the clicking of heels on the hardwood floor. "Darling, are you all right?" She heard her grandmother close the door and near her bed.

Kate rolled onto her back, reached for the bedside lamp, and clicked it on. The small light brightened things up a bit. She found her grandmother staring down at her from the foot of her bed.

"Carol said you had a headache. I just wanted to check." Her grandmother neared her. "You look pale. Are you all right?"

"I'm fine, Grandmother—just a headache. No fussing now." The last thing that Kate needed was someone, anyone, and especially her grandmother, fussing over her.

Katherine walked over, sat on the edge of the bed, and brought a hand to Kate's forehead. "You're not warm. But you are pale." She moved to get up. "Perhaps, I should call up Linc or Perry—"

Kate grasped her wrist. "No, Gran. I'm fine. Really. Headache and tired, that is all." She wouldn't worry her grandmother on a night she planned for the last three months.

Katherine studied her. Those vivid green eyes roamed over her, studying her, as if doing her own checkup. "Are you sure that's all? I worry about you."

Kate squeezed her grandmother's hand. "I'm fine, Gran. Go back to your party and stop fussing. "

"It isn't the same without you," Katherine said.

"Grandmother, you have to stop worrying about me."

"Now how do I do that?"

"You're thinking about the accident, aren't you?"

"Now why would you say that? Of course, I'm not," Katherine said.

"Now why don't I believe you? Perhaps, it's because you have that worried look on your face I'm come to know so well," Kate said, her voice lowered. "I worried you terribly, Gran, didn't I? I'm sorry."

Katherine extended a hand and brushed the hair away from Kate's face. "It wasn't your fault. Things like that happen on a farm," she said. "I told you, it also happened to me."

"Afterward...was my fault," Kate said.

"No. It wasn't. You were grieving and you were in a great deal of pain." Katherine took her hands into hers. "It's over and done with. Let it be, darling. You're here. You're alive and you're well. That's all that matters. The rest is in the past."

Kate had another concern on her mind. "Grandmother, don't you ever get bored?"

Katherine released her. "Bored, with so much to do around the farm? Nonsense, darling, has life on this here farm ever been that? Never."

Kate couldn't help but be concerned for her grandmother, especially after the accident two years before. She didn't want to worry her grandmother needlessly. She also didn't want her grandmother to ever be alone. "But you must get lonely. Grandfather is dead nearly twenty years now. I mean—"

"How can I get lonely when I have you?"

"That's not what I mean—maybe you'd like the farm back to run?"

"Never. I gave it to you, just as your father would have wanted. I'm fine with my charity work."

"Maybe—it isn't enough."

Katherine eyed her and grasped Kate's hands into hers. "Darling, what is all this about? Really? Is something bothering you?"

"I watched you tonight. You were in your element and all the men were drooling over you."

Katherine laughed—a deep throaty laugh. "Oh, darling, men

are so easily manipulated. I told you that. I'm a widow, I'm rich, and I look good for my age—astonishingly good, I might add. Men desire women. They drool over us. That's what they do. Show them a little cleavage and they'll eat out of your hand."

Kate hoped she wasn't blushing. Her grandmother could be so forthright, especially when she wasn't prepared for it. "You look astonishingly good for any age, Gran, and I understand what you're saying. I just think you should just get out more. Meet someone. Uncle Linc is crazy about you—"

"I see. You're worried your old grandmother's life is incomplete without a man in it? Is that it? You're not worried about my sex life, are you, darling?"

Kate averted her glance. She coughed into her hand and cleared her throat before she could speak again. "I—I'd never say that. A woman doesn't need a man to make her life complete. You taught me that and I believe it. I just want you to be happy."

Katherine grinned and touched Kate's cheek. "Darling, I am happy as long as you are. Now stop fussing. That's my job. Get some sleep and no more nonsense talk about men. I'm quite happy with my life the way it is."

"Yes, Gran. On one condition," Kate said, eyeing the bravest and toughest person she'd ever known. She couldn't just leave the recent occurrence alone without saying something about it.

Katherine stared at her with wide eyes. "And what's that, darling?"

"About what happened earlier tonight with Sam—"

Her grandmother's eyes darkened over and her tone was short. "That doesn't concern you."

"But you were angry, very angry. I never saw you so angry."

Katherine neared her. "Darling, it's very important that you know that I would do anything to protect you."

"I know that, and what does that mean?"

"Get some sleep." Katherine leaned forward, kissed Kate gently on the forehead, and stepped back. "It's been a long day. You need your sleep to get rid of that headache."

"Gran, I'd really like to know. If something's wrong—"

"Nothing's wrong, darling. What could possibly be wrong? There's positively no need to discuss it. It's over and done with. Sleep now."

Kate nodded. "All right, Gran, as long as you promise to go back to your party and not fuss about me."

Katherine studied her then leaned forward and kissed her on the cheek. "All right, darling. Call for me if you need anything. Promise?"

"I promise, Gran. Now go on."

Katherine moved to the door, opened it, and looked back at her.

"Good night, Gran." Kate shut off the light and rolled over. After a few moments, the door opened and closed. After a few more moments, she heard footsteps walk away from the door.

ဗာၺၧ

Kate couldn't breathe. Where was she? Darkness surrounded her, total blackness. Not even a bright light could cut through it. She was drowning in fluid, suffocating her. She couldn't see. There were noises, voices yelling. Who were they? She didn't recognize them. Why were they yelling? What was going on? Where was she? Why couldn't she see anything? What was happening? Why was she so…scared? What was that loud noise?

"*No! No!* Help me!" she screamed and sat up in bed in an instant.

She was breathing so rapidly she lost all sense of where she was for a few moments. She could hear her heart pounding in her ears, pulsating.

Only when the door to her room swung open and she heard the familiar voice did she begin to settle down.

"Kate, darling, what is it? Are you all right?" Katherine rushed in and flipped the light switch on just inside the room. She dashed to the bed and sat down on the edge of it. Her eyes searched Kate—the worried look evident in the wide eyes and arched brows.

The bright lights hurt Kate's eyes momentarily. "I'm fine."

Katherine caressed her cheek, those eyes of hers roaming over her. "You've been crying."

Kate brought her hands up to her cheeks. They were damp. She wiped her eyes with her hands. "It was just a nightmare."

Katherine took her hands into hers. "Want to talk about it?"

Kate forced a laugh. "It was just a nightmare, Gran. That's all."

Katherine brushed the locks of hair away from Kate's face. "You're soaking wet, too."

"W—what?" Kate felt her nightgown top and realized she was. "I must have been sweating."

"You need to change."

"I will," Kate said.

Katherine eyed her. "Darling, are you sure you're all right?"

"I'm fine, Gran. You worry about me too much."

"That is a grandmother's prerogative. Are you sure you don't want to talk about it?" Katherine said and placed a reassuring hand on her granddaughter's shoulder. "It might help, darling. Was it—about the accident again?"

"No. It was…different. I don't remember having this one before."

Katherine held her hands on her lap. "How so?"

"That's it. I don't really know. I heard voices…shouting…I didn't recognize them. I heard a loud bang…a car…a shotgun…I'm not sure which. It went over and over and over again in replay. Silly, huh?" She noticed her grandmother's stare had turned to concern. "Gran, are you all right? You look…spooked. It was just a nightmare."

"Of course it was, darling. I just worry about you. I don't want to lose you."

"Lose me? Gran, where am I going? The accident was just that. Plus, this is my house, too. I'm not going anywhere. How are you going to lose me?"

Katherine cupped her chin in her hand and sighed. "One day you're going to get married again and decide you no longer want to live with your old grandmother anymore."

"First of all, you're not old. You run circles around me most times." Kate took her hand into hers. "Second, I didn't move out when I married Adam. Do you really think I would abandon my home in the future, or you? You raised me. I'm not going anywhere. Now, I'm fine. Go back to bed."

Her grandmother stared at her. She released her hands, moved to the door, and then stopped. "If you need me darling, I'm right across the hall."

"I know where you are, Gran. Now go on. We have a farm to run. Can't stay up all night now."

Katherine's eyebrows rose and she grinned. "I had that coming, I guess."

"Sounds strange hearing your words come out of my mouth, doesn't it? You had to figure they'd come back your way some day. I waited my entire life to say that to you."

Katherine forced a grin and shook her head. She raised her hand at her and pointed in the air. "Go to sleep, darling. And change out of those wet clothes now."

"Yes, Grandmother, I will."

Katherine hesitated then opened and closed the door behind her.

Kate waited a moment before she got out of bed. If experience taught her anything about her grandmother, Katherine was waiting on the other side for a few moments to ensure that she didn't need her. She couldn't love her grandmother anymore if she had tried. A few moments later, she heard the footsteps head away from her room.

☙❧☙

Back in her massive bedroom, Katherine pushed her long hair out of the way of her neck. She picked up the phone and pressed a few familiar numbers. It rang a few times and the familiar male voice answered.

"H—hello? Yes?"

"It's Katherine."

"Katherine? What's wrong?" he asked.

"Kate had a nightmare," she said.

"W—what?" Lincoln said. "You're calling me for that? What time is it?"

"It doesn't matter. Can babies remember things?" she demanded.

"W—what? Katherine." She could hear his exasperation. "What is going on?"

"I said, can babies remember things—from their past? Yes or no?"

He sighed. "Just tell me what is wrong."

"She had a nightmare—about that night. Can she remember or not? Just answer me."

"Newborn babies can't remember anything, Katherine," Lincoln said.

"Are you sure? You always say you're just an old country doctor. What if you're wrong?"

"Katherine." He raised his voice. "Calm down. Babies don't remember things from when they were born. Trust me on this. If you don't believe me, then do some research. You have a computer—"

"Research? I don't touch a computer unless I have to. That is why I have you," she shot back.

"Then trust me," Lincoln said. "You trusted me then. Get some sleep. Relax. It was just a nightmare. I promise."

"Fine. Good night." She hung up and sighed. She hoped he was right, but what if he wasn't? She couldn't stand the thought of the alternative. "It was just a nightmare," she told herself. "Of course it was. Of course." What else could it be? What if it wasn't? No, she wouldn't deal with the possibility. The past was the past. They buried it a long time ago.

৫৩৫৩

Kate eyed her grandmother the next day as they enjoyed lunch together in the smaller informal dining room. Dinner was always served in the formal dining room, but not breakfast and lunch. Her grandmother said nothing, which was most unusual. It was the same thing at breakfast. She debated bringing up the subject again, about Sam, but decided to let it lie, for now anyway. If she wanted to find out anything, she'd have to go about it another way. But there was always a chance.

"Gran, about yesterday—with Sam—"

"I told you to let that go. It doesn't concern you. I won't discuss it." She shot to her feet. "I have things to tend to and so do you."

Kate nodded, reluctantly. "Okay, Gran. I'm going to go see the foals again after my chores." She walked around the table, gave her grandmother a gentle peck on the cheek, and eyed her cautiously.

Her grandmother stood there, her face and upper lip stiff. She didn't even look Kate's way. Her reaction caused a shudder.

"Why don't you do that, darling? An excellent idea and I can finish my chores. I went over the checks for the donations from the party. We did extremely well this year," Katherine said. "Oh, and by the way, I called Daniel Spencer. He's willing to buy the foals when they're ready. For a very good price, I might add."

"No, Gran," Kate said. "I'm not selling them. I'm keeping these two."

"Darling, whatever for? This is what we do. We breed horses

and then sell them," Katherine asked. "This is a working farm, after all."

"These, I want to keep," Kate said.

"Of course, darling, if that is what you want."

"It is. Thank you, Gran."

Kate walked to the doorway. Her grandmother didn't look up but remained transfixed. Something wasn't right here. It was a feeling more than anything else—certainly nothing to place a finger on. Her grandmother wasn't herself. Kate stepped outside, stopped for just a moment, and then headed toward the front door and swung it open. She walked outside onto the porch and down the five steps onto the concrete walk.

It was warmer than yesterday. Summer would soon arrive and, with it, the hot, humid heat known throughout the South— the warm humid air that made the grass green, the flowers bloom, and the inhabitants of the Magnolia state retreat inside to seek the comfort of air conditioning and a never-ending supply of sweet tea.

☾☽☾

After a couple of hours of checking the fence line and counting the cattle, Kate drove back to the barn and parked the beat up blue Ford pickup just outside. The fresh air felt good on her skin and in her lungs. She snapped her fingers. She forgot to call Dinah again today. *What is going on with me? I've never been this forgetful before. Perhaps, I'm working too hard or have too many things on my mind.* But a working farm didn't run itself and grandmother relied on her. She grinned. Not that her grandmother needed any help, but as far as running it was concerned, Katherine gave her free rein. Had Kate's father lived, he would be running things. Had her father lived, things would, no doubt, be different. How different was the question? She never really thought about her father before. Her parents had died in separate accidents when she was a baby and that was a long time ago. After seeing the foals, she was going to follow up on what she meant to do last night.

She headed into the stall where their foreman, Carl, evidently just brought in the foals from their exercise.

"Evening, Carl."

He hung up a rope on a nearby hook on the wall and faced

her. "Evening, Miss Kate. Come to see the babies?"

"I have." She leaned on the wooden gate to the corral and admired the small muscled animals and their mama. "They look happy."

"They are and doing fine. Just had 'em out with their mama and they did really well," he boasted.

"Good. I'm glad."

"Miss Katherine hasn't been down since they were born. That's not like her. Not like her at all. She's not ill, is she?"

"No, but you would know better than I would since you've been working here longer than I've been around," Kate said.

"Yeah, reckon I would." He scratched his forehead then reached for a handkerchief from his back pocket and wiped his brow. "It's going to heat up real quick. I can feel it."

"You're right. I feel it, too."

"You know you two ladies don't have to worry about these here foals. They're healthy and happy. Of course, you know better than I do, Miss Kate."

"It's not every day twins are born safely," she said.

"Over concerned is what you are and you don't have to be with me around." He stuffed the handkerchief back into his pocket. "I get it, though. But I don't want either of you worrying now. When it comes to horses—"

"'I know everything there is to know and if I don't know it, it's because it ain't so,'" she mimicked.

He furrowed his brows at her and grinned. "Okay, Miss Kate. I reckon I had that coming."

"I'm going to sit with the foals awhile. Go get something to eat," she said.

"Eat," he asked. "What time is it?"

"When are you going to get a watch?" she scolded.

"I do mighty fine without one, thank you very much."

"Except when it comes to eating," she scolded again. "One of these days, Carol is just going to put your food straight from the stove into the trash can."

"All right, Miss Kate. I'm on my way." He moved to leave. "If you're not here when I get back, have a good evening."

"I will."

She removed the rope tie off the gate and stepped inside the stall. The foals were settling down around their mother. The mare was sitting down on her haunches, taking it all in. She was beau-

tiful and majestic, pure white in color. The foals were her fourth
litter born to her in the last six years. These foals were her second
set of twins. Delta Darling was a prize horse. Her blue ribbons
covered the wall in the barn. Standing Tall was the stud. He was
a handsome black stallion, fifteen years of age. He was their
pride of the farm—a show horse champion. Katherine had turned
down many offers to purchase him from as far away as Dubai,
Saudi Arabia and Devonshire, England. His blue ribbons covered
the wall next to Delta Darling's. Their yearlings could fetch an
even heftier price, as the yearlings before them had done. That is
if they sold them, which she wasn't going to do. Not this time.

ભʀભʀ

After her chores, Kate changed from her work dungarees into
a fresh pair of jeans and an oversized red sweatshirt and made her
way to Maddy's house. In the pickup, it took a whole five
minutes to get to their place on the other side of the farm. The old
farmhouse sat right near the road, just on the edge of Magnolia
Lane Farm. Kate walked up to the door and knocked. For the first
time, it occurred to her that she had never been to Maddy and
Sam's house before. How was that possible? Probably because
she never had a reason to be here before today. Well, now she
did. Something happened yesterday and she couldn't leave it
alone. She needed to know what it was that had put her grandmother in such an erratic state. Curiosity drove Kate.

The door opened slowly and she saw Sam seated at the table
in the kitchen, off to the right of the hallway. He held a cloth to
his mouth when Sam's mother, Maddy let her in. Maddy was a
slim woman about five feet and four inches tall. Her black hair
was short and framed her face perfectly. She never noticed how
beautiful the older woman was until now when they were close
up. Her pecan colored skin was flawless and had a youthful glow.

Sam moved to stand up when he saw her. She waved for him
to sit back down and he did.

"Forgive the intrusion," Kate began. "I wanted to check on
Sam."

"There was no need for that. I'm fine," he replied.

"Good. Now you can tell me what happened last night," Kate
said.

"Nothing for you to worry about," Sam said.

"He's okay, child," Maddy interjected. "That's all that matters."

"Nothing happened?" Elsa chided as she entered the room, went to sit down next to him, and examined his face. "Sam, look at your face. I came home as soon as Carol told me last night and still I couldn't stop it from bruising."

"I told her not to say anything—" Sam said.

"What happened last night, Sam?" Kate interrupted as she took a step forward. "I'd like to know."

"I'm fine. Really," he said. He took Elsa's hand into his and avoided looking at Kate.

"You don't look fine." Kate saw a large purple bruise on the left side of his face, between his eye and cheek, and butterfly stitches. "And I never saw my grandmother so angry, ever. What happened?" She wouldn't back down—this was serious to her.

"I'll tell you what happened," Elsa said. "Your grandmother has gone insane!"

Sam shot to his feet. "Sit down, woman. You have no idea. Now be quiet."

"I will not. She deserves to know the truth," Elsa said. "And now is as good as any time to tell her. Why does she hate my Sam so much? And Maddy? Do you know?"

"Shush, child," Maddy said.

"Tell me what happened last night," Kate pressed. She gave the old house a quick glance. It was comfortably furnished. One wall across from them had framed photos of different shapes and sizes. And there were books that lined another wall—lots of books. The house was larger inside than it looked from the outside.

"It really is nothing for you to worry about," Maddy told her. "It was just a misunderstanding."

"I'm sorry, Maddy, but I don't believe that. I don't think Elsa does either," Kate asserted. "My grandmother was livid. I demand an explanation."

"It's time, Mama," Sam said. "You have to tell her."

"No, it's not," Maddy scolded and waved him back. "You hush now—"

"I'm not leaving here until someone tells me what happened," Kate said. "I know it was something, because my grandmother hit you, didn't she, Sam? Where else did that bruise come from?"

Kate heard Sam sigh, which confirmed it.

"Don't you dare," Maddy threatened.

"I'm sorry, Mama, it's time. I can't hide the truth from her anymore or from my wife." He looked at Kate. "Did you read your mother's journal?"

"Wh—what?" She looked closer at him. "How did you know about that?"

"She told me. That's why Miss Katherine was so angry. She found out that you were in the attic," Sam said.

"So? I was in the attic," Kate said.

"No one is allowed up there. No one," Sam said.

"Certainly that doesn't apply to me—"

"Especially you," Sam said.

Kate eyed him. "Especially me? W—what? Why?"

"It's because of your mother," Maddy said calmly.

"What about my mother?" Kate's eyes remained on Sam. "What does the attic, and a few pages in her journal, have to do with my grandmother losing her temper and striking you?"

"Because your mother was Black," he shot out. "I'm sorry—I didn't mean to say it that way." He shook his head. "It's just—"

"Sam," Maddy scolded.

"Ex—cuse me?" Kate said and stared at him. "Just what? My mother was what?"

"It's true, child," Maddy said as she took a cautionary step toward her. "I can't keep quiet anymore. I'm sorry, child."

"Wh—what? What are you talking about?" Kate said and stared at him.

"We're your family, your mother's family. That is why we're here," Maddy said. "Have always been here, for you."

Kate froze. Everything froze in time. Then she faced Maddy and spoke. "Why would you tell me such a lie? What have I done to you?" Kate asked. "I've known you and Sam for my whole life—"

"It's not a lie, child. It's the truth," Maddy said.

"Of course, it's a lie. Look at me. I'm White. I'm not Black."

Maddy stepped toward her. "You have what we used to call in the old days—good skin. Like your mother did—she had good skin too. You both can pass for white. You can because you are half-White, but the other half is Black." She brought a hand to her chest. "My half."

Kate took a step back. Her stomach was tightening up. Bile rose up in the back of her throat and she swallowed hard to get it back down. "What are you talking about? What makes you say such lies? My mother wasn't Black—and what do you know about it anyway? What makes you say such a thing?"

"Because, Kate," Maddy declared. "Your mama was my baby girl—Livie—Olivia."

Kate swallowed hard again, but the sour taste of bile lingered. She glanced at Sam who nodded. "You had to be told, especially after last night," he said. "I'm sorry, Kate. We should have told you sooner."

"I—don't believe you. You're lying. You're all lying," Kate accused.

"Why would we lie to you? For what possible reason?" Maddy asked.

"I—I don't know why. But you are," Kate said. "That's why my grandmother was so angry. You told her this lie—but why? Sam, answer me."

"It's not a lie. Your mama was my daughter. I'm your grandmother," Maddy said.

"You're lying," Kate said. "It's not true. I'm White."

"Yes, half-White. Half-Black," Maddy said. She reached out to touch her, but Kate pulled back. "I can imagine how you must feel—"

"Don't touch me! I'm going to tell my grandmother what you said."

Sam shot to his feet. "No, don't!"

"Why not? Because you're lying, right? I've known you, Maddy and Sam, my whole life. If this was true, why didn't you ever tell me? Because it's a lie, that's why."

"No, because it's the truth and Mama and Daddy swore never to tell anyone. I swore too. She'll kick us off the plantation," Sam said. "We'll lose everything. We'll have to leave here, leave you."

Kate spun on him. "W—what the hell are you talking about? This is your house, your land. Why would she throw you out, except for the lies you're telling me now?"

"What did the journal say?" Sam asked.

"Wh—what?" His question startled her. "Only that my grandmother hated her so. Hated my mother so much. And my mother's parents hated my father—"

"Because your mother was Black," Sam told her. "And your father was White."

"No—No. You're lying," Kate said. "No. It's not true. It isn't."

"No, child," Maddy said. "We're telling you the truth. Miss Katherine never meant for you to know, ever. None of us did. We all swore never to tell you. If we ever did, she'd evict us."

"You're lying. You're lying. This isn't true," Kate declared. "It isn't. It just can't be. It isn't possible."

Kate watched as the older woman went to the wall behind her and removed a wooden frame. She brought it over and placed it on the table before her. "Do you recognize anyone in this photo, child?"

Kate stared at her and then looked down at the color photo. In it were about a dozen persons, all were either black as ebony, or brown as caramel, except one. One little girl with ponytails and brown hair stood out from all the rest because she was clearly not Black. She was White. Kate stared at her. Who was she? She didn't recognize her. She looked up at Maddy. "No. Who are they?"

"This was a family photo taken here. A long time ago. The little girl is your mother," Maddy said. "My baby, Olivia. She was seven here."

Kate crumbled inside. She stared at the photo. *My mother?* Something tugged at her—a strong feeling from inside her gut. She reached out her hand to touch the spot where the little girl stood, but instead pulled back. Knots twisted her stomach now. Tears were building within her eyes. "No. No. No. No." Her mind was turning into mush and her heart was racing, thumping and threatening to jump from her mouth. "This isn't true." She backed up. "You're all lying. Lying." She looked at Maddy then moved to the door. "I don't believe you. None of you."

"Don't go, Kate, wait," Maddy called. "Please, Kate."

The door shut behind her. Sam moved to follow her. "Let her go, Sam," Maddy said.

"But, Mama, there's more to tell her," Sam said.

"I think she's heard enough for tonight. Let her go. She needs to…absorb what we told her."

"And Katherine? What do we do about her?"

"We'll deal with her when we have to," Maddy said. "We broke our word. We'll accept the punishment."

"But this is *our* house. We were all born here," Sam protested.

"It was never our house. Not since—that night. Now, we have

to be here for Kate," she reminded him. "We owe her that."

"Sam," Elsa said. "Is there something I need to know?" She grabbed his shirt collar. "What is this all about? Tell me. It can't be true."

"Remember I told you my sister died in childbirth," he said.

"Yes, so?"

"She was Kate's mother," he said.

"Don't be silly. Kate is White—"

"So was my sister, at least she passed for being White. You heard Mama. It's all true, and there's more."

Elsa glanced at Maddy and then back at Sam. "So Kate is your niece? Our niece? How could you not tell me any of this, Sam, how could you?"

"Sit down, Elsa," Maddy said. "We'll tell you everything, but you can't tell a soul. No one. Ever."

"Sam?" Elsa asked.

He took her hand and guided her to the chair next to him. "Sit down, honey, and I'll try and explain." Would his wife believe him? Would she listen? Would she care? Or would she leave him? He'd soon find out as he told her the whole family secret.

Chapter 4

Kate wandered on back to the barn and went in to check on the foals, leaving the pickup truck where she parked it, just outside. The foals were both sleeping curled up against their mother's broad chest. She envied them their safety. Her life had just turned upside down. If it was true, what they just told her, who was she? The reality was there before her. Why would they lie? What was their motivation? She had known them for as long as she could remember—longer than that. Why would they lie? People didn't just do that. Did they? And if it was true? She looked down at her hands, both of them, front and back. She was White. White. There was no denying that. There was no question. She wasn't as ivory white as her grandmother was. She had more of an olive tint to her skin.

She sat down in the paddock and leaned her head against the wall. She had to talk to her grandmother. She had to, but what if what they said was true? What if? As stressed as she was, she couldn't fight the fatigue that drowned her now.

An hour later, she awakened to Carl's voice, "Miss Kate," he called from outside the stall. "Are you in here?"

"Y—yes." She came to her feet. "I'm here." She brushed off the loose straw and dirt.

"Checking on the babies again?" he asked.

"Yes, I have to go." She brushed past him and out of the barn.

❧❦❧

Kate decided to take things in hand and went to see Uncle Lincoln Castle before attempting to discuss anything again with her grandmother. Lincoln was their oldest and dearest family friend. He was one of her grandfather's best friends. He was the family doctor privy to a world of things normal outsiders wouldn't know. She wondered if he knew anything about what Maddy and Sam told her. She knew he brought her into the world the day she was born. How much did he know? How much would he tell her? There was only one way to find out and only one way to do it. He would certainly be easier to deal with than her grandmother. If there was one thing she knew, if Katherine Thayer didn't want to talk, she wouldn't.

He welcomed her into the renovated farmhouse when she rang the doorbell.

"I'd like to speak with you, Uncle Lincoln," she said. "It's important."

"Come in, Kate. Always glad to see you. You're not feeling ill, are you?"

"No. Nothing like that." She walked in and moved to his office in the back of the house. "I'd like to talk to you about the night my mother died," she said.

She noticed she had rattled him when he stopped. Good. Maybe it'd make it easier for her to extract information from him.

He moved forward after a long moment. "What about it?"

She sat down in front of his desk. "Tell me."

"That was a long time ago." He ran a hand through his cropped white hair. "Why bring it up now?"

"I met my mother's family," she said.

He swallowed hard. "I'm not sure I know what you mean." He moved toward his desk. "I have work to do—"

"I know I'm Black," she said. "I know my mother was Black. The secret is out."

He stopped alongside his desk and said nothing.

The silence pushed down on her ears as if someone was squeezing her head. It compelled her to speak. "The question is, what else is there that I don't know?"

"Maybe you should discuss this with your grandmother—"

"I will. For now, I'm discussing it with you. Is there anything I should know?" she asked.

"How do you know about Maddy? Your mother?"

"Maddy and Sam told me," she said.

He faced her with a look of disbelief. "They—told you? Then they told you about your sister, too?"

"What sister? I don't have a sister."

He averted his gaze.

"Uncle Linc—what sister? I don't have a sister."

"No, not anymore." His voice was just above a whisper. He faced her. He hesitated. She noticed his lips tremble as he spoke. "Your sister was stillborn. She was your older sister."

Emptiness pervaded her. "I see." It was all she could say.

"I'm sorry, Kate. We should have told you, but she was dead. There was never any need to do so."

"Why did you lie to me? Why did you keep this a secret? I had a right to know," she said.

"Yes, you did. And I know you're upset—"

"You let my mother die too that night. The night of the car accident, didn't you?"

"No," he shot back. "I tried to save her. She was bleeding too heavily, too fast. Don't you think I have wondered all these years if she would be here now if only we were able to get her to the hospital? There was no time."

She eyed him. "Why wasn't there time? The hospital is only ten minutes away." And then it hit her. She sighed deeply. "She didn't die in a car accident, did she?"

He looked away.

"Did she?" she demanded and leaned forward in her chair.

He pursed his lips before he spoke. "No, Kate. She didn't."

She sat tall in the chair. "H—how?" She swallowed hard and coughed to clear her throat. "How?"

"It was in childbirth. She died just after you were born. Her water broke—and then you came—I tried to save your mother. I was desperate to save her—for Jax—for you. I swear to you, Kate. It was an accident."

"But not a car accident. Why? Why did you and Gran lie to me? Why?" It was too damn surreal and unbelievable. All this time—she thought—she believed—and in the end, it was a lie, another stupid lie. "And why did you care so much about my mother? My father? Me? You're just a family friend."

"No, Kate." He took a deep breath and released it, slowly. He slowly raised his gaze and leveled off with her. "I'm your grandfather. Jax was my son. I'm sorry. I didn't mean for you to know like this. You were never to know. I swore never to tell you, to hurt you," Lincoln said. "Or upset your life."

"That's—not possible. That's not true," Kate said. "You're lying. You're all lying to me. Why?"

"It's not a lie," he said. "We did lie to you, but this isn't."

Kate stared at him. He spun away from her, scuffled behind to his metal file cabinet, and leaned against it. For the first time, Kate saw how really old he was. "I think you better explain," she told him.

"Your grandfather, Jackson, wasn't your grandfather," he said and didn't look at her. "I know. My father was the Thayer family physician for years. I worked with him while in and out of med school and succeeded him." He shook his head slowly, his slightly wrinkled hands rested on the edge of the big wooden desk. "Your grandmother and I—" He turned toward her. "Katherine and I—we were—lovers—for a long time."

Kate felt a deep kick into her stomach and back. For a moment, she couldn't breathe. And when she was able to speak, all she could say was, "E—excuse me?"

"I'm sorry. You shouldn't have found out this way." He stepped toward her and leaned against the desk, tall and strong. He looked away and his eyes appeared to see somewhere long ago. The words caught in his throat. "It happened so long ago, so easily really. Your grandfather Jackson was away so often. He didn't know. I loved her, your grandmother. Katherine wanted a child more than anything. I was already in love with her, you see, from the moment I met her. She was—" He faced her. "—is a beautiful, stunning woman." Warmth emanated from his words. "Jackson never knew. Your father never knew. I promised her that I would never speak of it—that you would never know, at least not like this. I'm sorry, you shouldn't have been told this way." He took a step toward her. "You see, your sister was my flesh and blood too—my granddaughter. I loved your mother, too. She was Jax's wife. I knew her for her whole life."

Heat began to fill her cheeks. She flexed her wrists and clenched them tightly, determined not to falter. She softened her words. "I don't know what to say. I just don't."

He half-turned toward her. The lines on his face deepened before her eyes. He seemed to age twenty years at that moment. "I love her—Katherine. I always have. I always will." He half-smiled. "I love you too. I loved her too, your sister."

Kate shot to her feet. "I have to go." She couldn't think. She couldn't speak. Millions of questions, thoughts, and not one answer presented itself to her. Secrets and lies—Lies and secrets. That is what her life was now. The truth that she knew no longer existed. Instead, the truth that persisted for thirty years finally reared its head.

☙❧☙

Kate had no choice now. She had to know more. She had to know the truth. She went home. It was the only place in the entire world she had ever felt safe and secure, but not anymore. Whatever had occurred in her life before, the good and the bad, Kate knew she always had home to go to. Now, she wasn't so sure. The life she had known for so long had changed in the blink of an eye, and for more than one reason. The persons she had known forever had lied to her and kept secrets from her. Worst of all, the one person she had cherished most in her life and trusted implicitly, deceived her.

Her hometown of Thayersville sat midway between the smaller sister cities of Yazoo City and Benton in the northwestern part of Mississippi in Yazoo County. Yazoo County was the largest county in the state of Mississippi and the most densely populated. She appreciated the small size of just 15,000 people. Townspeople often remarked that there were more horses and cattle than people. And that was okay with her. One could be from one side of town to the other in just five minutes, ten if there was traffic. People who lived in the larger cities of Jackson and Madison couldn't boast that. Of course, that was when the trains coming into and out of town didn't block your route. In that case, there was no telling how long it would take.

Mature magnolia trees lined the driveway from just off the road until about one hundred feet short of the house. Hence, the farm's name. Scattered about the property were aged weeping willows and live oaks with hanging moss. With the exception of some trees, Kudzu wrapped most of the trees. Kudzu was a vine imported from Japan years before, and just took over, until it now was a familiar staple in the Southern state. She drove slowly along the asphalt drive, slower than normal. The usual ten-minute drive from Lincoln's office seemed more like an hour long today—twice as long from the road turnoff to home too. Time just seemed to stand still. There was really no reason to rush home. Her grandmother would be less than thrilled about a sudden change in routine. Her grandmother Katherine Eleanor Beauregard Thayer IV didn't handle change well, unless she was the one making the change. But right now, Kate could care less about what Katherine wanted.

She entered the long driveway from Thayer Lane off Highway

forty-nine and stared at the building she'd called home for her entire life. The old antebellum house with details reminiscent of the Parthenon—stately, pillared Greek revival homes she long admired, reflecting a passion for antiquity—was imposing to her today as she neared it. Six white columns were the first thing any visitor would notice on the white mansion. There they stood as if soldiers on watch, guarding the inhabitants inside. Ironically, during the Civil War, Magnolia Lane Farm was the headquarters of a lesser known Confederate General, John Lee Knox, for a short time. In 1863, a brief battle was fought in the front yard. Bullet holes could still be seen in two of the columns and one of the walls. She almost didn't recognize the magnificent building, her mind diverted by other things.

She pulled up to the end of the driveway, just short of the six car garage, and parked next to her grandmother's shiny new blue metallic Cadillac Sedan. She took a deep, slow breath before she shut off the pickup. She opened the driver door, stepped out, made her way up the five front steps, opened the front door, and ambled inside. The solid oak door seemed heavier than usual. She took one last look outside at the place she called home, turned away, slammed the door hard, and stormed into the parlor.

There she was. Her grandmother stood by the massive stone fireplace staring up at her husband's face—the larger than life size portrait of Jackson Atticus Thayer IV. Kate couldn't help but laugh at the irony of it all.

Katherine faced her. Her face was rigid. She was clearly not amused. "Where have you been? You're late for dinner. You know how I detest tardiness. "

"And lies?"

Katherine eyed her. "What?"

Kate went to the bar and began to pour a drink. Undecided at first, she quickly poured an inch of Grand Marnier into a glass. "Tell me, Grandmother." She spun on her heel to face the formidable woman she had admired for so long—too long, perhaps. "How do you feel about lies?"

Katherine glared. "That is a stupid question," she snapped. "I detest lies. You know that."

Kate gulped her drink, hoping for the courage to speak the truth without wavering and choosing the steps of the argument wisely. "I wondered, since you have told so many yourself." She moved to pour another.

Katherine rushed toward her and snatched the glass from her hand. "Are you drunk? You know I abhor drunks."

"No. I'm not drunk, though I wish I were," Kate shot back.

Katherine's eyes darkened and widened and she placed the glass back on the bar. "We're going in for dinner. You need to get dressed—"

"No. Not until we discuss your lies. All of them."

Katherine spun on her heel to face her. "What are you going on about? What lies? I never lied to you!" She turned away.

"Tell me about my sister, Grandmother."

Katherine stopped. Then, suddenly, she turned and said calmly. "Your what?"

"My sister."

"You don't have a sister," Katherine said matter-of-factly.

"But I did. I spoke with Uncle Linc," Kate said. "He told me she was stillborn. Why didn't you tell me I had a sister?"

Katherine spun away from her, dismissing the statement with a wave of her hand. "The man is a fool. He shouldn't have said anything. It's all in the past."

"Uncle Linc. Is that why you slept with him? He told me he was my grandfather—"

Katherine faced her. Her eyes widened. "He told you that? He's a liar!"

"Is he? Why would he lie about that?" Kate shot back. "It doesn't make sense."

"He's a man. Why do they do any of the things they do?"

"I'd like to know the truth—"

"Stop this at once!" Katherine bellowed.

"No. I want to know the truth. Is he my grandfather?"

"No, of course not!" Katherine snapped and stepped away. She sighed and faced her. "Sometimes, a woman has to tell a man some lies to get him to do what she wants him to. That's all. You were married—you know."

"In the short two years I had with Adam, I never lied to him, so no, I don't know. Why don't you tell me?" Kate said.

Katherine waved her hand again. "Don't be foolish, darling. He's not your grandfather." She brought up a hand to her chest. "I should know."

"So you didn't have an affair with him? He lied to me. Why would he do that?"

Katherine glared at her, the green eyes turning icy. Kate had never seen that look—ever—not even the night before. "What I did, or didn't do before you were born, or after, is none of your business, young lady." Katherine spun away and moved to leave. "Enough of this. We're going into dinner. Now."

Kate blocked her path. "I'm not finished. I want to know the truth—"

"This conversation ends here. Is that clear?"

"Is that your final word on it?" Kate asked.

"Yes. It is. It is time for dinner. You don't have to dress. I'll allow it this once." Katherine walked away with her head held high, but before she was out of the room, Kate had to speak.

"I love you very much, Grandmother," Kate said. "But this discussion isn't over."

Katherine stopped at the door.

Kate stepped up to her. "For so long it was only the two of us. I trusted you implicitly and never doubted you, once. I would have done anything for you."

Katherine faced her, perplexed and her voice softened, "I love you. We can get past this."

"No, I don't think so." Kate leaned forward and placed a gentle kiss on her cheek. "You lied to me, Grandmother. Besides, I'm Black—and you can't stand that."

Katherine nearly fainted. She had to grip the doorknob for support. "Darling, you're not Black. Whoever told you that is a liar, can't you see that?"

"No, Gran, you lied. I know how my mother really died. I spoke with Maddy and Sam. I know Maddy is my grandmother. Now I know why you hold fundraisers here for the poor every year," Kate said and the words just flew out. "You feel guilty for lying to me. You can't live with yourself, so you have to make up for it, don't you? You're the liar, Grandmother. You have a guilty conscience and can't live with it. How do you do it? How could you? What were you thinking? Who the hell are you? What else have you lied about, Grandmother? What other lies have you told me? What else aren't you telling me? Why did you hate my mother so much? Why the lies, Grandmother? Why—"

The slap across her face was out of nowhere. Kate took two steps back. "Who are you?"

"I am still your grandmother, young lady, and don't you forget it," she snapped. "I will not tolerate impertinence in my house. Pull yourself together this minute."

Kate brought up her hand, held it against her wounded cheek, and ran from the room.

Katherine reached out to her but it was too late. Instead, she placed her hand on the doorknob.

The last thing in the world she ever wanted was to hurt Kate. She couldn't let the night end this way. She could have avoided all this. She shouldn't have been so nice to Maddy and George. This was the repayment for her kindness.

Chapter 5

Kate stormed into her room, slammed the door behind her, and locked it. She placed her hands palm down on it and let her weight hold it. She couldn't help but stare at her hands. Kate never thought about skin color before, or the different shades that made up different people, until now. She never thought about her grandmother's lily-white skin compared to her olive-oil complexion. Of course, she thought about it a great deal now. How could she not?

From the photos around the house, she saw that her father and grandfather were White, but not as light as Katherine. Yet, Kate was darker than all of them, and now she knew why. It made perfect sense now.

It just didn't matter. She spent her entire life surrounded by Colored people. They were all hard-working and loyal. All their employees, except Carl were Colored. Was that intentional on Katherine's part, as Kate had accused her? Did her grandmother feel guilty for what they all did? Did any of them feel guilty at all? Was her grandmother as racist as she seemed, or was it just hatred for Maddy? If it was racism, why would her grandmother surround herself and Kate with Colored employees and treat them civilly? It just didn't make sense at all. Of course, none of it made sense. Sense began to go out the window along with stability the day she discovered her mother's journal.

She dragged herself over to her hundred-year-old writing desk and slumped into the chair. Gripping the sterling silver frame in her hands, she ran one hand over the glass, as if the young man beneath it could feel her touch. "I miss you, Adam. I wish you were here."

The blue eyes stared up at her. She missed his smile and his strength. "I wish you were here, darling, I need so much to speak with you. So much has happened in my life—would you still love me had you known the family secret? Secrets about me?" She missed his embrace. She placed the frame gently onto the desk. "I'm scared. I may have to go away, and I am...scared." She grinned to herself. "I wonder what you would tell me—go for it! Do what your heart tells you to do—like when I married you. I followed my heart. I never regretted it, but I miss you so."

She extended her hand out to the sterling silver hand mirror that lay next to it. It was a matched set. She took a slow, deep breath and picked it up. She held the handle in one hand while running her fingers of her other hand along the rim. "I remember when you gave this to me." She turned it over to read the inscription: *To my darling Kate, Let us look forward to many years together. Love always, Adam.* She had to swallow to rid her throat of the lump that was forming.

Her thoughts went to the last morning they had shared together as husband and wife—before the accident—when she lost him two years before. She remembered their last day together vividly. It was etched into her memory for eternity. As usual, for their brief Saturday mornings together, they had just finished making love under their favorite live oak tree, dripping with Spanish moss, before he went to work that day at the local hospital. It was one of the rare times they had together away from the farm, her grandmother, and staff, and they cherished it. Like Adam, she valued privacy, and though Gran was great at not intruding upon their privacy, Kate knew he valued their time alone together...

∽✺∾

She lay back atop the blanket. He was on his side, leaning on a bent elbow, and stared down at her. His long lean fingers ran across her lips and down along the nape of her neck.

"I love you, Kate, very much." He leaned over her and placed his lips over hers then released her. "I don't want to leave you today. I'll miss you." He ran his fingers along her cheek and rested them on her chin. "You mean the world to me."

She reached out to him and ran her fingers through his short, thick brown hair. His blue eyes sparkled under the bright sunlight. "I love you, too. And I don't want you to go, but—" She took his hand in hers and brought it to her lips. "I know you have to."

The last thing she wanted to do was let him go. For once, she wanted to spend a day in bed with him making love, just as they did on their honeymoon. With Adam going to medical school and working full time at the local hospital, time with him was rare.

Times, like this morning, she cherished, but she knew how much he wanted to complete his studies. He had supported her through veterinary school, even waiting until she graduated until they were married. He told her he didn't want their marriage to interfere with her career. How could she not do the same for him?

He brushed her hair away from her face. "In another year, I'll be done with all of this and then we can go on with our lives. I promise."

She brought up her hands to his face. "Can you stay with me a little while longer?"

He did, but as a result, he was late to leave for work. He sat up and dressed. "If I don't hurry, I'll be late."

She sat up aside from him and dressed quickly. He helped her to her feet.

"We can take a shortcut and get to your car in time to get you to work, no problem."

He took her into his arms. "Does it give us time for some more loving?"

She laughed. She wanted him again more than anything, but she had to be realistic. "Not anymore it won't."

"Well, we better get going then. The sooner I get to work, the sooner I get home to you."

They walked to their horses and he helped her get on the palomino's back and into the saddle. He, in turn, climbed up into the saddle on the quarter horse's back. "Race you to the driveway," he said and took off at full gallop toward the house.

She laughed. Kate followed him across the pasture. Little did she know that it would be the last time. He wasn't far ahead of her when she saw Adam and his horse move to jump over the gulley. Kate didn't see anything, but something spooked his horse. It all happened so fast. It appeared to happen in slow motion. She saw the stud veer backward and heard Adam shout something back to her. Adam and the stud almost moved as one as the horse veered backward onto its hind legs and fell back, throwing Adam to the ground. By time she reached them just seconds later, her horse stopped just short of the gulley and threw her forward.

That was the last thing she remembered until she woke up in the hospital and saw her grandmother's face.

c⁄ɔc⁄ɔ

She stared at his photo and shut her eyes briefly at the memory that elicited both joy and sadness. "I miss you so much." Her fingers ran along his cheeks and rested on his mouth. "We didn't have much time together, did we? But we had fun when we did. Studying to be a doctor wasn't easy for you, I know. And I know why you lived here when you didn't want to. Getting out from your father's shadow wasn't easy, but people loved you here. I know you didn't want to live here at first, but I thank you for doing so. Would you be alive had we lived on our own, away from here? I wonder that all the time. Not as much as I used to. I'd like to think I'm older, wiser, and stronger than I was when you died. I hope so, anyway. I didn't handle things too well back then. If it wasn't for Gran, I don't know where I'd be right now. Gran—" She forced a small laugh. "I don't know if I can trust her anymore, Adam. I just don't know if I can trust anyone anymore. They lied to me, darling, all of them. People I've known forever. I'd know what you'd say and what I should do, but forgiving and forgetting is not so easy when you're furious, as well as scared. I wish you were here. You always made me feel safe. I miss your arms around me."

Slowly she flipped the mirror over, lifted it up, and looked into it. With her left hand, she held it up. She brought up her right hand and raised it to her cheek, ran her fingers along her face, her lips, and her neck, and examined her reflection. "I don't look any different." She set the mirror down and examined her hands, first the top and then her palms. She ran one hand along one arm and the other hand along the other arm. "I don't feel any different." She opened her hands and set them flat onto the desk, palms down.

She reached into her top desk draw and pulled out the journal. Running her fingers over the cover, she flipped it open to a random page and stared at the writing. It was her mother's handwriting. "Oh, Mama, Daddy, I miss you. I wish you were here. What happened? What really happened? Why did you leave me?"

The knocking on the door jarred her back down to the reality of it all. She knew who it was and wouldn't answer.

The knock repeated. She heard the doorknob struggle to turn. "Kate, open this door. We need to talk. Open this door, now," Katherine said. "Darling, please."

Kate stared at her husband's photo as she tried to block out the realities shoved into her life over the last two days. She didn't want to speak with her grandmother, not if it meant arguing with her and not getting the answers she desperately needed.

"Katherine Caroline Thayer, open this door now! I insist you do as I say!" her grandmother yelled.

Kate heard fear in her voice. She rarely heard fear in her voice, at least not in a long time.

"Carol, get me the key to this door now!" she heard her grandmother yell and resume the knocking, and then it turned to banging. "Darling, I insist you answer me, now! Kate, Katherine, do you hear me?" There was urgency in her voice.

Kate set the journal back in the drawer. She dragged herself onto her feet and shuffled toward the door, just as it slammed wide open.

Katherine rushed to her and seized her by the shoulders. "Are you all right? Have you been drinking?" Her fierce green eyes scanned the room. Carol waited in the doorway. "Answer me! What do you think you were doing locking yourself up in your room and not responding? Answer me!"

"I'm fine, Grandmother." Kate pulled away from her. She shuffled to the king-sized bed and sat down on its edge. "As well as can be expected, considering."

"You may go, Carol," Katherine said and sighed.

"Miss Kate?" Carol asked.

"It's all right, Carol. Thank you."

Carol hesitated, then stepped out, and closed the door behind her.

Katherine brought up her hands, joined them together as she brought them up to her chest, and rested them there near her heart. She neared the bed and sat down beside her. "Darling, all I've ever done was to try and protect you."

Kate stared at the hardwood floor. "Protect me? From what? My mother's family?"

"Yes and this awful secret. Before you judge me, you need to ask yourself, why didn't your mother's family ever tell you the truth? They knew about you. Did they ever tell you who you were before now?"

Kate considered that and had to face that truth. "No," she said. Katherine was right about that.

Katherine reached out a hand and brushed Kate's hair with her fingers. "Darling, I love you. You must know that. I have no regrets—certainly not in protecting you. You must think about this clearly. Once you embrace your mother's Black family. Once you acknowledge being Black, there is no going back."

"What do you mean by that?"

"They're lazy, shiftless—no good," Katherine said. "They can't be trusted."

Kate faced her. "That's not true, Gran. That's a stereotype and you know it."

"No, it's true." Katherine brought a hand up to her chest. "Believe me, I know."

"Why do you hate them so?" Kate asked. "What is this all really about?"

"They're Black. Do I need another reason than that?"

"Yes. You do." Kate eyed her grandmother. "Why the secrets and lies, Grandmother? Why lie about how my mother died? She didn't die in a car accident. She died in childbirth—my birth."

Katherine sighed. "It was necessary. There was no need for you to know the sad, horrible truth of that. It would only sadden you."

"But why?" Kate reached out a hand to touch her grandmother's elbow. "Why were you so concerned about me just now?"

"I don't know what you mean."

Kate studied her to find any clue as to what was going on. Sometimes actions revealed more than words ever could. "I saw your face, Grandmother. Tell me the truth. What were you afraid of?"

Her grandmother stood up. "Nothing, I don't know what you're talking about. It's just..." Katherine slipped. "Your father..."

"What about my father? He died in a riding accident. You said so." Kate grasped her wrist. "Or was that a lie, too? Please, Grandmother, just this once, can't you tell me the truth?"

Katherine turned away from her. Her hands fell to her sides and folded into balls. "Your father did the same thing the night your mother died. He locked himself in his room and drank. He killed himself."

Kate sat back, stunned again. "So it was a lie."

Katherine sighed. "Not exactly."

"What happened? Tell me, please, I need to know, Gran."

Katherine faced her. Her eyes avoided Kate and her lips quivered. She wrung her hands across her chest. "It was her—your mother. She bewitched him. She took him away from me. My child—my son—my baby boy—your father."

Kate was terrified of the truth but needed to know—she was desperate to know. For it to rattle her grandmother, Kate knew it couldn't be good. "Tell me, please, I want to know."

"For what possible reason? For what good? It's all over. In the past."

In order to go forward, Kate had to ignore the pain in the other woman's eyes. "I need to know, Gran. I need the truth."

Her grandmother's voice deepened. "It was right after she died. That woman—your mother. He went into their room and locked the door." She began to pace the room, slowly at first. "I went back to him and knocked on the door. He didn't answer. I decided to wait until morning—let him sleep. Recover from her death." She stopped at the dresser. "There was an awful noise in the middle of the night—a loud bang. I knew what it was at once—a shotgun blast." She brought her hands up to her face, covered her ears, and shut her eyes. "The door was locked. We couldn't get in. George, Jackson, and Lincoln broke the door in. When we stepped inside—he lay on the bed—my boy—my son—my child—your father. He lay on top of her." She opened her eyes and glared. "He killed himself over her—your mother— that woman. He left a note that he couldn't bear to live without her." She lowered her hands. "He had everything. He was everything—my everything and he killed himself over her." Katherine turned away.

Kate swallowed hard. Some of it made sense now—her grandmother's hatred for her mother. "T—that's why you keep their room locked and the nursery they made for me. It saddens you."

Her grandmother faced her. "There's nothing in those two rooms but sadness. There is no need to go in there, ever."

"So," Kate admitted, "my father didn't love me enough to stay—to be here for me. Why did you lie to me about how he died?"

"I was trying to protect you. You didn't need to know any of this. That is all I have ever done for you. I will not apologize for it." Katherine walked over to her and took her hands in hers. "It is all over now. In the past and we have to move on from all of it, all of this. We can get past this. No one knows. No one has to. And those that do, will never say anything. I made sure of that." Katherine hugged her tightly.

Kate pulled back from her. "You mean silencing Maddy and Sam?"

"Yes, and they won't talk."

"Gran, you can't expect me to ignore that I'm Black. Ignore who I am and what I found out."

"Yes, I do darling. You have to."

"Gran, I can't do that. That'd be ignoring my mother. My mother was Black. I'm not ashamed of that. My father, your son loved her. Her parents are Black. I'm Black. It's who I am now."

"You're only half-Black!" Katherine sighed in frustration. She was clearly exasperated. "I'm sorry, darling."

"Don't be. I'm not," Kate said. "I'm stunned. I'm confused by it all, but I'm not sorry. It doesn't bother me."

"Well, it bothers me and it should bother you!" Katherine snapped.

"It doesn't, Gran, and I don't understand why it bothers you. Why should it bother me?"

"You grew up in a different time. You wouldn't understand."

"Then explain it to me, please. I want to know. I want to understand."

"You can't."

"I'm willing to try," Kate said. "Gran, could you do that, ignore your mother? Did you love your mother?"

"Of course I did," Katherine shot back.

"And I love mine. Just because I never knew her doesn't mean I love her any less. My father loved her. He didn't care she was Black. He didn't care his child would be."

Her grandmother sighed again and was clearly frustrated with her but did well in holding it back. "Did Maddy tell you how much she and George were against your father marrying your mother? How much they hated him because he was White?"

"No, she didn't, but—" But it was in her mother's journal. Her parents hated him.

"Well, she should have. She is anything but an angel. She didn't want her daughter, your mother, anywhere near a white man, which is pretty funny coming from her."

"What do you mean by that?" Kate asked. "Did she hurt you?"

"It doesn't matter now. It's in the past."

"Grandmother, I really want to know. I need to know. And what is the big deal anyway? This is the year 2015. We have a mixed race president-the first one—"

"Black president," Katherine corrected.

"'Wh—what?" Kate asked.

"He chose to be Black on his census, not mixed race."

"Gran, what does that mean?" Kate asked. "What does that have to do with anything?"

"You're either Black or White. You can't be both. Both sides won't accept you. He knows that. He chose to be Black to get the Black vote and he did."

Kate laughed. "That's archaic thinking, Gran."

"No, darling. In some places to a lot of people, it is not. I don't want you to be hurt. Darling, people can be cruel. They'll say awful things." Katherine shot to her feet and spun around to face her. She waved her hands at Kate for emphasis. "Darling, you just don't understand the harsh realities of life. I've protected you from all of that!"

"You're overreacting, Gran."

Kate saw her grandmother's eyes blaze at the remark and then, as if by magic, her grandmother calmed herself and spoke in a low voice. "No, darling. I think not."

"Grandmother, I'm thirty years old. I haven't lived in a bubble. I've lived in other places. I've traveled. I've been married and widowed. I know enough about life to know how cruel it can be, but not anywhere as cruel as a family that lies and keeps things secret. I can't help wondering if there is anything else you and Maddy are hiding from me? Is there?"

Katherine went back to her. Her eyes softened. "I asked you earlier—did Maddy and Sam ever come to you before today and tell you they were your Black family? Did they ever tell you that your mother was Black? Did they?" Katherine placed her hand on Kate's shoulder. "It was because you were White."

Kate stared at her grandmother. Was that it? Was that the real reason behind their keeping the secret? For lying to her all these years? "They said you would kick them off the property, out of their house if they ever told me the truth."

"Is that what they said? George and Maddy wanted no part of

a White baby or a half-White baby. I'm so sorry, darling, to be so blunt. The last thing in the world I ever wanted was to hurt you, but you wanted to know. Darling, your grandfather and I wanted you because you were White, so we kept you."

"Half-White, and what do you mean, you kept me?"

Katherine spun away. "I'm sorry, darling. I can't discuss this anymore. It's too painful. You'll have to just accept what I told you and let it be. Or get the rest from Maddy. See how much truth she tells you. You have to trust me that I know what is best for you and let this go. Some things are better left as they are. No one knows about this. No one knows you are half-Black. No one ever need know. Leave it alone." She reached out a hand and caressed Kate's cheek. "Don't ever lock yourself in your room again, darling. Please. Promise me." She then moved toward the door. "Let it go. Leave it be, darling, please. I'll have Carol bring you up a tray with some warm milk." She shut the door behind her.

"But I know, Gran," Kate murmured. "I know."

And she needed to know if there was more, and if there was, she needed to know all of it. She sensed there was more without Katherine telling her. There just had to be by the way her grandmother held back. *What did she mean by...she kept me?*

Chapter 6

With all that happened today, with all that she learned, with all the things said, and all the things that weren't said to her, Kate knew she would not be able to eat or sleep without finishing what she had already started, no matter how tired she was.

Forget about trying to get some sleep. Kate wasted no time in going back to visit with her mother's family. She was so angry, she made it to Maddy's house on foot in just ten minutes. She didn't even knock before she swung open the front door.

"I'd like to speak with you Maddy," she said.

Sam, Elsa, and Maddy sat at the round wooden table in the kitchen off to the side of the short hallway. Neither one of them looked surprised to see her.

"Of course, child. Come in," Maddy said.

"Alone," Kate said. "Please."

Sam and Elsa hesitated and then got up and left the room.

"Sit down, child," Maddy said.

"First off, I'm no longer a child." Kate remained standing. "Tell me about the night my mother died."

"I already told you all I know."

Kate pulled out a chair. "That's just it, Maddy. I don't think you did."

"I haven't lied to you."

Kate leaned toward her. "That's just it, Maddy. I think you have. I want to know why my grandmother hates you so much. Why she hated my mother so much, and you and George, why did you hate my father?"

"I don't know," Maddy said and turned away. "I told you everything."

"Pardon me, Maddy, I don't believe you."

"Maybe you should ask her—Katherine," Maddy countered.

"I know you and George didn't like my father. Now, I'm asking you. I want to know and I want to know now." Kate folded her arms across her chest. "And I'm not leaving until you tell me."

Maddy turned around and stared at the floor. "It was—a long time ago. It's not worth talking about."

Kate studied her. "What was a long time ago?"

"Some things are better left buried. I'm sure Katherine agrees with that."

Kate took a step forward. "She said to ask you. I'm asking."

Maddy's eyes widened and she shook her head. She sighed, removed her reading glasses, and set them down on the table before her. "Child—"

"I told you, I'm not a child," Kate said. "Second, you want me to accept you as my grandmother—believe what you said? Then you owe it to me to tell me the truth." Kate slapped her hand on the wood table. "Now, Maddy. Please. If you care anything about me, tell me, please."

Maddy jumped at the sudden sound and shifted in her seat. Kate saw her mull it over.

"You're right. You're not a child anymore. Not for a long time." Maddy got up and walked to the sink. "No more secrets." She sighed and closed her eyes for just a second then spoke. "I knew your grandfather—Jackson—for a while." Her lower lip began to tremble. "We were lovers."

Kate caught her breath. That certainly explained a few things—Katherine's hatred for Maddy. *Oh God, no…*the worst thought came to mind.

Maddy went on. "Please don't judge me, child. I was young, my husband—your grandfather George—and I were having problems. Your grandfather, Jackson, and Katherine were having problems too. It just happened. We were there for one another—while it lasted."

Kate had to interrupt. "Please, don't tell me he fathered Sam or—my mother." That would be more than Kate wanted to know.

"No," Maddy said. "My husband, your grandfather George, was their father. The children were already born."

Kate hadn't realized she had held her breath until she heard herself sigh in relief.

"I was in love with Jackson," Maddy continued. "Maybe in another place and time, we could have been together. I was willing to leave my husband. Then one day, Jackson ended it. I was heartbroken. I was furious." She returned to the table and sat down. "He said your grandmother had found out and threatened to divorce him and take your father away. He couldn't allow that. I guess he had no choice, but he broke my heart. The last thing I wanted for my daughter, your mother, was to fall in love with a White man, like I did. I didn't want her hurt, least of all by Jackson's son."

"My grandfather was married. You were married. My father wasn't," Kate said. "And from what I hear, my father was nothing like his father."

"No. He wasn't. He was a fine young man, a good friend to Sam, the older brother he never had. "

"But that didn't matter to you, did it?"

"He was White, Kate. He was Jackson's son. Your mother wasn't for him."

Kate couldn't believe what she heard. She banged her fist on the table. "Says who? You? Katherine? My grandfathers? That wasn't up to any of you to decide! Wow, both of you are something else. You're more alike than you realize, do you know that? Tell me, Maddy, do the two of you, Katherine and you, conspire here together at night while I sleep?"

"W—hat? Of course not. I hate your grandmother."

"And she hates you. Tell me. Did my parents know of your animosity for each other?"

"Of course, they knew we didn't like each other and we were against them being togeth—"

"And against them marrying each other?" Kate cut her off. "I know all about that."

"It was a different time, a different place. If they were somewhere else—"

"And if they'd had different parents. It was 1984, Maddy, not the sixties, and they got married, anyway, in spite of you, all of you." Kate couldn't have been more proud. She never knew them, but she couldn't have loved them more had she tried.

"Yes, they did, but please don't judge me, Kate."

"Judge you? I don't even know you. And right now, I'm not sure I want to. Tell me, is there anything else I should know?" Kate demanded.

"Kate, you don't understand."

"You're right! I don't! Answer my question. Is there any more secrets?" Kate asked. "Anything else I need to know?"

Maddy hesitated.

"Is there, Maddy?"

Maddy stared at the table for a few moments and then glanced up. "It's about—your sister."

"What about her? She was stillborn."

"No," Maddy said. "She wasn't."

Kate felt the anger rolling into a ball in her stomach. "Go on," she growled. Somehow, she already knew. Somehow, there had always been a pit in the bottom of her stomach, something she could never digest. Somehow, there was something always missing from her life aside from her parents.

"She was sent away. Katherine didn't want her around," Maddy said. "None of us did."

"Why not? She kept me."

"Your sister was Black. Black as I am. I guess she didn't want a reminder."

"Of your affair with her husband? Unbelievable! You both hid all this from me. You're no better than she is."

Maddy held up her hands. "Kate, please—"

"Tell me, what was the price for your silence, your lies? I really want to know. Was it this house? This property, as Sam said earlier? Are you telling me you sold your granddaughters out for material things?"

"I swore an oath to protect you, from the truth," Maddy objected.

"Protect me? From the truth? Your truth or hers? Where is my sister?" Kate demanded.

"I don't know. I haven't seen her since that night you were both born."

"Both born? What do you mean both born? We were born the same night? We couldn't have been. Unless—we were twins?" Kate said.

"Yes. She was born first. You came along a little while later. You were both so small, so quiet."

Kate sat back in the chair, trying to take it all in while fighting for composure. She didn't know whether to run or stay, to explode or remain calm. This was more than she expected to learn. Her sister. Her sister wasn't dead.

Kate swallowed hard. "Twins?"

"Yes. Fraternal twins, your mother wasn't strong enough for

both of you. Doctor Castle did everything he could for her. I was there. I know." She brought her hand to her chest. "Olivia died—just after you were born."

Lincoln was there? Of course he was, their family doctor and close family friend. "Why did you all lie to me? Why did you all hide this from me? Why?"

"Kate, we swore an oath."

"To give my sister away?"

"Yes. As I said, to protect you."

"You mean to protect you. Did you ever once think about telling me the truth? Once? In all these years?"

"Once or twice—I thought about it—but…"

"But?"

"I agreed with Katherine. The damage had already been done. There was no need to dredge up the past. You were so happy. We could stay here and be close to you, to see you grow up. We were just trying to protect you. We agreed that it would be easier for you to believe you were an only child rather than tell you she was stillborn. We all wanted you to be happy."

"Happy? My sister wasn't stillborn! You lied to me!" Kate leaned forward. "Look at me, Maddy! Do I look happy?"

"No, but you never were supposed to find out. Never."

"Well, that certainly has changed, hasn't it? Where is my sister?"

"I don't know. I really don't. Katherine didn't want to know either. I did later on, but it was too late."

"So the four of you conspire together—and you had an affair with my grandfather. Now I know why Katherine hates you. Makes sense. Some of it."

"She wasn't exactly an angel herself," Maddy said.

"What do you mean by that?"

"It's not for me to say."

"You're right. I think you'd said enough, just not in time. But I'd like to know, just the same anyway."

Maddy nodded. "Your grandmother had a few affairs while she was married. To whom, I won't say. That is up to her to tell you."

"Is that why you felt it okay to have an affair with her husband?"

"I told you—we were both having problems. It just happened. That's all," Maddy explained.

"Let me guess, one of them was Doctor Lincoln," Kate said.

"Yes—how?"

Kate heard the shock in Maddy's voice. "Does it matter?" Kate sighed at it all—Katherine did lie about Lincoln. "I don't know if I believe anything either of you say. I don't know—"

"Kate, child." Maddy reached out to touch her. "Please—"

Kate pulled back. "You know, all you had to do was tell me the truth. We were family. Now it's too late."

"It's never too late. We are family."

Kate shook her head. "You don't know me at all, and I don't know you, and right now, I'm not sure I want to."

"Kate, please—"

"Tell me something, Maddy. Katherine and Jackson kept me?"

"Yes."

"Because I was White?" Kate concluded. "Or looked White?"

"Because you were born White, yes."

"Why didn't you and George keep my sister?"

Maddy didn't answer and turned away from her.

"I'm going to try and find my sister, but as for the rest of you, to hell with all of you!"

Kate stood up so quickly that the chair flipped over backward onto the hardwood floor. The crashing sound slashed through the silence. She was so filled with confusion and anger that threatened to consume her, the sound didn't even faze her. She rushed from the house and slammed the door behind her.

❧

Kate rushed away from the house and stormed up the long road back to the big house. Seeing Maddy confused her even more than before and made her even angrier. Knowing Katherine lied about her affair with Lincoln incensed Kate. Was Lincoln really her grandfather? Or was it merely another lie? Could she believe anything Katherine said to her now? Maddy? Of course, that question wasn't nearly as important as what really pressed on her. Where was her sister? Did Maddy really know and not tell her? Did Katherine know? Did anyone know?

There were so many questions and the more she asked the more she discovered. Would there be an end to it all? Her mother's journal wasn't very long, or very informative. In a few pages, it said more than she could have imagined, but not enough to tell her what she needed to know. Her grandparents hated her parents. They didn't approve of their children's love for one another, their marriage, or their baby that was on the way. The grandparents, it seemed, had their own plans for their grandchild, and evidently they made good on it, at least some of it.

She should go home and try to sleep. She knew that. It had been a long day. She needed to rest, especially since she didn't know what was exactly wrong with her. Perhaps, she was just tired and dehydrated. She knew enough about lab work to know that some irregularities would show up when one was dehydrated. Uncle Linc was just a bit overcautious because he was limited in what he knew. But she knew she couldn't sleep. How could she sleep after all she just discovered? How? Besides, the last thing she wanted to do was chance seeing Katherine again when she was so angry. The rage that was building inside her terrified her.

Instead, she stopped inside the barn after the fifteen-minute walk back. She walked slowly on her return in order to give her time to think. She never paced before, but tonight she found herself doing just that. She wanted to hit something, someone, or throw something against the wall. But she wouldn't. That wasn't rational and it wouldn't achieve anything, especially when what she wanted to do eluded her. Besides, there was still one more person she needed to visit. It was nearly ten now, but she didn't care. She stormed to her car, a two-door Mustang GT convertible, and pulled the set of spare keys from under her seat. She started the car and eased it down the long driveway onto Thayer Lane and then onto the main highway Forty-Nine. Highway 49 and Highway 16 were the crossroads and the home of the Blues. Ironic, since today it had been become her crossroads too. Once she was on the road, she sped on toward Lincoln's house. If anyone knew, it might be him. In fact, if she was right, it was him.

ↄ◌ↄ

Before she knew it, she found herself back at Lincoln's renovated farmhouse ten minutes later. She knew she had to maintain control, but this matter was more important.

She knocked on the door and rang the bell three times in a row. She knocked again and rang the bell until someone answered. Lincoln often retired early as he began with early days.

She yelled through the door. "Open the door, Uncle Linc! I need to speak with you!"

She saw the light behind the drapes go on in the living room.

Lincoln opened the door. His white hair was disheveled and he had come to the door in a long robe and slippers.

She brushed past him. "Where is she?" She had no time for cordiality.

"Where is who?" he asked and brought up a hand to comb his hair with it. "What time is it?"

She led the way into the parlor off the short hall.

He followed. "Kate, what's this about? Are you ill?"

She pushed away his concern for her safety. "Where is she?"

"Kate, what are you doing here so late? Is your grandmother all right?"

She spun on her heel and faced him, cutting him short of his steps. "That wasn't the question, Uncle Lincoln. The question should be, is my sister all right?"

He couldn't match her gaze and turned away. "What are you talking about? I told you—"

"I know what you told me, Uncle Linc, but I don't believe you. Maddy told me the truth. My sister wasn't stillborn. She's alive, so where the hell is she? Did you kill her? Since she wasn't stillborn, you must have killed her."

"W—what? Of course not. I told you—"

"I know what you told me. Where is she?" She folded her arms across her chest and planted her feet firmly on the hardwood floor. She wasn't going anywhere until she got what she came for. "I'm not going anywhere until you tell me the truth." She plopped down on the burgundy leather sofa. "And I don't want Katherine's truth or Maddy's. I want to know where she is. The rest I'll find out later. You know, don't you, or did you kill her? You'd do anything for my grandmother, wouldn't you? There is no other explanation. You must have killed her then, because she wasn't stillborn."

"No. I didn't. I told you—" He walked over and sat down on the matching sofa across from her. She saw the defeat on his face. She didn't care. Right now, the only persons she cared about was herself and her abandoned sister.

"What happened?" Kate said. "You'd do anything for my grandmother. So did you kill her? Did you kill my sister?"

"No, I couldn't. I told you—"

"Then where is she? Tell me. Please. Where can I find her?"

He shook his head. "I gave my word to Katherine. I won't betray your grandmother."

"But you'll betray me? My sister? Your supposed grandchildren? I need to find my sister. What my grandmother did was wrong. What you all did was wrong." She reached out and grabbed his collar. "If you care about me, tell me where to look for her." She released him. "Please. What really happened that night? That night we were born. Did my grandmother want her dead?"

"No, Kate, I know you're upset—"

"You delivered her. You took her away or you killed her, which is it? There can only be one answer."

"She isn't dead, but I don't know where she is," he said, avoiding her gaze.

"I don't believe you, Uncle Linc. You told me she was stillborn, which was a lie. You're a liar just like my grandmother and you killed my sister for her, didn't you? "

"No! I didn't kill her!" He took a breath. "Your grandparents didn't want her. I sent her up north to an orphanage there, to give her a chance," he said. "I didn't harm her. I swear."

"Which grandparents? Katherine and Jackson, or Maddy and George?" she asked.

"Both, Kate." She heard him sigh. "Neither wanted you or her. Neither. Maddy and George didn't want you or her. Neither did Katherine and Jackson. We weren't expecting twins."

She leaned back against the sofa. Astonishment filled every pore and burrowed into her heart. Was it possible for a heart to stop and still be alive? For a long moment, she swore hers did just that.

"They didn't want her—or me?" she asked. Her throat went dry. "Our grandparents didn't want us? Both our grandparents? Our mother's parents didn't want their grandchild either? Is that what you're telling me?"

This was all too incredible to hear. No wonder Maddy couldn't tell her. *Is this what they meant by seeing your world come to an end?* For everything she knew did just that. It ended.

"Yes, Kate. Neither wanted you or your sister. Neither wanted a mixed-race baby," he said. "I'm sorry. They didn't, except when Katherine and Jackson—when she saw you. Katherine wasn't about to give you up. They kept you. Your sister was already gone from the house by then and on her way up north."

She heard the pain in his voice, but it was nothing compared to the pain in her heart. Is this what it felt like to be stabbed? She heard Katherine's words again, '*We kept you.*' Now she knew what she meant.

He reached out to touch her arm.

"Don't touch me." She pulled back. "My grandparents didn't want either one of us? Is that what you're saying? Is that what you're telling me? My grandparents, all of them—are racist?"

She saw him recoil from her. "I'm sorry, Kate, but you wanted to know."

She snapped to her feet and turned toward the fireplace. It was as cold and barren as she was right now. "I trusted all of you." She glared at him. "I loved all of you. I've known every one of you for my entire life." Her words were strained and full of pain. She heard them echo in her ears. She never felt as alone as she did now.

He brought up his hands and folded them across his chest. "I'm sorry, Kate. You were never supposed to know any of this. Ever."

She ignored him. She had heard that before. Three times— from both grandmothers and him. Same dialogue which was obviously rehearsed. That was the only way to explain it.

Liars. All of them.

"M—Maddy said…" She tried to absorb what she just heard and keep her thoughts on track. There was even less sense to things now and so many more questions. "Maddy said she is Black. My sister looks Black."

"She did. She was." He shook his head. "She is. I guess. I haven't seen her since you were both born."

Kate caught her breath. She needed to be in control. She had to be to get what she came for. All sorts of thoughts and questions flooded her. There were so many she could only voice one—the one that pressed on her most, the one she came to get the answer to. "Where is she? Do you know?"

"Do Katherine and Maddy want you to know?" he asked.

"To hell with what they want! Do you really think I care what they want?" She felt herself losing control and she didn't want to do that. If not for her upbringing—It terrified her that if she was someone else, she could strike this old man down right now. "I want to know. You owe me. You owe my sister. You let our mother die!"

"I told you." He stood up. "I tried to save her. She was fragile. I did. I tried to save her. I swear." She heard remorse in his voice. "And I couldn't hurt your sister any more than I could hurt you. I didn't—I—"

"But you did hurt me, Lincoln, and my sister. You hurt both of us." Only one thought pushed her onward. Heat began to fill her cheeks. She flexed her fists and clenched them tightly determined not to falter, but she softened her words and sat down on the sofa. "Do you know where she is or not?

For a moment, he didn't speak. Then he lifted his gaze to her, slowly nodded, sank into the sofa, and covered his face with his hands.

"Tell me. And it better be the truth, Uncle Linc."

Chapter 7

Katherine couldn't sleep and went to check on Kate. Just in case, she knocked on the door and then entered when there was no answer. As usual, she left the door open in order for the hall light to make its way into the room. She didn't want to take a chance and wake Kate if she was sleeping. After all that occurred today, she had to ensure that Kate was all right. Her granddaughter could never sleep when something troubled her. She did expect Kate to be awake, but she wasn't, and Katherine soon discovered why, as she approached her granddaughter's bed.

On the bedside table was a small bottle. "Sleeping pills?" she whispered. She closed her eyes for a moment and sighed. *Oh God, darling, I thought we discussed this.* She took the bottle to the hall to read the bottle in the light. They were sleeping pills from over the counter. She went to Kate's bedside table and set the bottle back down. Slowly she opened the draw to look inside and found nothing, as she expected. She went into the bathroom, closed the door, and flicked on the light. Inside the medicine chest, she looked again, but found nothing.

She closed her eyes for a moment and sighed in relief at finding nothing she expected to find. She shut off the light and eased out of the bathroom and back to Kate's bedside. Of course, she had to allow the sleeping pills this time, after all that Kate went through today. She needed to sleep. *Darling, please just let things be. Just leave sleeping dogs lie. Some things are just better left alone—*

Kate's sudden movement startled her. Kate rolled over from her side onto her stomach. Suddenly she started fidgeting in her sleep. Her eyes began to flutter and she began to whimper.

Katherine stepped toward her, reached out, placed a hand on her shoulder, and spoke softly. "Easy, darling. Sleep now, darling. You're safe," she said. "Grandmother is here. Sleep."

In reflex, under her grandmother's touch, Kate's sleeping form calmed down immediately. Katherine leaned over and brushed away the strands of stray hair from her granddaughter's face. Her skin was warm to her touch. Katherine raised her fingers to her own lips, kissed them, and then touched Kate's lips with them. "You sleep now, darling. We'll talk about all of this tomorrow and what we're going to do," she whispered. "We'll fix this. I promise. You rest now." She ambled her way back to the doorway, gave one long look over her shoulder, and shut the door behind her. She held onto the doorknob and leaned against the door. "This too shall pass," she said.

୧୬୧

First thing in the morning before anyone else was up, Kate showered, dressed, and went down to the barn. The twin foals were snuggled against their mother. Delta Darling was preening herself. She was busy licking her foreleg. Kate admired the beauty of them, their majesty. Their lives were so simple. Someone else, such as she and her grandmother, would decide their fate. They didn't have to worry about choices and they certainly didn't have secrets in their lives.

"They're doing just fine, Miss Kate," Carl said from behind her.

She was so engrossed in admiring the horse family she hadn't heard him enter or expected him so early. "I know. I just want to be sure. The first two weeks are the most crucial for mother and twins."

"You said, but they're fine. They're in good hands. Mine," he said. "And yours. You're up mighty early. It's not even light out yet."

She appreciated his levity. Life was so simple for him too. He had room and board and he had a job and security. He had stability. He knew where he was and what he was doing. She and her grandmother told him what to do, what to expect, and he saw that it was taken care of.

"So are you," she said.

"Yeah...well. I was concerned about them too. They're beautiful, Miss Kate."

"Agreed."

"Your grandmother is set to fetch a good price for these two," he said.

"No. I don't think so."

"No?"

"I'm keeping them."

"Good answer. They are your horses, miss."

"Yes. Yes they are." She leaned over and patted Delta on the head. Delta nuzzled in her hand. "I want you to take extra special care of them, lady." She withdrew an apple from a closed metal bin on the wall. From the back pocket of her jeans, she withdrew a small pocketknife. Slowly, she cut pieces off the apple and handed a piece to the mare. The mare greedily took it, chewed, and swallowed.

Kate climbed over the wooden fence and jumped down. The two foals woke up and looked up at her. She knelt down and handed out a piece of apple in the palm of her hand. The black foal moved to stand and took the apple from her. It turned around and brought the apple piece back to the other twin. The two foals nibbled at it until it was completely gone. The mare nuzzled them and they lay down against her again. This time Kate moved closer and cut three pieces of apple, one large and two small. She slid along the ground until she was just next to them. With an outstretched hand, Kate offered them the pieces. This time the smaller white foal got up first, still a bit wobbly on its skinny legs, took the piece, and nibbled on it in her hand. The black foal copied it. The mare watched and, when her babies were finished, she consumed the large piece. She neighed and the two foals went back to her. She nuzzled them and placed her head on them and they went to sleep. For a long moment, Kate envied them. The twin foals had a mother's love and protection. It was something she never had and never would. They were beautiful and she couldn't help but admire them—the mare's love and care for her foals and their beauty.

She leaned over, hugged them tight, and then stood up.

Carl tilted his head at her. "You say that as if you're going somewhere."

"Maybe. I just might. For a little while. You'll take care of them for me? Keep them safe?"

"Of course I will. You know that," he said. "Are you all right, Kate? You seem…different today. Not yourself."

Was that ironic or what? "How long have you known me, Carl?"

"All right, I'll play. Your entire life. Thirty years. Why?"

"You said I seem different, how? Do I look any different to you? Sound any different?"

"No. I just meant you seem preoccupied with something, and it's not the foals."

He was right about that. "Watch over them for me," she said and turned to leave.

"I will."

ɛ·ɔɛ·ɔ

Katherine went down to the dining room to join Kate for breakfast. She was prepared to be firm but gentle with Kate. Kate had to let things go. She just had to. Katherine would ensure she would and would deal with Maddy and Sam later.

As usual, Kate would begin her day with chores then return to the house and share breakfast with her grandmother and they would talk. That was their routine. It was the staple for their day. Why should today be any different? Kate was a sensible young woman. Katherine had every faith in her that she would do the right thing, according to her grandmother's wishes. She always had done so before. Of course, Kate could sometimes be stubborn, but she was level headed and Katherine knew that, in the end, her granddaughter would listen to reason. She always had before. Kate was not the sort of person to let her emotions run things and Katherine took great pride in that.

She sauntered into the dining room to begin her discussion with Kate but there was no sign of her. As usual, Carol scurried in with a pot of coffee and proceeded to fill a cup in place in Katherine's spot at the head of the table. After adding a bit of crème and sugar, Katherine took her seat and sipped.

She picked up the folded newspaper from beside her plate and began reading. Every morning she and Kate read the *Wall Street Journal*, the *New York Times*, and the *Thayersville Gazette*, and discussed business and affairs about things that concerned the farm and things in general. Katherine believed that a woman should be prepared to run the world, if need be, and she instilled that in her granddaughter. Women had been trod upon, ignored, and taken advantage of for far too long, and her granddaughter knew, from a baby, that she was important. Her thoughts mattered and no one would ever tell her different. No man would ever make Kate a doormat. Never leave anything for a man to do something that you can do, she often told Kate. That was the reason the state of the nation and the world was in such a mess. Sadly, men ran everything. Despite it being 2015, it was still a man's world and they still didn't know how to run things properly.

She glanced at the clock. It was nine a.m. and Kate should be here any minute. Katherine opened to the business section and scanned the stock pages, paying close attention to the stock they owned in various business entities. Ten minutes later when she glanced at the clock again, there was still no sign of Kate. This wasn't at all like her. First, last night with being late for dinner and now this. Of course, last night Kate had a good reason for being late.

Carol came in, but before she spoke, Katherine did, "Have you seen Miss Kate this morning?"

"I did, Miss Katherine. She went out to the barn to check on the foals after chores."

"Did you see her return?"

Carol thought for a moment. "No, but I was busy cooking. Elsa is off today."

"Fine. Bring me the phone please."

Carol took the cordless receiver off the wall phone from behind her, brought it over, and handed it to Katherine. "Do you still want me to wait on Miss Kate or serve you?"

Katherine stared and didn't answer. Carol nodded. Katherine had a routine and Carol knew it, but sometimes she had to remind her. Unless one was away, or ill, Katherine and Kate always dined together.

The first call was the obvious one to make, but instead of Kate she received the voice mail and left a message, "Darling, it's Grandmother. Where are you, darling? You're late for breakfast and I'm worried about you. Call me when you get this or please be here. I love you, darling." She hung up. She hated the modern technology, no matter how convenient it could be. It was all so impersonal and trite.

Katherine dialed the barn and waited. She tapped her fingers on the edge of the saucer.

"Hello, Carl here?" the voice answered after four rings.

"Morning, Carl, Mrs. Thayer here. Is Kate there?"

"Morning, Miss Katherine. No, she isn't. She was earlier, though. Checking on the foals and mare."

"Did she go riding or onto other chores?"

"Nope. I saw her heading back toward the house. Is there a problem, Miss Katherine?"

His reply concerned her. "I'm not sure."

"You want me to ride out and check around for her?"

"Yes, I would, Carl. Thank you. Call me when you find her."

"I will. I'll have her call you straight away." He hung up.

She ended the call and set the phone down next to her coffee cup. For a brief moment, anxiety gripped her and she had to catch her breath. The last time that Kate had been unaccounted for was when the riding accident had occurred two years before. Had she gone riding this morning and was there was another accident? After yesterday, Kate may not be thinking clearly, but that would be so unlike her. Or was it because of yesterday that Kate wasn't here?

Katherine came to her feet. "Carol," she called.

After a moment, Carol scurried into the dining room and wiped her hands on her waist apron as she entered. "Yes, Miss Katherine?"

"When you saw Miss Kate this morning, was she all right?"

"Y—yes. She was fine. She didn't want anything from the kitchen but she was fine. Is everything all right, Miss Katherine?"

"Did she say anything to you?"

"No, should she have?"

"Are you sure she didn't say anything to you?" Katherine asked. "Anything at all?"

"No, Miss Katherine. Nothing at all."

"I want you to call her friends. Every one of them. See if they're seen her."

"Yes, Miss Katherine."

"Beginning this minute," Katherine ordered. "And tell Carl to have our hands look for her too. All of them."

Katherine leaned on the edge of the table and tried to think rationally. Where could Kate be? Of course, Kate wouldn't do anything foolish, would she?

After last night, though, anything was possible. Could it be that she went back to see them? Again? But for what possible reason? They already told her the dreaded secret they swore never to reveal—Oh, no, they wouldn't. They swore—but they swore never to tell her anything and then they did. They couldn't—

Just then the phone rang and she snatched it and pressed the talk button. "Kate, darling, where are you—"

But it wasn't Kate. "I'm sorry, Katherine. I should have called last night, but I was pretty shaken up," Lincoln said.

"Whatever are you going on about?" she demanded.

"Kate was here and she was very upset."

"When? When was she there? She said she went to see you earlier in the day. Why did you tell her you were her grandfather?"

He cut her off. "She knows, Katherine. She was here last night."

"Knows what? That she's half-Black? I know that. She said Maddy and Sam told her. We were going to discuss it this morning—" *Last night? After we spoke? After I told her to let it go?*

He cut her off again. "No. She knows about her sister. All of it."

Katherine's legs went weak under her. She sank into the wooden chair and nearly dropped the phone, but caught it with the aid of her other hand. Her hand began to shake and she had to hold the phone with both hands. She swallowed hard, but the lump wouldn't go down. "W—what? What did you just say?"

"She knows about her sister, Katherine. I had to tell her. I had no choice."

"How on earth?" Katherine exclaimed. "You swore to me never to say anything. We all swore that night."

"Maddy told her about her sister not being stillborn. Kate was furious when she got here. I never saw her like that. She looked like Jax did that night. She scared me. I had to tell her the truth. My God, Katherine, we were wrong. We were all wrong about this."

Carol ran in at the sound of Katherine's raised voice. Katherine waved her away and Carol scurried back out of the room.

"Where is she now?" Katherine said.

"She's not at home?"

"No she isn't at home," she shot back. "Did she say anything about what she was going to do? Where she was going?"

Silence.

"Lincoln, what did she say to you?"

He finally spoke. "She wanted to know where her sister was."

"And? What did you say?" Katherine demanded.

"I told her I don't know," he said and she heard the exhaustion in his voice, but he was not her concern. Kate was.

"Well it's true, isn't it? You don't know." She began to ramble. "How could you? It's been thirty years. Anything could have happened to her. I told you what to do."

"She didn't believe me," he said,

"So you lied again? Right? I mean—you don't know so what could you possibly tell her?" Katherine demanded. "And you wouldn't tell her the truth?"

His voice was shaky. "No—of course not."

"Good. If she contacts you again, tell her to come home. I need to talk with her. I need to fix this," she said and hung up. She closed her eyes for a moment, slowly inhaled a deep breath, and exhaled. Her hands were still shaking but were leveling off. "Oh Kate, what have you done? Where are you? What are you going to do?" *I should have told you the truth—*

But it was too late for regrets.

There was only one thing left to do now. There was only one place left to go and see what other foolishness occurred last night. Now she knew why Kate had needed sleeping pills to get to sleep. The secrets Katherine had held together for so long, out of sight and out of mind, had just exploded and collided head on. However would she contain this now? However would she fix this?

Chapter 8

Katherine rushed into the kitchen and snatched a set of keys from the hook so fast Carol didn't know what to think. In an instant, she was in the blue Ford pickup and racing down the drive away from the house. Five minutes later, she was across the farm on the road in front of a house she hadn't been in years.

Without knocking, she pushed open the door, rushed past Elsa, and stormed up to Maddy. Elsa and Maddy were standing in the kitchen, talking, when Katherine burst in. From their expressions, both the women were clearly stunned to see her.

"Where is she?" Katherine demanded. She had no patience for lies.

"Who?" Maddy asked. "What's going on? What are you doing here?"

Katherine saw the shock on the other woman's face. "What do you mean who?" she snapped. "What other reason would I come down here to see you? Kate—where is she?"

"Kate? She's not here," Elsa interjected. "What makes you think she'd be here?"

"Thank you, Elsa, but I wasn't speaking to you." Katherine faced Maddy. "Where is she, Maddy? What exactly did you say to her last night? I was foolish enough to think she'd drop it, but she didn't. Now where is she?"

Sam entered the kitchen from the living room. "She's not here. We haven't seen her since last night."

"You expect me to believe you?" Katherine snapped.

"It's true," Elsa said. "They only told her the truth."

Katherine ignored Elsa—her focus was on Maddy and Sam. "Where is she? Maybe she's with your people."

"My people?" Maddy said. "I think she'd stand out, don't you?"

"You just couldn't keep that big Black mouth quiet—" Katherine hollered.

Sam stepped in from the side. "Careful, Miss Katherine, this is our home—"

Katherine faced him. "On my farm, my land. I let you stay here, as long as you never said anything to Kate. You just couldn't hold back, could you?"

"*I* told Kate," Sam snapped. "It was time."

Katherine wasn't impressed. "It was never the time. She never needed to know." She faced Maddy. "You gave me your word, and I believed it."

"We both lost our children. Do we want to lose Kate, too?" Maddy said.

"My son killed himself because of her—your daughter."

"And my baby died in childbirth," Maddy shot back. "We need to put our differences aside and find Kate."

"We wouldn't have to find her if you just kept quiet," Katherine pointed out. "This is all your fault. Every bit of it."

"Believe what you will, but we must join forces," Maddy said.

"Where is she?" Katherine demanded and slammed her hand down hard on the table.

"I don't know," Maddy said.

"If you're lying to me, Maddy, I swear I'll tear this house down with all of you in it."

Maddy stood tall before her, which was no match for Katherine's height. "I said I don't know. She wanted to know where her sister was. I don't know, do I? Oh my God, what have we done?"

"What have we done?" Katherine shouted. "You just couldn't keep your big mouth shut, could you? You swore. You promised. We all did," Katherine said.

"Sam is right. It was time she knew," Maddy said.

"That wasn't up to you to decide," Katherine shot back and stamped her foot.

"I lost my baby girl that night!"

"And I lost my son! Isn't that enough?" Katherine moved to leave but spun around instead. "If anything happens to her, Maddy, I swear I'll have this house torn down around you and this land burned to the dirt!" Katherine stormed out and slammed the door behind her.

Maddy faced her son. "Sam?"

"I don't know where she is, Mama. I haven't seen her since she was here last night."

"We need to find her, son. We need to spread the word to find her. She was so angry last night. I hadn't seen that kind of look since the night your sister ran off and married Jax when we forbid her to see him anymore." Maddy went to the family photo on the wall—the one she had shown Kate the night before. She stared at the little girl in it. "My baby's babies are all grown up and I don't know them at all," she said. "We have to find Kate, Sam."

"I will, Mama, I promise," he said without hesitation.

"How, son?" She glanced at the rest of the photos on the wall that she had made into a shrine for Olivia.

He came up behind her. "I don't know, Mama. I'll check around. I'll check the train stations, the bus stations. I'll find her."

"We don't even know where to begin. If she even left town," Maddy said.

"I'll ask around," he said. He kissed her on the cheek then went back to Elsa. "I'm going to see if I can find her," he whispered to his wife.

"How? Where?" Elsa said. "How are you going to find her?"

"I don't know. Stay with Mama." He took her hands and kissed her slowly. "I love you, baby."

He grabbed a jacket from the hook near the front door and was gone a moment later.

Elsa went to Maddy's side.

Maddy placed her hand on an eight by ten inch photo of her daughter on the center of the wall. Her daughter was on one side of the color photo. The other side was missing—torn off. "This was her wedding photo when she married Jax," she said.

"I know, Mama. She's beautiful," Elsa said. "Let's sit down."

"She was so beautiful. George cut Jax out of it because he didn't want a White man in his house looking down at him. I only could put the photos up of her, after—after he died. He wouldn't have it." She leaned forward and kissed the photo of Olivia. "She gave us a copy of her wedding photo even though we were against her marriage." She shook her head. "Her little girl—if something happens to Kate—to…"

"Sam will find Kate. You know he will," Elsa said. "If anyone can, Sam can." She placed a hand on Maddy's back and rubbed it in small circles.

"George never really accepted Livie looking so White," Maddy told her. "He thought I had cheated on him with another and she wasn't his. But look at her. He just refused to see. She was her daddy's little girl. Strong chin, her daddy's eyes, and his mouth. And she was just as stubborn as he was. He was such a fool." Maddy turned to face her. "Don't be angry with Sam. He never told you anything because we made him swear never to tell anyone."

"I'm not. I love Sam," Elsa said. "I understand, Mama."

"Do you? Really? I'm glad. Not everyone could." Maddy turned back to the photos. "So much time has been lost. Things were so different back then. Even now, things aren't the way God intended them to be. I couldn't blame him really—George. Mister Jackson could be hard on him with work, but his son, Jax, he was nothing like his father. Funny thing is after our baby died, George refused to talk about Livie, but I would hear him crying when he thought I wasn't in the house, or when he thought I was sleeping. He'd never talk to me about it. He was the best blacksmith in the county, the state. Foolish, proud, stubborn man. He refused to move with the times." Maddy brought up a hand and touched her daughter-in-law's cheek. "You and Livie would have been such good friends. I know it. You're so much like her. You are patient, understanding, kind yet stubborn, and you both love Sam. He idolized her, you know, his sister."

Elsa took her mother-in-law's hand in hers. "Yes, Mama, I know we would have been. I know."

"You're so good for my boy," Maddy said. "Sam loves you."

"I know, Mama, and I love him. You should sit down."

"Why couldn't we accept Livie's choice? Why were we so horrible to them? Why were we so wrong?" Maddy couldn't hold back. "I miss my baby." She let the tears fall. Her heart began to race. Her mouth became dry. Her legs became deadwood. "Did I ever tell you how she defied us? How she and Jax ran away and got married?"

"No, Mama. You haven't."

"I was there, at home, waiting for her so that we could sit down to dinner. She was always late for dinner and her daddy was already so angry. He liked dinner on time. I remember this particular night because I met her at the door when she came in…"

❦❦❦

Maddy met her at the door. "Where have you been, child? You're ten minutes late. Your daddy is fit to be tied. You know how he hates to be kept waiting."

Livie didn't get a chance to speak before she heard her father's booming voice from behind. "Damn it, girl, where have you been?"

"With friends," she said.

"What friends?" he demanded. He was furious. He was always furious when he wasn't obeyed and lately Olivia stopped obeying him. He stepped up to her. "You were with that Thayer boy again, weren't you? I told you to stay away from him. I won't have my daughter carrying on with no White boy."

Olivia stuck out her chin and met him head on. "First off, Daddy, Jax is no boy and we love each other. When we graduate from college, we're going to be married."

George snapped and struck out at her face with one large powerful blow. "Like hell, you will!"

She reeled back and grasped her mouth. She looked at her mama, but Maddy merely turned away.

"To hell with all of you then. I love him," she said and stormed from the house.

George ran after her and then came back for the truck keys and they both rushed after her. They knew exactly where she was going and they followed her.

As Maddy and George pulled up into the long driveway and neared the house, they saw her on the steps. Jax met her there. She rushed into his arms and he held her close.

George sped to the bottom of the steps, stopped the truck, and got out. He moved to grab Livie, but Jax blocked his path. George was a big man. Years of forming iron for Magnolia Lane Farm had made him into a muscular man. He stood six feet and didn't have an ounce of fat on his body.

Jax wasn't small either. He stood six feet and four inches tall and earned his muscles from working on the farm from his youth, sometimes right alongside George. When Jax supervised the farm workers, he got right into the throes of it, working alongside his employees. Loading hay bales and breaking horses weren't beneath him, as they were for his father. He played football through high school and college. If anyone was a match for taking on George, it was Livie's knight in shining armor.

"You're coming home, girl, now," George said.

Olivia moved from around Jax. "It's all right, Jax. I'll be back. I don't want a fuss. I'm all right now."

George grabbed for her arm. She lifted her head for just a moment and Jax saw her face. He shoved George back and pulled her to him. "Who did this to you?" Jax demanded. "Did your father hit you? Because of us?"

She lowered her head. Jax pushed her behind him. "You're staying here with me."

"You turn her over now, boy," George said. "I have no quarrel with you."

"You better go home, George," Jax said.

"You may be my boss, but this is personal. Step aside. I don't want to hurt you, boy," George said.

Maddy stepped forward. "Just let it be, George, please."

"Shut up, woman. Get in the truck," George ordered, but Maddy didn't obey.

George took a step forward to grab Olivia but Jax held his ground. "Go home, George."

"She is my daughter."

"She is going to be my wife," Jax said.

"Like hell, she is!"

George reached out and grabbed her hair. Jax made a fist and slammed it hard into the other man's face. George went down onto his back. He was obviously stunned for he didn't move.

"Jax, don't!" Olivia yelled and brought her hands to her face. "Daddy, just go home. Please!"

Jax leaned over George. "I've known you for my whole life, but if you ever lay a hand on her again, I'll break your neck." Jax stood up, moved to take Livie up the steps, and stopped. He came face to face with his father aiming one of the family prized shotguns over his shoulder behind him.

"We're not going to have any problems here, are we, George?" Jackson said and didn't even look at his son.

Jax turned to find George just behind him with his hands clenched into raised fists.

George took a step back and held up his hands in surrender. "This is family business, Mister Jackson. I have no quarrel with you. I just want to take my daughter home. That's all. Your son here got in the way. He can be a hothead sometimes, you know." George feigned a laugh.

Jackson didn't waver and neither did the muzzle of the classic 1913 LC Smith 12 gauge side by side shotgun. "If memory serves me correctly, George, you have quite a hothead on your shoulders too. Now maybe it's best if you go home."

"Not without Olivia. You know as much as I do they don't belong together. Now they're talking marriage. You want that, Mister Jackson? 'Cause I don't," George said.

Jax took Olivia's hand into his. "We're going inside," he told his father.

Jackson eyed him and lowered the gun. "She's welcome to stay here until her daddy calms down."

"We're getting married, Dad. I told you. Right after we both graduate," Jax said.

"No. You're not. Think sense, son. You're not marrying a Colored girl," Jackson said. "No offense to Olivia, I've seen her grow up, but no way, son."

"We love each other," Jax said.

"End it. Now. Here. Let her go home," Jackson ordered. "You go in the house."

Jax looked at Katherine. "Mama?"

She shook her head. "No, Jax."

Jax led Olivia to the side of the porch just within earshot of the others. "Do you love me?" he asked her.

"With all my heart."

"Do you—do you want to end it? Do you want to—to not see me anymore?" he asked.

She took his large hands into hers and kissed them. "I love you, Jax, always and forever. I don't want to be anywhere else, or with anyone else."

He grinned. "Do you still want to marry me?"

"More than ever."

"Do you trust me?"

She grinned. "Absolutely."

"Then come with me." He lifted her up over the porch railing. They both ran to his small expensive silver sports car, jumped into it, and sped out of the driveway and out of sight.

∾∾∾

"I think Jax meant for us to hear everything he said to Livie that night because I heard his every word. I also think we were all too stunned to move when they did that. When they ran away. We didn't see them for a week. We didn't hear a word from either of them. We didn't know if they were alive or dead. And then they finally came home. They married in Las Vegas and they were so happy. Right from the start, we made their lives miserable and tried to break them up. And when Livie said she was pregnant a little while later, we were even worse to them. All we wanted was for them to be apart from each other. We didn't care how we did it. We were so wrong, so horrible." She looked at Elsa. "Do you hate me?"

Elsa took a breath. "You were all wrong, Mama. They obviously loved one another very much, but I wasn't there. And that was a long time ago. Yes, you were all wrong, but no, I don't hate you. I could never hate you."

"All I ever wanted was for my two babies to be happy, and Livie was. Why couldn't we see that and just be happy for her, for them?"

Elsa took her into her arms. "Let's sit down, Mama. You should sit."

Maddy cried for the thirty years lost, and the years before, and for the present. "My baby was only twenty, only twenty when we lost her." Her legs went weak under her, but Elsa caught her before she fell to the ground and helped her over to the nearby wing chair.

"Sit down, Mama." Elsa released her into the chair. "I'll get you some tea."

Maddy grabbed her wrist. "No, child. No tea. Sit with me. Just for a little while."

"All right, Mama." Elsa sat in the rocker right next to her and held her hand. "I'll sit with you for as long as you want."

cςεσ

Katherine sped the pick-up truck into the drive directly in front of the garage and barely missed hitting the steel door. She hadn't felt so angry in such a long time and here in the span of thirty-six hours fury consumed her more than it had since thirty years before. For a long moment, she sat there behind the wheel and considered the options. She had raised Kate to be a strong independent woman. As a result, Kate wouldn't yield to anyone, not even to her, not unless she wanted to. Katherine closed her eyes. *'Be careful what you ask for,'* rang in her ears. However, Katherine had to remember that Kate knew that her grandmother loved her and had her best interest at heart, always. Katherine had to take comfort in that.

She knew she couldn't let her emotions get the best of her. Emotions were weakening and the downfall of those who let it consume them. She couldn't let her concern get out of hand. She had a farm to run. She had to take care of things until Kate regained control of her senses and returned. Until then, Katherine would be the caretaker, as she was before when Kate was just a child and too young to take over. The second time, when Kate was away at school and couldn't take over until she had graduated, married, and returned from her two years abroad and in New York with Adam. Then Katherine had turned over full operation and trust to her. Then again, two years before she had to be caretaker when Kate was incapacitated and bedridden for eight weeks and the long recovery after.

Kate was an intelligent woman. Katherine had taught her self-reliance. She'd have to trust that Kate wouldn't do anything foolish and would come home when she was ready. Until then, Katherine would have to run things again. No big deal. Kate would be back soon. Katherine knew it. And things would be back to normal. She would see to that.

She went up to her room and changed into a pair of old jeans, and a long-sleeved farm shirt. She grabbed a bush hat and a pair of leather gloves from off the shelf of her closet.

Downstairs, she grabbed a pair of rubber boots from the entryway closet and headed to the front door right past Carol.

"Miss Katherine? Aren't you going to eat lunch? I have it ready? You didn't eat any breakfast—"

"No time, Carol. I'll see you at dinner. If you need me, I'll be working outside," Katherine said and shut the door.

"Outside?" Carol said. Since when did she work outside? Not since she turned the farm over to Kate. That was Miss Kate's domain, when she was here, anyway.

৵৩৵৩

Katherine went into barn, straight to the back wall that held a dozen hooks. She took a clipboard off one. With her other hand, she raised her reading glasses from the strap around her neck, placed them on her nose, and began to peruse the sheets.

Carl came in from the back where the workshop was located. He was whistling a tune she didn't recognize. He stopped when he saw her. "M—Miss Katherine? Morning. Anything I can help you with?"

Without looking up, she answered, "No. Nothing."

"Um—I'm sorry, I just don't usually see you down here anymore. Here to check on the foals? They're doing—"

"No, Carl," she cut him off. "A farm doesn't run by itself. I'm here to see what needs to be done today."

"Oh, well, that's all right then." He moved to leave then stopped. "Pardon me, Miss Katherine, I can take care of anything that needs doing until Miss Kate returns."

"Returns? What do you mean returns? What makes you think she's gone?" she snapped.

"Well, what I mean to say—look—nothing, Miss Katherine. Nothing at all. Slip of the tongue. That's all. I better get to mending those downed fences."

"You do that, Carl. Run along now. I'll be fine."

He waited. "Are you sure you don't want me to help you with something?"

She glanced up. "Carl, this is my farm, is it not?"

"Well, yes, ma'am."

"Do I look as if I require your assistance?" she said.

"Well, no, ma'am, just thought…well, Miss Kate has her way of doing things, that's all."

Katherine faced him. "And you think I'm going to interfere with her routine?"

He raised his hands in the air. "No, ma'am, the routine she learned from you. Just want to make sure you know how she runs things."

"I'm sure I can figure out her system, Carl, since as you said, she learned her routine from me. Thank you, Carl."

"You're not going to try and break a horse or something like that while I'm gone, are you?" he asked and then gave a small laugh.

"Are you being flippant with me, Carl?"

"Who me?" he said. "No, ma'am. Not a chance. Just a little joke."

"Very little, Carl. You may go now," she said.

He nodded and moved to say something more.

"I'll call you, Carl, should I have any questions," she finished for him.

"Y—yes, ma'am," he said. He scratched his head under his cowboy hat and headed out.

"Men," she grumbled. "Still think women are helpless. What a crock! Had I left it to the men, this farm would no longer exist."

Of course, there had been a price to pay to run it as she wanted to and do as she pleased with it, and everything else. But it was well worth it, especially since Jackson had died long before she did. She had no one to answer to now. Not now. Not ever.

ഌഈഌ

Sam checked the bus and train stations in every town beginning in Thayersville and an hour's drive out to include the larger cities of Jackson, Vicksburg, and a final stop in the smaller nearby city of Yazoo City. Finally, he saw a young White woman on the platform in downtown Yazoo City, a twenty-minute drive from home. Yazoo didn't have a train station, just a stop with a roof and bench.

Was he seeing things or was it really her? All he could see was her profile, and he was about a hundred feet away, but she closely resembled his niece. She was tall and slender with long sandy blond hair that fell to her shoulders. He greatly hoped it was her. He'd run out of places to look, except for the airports, but if she was anything like her mother, the train or bus stops were a better bet.

"Thank God. It is you," he said as he caught up with her.

She didn't face him. "What are you doing here, Sam? Go home."

"Everyone is looking for you," he said, obviously having run to catch her since he was breathing rapidly, and his limp was more pronounced than usual.

"Let them look," she said.

He reached out to lay a hand on her shoulder.

"Don't touch me, Sam," she snapped.

He backed up. "I'm sorry, Kate. For everything. I swear. I'm so sorry. You have to come home. Everyone is worried about you."

"Let them worry." She wanted so much to hate him, all of them and yet, she couldn't. However, anger did consume her—

for now, she couldn't push it aside. She turned away. "Go home, Sam."

"Where are you going? Maybe I can come with you?" he said. "Look after you."

"You mean like you did for my mother?" she snapped.

"That's not fair. There isn't a day goes by that I don't kick myself for letting her get involved with him—I mean—"

"You mean my father? So you didn't like him?" Kate said.

That was enough for her. Was he racist too? She hadn't realized. How could she be wrong about so many people close to her?

Sam pursed his lips together. "I didn't say that. I didn't mean—look, your father was a good man, a friend. We grew up together, the three of us, but he wasn't for her—"

"Because he was White?" Kate said. "Or because she was Black?"

"I didn't say that, Kate—"

She cut him off. "You didn't have to. I know the truth Sam. I know everything. Neither of our grandparents wanted us born because we were "mixed race," and when we were born, they still didn't want us. Funny thing is, Katherine and Jackson kept me, but no one kept my sister. No one, not even my Black grandparents."

"She was stillborn, Kate."

She laughed. "Is that what they told you?"

"What do you mean by that?"

"Just go home, Sam. I really don't want to see any of you right now."

"Kate, don't get me wrong," Sam said. "Back then, I believed our people should just stick to their own kind."

"Our people? White people or Black people?" Kate said.

He sighed. "Both. Trouble happens when you mix them."

"Trouble? Like my sister and me? Trouble? Is that what you mean? You're incredible!"

"No, of course not. We love you, both of you. You're our family. Look, Kate, you're getting it all wrong."

"Family? No. I don't think so. I understand everything now. I think you should stay here." Kate glanced at her watch.

Sam took a step toward her. "I'm sorry. Look, I gave my word to both your mama and daddy to look after you, before you was born. I couldn't protect your mama. Let me at least be here for you. Please."

Kate eyed him. "Why?"

"Because you're my niece and I love you. I know you don't believe me, but it's true."

"Even though I'm half-White."

"I don't care about that. I never did, except, back then, like I said, I thought your mama, Livie should have married someone else, not your daddy."

"Do you think she'd still be alive had she married someone else?"

"Yes…maybe…I don't know. I thought so back then," he said.

"Did my mother love anyone else?"

"No. Not a soul."

"Go home," she said.

"Kate, I understand you're angry—"

She turned on him. "You understand nothing! How could you? You don't know me! And I don't know you!"

He remained calm. "I'm family, Kate. We're family."

She took a step toward him. He remained still—unruffled by her temper.

"Family? What family? Families don't keep secrets and lie to one another, Sam!"

"Every family has secrets—and lies," he said. "We're no different."

"Like hell, we're not!" She took a deep breath. Her heart was racing. She knew her blood pressure was up. *Calm down*, she said. *This isn't you.* "Families don't hate each other because of the color of their skin. Families don't break up families. Go home, Sam. Just go home." She turned away and took a deep, slow breath. Normally a calm person, this sudden rage that grew inside frightened and unsettled her. "Just go home, Sam," she said softly. "I don't want you here."

"Okay," he said, but from the corner of her eye, she saw that he wasn't leaving.

"What are you doing?"

"Waiting for the train," he said nonchalantly.

"I said go home. I don't want you here."

"This is a free country, Kate. I can go anywhere I want. You don't own the train," he said.

She sighed in frustration and let go of the hostility, temporarily. "Fine. Whatever." She faced him. He was eyeing her, but didn't say a word. "You're going to follow me, aren't you? No matter what I say?"

"If that is what it takes, Kate, yes. You're not the only stubborn one in this family," he said.

She shook her head in disbelief. She thought she knew him—this man who stood before her. This man with the caramel skin and eyes to match and stood merely seven inches taller than she stood. He was six feet, four inches tall. Of course, she didn't really know him at all. "All right. You can come with me."

"Where are we going?" he asked.

"Does it matter?"

"No," he said. "This will be good for me. Haven't been on a train in years. Not since, I left for West Point. Why didn't you take a plane?" he asked. "It'd be faster to get you to wherever you are going."

"I don't fly," she said.

He studied her and then his eyes brightened, as if he knew the answer to a secret. He nodded and grinned. What else did he know that she didn't? She had to know.

"Something amusing?" she asked.

"Nope, not a thing."

Kate glanced at her watch. The distant noise of an oncoming train interrupted her thoughts. They both moved to pick up her small case but he reached it first.

"I'd really like to come with you," Sam said.

"What if I said I was leaving Mississippi?"

"Then I definitely should come along. I haven't been out of Mississippi since I was in the army."

The train made its entrance into the station. She knew it would be as difficult for him to hear her as it would be to speak. All she could do was nod.

Chapter 9

Back at the plantation, later that evening, Katherine questioned the staff and dismissed them, except for Carol. Katherine couldn't help but pace and she didn't care who knew about it. "Anything from her friends?" she demanded.

"No, Miss Katherine. No one has seen her since the party the other night," Carol said.

"Are you sure she didn't say anything to you last night? Anything?"

"I'm sure, Miss Katherine. I took up a tray last night just like you told me to."

"What did she say to you? Exactly?"

"Thank you, but she wasn't hungry."

"That's all?"

"Yes, Miss Katherine. That and to take the tray away and good night."

"Thank you, Carol."

Carol nodded and moved to leave.

"Wait a minute," Katherine said. "Where's Sam?"

"I don't know, Miss Katherine."

"Never mind. Thank you."

Carol scurried from the room. Katherine paced the room then stopped to stare up at her husband's portrait. She walked over to the bar, picked up a near half bottle of whisky, and flung it up at the painting. The bottle broke. Shards of glass and the alcohol streamed down the front of the painting onto the mantel below.

Carol scurried back in at the sound and moved to clean it up.

"Leave it," Katherine said.

Carol nodded and scurried back out.

Katherine walked over to the large fish tanks Kate kept against the wall. If she remembered correctly, there was one marine tank and one tropical and both were fifty-five gallons each.

She couldn't remember the types of fish inside. The feeder and lights were set on timers, which wasn't a good sign. Kate only set them when she went away. It was set for two weeks. Is that how long Kate planned to be gone? Where was she and what would she be doing for two weeks? That concerned her deeply. It was so unlike her to do this.

The phone rang and Katherine moved toward it. She snatched up the receiver. "Kate?"

"Sorry, Miss Katherine," Carl said. "Just me. We've covered the whole place and there is no sign of her anywhere, which is a good sign."

Katherine's heart skipped a beat. "Fine, Carl. Thank you. Let me know when she shows up." She hung up the phone and held onto it. She hung her head, said a small prayer, and then looked up at the portrait of her husband.

She picked up the phone and dialed Maddy.

"Have you found her yet?" Katherine asked. "Has anyone seen her?"

"No. Sam hasn't returned yet," Maddy said. "Katherine, I think we should—"

"Call me when you find her or hear anything." Katherine slammed down the phone. She glanced up at her husband's portrait now wet with liquor. "Bastard. You men make the mess and we women always have to clean it up, don't we? I'll never regret protecting Kate, never, but in the process I think I may have chased her away and you were no help at all."

She picked up the phone receiver and pressed the button for the internal line. She didn't have to say anything, Carol entered within less than a half a minute. "Yes, Miss Katherine?"

"I want this portrait removed and discarded." Katherine saw the puzzled look on Carol's face.

"Miss Katherine?"

"Tomorrow morning, first thing, have it taken down and burned."

"Are you sure about that, Miss Katherine?"

Katherine walked to her and placed a hand on her shoulder. "Just do it, please. Get rid of it, Carol."

"Yes, ma'am," Carol said and watched Katherine exit the room.

Carol walked over to the fireplace and began cleaning up the broken pieces of the liquor bottle. She stopped and looked up at the portrait. "You must have really pissed her off," she said to the portrait. "I really never heard anything good about you and the way you treated my mistress. I certainly won't miss your face looking down at me anymore." She stuck her tongue out at it and went back to her work.

∽∾∽

A little while later, Carol went into make Kate's bed when she found the white envelope on it. She stared at it and was afraid to touch it.

Finally, she lifted it off the pillow and stared at it.

Elsa came by and noticed Carol standing near the bed. "Carol?"

Carol turned. Her usual smile was absent.

"Are you all right? You seem…spooked," Elsa said.

"I—I found this on Miss Kate's pillow. It's addressed to Miss Katherine."

"So just give it to her."

"What if it's bad news?"

"What would make you say that?" Elsa asked. It probably was, but how would Carol know?

"Miss Kate isn't here. She left no word and left. Miss Katherine isn't herself. She went to work outside to do chores. She hasn't done that since she turned the farm over to Miss Kate three years ago. Should I give it to her?"

"What do you think?"

Carol sighed. "Yes, but before, or after dinner?"

"If I were you, I'd wait until after."

Carol sighed again. "Yes, I suppose so. She'll be upset either way. At least she'd have eaten first. No good to get all angry on an empty stomach. Thank you, Elsa."

Elsa went to move on.

"Elsa," Carol called.

"Is Miss Kate all right?"

"I'm sure she's fine," Elsa said and fervently hoped so. Where she even was, was anyone's guess. All Elsa knew was that she was worried about both her niece and her husband.

∽∾∽

When the train pulled into the tiny station in Yazoo city, it rolled to a stop and a middle-aged Black man stepped down. As she neared him a voice came from the train's loudspeakers. "Welcome aboard Train 21 *City Of Lights* to Chicago. Please have your tickets ready for our porter to collect."

"Evening, miss?" he said and tipped his pillbox hat at her. "Anyone having sleeper reservations, please step forward."

Kate was one of three passengers to step forward. She was one of five plus Sam present. She was closest and handed the porter her ticket. He examined it, ripped off part of it, and placed it in his shirt jacket.

"Thank you, Miss Thayer. I see you have a reservation in one of our Superliner Bedrooms. Good choice. Your room is available on the Upper Level of the car behind me. You can go right in and we'll come by and check on you."

"Thank you," she said. "I need to purchase another ticket—" she began.

"We're traveling together," Sam added. "I don't have a ticket."

The porter checked his small handheld console. "I'm sorry. We're all out of sleeper rooms to Chicago. You can buy a seat ticket only."

"That's fine," Sam said. "I'll take it."

Sam took out his wallet, withdrew a credit card, and handed it to him. The porter scanned the card and returned it to him. "Thank you, Mister Johnson," the man said. "The name's John should you need anything. You'll have your own porter for your car during the trip. Have a safe trip."

Kate walked to the car, grabbed the handrail, and stepped up. Sam was right behind her with her bag. She walked down the passageway, headed upstairs to the second level, and found her berth without difficulty. She stepped inside and waited for Sam. He hesitated. Another porter came by and introduced himself as George.

"I can show you around inside if you need," he said. "Not my car, but we share work when we have to.

"Thank you, George," Kate said. "That's fine, but that won't be necessary. I'm fine."

"Fine, ma'am. Dinner for your room is at seven thirty, Miss Thayer. Just proceed to the dining car and they'll take care of you."

He faced Sam. "And you, sir?"

"I don't have a room," Sam said.

"No problem. I'll show you where you sit."

Sam nodded at her. "I'll let you get settled and see you later."

"Fine, Sam."

Sam followed the porter out.

Kate closed the door and leaned against it. For the first time since yesterday, she had a chance to catch her breath. To slow down and think about what she was doing. That wasn't like her at all. Of course, her life had suddenly changed drastically over the course of a couple of days. And only a slight portion of it had anything to do with her appointment with Doctor Lincoln Castle. In the blink of an eye, everything she had known had been thrown upside down. How was it possible?

She ambled over to the sofa and sank down into it. She withdrew her cell phone from her purse and opened it to find there were twenty-two messages for her. Though she knew that most of them were probably from Katherine, she pressed to play the latest one anyway. It had come in thirty minutes earlier.

"Darling, where are you?" Katherine said. "I'm worried about you? Are you all right? Are you eating? Darling, please call me when you get this message. Whatever is bothering you, we can fix this. I promise. All you have to do is tell me what it is. Please, darling, call me."

Kate ended the call, pushed a number from her directory, and made one final call she needed to tend to. She also set her cell phone alarm clock to wake her promptly in the morning. She shut off the cell phone volume, switched it to vibration, and returned it to her purse. She leaned her head back against the head cushion and glanced out the window just as the train jerked and stirred into motion.

She can fix this? All I have to do is tell her what is wrong. Ha. As if her grandmother didn't know. They all knew—that was the problem. Fix it? As if she could.

She closed her eyes for a moment. That was all.

ⅇⅇ

Later back at the manor house, Carol went back up to Katherine's room. "Miss Katherine, will you be coming down for dinner or shall I bring you up a tray?" Silence met her. "'Miss Katherine," Carol reached out a hand and touched her shoulder causing both women to jump.

"Carol? What is it?" Katherine said. "Have you heard from Sam? Kate?" She hadn't even heard the other woman enter.

"No, ma'am, it's almost dinner time. Will you be coming downstairs, or should I bring you a tray?"

"I'm not hungry."

"Yes, ma'am, but you have to eat."

"I said, I'm not hungry, Carol!"

"Yes, ma'am." Carol started to turn away.

Katherine sighed. She didn't mean to frighten Carol or be harsh to her. "Carol." Carol stopped and faced her. "Thank you. I'm just not very hungry."

Carol forced a weary grin. "Well, I'll let you miss dinner this one time as long as you try to eat something a little later on, okay, Miss Katherine? You really need to keep up your strength. Miss Kate wouldn't be too happy with you if you let yourself get sick."

Katherine eyed the younger woman. Carol was a fine young woman. She had no regrets over hiring her, even when no other woman in the county, White or Black, would hire her simply because her father had been a convicted murderer. He had been executed before Carol had even been born. It wasn't Carol's fault who her father had been. It certainly didn't matter to Katherine. After twenty-one years in her employ, Carol, on more than one occasion, proved to be competent and loyal to her and Kate. What more could an employer ask for?

"We'll see. Go on," Katherine told her.

"Miss Katherine—are you all right?" Carol studied her. "Should I call Doctor Lincoln?"

"No. I'm fine."

"Are you sure?"

"Go on, I said. And Carol, go ahead and bring me up a tray, please."

Carol grinned. "Yes, Miss Katherine. Coming right up."

Katherine wasn't really hungry, but Carol was correct. She had to keep up her strength for when Kate returned. She needed all her strength and resilience to help Kate get through this bump, as when she stood by Kate two years ago.

She could only hope that Kate was eating right. Better yet, she hoped that Kate was eating at all. The girl could be quite reluctant when it came to eating regularly. She had to be kept to a routine to ensure she would, which is why Katherine insisted on one at home. The girl wouldn't eat at all if not for the routine. Everything else in life took precedence. Kate's mind could often work quicker than any computer. Her mind would tend to other things that needed her attention first before she took care of herself. Whether it was overseeing the sale of horses, ensuring the workers harvested the cotton crop on time, or that the cattle got fed and watered, Kate took everything seriously. Katherine was proud of her, but it often drove her to worry about her, as well.

༼ン༽

Back aboard the train going north from down South, downstairs on the lower level of the passenger train car, the porter George led Sam to his seat. Before George left, Sam spoke. "The dinner time you gave my niece, is that for everybody on board?"

"No, sir. Just for our sleeper guests."

"I see," Sam said. "Is there any way I can get dinner reservations? This is a reunion for my niece and me and it's important." He was more concerned about her safety than he was about dinner.

"I'm sorry, sir."

"Nothing available for a veteran?" Sam said. "I'll pay for the seat."

"Ex-military?" George asked.

"Retired army."

"Really?" George's eyes lit up. "My son is in the army. Just went to OCS. I'll tell you what—it's irregular, but I'll see what I can do for you."

"I appreciate it. Thank you," Sam said and extended his hand. George took his hand in a friendly shake. "And good for your son. Congratulations. I'm sure he'll graduate top of his class."

"Thank you, sir. We hope so. He's all gung ho about it," George said and moved on his way forward.

Sam nodded at the older White man seated near the window next to him. The man was dressed in a gray suit and red bow tie. Black framed glasses sat on the edge of his nose. The man set down the book he was reading and extended his hand. "The name's Jim. Jim Hooper."

Sam leaned forward, extended his hand, and introduced himself.

"Have a seat, son. I don't think you're going to grow any-more," the man said.

Sam sat down. His leg was bothering him, but he didn't want to show it. Instead, he angled it just to be out of the aisle, but not sticking out too far. His discomfort must have shown because the man noticed.

"You all right son? Leg bothering you?"

"A little. Old injury," Sam said.

"Military or sports?"

"Army."

"I knew it," the old man said. "My son-in-law was in the Marines. He was killed when a land mine exploded under the personnel carrier. Twenty marines died that day."

That touched Sam deeply. He sighed and shut his eyes for a moment. "I'm sorry to hear that, sir." He remembered his war time days, way too vividly sometimes, and wished he could forget.

"Me too," Jim said. "He was a fine young man, just thirty-one. Just had his funeral last week and now we're heading home. I hate flying, so here we are."

"Are you alone?" Sam asked.

"Nah, gave my daughter the sleeper car. A young woman needs her privacy, especially if she wants to cry. She doesn't want me to see, but I know. They were married for six years. Met in college. I'm going to miss him."

"I can imagine," Sam said. "It's rough. I know." How many funerals did he attend since the United States entered Afghanistan and Iraq? He'd lost count.

"Were you in Afghanistan or Iraq?"

"Both," Sam said.

The old man nodded. Sam saw the pained look in his eyes as he tried not to stare at Sam's bruise. "My son-in-law too. Three tours in each place. He was due to come home again a month before—then boom it happened." He clapped his hands for emphasis.

Sam flinched and shifted in his seat. He swore his heart skipped a few beats. He didn't realize just how touchy he still was after resigning his commission two years earlier.

"I'm sorry, son," Jim said. "Didn't mean to make you jump. I should know better. I was in Vietnam. Took me ten years to get over that mess. I'm sorry."

"No problem, sir," Sam lied. "None at all." He had to maintain his grip. It seemed that all this stuff with Kate and the family made him more sensitive to everything.

"You have family with you?" Jim asked.

"My niece." Sam felt warmth fill him when he said it and felt his heart skip a beat. He never had a chance to say it out in the open before. "She has a sleeper car too. You're right about privacy."

"That's nice—seeing an uncle and niece traveling together. I used to take my nieces to a lot of places when they were little, but then they grew up and didn't want to travel with this old man anymore."

"That's too bad." Sam really didn't know what to say. The man was nice enough, but Sam hoped he wouldn't talk all the way up North.

"Well, I've said enough. I didn't mean to go on, but I've been on here since New Orleans and no one to talk to. I'll just go back to my book and let you be, if you don't mind?"

"Not at all, sir," Sam said both relieved and a little bit guilty for thinking so rudely. "It's been a pleasure."

The man nodded and put his focus back on reading a very big book, *War and Peace* by Tolstoy.

Sam leaned back in the chair grateful for the silence, except for the slight jerking and clanging sound of the train in motion. He didn't mean to doze off.

"You're all set, Mr. Johnson." The porter returned and woke him. "You'll be enjoying dinner with your niece at seven thirty in the dining car. Enjoy your meal. If I can be of any further assistance, just ask for me, George, or any porter. We'll be glad to help."

Sam extended his hand. "Thank you, George. I appreciate it."

The old man nodded and smiled. "Don't have to thank me, sir. Your reservations were already made. Your niece called them in a little while ago to ensure you had them. Have a good night," George said and moved on his way.

She did? Shocked, all Sam could do was shake his head. He sighed in admiration. She definitely was a woman of action—even more like her mother. Olivia would be so proud. He certainly was.

He saw her grow up when he visited on leave, but it wasn't the same, being in the background, the son of an employee then ex-employee, but it was better than nothing. At least he was able to see her.

He glanced at his gold watch. After seven already? Where did the time go? He took a deep breath. He knew Kate was going to want to speak with him, about what exactly he didn't know but he could guess. And of course, he'd have to tell her the truth. No more lies. He swore that when she nearly died two years before.

He felt a twinge in his leg and stood up to relieve it, but it didn't help so he walked up and down the car a few times before he went upstairs to go fetch Kate. He hoped she wouldn't mind joining him for dinner. He shouldn't have presumed. He realized that now. What if she didn't want him to join her? She had every right to refuse. What if she made the reservations simply to be nice? Of course, the worse thing she could do was tell him no. With that in mind, he made his way to her cabin and knocked. No answer so he knocked again. No answer. He knocked a third time, louder this time.

℮∕ͻ℮∕ͻ

Back at the manor house in Mississippi, in her master bedroom suite, Katherine went to her nightstand and picked up the phone to ensure there was a dial tone. She couldn't even imagine where Kate was. She could be anywhere. Katherine began pacing back and forth. All sorts of things began to form in her mind and her concern for Kate grew. What if something happened to Kate? What if she was going to do something foolish? Why hadn't she called back? Katherine's thoughts were interrupted by a knock on the door.

Carol entered when told to, walked over to her, and began cleaning up the tray.

"I'm so glad that you ate," she said.

"It was delicious, Carol. As usual. Thank you."

Carol lifted the tray, carried it to the dresser near the door, and set it down. She stopped a moment with her back to Katherine and then walked back to her. Carol reached into her apron, retrieved a white envelope, and held it held out to her. She took a breath and waited.

"What's this, Carol?" Katherine asked.

"I—I found it this afternoon when I went to make Miss Kate's bed. It's addressed to you."

Katherine shot to her feet. "This afternoon? Where has it been all this time?"

"I thought—it would be best to wait until after you ate something," Carol said.

"You thought?" Katherine exclaimed. "You thought? I don't pay you to think, Carol!"

Katherine snatched the envelope from her and stared at it. Fear gripped at her throat and at her heart. Slowly, she reached down, raised her eye glasses from around her neck to her nose, and read the address to her on the outside of the envelope. She immediately recognized Kate's elegant handwriting on the envelope and inside on Kate's personalized stationery sheet.

> *Grandmother, I love you, but I don't agree with you or Maddy or my grandfathers. Not with any of you. I'm sorry that all of you didn't like my parents getting married, but they did. Tell me, Grandmother, had I been born Black, would you have discarded me too?*

Katherine nearly collapsed where she stood. Carol must have noticed because she rushed to her side and grabbed hold of her from behind.

"Miss Katherine, are you all right? Shall I call Doctor Lincoln?"

"No, just help me to the bed," Katherine said as she tried to regain control of her breathing.

Carol eased her over and Katherine sank down on the edge.

"Where is Sam?" Katherine asked.

"No one knows. He's not answering his phone. I did send for Elsa, Miss Katherine. Is there anything else? Are you sure you don't want me to call Doctor Lincoln?"

Katherine grasped the other woman's wrist with her free hand. "No, Carol. Thank you. I'm sorry. I didn't mean to yell at you." She extended a hand and patted Carol's shoulder. "You can go."

Carol hesitated and then walked to the door and stopped.

"Go on, Carol. I'm fine now," Katherine repeated. "And no calls to Doctor Lincoln."

Katherine crumbled the note and brought it up in her hand against her chest. She brought her other hand up and buried her face in it.

There was another knock on the door. Katherine lifted her head and took a breath. She wouldn't reveal her true feelings to anyone. "Come in."

Elsa entered and walked up to her. "Miss Katherine, you wanted to see me?"

"I need to speak with Sam."

"I don't know where he is. I haven't been able to get a hold of him."

"Still? And Maddy?"

"She doesn't know either. He didn't say a word. We assume he's still looking for Kate."

"Is he with Kate?"

"I don't know. I would think so, if he found her. But he didn't say anything to us. If he is, you don't have to worry. He won't let anything happen to her." Elsa took a step forward. "We know you're angry, but Sam and Maddy did the right thing. They both agreed. It was time she knew. Too many years have passed already—"

Katherine shot to her feet. Elsa stepped backward quickly. For a moment, they stared at one another. Then Katherine sank back down onto the edge of the bed. "You can go, Elsa. But when you hear from Sam, I want to know. I don't care what time it is."

"I will."

Elsa stared at her. The formidable Katherine sat holding her fist against her chest and stared out into space. Elsa could see the tip of paper sticking out of the older woman's fist and wondered what was in the letter Carol found? Would Carol know? If she did, she most likely wouldn't say anything, as Carol was loyal to Katherine and Kate. Where was Sam? It wasn't like her husband to just disappear without a word. It certainly wasn't like him not to answer his cell phone. Was he all right? Was Kate? Had they done the right thing after all by revealing the truth to Kate? Or was it a big mistake?

She stepped out into the hall and carefully closed the door behind her. She pulled a cell phone out of her pocket and dialed. No answer. She decided to leave another message, "Sam, honey, where are you? We're all worried about you and Kate. Please call me when you can. I'm really worried about you. Are you with Kate? Where are you? Call me. Please." She pushed the end button.

Elsa loved Sam more than life itself. When she first met him in 1992, he was a major in the army and very much a gentleman. She was a nurse and he was visiting a friend in the army hospital in Germany, the very same friend that she was tending. A week later, the friend died from complications of massive infection. She comforted Sam, and one thing led to another. They were married a year later. She remembered it fondly. It took him five times to propose to her before she finally broke down and said yes. Her parents didn't mind that he was a Black man. They seemed more concerned that he was an American Army officer and they might not see their daughter again. Her father was re-tired U.S. Army and familiar with the routine of moving around. He didn't want that for his only child.

As it turned out they had very little to worry about. Sam was very much the family man and every year they spent his thirty days of leave half in the States with his mother and the other half in Germany with her parents.

Except for his deployments abroad, they weren't separated. This separation from him now was killing her, especially since she had no idea what was going on. And the unknown was what worried her most of all. All she could do was pray for his safe return with Kate.

She went back to Katherine's room and slowly opened the door to take a peek. Katherine hadn't moved from the bed.

Chapter 10

Elsa went downstairs and into the kitchen. Carol turned to face her. "Elsa, what is going on with Miss Katherine? She's acting...weird. So is Miss Maddy? She's called up here all day asking about Miss Kate. I don't know what to tell her."

"I don't know," Elsa said. "What do you mean?"

"I gave Miss Katherine the note from Miss Kate and she nearly collapsed onto the floor. She wouldn't let me call Doctor Lincoln. She scared me to death."

"I just spoke with her. All she did was stare at me. She jumped out at me then she sat down. She scared me, too. You have any idea what was in the note?"

"No," Carol said. "Does this have anything to do with Miss Kate's parents?"

"What do you mean?" Elsa asked. Sam said no one, no one but his parents, Olivia's parents, Doctor Lincoln, and his sister Betsy knew about that awful night.

"I don't know. I know they died when she was a baby way before I came here. It's just a feeling..."

"Well, you keep that feeling to yourself, okay? Don't you fret. You just do your job and I'll do mine. Okay?" Elsa said.

"I'm worried about Miss Katherine."

"Worried? Why?"

"I know she's not the easiest woman in the world to get along with, but she's always been good to me."

Elsa placed a hand on the other women's shoulder. "I know."

"She gave me a job when no other woman would hire me because I was too young. She gave me a place to live, food to eat, and a paycheck. I'm just worried about her."

"I'm glad she was good to you," Elsa said. "Now don't fret. I'm going home. You should turn in too. It's been a long day."

Carol nodded and went back to cleaning things up for the night. Neither she nor Katherine could stand a dirty, untidy kitchen.

e⁄ɔc⁄ɔ

Inside, her sleeper room aboard the train, Kate startled awake at the sound she heard in her head. Did she hear a knock or was it a dream? There it was again. It was no dream.

Then she heard the voice. "Kate, are you all right in there. It's Sam. I came to pick you to go to dinner. Kate…"

Sam? What time was it? She glanced at her gold watch and saw the time, almost seven thirty. She got up, went to the door, and opened it. There he stood with a slight grin on his face. "Hope you don't mind, Miss—" He stopped. "Kate, I thought we could have dinner together, if that is all right with you, seeing how you already made the reservations?"

"They told you? I wanted it to be a surprise. I hate eating alone. Hope you don't mind?"

"No."

"Good." She hoped she'd be able to eat. She still didn't have much of an appetite. "Fine, Sam. Let's go." She dashed back to the cabin and retrieved her purse. She exited, closed the sliding door behind her, and locked it.

e⁄ɔc⁄ɔ

When Sam and Kate entered the dining car, a porter immediately greeted them, a young Black man about twenty five. He looked for their names on a list, took them directly to their seats, and departed.

They sat down across from two young men who appeared not to be able to stop giggling. Sam moved to introduce himself but they ignored him. He studied them for a few moments. Kate didn't appreciate their rudeness. Her grandmother brought her up to be polite. When you spoke to someone for a while or was seated with someone, the rules of etiquette were observed. Of course, not everyone behaved like that anymore. It was obvious these two didn't. Or was it something else? She hoped it wasn't what she was thinking. That would make her very angry.

"Excuse me." Sam stood up. "I'll be right back."

Kate watched him leave and wondered where he was going. The two young White men eyed her, giggled louder, and poked each other's shoulder with a finger.

"Miss," the freckled one with blond hair asked. "Who's the nigger with you? Friend or foe or both?" He giggled again.

Kate couldn't say anything for a moment. She was just too astonished. "Wh—what? Excuse me? What you did you say?"

The other boy with brown hair spoke, "Sorry, miss." He giggled too. "You have to excuse my friend. He's a little drunk."

"How old are you two?"

They didn't look older than eighteen, and had acne breakouts on their cheeks, but she knew better than anyone that looks could be deceiving.

"We're old enough," the rude one said.

Sam returned just as the rude one spoke again and pointed, "Hey look, it's the Jolly Giant Nigger."

Kate shot to her feet so that she was between Sam and them.

A porter was with Sam. "Is there a problem, miss?"

"Yes," she said without facing him. "We'd like to change our seat."

"Of course, your uncle asked too. We have another place for you over here, if you both come with me."

Kate moved to leave. The two young men said nothing, which was a good thing. She swore she could feel her blood boiling in her veins. If they said one more thing...

Sam stood aside to let her exit and then she heard the young man. "Goodbye now, Uncle Tom." Giggling. "Enjoy your meal, Uncle Tom, so nice to see you." More giggling. "Dumb nigg—"

He didn't have a chance to finish. Kate snatched the water glass from the table, threw the water at him, slammed the empty glass down hard on the table directly in front of him, and glared into his eyes. "You disgust me! It's people like you who have turned this world into shit!"

She didn't know what she looked like and she didn't care, but she could tell that it scared the hell out of them. The giggling stopped. They suddenly sobered up. They stared and clenched their mouths shut. Their eyes widened.

"Your parents should be embarrassed by you," she went on. "I know I would be! If you can't say anything nice, just keep your mouth shut!"

When she was sure they were speechless, she stormed away to follow the porter a few tables away. By time she got there, she had forced herself to calm down a bit and sat down, but obviously not calm enough. Slowly, she released her fists. At the new table sat two elderly women across from them.

"You all right, honey? You're all red." The Black lady with curly white hair spoke first. "Don't let those boys get to you. They've been like that for a while before you came in. I don't know why they let them stay. It's sad what this world is coming to. Sit down and relax." She giggled. "Oh, where are my manners? I'm Rosie Carter. This here is my friend Betty Silva."

"You'll have to excuse us," Betty, the other lady, White with short curly white hair, said. "We're best friends since high school and once a year we travel to see each other." She stopped and glanced behind Kate. "Oh, look. They're finally taking those rude boys away."

The other passengers clapped at the boys' departure.

Kate and Sam glanced over and saw three porters and a conductor escorting the two rude young men out of the car amongst protests of, "We didn't do anything. This is America. We can speak up if we want to. Get your hands off of me you, dumb nigger!"

Sam moved to step away but Kate, fearing the worst, caught his hand and he stopped where he stood. Once the boys were gone from the car and it was silent again, she released him.

Rosie brought her hand to her chest. "I live in Chicago, Betty in New Orleans. Once a year one of us flies to the other and then we ride the train back after we spend time shopping and visiting each other. It's so much fun. Girl time. With our husbands dead and children grown, it's just us now."

"It's quite fun," Betty added with a chuckle. "We spend time at each other's houses and then head back home."

Kate appreciated the respite from other thoughts. "That's nice, ladies. I love it." She extended her hand. "I'm Kate Thayer. This is my uncle, Sam Johnson."

The women took turns shaking her and Sam's hand. These women were happy and it was contagious.

"So nice to meet you both," Rosie said. "You should really sit down, Sam. You're already too big of a boy to grow anymore."

Sam grinned. "Yes, ma'am," he said and sat down in the aisle seat next to Kate.

"Now you two go on with your talk and your meal and don't mind us. We have so much to get caught up on. Hope you don't mind. We don't want to be rude," Betty said.

"No, ma'am," Kate said. "Not at all. You two go on." They impressed her by their vitality and care for one another. "If you don't mind me asking, how long have been friends?"

Rosie brought her hands up to her lips and eyed her friend. "Jesus…it must be nearly seventy years…yes, right, Betty?"

"We were fifteen. We're eighty five now. Yes, Rosie, seventy years," Betty said after doing some mental math. "Of course, back then we couldn't go to the same high school. We met at each other's houses. Our friendship was a secret from our family and friends."

"And our friendship endured," Rosie said.

Kate smiled. "Obviously. I'm impressed. That's a long time. You've must have seen a lot changes in the world."

"Oh, honey," Rosie said. "You have no idea."

Betty added, "Some were good and some were bad—mostly good—not all. Take, for instance, those two boys that were over there. Came from a bad home. No respect for their elders. No one. And that is the youth of this country. Sad."

"But that's fine," Rosie added. "Not all people are like that, are they, honey? Look at you and your uncle. That's progress." Rosie winked. "Just what Doctor King wanted. For all of us to live together, peacefully, and look past the color of skin." She reached out and patted Kate's hand. "You are our future. God bless you and your uncle, and your mama and daddy."

Kate stared at her. It was as if her eyes were opened for the first time. Could this woman, this stranger see right through her? She knew that wasn't possible, but it was just too coincidental to ignore. For a moment, being with the two rude young men had soured her. But these women instilled the hope she always had. "Thank you, ma'am. You too."

The women smiled and went back to chatting and laughing with each other.

There they sat, together, one Black woman and one White woman—friends for seventy years. Wow. How was that possible? They had been through the sixties, the civil rights movement. They had been friends when they shouldn't, or couldn't have been. It amazed her. It enthralled her. It saddened her. Why couldn't her family, her grandparents had been more like these two women? After her encounter with those two young men, she figured Katherine had been right after all and that was depressing. But these two women showed her what she already knew. Bigotry didn't have to happen. It was a choice one made.

"What happened over there, Kate?" Sam asked. "When I left the table?"

"Nothing," she said.

"It didn't seem like nothing to me or these two ladies. Did they get out of line with you?" he asked.

"I'm old enough to take care of myself, Sam. Thank you. And no, they didn't get out of line. They were fools," she snapped and then took a breath. "I'm sorry. I didn't mean to snap at you."

"I'm proud of you," he said.

"For what? Losing my temper?"

"For standing up and saying something," he said. "Most people don't. That's why they get away with it. I did hear some of what they said."

"Well, I don't tolerate fools," she said. "I have no patience for them."

"You sound like your grandmother."

She turned to him. "Would that be my White grandmother, or my Black grandmother? Which one is more racist, I wonder?"

"Kate, you don't understand—"

"No, I don't. Look at these women. Friends through the civil rights days, Sam." She turned away.

"Your grandmothers have changed. They're not the same women," he said.

She faced him again. "Are you honestly sitting there defending them? I understand your mama, but Katherine?"

"Kate, that was a long time ago."

She shot to her feet. "Not long enough for me!" She stopped when she saw the two women turn to face her. "I'm sorry," she apologized to them and Sam. "Forgive me."

The two women nodded and, for a moment, they stared then went back to their discussion, but the tone had changed. She heard it. She felt it.

Kate slowly sat back down.

"I'm sorry, Kate. I didn't mean to upset you," Sam said.

"No, I'm sorry. I'm so angry, I forgot where I am. I usually don't behave this way. I want to discuss this, but not here," she said. "No more talk about family."

Sam nodded. The porter brought the first course of their meal. Sam ate hungrily and she just picked at it.

"You need to eat something," he said.

"I'm not hungry."

"Kate, please try to eat something. Just a little bit."

"You're not my father, Sam!" she snapped again and sighed.

"No. I'm not. I'm sorry," he said in a lowered voice that sounded to her like regret. "Just concerned. You need to eat something or you'll get sick." He sighed. "I'm sorry, Kate. I wasn't trying to be your father. I'm not Jax."

His concern touched her deeply. He had always been there for her, before she knew who he really was. She reached out a hand and placed it on his. "I'm sorry, Sam. I'm having a difficult time with all of this. That's all. The lies, the secrets, the bigotry in my own family—"

He said nothing. He just clasped her hand in his large one.

Kate glanced up and saw the two elderly women smile and nod at them, as if they had approved and then they went back to their usual, cheerful chatty selves.

Kate released Sam, cut two pieces of chicken, and ate them. She ate four pieces of the cooked carrots and set her plate aside. She took a few sips of water and set the glass down.

The porter came by and tended to the elderly women first. He then moved to them and collected their plates. "Is everything all right, miss? You barely ate?"

"Thank you. Everything was fine. I'm just not very hungry. I'd like some coffee, please," she said.

"And you, sir?"

"Nothing for me. Thank you," Sam said.

Sam waited for the porter to leave. "Coffee? Isn't it kind of late for that?"

She raised a hand. "Don't."

Sam clasped his hands on the table. The two elderly women stood up and approached them arm in arm. "We are calling it a night. Past our bed time." Betty spoke first. "Don't want to get kicked out of here for lingering too long."

"It was a pleasure meeting with both of you," Rosie said. "You have a safe trip and be good to one another. Life is too short for regrets." She brought a hand to her chest. "Believe me, we know."

"Good night now," they said in unison and headed out of the car.

"That could have been my grandmothers," Kate said. "Do you realize that?"

Sam nodded. "Same thought came to me too. Seventy years…wow."

"Black and White," Kate said. "They don't even mind. They're friends."

The porter returned with a pot and filled her cup. "Anything else, miss, sir? Dessert?"

Kate was lost in what could have been. Have no regrets, the two women had said. She had only one—of what might have been if only she had known. Other than that, she had no regrets. Of course, had she known, would it have made a difference? Would it have changed anything? Her grandparents were who they were. How could she have changed that? Evidently, it wouldn't have mattered at all.

"No thank you," Sam finally said. "We're fine."

She stared at the steam floating from the cup of hot coffee—black coffee and the irony of her preference for it that way, untouched, unflavored, and just that—black. Cautiously, she lifted the cup to her lips, sipped, and then set the cup down.

"Where did you go, earlier, when you left the first table?" she asked.

"Those boys were drunk. I went to tell the porter and to get us another table. I didn't want you sitting near them," he said.

"Why? How did you know they were drunk?"

"I've commanded battalions of men. I know."

"Why didn't you want us sitting there?" she asked. "Me sitting there with them?"

"I had a feeling. I knew they'd be stupid. I wanted to protect you from that," he said.

"From what? Their bigotry?" she asked and took another sip of coffee.

"Yes."

"How did you know they'd act like that?"

He shook his head. "Call it instinct. People do, that's all."

"And?"

"Kate, leave it be."

"No." She reached out to his large hand. "Tell me."

He eyed her hand on his. "We're a large Black older man and a young White woman traveling together."

"So?"

He turned to her. "You really don't understand, do you?"

"Enlighten me," she said and took another sip of the coffee.

"People say things," he said. "People can be cruel."

"I know that. I'm not a fool."

"What you are is too good, too nice, like your mama. Those boys—they're not the only ones that think like that," he said.

"I know that, Sam. My grandparents think like that," she snapped and turned away.

He grasped her hand. "No."

She faced him.

"Your grandparents are not strangers, Kate. Strangers have no limits. What do you think would have happened if you had not scared the bejesus out of those two young fools? Had I not gone to get the porter?"

"You mean, aside from you maybe pummeling them into the ground?" she said.

He sat up tall. "Is that what you think of me?"

"Careful, Uncle, hear my words. Don't assume. I know you would have protected me. That is what I know," she said. "You always have, even when I didn't know who you really were. I didn't forget that."

He relaxed.

"Now, if I was able to hold you back," she said. "I would have pummeled them into the floor and into the tracks beneath us."

He grinned. "That's not what I meant, Kate."

"I know what you meant. They would have become worse, out of control, until someone stopped them. I'm not naive, Sam. I just—"

"You never had to face it before. You never had to deal with it before," he finished for her.

"No, I haven't. How could I?" She glanced at her watch. She needed to talk, but this wasn't what she had in mind. "It's nine o'clock. I'm turning in." She stood up.

"I'll walk you back," he said and copied her.

"Afraid I'll get lost?"

"Maybe. Maybe, I'm just being the overprotective uncle."

"I can live with that." She led the way out and to her cabin, acknowledging a few people they passed in the passageway going the opposite way.

At her cabin, she opened the door.

"Well…" he said. "I guess I'll say good night."

"No, Sam. Not that easy. We need to talk," she said and indicated that he should enter inside. "You're here now. Come in."

He nodded. He stepped in and the small room immediately shrunk around his bulk. "These rooms aren't made for a big guy like me."

"Evidently," she said. She shut the door behind him. "Do you still want to accompany me to where I'm going?"

"Yes, I said I would."

"Then sit down, Sam." She moved to the chair recliner and sat down. "Please." She indicated the sofa across from her. She knew it'd be more comfortable for him. He walked over to the sofa. She noticed that his slight limp was a bit more pronounced this evening. "Sam, are you all right? Is your leg bothering you?"

"No. I'm fine. Just a little stiff is all." He sat down slowly.

"Good. Then there's a price you have to pay for me allowing you to come along with me."

"Okay. Name it."

"You'll have to tell me about my parents."

"I wouldn't even know where to start," he said. "I don't know much."

"Tell me what you do." She unlatched the fold down table and set it up between them.

"You tell me where we're going," he countered.

"Agreed. You first," she said.

"Just like that? No negotiation."

"We just did, Uncle. You can tell me what I want to know and accompany me." She folded her arms across her chest. "Or you ride with me to the next station, get off, and I go on alone if you don't tell me."

He nodded. "Seems fair."

She took a bottle of water from the drink holder next to the table and handed it to him. "Tell me about my mother."

He took the bottle of water and set it down on the table. He raised a hand to scratch the back of his neck. "What do you want to know?"

"Everything," she said and retrieved the other bottle of water closest to her for herself. She unscrewed the cap and took a few sips and then recapped it and set in the holder. "And please, no more lies."

"No lies, Kate." He looked at her with his dark caramel eyes then glanced away. His lower lip trembled a bit. "She was my older sister and I idolized her. She was beautiful, funny, and smart." He faced her with a grin. "And she liked to draw and paint. She was really good too. She won a full scholarship to attend Old Miss."

Old Miss was the nickname for the University of Mississippi in Oxford Mississippi. It was also the alma mater of her grandparents Jackson and Katherine and her father. "Please, go on." She wanted to hear more. She needed to. She didn't know any of it. How could she? No one spoke about her mother, ever. It wasn't like she could have sought out Maddy and Sam to ask about her earlier when she didn't even know they were family.

"She loved your daddy so much," he said. "She didn't care he was White and he didn't care she was Black. They really loved each other. I didn't think much about it back then, but thinking about it now, I could see it in their eyes when they looked at each other. The way Elsa and I look at each other. The way he treated her. You just knew. You understand? We saw it in the way you and Adam looked at each other. The way he treated you with respect."

"I do." She had shared that same love with Adam. "I understand." With so much to think about lately, she hadn't thought about him since she had left the house to see Maddy a second time.

"When my mama and daddy, Maddy and George, forbid her to see him anymore, she tore out of the house. They ran away and got married. Wow! Our parents, his parents—" He snickered. "They were all furious. I wasn't there, but I heard about it when my father ranted about it. He died a few months later from a heart attack. Mama thought his heart was broken. Maybe it was, but your mama couldn't be told what to do. I admired her guts though, at the time, I thought she was a fool. Now, I understand."

"Go on. Tell me about my father. Why did you hate him? It couldn't be just because he was White." Kate leaned forward in her seat. "Your wife is White."

He sighed and lowered his eyes. "Not just that, but yes, back then. It's a long story. You didn't give me a chance to explain—"

"It is fourteen hours until we get to Chicago," she said.

"Is that were we're going then?"

"Maybe."

He looked up. "Kate," He sighed deeply. He looked tired. "Some things should be left in the past—"

"Not when it is a part of my life and I want to know about it." She reached out and grasped his hand into hers. "Please, Sam, there's so much I don't know and I need to."

He studied her and his eyes brightened. "Just like your mama. I couldn't say no to her either. Most of the time." He sat up tall in his chair but averted his eyes. "My mama and your grandfather, Jackson, a long time ago—"

"Had an affair. I know. She told me."

"She told you?" He sighed and shook his head. She could tell that he hadn't expected that. "I loved my daddy," he said. "I hated Mama for it, especially for it being with a White man, the boss man. I was so angry. I guess I hated your father for that too. And for taking my sister away. And then when she died, I blamed them both."

"Were you there that night? The night I was born? The night she died?" she asked.

He shook his head. "No. I was away at West Point. I didn't know until Mama called the next day. She told me what happened. I cried for two hours. I swore to hurt your daddy, but then she told me he had killed himself that night. That he had left a note, that he couldn't live without her." His shoulders drooped. "I was shocked by it all. He had been a good friend to me, but I thought that he wasn't for my sister. I was wrong. I was so wrong."

He looked at her. She could see tears welling at the base of his eyelids.

"I'm sorry, Kate. I'm so sorry. I always wondered if they'd both still be alive if they had some support from all of us, from me. Your mama was so fragile sometimes. She almost died when she was a baby."

"You didn't kill my parents. If anyone did, it was me," Kate said as she felt a void begin to form in the pit of her stomach. "She died after giving birth to me. If it was anyone's fault, it was mine." She turned away.

"No, it wasn't and you know it," Sam said. "It wasn't anyone's fault that your mama died. It just happened. I know that now. So should you. You're a doctor. She just wasn't very strong. And your daddy loved her. I know that now, too."

"She just wasn't strong enough for twins."

"No, she just wasn't very strong, physically. Fact is, Doctor Lincoln told her it'd be dangerous. She wouldn't listen. Too stubborn your mother was, just like you. And everything is going to be just fine. I feel it."

She faced him and tasted the saltiness of tears in her throat. "What makes you so sure?"

"I believe in God and his son Jesus. I don't know why they took my sister so young, and your daddy. But you're here and you're beautiful. And I couldn't imagine life without you in it."

"Even though I'm half-White?"

He sighed and shook his head. "All I see is my niece, not Black or White. You're my sister's little girl and that is all I care about. If it takes me the rest of my life, I will make it up to you. I swear on my life. You are a good person. You have a good soul. I love you, Kate."

His words touched the deep recesses she dared not enter, but it was too late. The tears broke through and she had to cry and get them out. *Oh, Mama. Daddy. I wish—I knew you.* She laid her head down on her hands on the table. She felt herself tremble and then felt Sam's large arms hug her against him. His warm breath was against her ears, her neck.

"It's all right, Kate. It's going to be fine. I promise. I'm here for you, to do whatever it is you need to. Don't be scared. I won't let anyone hurt you. You're my sister's little girl all grown up. I wish she could see you now. She'd be so very proud. They both would."

"I didn't know them, Sam, but I miss my parents, so much."

"I know what you mean. I'm a lot older than you and I still miss my father and Livie."

She cried and he held her. She wiped her eyes and sat up. "Thank you, Sam. I needed to hear that." She attempted humor. "Uncle Sam? Do I really have to call you that now?"

The moment of levity felt good.

"Kate, you can call me whatever you want. Just don't call me late for dinner. Okay?"

She laughed. He did, too. The release was just what she need-ed and she could see that he did, too.

"I wish I could believe you—what you said," she said.

"What makes you think you can't?"

"Because all of you lied to me, Sam, and kept things from me that I deserved to know. Even now."

"What do you mean? I told you the truth," he said.

"No. Not all of it."

"Kate, I swear to you."

"You didn't because my sister is alive and living in NYC, which is where we are going."

He clasped her hand. "That's impossible," he said. "Your sister is dead."

She pulled away from him. "No, she isn't."

"But Mama and Daddy said—Katherine said—Kate? Maddy said she was dead. She told me—"

"She wasn't stillborn, Sam," Kate said. She saw the shock and hurt in his eyes. "It was a lie. My grandparents lied about that. Maddy told me so the other night."

"When you came back and spoke to her alone? That's why you suddenly left?"

"Yes," she said. "She's alive, Sam, and I'm going to find her and do right by her."

He stared at her. "My mama lied to me? What's going on?"

She wiped her eyes. "You tell me. All of you lied to me."

"I don't know what to say. I swear to you I didn't know she was alive. How could I?" He turned away from her and sighed. "I thought I knew my parents."

"I thought I knew Katherine. Apparently not. I guess it just goes to show what they say. You never ever really know someone," she said.

She studied him. She wished she could trust him. She had to believe him. Her gut told her she could, but should she? Did his parents lie to him, too, as they had lied to her? It appeared so.

"How do you know where she is?" he asked incredulously. "How on earth did you find out?"

"Doctor Linc. He checked on her from time to time. See where she was. Make sure she was okay."

"Doctor Linc? How did he know?"

"That is another long story in itself."

"And we have time. Fourteen hours you said?" he said.

"Yes. Yes We do. But not tonight, Sam. I'm tired. You're tired."

He stood up. "Agreed. Not tonight. You need to sleep. And so do I," he said and headed toward the door.

His leg was bothering him, his jaw was clenched.

"You don't have to go sit up all night. There's plenty of space in this room for you."

"A young woman needs her privacy. Besides, I spent my career in the army. Sitting up all night in a cushy chair is heaven. I'll see you in the morning when we arrive." He headed toward the door.

"Sam, your leg—"

He placed his hand on the doorknob. "My leg will be just fine."

"Sam—" She had to say what she felt.

He stopped and faced her.

"I'm glad you're here," she said.

"Me too, kiddo. Me too," he said and forced a grin.

"Kiddo?" she asked. "You called me that when I was little. I remember," she said fondly.

"Yeah, I did." He opened the door. "Get some sleep. And lock this door."

She went to it and shut it behind him. Sleep would not come easy for her tonight. At least, not without a little help, but she didn't want to take that route. She didn't want to begin that cycle again. No, this time she wouldn't go that way. She went to her purse, pulled out her cell phone, and dialed a number from her directory.

While she waited, she thought about the pained look in Sam's eyes. She wanted so much to believe him. For as long as she could remember, Sam had always been in her life. But was he telling the truth? Did they lie to him also? He had to be telling the truth. That look in his eyes was too real to be anything but the truth.

Chapter 11

S am exited Kate's cabin, still stunned by what he just learned. How could his parents have lied to him too? It just wasn't possible, but there it was. Here he was, trying to justify to his niece that their actions were to protect her after they had done the wrong thing when, in fact, they had lied to protect themselves and their bigotry and hatred for a man, a boy that he had grown up with. He had deeply respected and admired Jax and, if he had been Black, he would have not had a problem with him marrying his sister. Of course, that was back then. Back when he knew nothing outside his cloistered world in Thayersville, Mississippi.

He waited outside the door until he heard it lock and then turned to head down the stairs to his seat in the lower level. The young porter, nearby when he exited, grinned at him.

"What's the matter, brother?" the porter said with a chuckle. "You seem down. Your honey kick you out, or was it just a booty call?"

The other man's dirty implication was too much for Sam to handle tonight. Way too much. It reached deep into a sore spot that was thirty years too old. He had learned better since then. In reflex, Sam seized the other man by his collar, off his feet, and slammed him up against the opposite wall. At a mere five feet eight inches tall and slim build, the porter didn't stand a chance to match the ex-football star from the West Point Military academy.

"What did you say?" Sam's voice deepened. He was breathing hard and trying to restrain himself.

The other man was terrified. Sam could see that in his wide eyes. He held up his hands in surrender. "Hey man, I didn't mean it. Jesus, brother, calm down."

"That lady in there is my niece," Sam said.

"Hey, whatever floats your boat."

"Not that it is any of your business, but she is and you need to shut your filthy mouth."

"Hey, man. I didn't know. I'm sorry. I just thought—"

"Thought what?" Sam snapped and tried to retain control of his temper. "You need to get your mind out of the gutter, or should I do it for you?

"No, man. Look, brother, how did I know? She's White and young. You're an older brother."

"One, I'm not your brother," Sam said. "Two, not that it is any of your business, but she's only half-White and my niece."

Sam saw the guy absorb that. "It's cool, man. I get it. I understand. I wouldn't want anyone talking about my niece like that. I'm sorry, man. Really."

Sam eyed him and lowered him slowly to the ground but held onto him. The last thing he wanted was for this guy to take off screaming down the passageway.

"I am sorry, man," the porter said. "I should keep my mouth shut. You're right. It's late. I'm tired. I'm sorry. You're a big guy—can you let go of me now?"

Sam eyed him and slowly released him.

"Look—" the porter said and clapped his hands together. "Let me make it up to you and your niece. I'll take you to your cabin and get you settled in. You hungry? Thirsty? Galley's closed but I can get something for you? Something for your niece? Anything. You name it."

"I don't have a cabin. And I'm not hungry or thirsty," Sam said. "And you stay away from my niece."

"Whatever you say, man, but no cabin? You're sitting up all the way? Well—look what's your destination? Chicago?"

"New York," Sam said.

"New York? Do you have a cabin on that train?"

"No. I'm going to get one when we board."

"You hope. Look, let me call on ahead and see what I can do. If they have one, I'll have them hold it for you and let you know in the morning. Okay?"

"Fine," Sam said. "Thank you."

"Good. I'll wake you and your niece up and get you seated and fed with a very goooooood breakfast to start your day." He extended his hand. "I am sorry, man. My name is Henry. Henry Williams and I really didn't mean any harm. Really."

Sam eyed the hand and then eyed the other man. His gut told him to calm down and he did. He extended his hand and shook the other man's. "Sam Johnson. My niece is Doctor Kate Thayer. You stay away from her."

"No problem, man—sir. You have my word. I know that's not saying a lot right now, but I'm really a nice guy, just a jerk sometimes. My wife says its only one of my faults."

"Yeah, I get you. Good night, Henry."

"Good night, Sam. See you first thing in the am. You need anything, anything at all, you call for ole Henry. I'm your man. Again, man—sir, I am really sorry."

Sam nodded and walked down the passageway to the car he'd be sitting up in. *You need to calm down, Sam. You could have broken the guy's neck then where would Kate be?* Kate was his first and only priority right now. She had to be. He owed her that. How could any of them have lied to her? It was all so wrong what they had done.

℮↗℈↗℈

It was nearly one in the morning in the manor house and Katherine still couldn't sleep. She had tossed and turned so many times that she had exhausted herself even more, but still she couldn't doze off. She sat up and sighed in frustration. The house just wasn't home without Kate in it. Not now, not when Kate was away at college, and not when Kate had spent two weeks in the hospital two years before. It was more of an occupied shell than a home and Katherine didn't like it.

Kate added youth and vitality to an otherwise lonely old house. This farm and the house that stood on it had been home to the Thayer family since eighteen-hundred-and-thirty. It had a lot of stories to tell—if it could talk. Thank God, it couldn't, for she was the subject of several of them. For the last fifty-three years, it had been her home and her home alone for the last twenty, except for Kate.

Now, as she walked back and forth down the long hall, from one end to the other, it was clear, once more, just how very desolate it was without Kate. Except for an occasional creek when she stepped on a certain floorboard, there wasn't another sound. Back outside her room, she stopped and took the few steps across to Kate's room from hers. She knocked on the door, as a force of habit, before she remembered that Kate wasn't in there. She entered and turned on the ceiling light by the light switch just inside the doorway. For a moment, she almost expected Kate to be there, either asleep or at her desk reading a new book—not necessarily new to the household, but new to Kate's eyes. The child loved to read anything and everything, a habit she had inherited from her father and his parents, but mainly from her.

Having married Jackson at just seventeen after early graduation from high school, Katherine had gone to college for just six months during which time she met and married Jackson after a whirlwind courtship. He had swept her off her feet, literally. At eighteen, she had given birth to Jackson Thayer V or Jax as he later came to be known. But being a mere housewife and mother was not enough for Katherine. She needed more. Her desires were many. Her thirst for knowledge was never-ending. Evidently, also in her granddaughter. Hence, the expansive library the home contained on the main floor of the house. Still, Kate couldn't get enough to read, and if that was her granddaughter's only addiction, she could live with that.

It was so different without her. Kate's bedroom lacked life without her. Katherine went to the large roll top desk against the wall. She'd had it custom made to fit a desktop computer system for Kate's sixteenth birthday. Of course, Kate now used a laptop. Katherine ran her fingertips along the cool metal of it. It was as cold and lifeless as the room it sat in. Without Kate, things just sat still. Time sat still. Morning would come and then after evening would follow, as days would go by, but there'd be no substance without Kate to help fill the days. Perhaps, without realizing it, without recalling when it occurred, Katherine had let herself live through Kate vicariously. If so, she did not mean to. She lived her own life, but since the death of her son Jax, and since the moment Kate entered her life, Katherine's life revolved around her, with her, for her. She sighed deeply. At least Kate didn't take the laptop and her closet remained as it was, which was a positive sign. Kate would return. *When* was the question. *Where* was she was another question. Two weeks? That couldn't be right. Perhaps, she just set the timers so she wouldn't forget it with all the other things on her mind. That made perfect sense. Though, Kate preferred to check on her fish to ensure they were safe and healthy and wouldn't set the timer. No, Katherine decided, the other explanation was a better one.

She walked over to the vacant bed and stared at it. How many nights had she entered this room when Kate was away at school or at a friend's house for the night? Still, it never felt as empty, as barren as it did tonight. She reached out and ran her hand along the crests of the pillowcase, felt the cool touch of it beneath her fingers, and sat down on the edge of the bed.

Kate would come home safe and sound. Katherine knew she would. She willed it to be so. She wouldn't deal with the alternative. What if Kate didn't return? No, there was no alternative, as far as she was concerned. Kate would return home and things would go back to normal. Katherine would do anything to make it so.

She remembered the first time she set eyes on Kate, the first time she held her...

⋅⋅⋅

The baby was born, the second one, but before Betsy took her away, Katherine wanted to see this one. And, when she did, she made her decision.

"Jackson," she said. "We're keeping this one."

Jackson declined. "Katherine, we agreed to send the child away, no matter what it was."

"She's White. I'm keeping her."

"Katherine, she's not White and we all agreed."

"Damn you all then. I'm keeping her. Are you saying I can't?"

Jackson sighed. "Fine. Whatever you want." He patted her shoulder.

"Look at her," Katherine said. "She's beautiful."

⋅⋅⋅

But Jackson didn't look at her, and he never really would, ever. The child was half-Black and that was all he cared about, which was ironic coming from him. She didn't care. She had enough love to give the child for both of them. All of them. Kate would never want for anything. Kate, yes, she would call the child Katherine Caroline Thayer after herself and her mother. Another woman ahead of her time and the first to teach her about survival in a man's world—how to play the game and win it.

The phone on Kate's bedside table rang her back to reality. She nearly knocked over the small lamp next to the phone as she reached for it.

"Hello," she asked and hoped fervently that it was Kate.

"Hello," said the unfamiliar male voice. "Is Daisy home?"

She knew no Daisy. "Sorry, but I think you have the wrong number."

"I'm sorry, ma'am. My apologies," the man said and hung up.

Katherine set the phone back into its cradle. She ran her hand along the soft comforter. It was cool and crisp. No doubt freshly laundered and pressed, as Carol knew how particular Katherine was about stuff like that. Once a week the linens were changed, washed, and pressed. Those peculiarities of hers seemed so minor in the scheme of things. All she wanted was for Kate to call, to tell her that she was safe and that she was coming home.

Katherine needed a diversion and farm work alone wasn't going to suffice. Kate was gone, which meant Katherine could indulge a bit more than she normally would and out in the open, which she never did when her granddaughter was home. Kate had an image of her grandmother that Katherine was determined to protect. There was never any need for Kate to know otherwise.

Katherine heard the pitter patter of tiny feet on the wood floor and turned just in time to see the cat enter. As if she wasn't there, Sterling ambled on over to Kate's writing desk and jumped unto the stand behind it situated between the desk and the window. He curled up inside the doughnut cat bed and proceeded to take a bath, licking his right paw and wiping his face with it.

Katherine stared at it. "How is it I tell Kate no animals in the house, and here you are?"

The cat stopped bathing its black fur for a moment to look up and meow at her. She walked over to it and stroked it behind the ear. The cat purred under her touch. "Tonight, you can sleep in here, but first thing in the morning you go out and stay out."

The cat meowed and went back to bathing.

Katherine sighed. This was her fault for giving Kate everything and anything she wanted growing up, such as the Rottweiler pup Katherine gave her on her fourth birthday after Kate fell in love with it at a friend's house the week before. Kate named the big-boned puppy Jasper. That clumsy little puppy followed Kate everywhere and grew into a solid muscled dog almost as big as a horse. He was her best friend and protector and lived until the ripe old age of fourteen. While he was alive, Katherine never had to worry about her granddaughter's safety. He died while Kate was home on summer break from college and her granddaughter was devastated. At least college took her away from that grief.

Katherine smiled and shook her head at the memory. From the moment he arrived, Jasper was relegated to the barn, but every night unbeknownst to her, Kate snuck out to bring him in for the night and put him back in the barn early every morning before anyone else was up. The charade lasted for three months until Katherine met the two of them one morning by the front door. When confronted with that, Kate stuck out her chin and merely answered, "He's just a baby, Gran, and he's scared out there all alone with the big horses, and he's my baby. Can't I bring him in at night? Please. He'll sleep in the doggie bed I made him and I'll put him out every morning just like I did? Please, Grandmother. Pretty please, Gran. I'll make sure he's a good boy. Please. I promise."

Of course, Katherine couldn't deny her and Jasper remained a house dog until he died. And Kate kept good to her word about him.

Being in the role of parent and grandparent wasn't an easy task, but Katherine had managed even when, as a child, Kate tried to bring in every injured or stray animal she found. The barn was one thing. Kate turned it into a hospital back then, but not the house. Of course, Katherine would never admit that she was trying to make up for all of the bad things that happened thirty-odd years before.

Tomorrow, she'd have to ask Carol about how the cat got in, though she already knew the answer to that. Twenty-two years older than Kate, Carol adored her and did anything Kate asked of her.

Katherine stood up, returned to her room, and lay back down. She didn't fight the exhaustion this time and, in several minutes, sleep swallowed her.

꿈꿈꿈

Maddy couldn't sleep. She tried, but it just wouldn't come. She counted sheep. She sat up and read a boring book. She even got up and made herself a cup of warm milk and, still, sleep eluded her. Now two and a half hours since she first laid her head onto her pillow, she stood by the front bay window, looking out into the pitch darkness. Farm land and trees surrounded her. In the distance, she could see a light from the big house, the manor house, the base of Magnolia Lane Farm, and guessed that sleep also did not visit Katherine this night either, and rightly so. Neither grandparent had done anything to be proud of, certainly not in their actions thirty years before.

Before their grandchildren were born, the four parents had already decided what was going to be done with him/her, the child of mixed races would be sent away. It had been a decision that the four adults had reached mutually and amicably for the first time in a long time. Neither wanted their child married to the other's child. It had all been so simple, too. They weren't concerned what their grown children wanted. What they wanted was what mattered. They would deal with their children about it. Back then, but now Maddy knew better. She was smarter and free of the chains of old views of bigotry. She was free of her husband's overpowering views of the same. She foolishly let him run things, as if he really knew best. What a fool she had been. Of course, it was so much easier just to go with the flow than to go against it. Now, she paid the price. One granddaughter was sent away, discarded like some worn out clothes, to where she didn't know. The other, Kate, didn't even know who she was, who her mother was, and who Maddy and Sam were. All these years, they had lived so close to her and said nothing. And now that they did, Kate wanted no part of them. And who could blame her? And now, no one knew where Kate was and if she was okay. All this tore a hole in Maddy's heart that would never heal.

"Mama," it was Elsa.

Maddy had hoped not to disturb her, but Elsa was such a light sleeper, probably left over from her days of being married to an army officer.

"Are you in here?" Elsa entered the parlor from off the hall and turned on the floor lamp just inside. She was bundled up in a long red robe that covered her ankles. Her long black hair flowed past the fluffy collar. "Mama." Elsa approached her. "What are you doing up in the middle of the night?"

"I couldn't sleep," Maddy said. "You should go back to bed."

Elsa shook her head. "I will when you do."

"That may not be for a while yet."

"Then I'll stay up for a while too."

"Elsa," Maddy began to scold her.

"I know what you're going to say." Elsa put an arm around her waist. "But I'm not. What's the harm? I can make us some hot cocoa. That might make you sleep."

"Only if you put some brandy in it," Maddy said.

"Mama, that's an excellent idea." Elsa kissed her cheek and moved away.

Maddy brought up her arms to wrap about her shoulders. "Why hasn't Sam called? This is so unlike him. Where is he?"

Elsa stopped and faced her. "I'm sure they're all right, Mama. He probably wants to make sure Kate is all right."

"If he has found her," Maddy said. "And if he is even with her."

"He would have called if he didn't find her," Elsa pointed out. "He would have come back if he didn't. I know Sam, Mama. The soldier in him wouldn't let him end the mission until he found her."

"You know Sam too well," Maddy said.

Her daughter-in-law was an angel. She had to be, for she didn't yell or leave when Sam and Maddy revealed the truth about Kate and the secrets and lies they told. Though the look of hurt and sadness showed on her face, there was also a joy along with it.

"I try," Elsa said. "Sometimes he can be so complicated. He wants to be perfect, and now I know why he was always so concerned about Kate. He always acted like what an uncle should be and now I know why."

"Elsa."

"No, Mama, I'm not angry. I understand. Really, I do. I just wish you both had trusted me enough to tell me sooner." Elsa raised a hand in the air. "I know why you didn't. If I didn't know, I wouldn't have to lie. I just wish it was so, that's all."

Maddy went up to her and took her hands into hers. "They say that history repeats itself. Do you believe that? To see if we have learned from past mistakes and not to make them again?"

"Yes, Mama, I do. Why?"

"My baby girl, Livie, married a White man and we didn't approve. We rejected her children because they were neither Black nor White. My son married a White woman whom I adore. I'm so ashamed. I never saw myself as a bigot even when we forbade Livie to see Jax anymore. It was the way things always were. The way George and I wanted them to be. But we were wrong, so very wrong. We were. And if my eyes didn't open because of what we did, I wouldn't know you now, or love you. I love you, Elsa, just as if you were my own."

Elsa stepped closer and into Maddy's waiting arms. "Oh, Mama."

"Do you think God can forgive me?" Maddy said while brushing her daughter-in-law's hair with her fingers. "Do you think Kate can—and the other, should Kate find her?"

Elsa pulled back and stared at her. "Other? What other, Mama? What are you saying?"

Maddy took her hand. "Make us some cocoa and I'll tell you what I never told, Sam. Kate had a sister. We told him she was stillborn, but she wasn't. I finally told Kate the truth. That look on her face." She released Elsa and brought her hands to cover her mouth. "I'll never forget that look. She looked so much like her mama, Livie, the night her daddy and I forbade her to see Jax anymore. If looks could kill…"

"Oh, Mama." Elsa's expression changed to sadness. "What have you done?" Elsa took her hands into hers. "What happened?"

"Do you think God can forgive? Really forgive?" Maddy said.

Elsa led her over to the sofa. "I can't answer that, Mama. I don't know, but I do know that, with God, all things are possible. Look at us."

Maddy couldn't help but grin at her. "Yes, look at us."

Maddy hugged her tightly. She couldn't imagine her life without Elsa in it. Though, sadly had her husband George still been alive, she knew it wouldn't be. He wouldn't have welcomed Elsa with open arms and she would have lost Sam and Elsa or both, just as she had lost Olivia and Jax, just as she had lost Kate and her sister. Something terrible was going to come from all of this. She just felt it.

"Sit down, Mama. I'll get the cocoa and we can talk."

Maddy released her and sat down. Suddenly, she couldn't hold back anymore. She raised her hands, buried her face in them, and let the tears fall where they lay.

Elsa went to her and hugged her. "Oh, Mama, it'll be fine. You'll see. It will be."

She sat down and Maddy fell against her. Maddy couldn't help but regret the choices made when she was younger. The sudden death of her daughter had changed her. It certainly had changed her relationship with her husband, George. She grew to resent him. It must have changed him too, because within the year after their daughter's death, he had died of a heart attack. He was ten years older than Maddy. He was fifty one when he died.

☙☙☙

Aboard the train, Sam sat back in his seat and glanced around. Most of the other passengers were asleep, pretending to be, or reading. He couldn't do anything. His leg was sore. It hadn't bothered him like this since just after the initial injury. He forgot his pain pills when he left home so he'd have to grin and bear it. He glanced at the old man next to him. Mr. Hooper was fast asleep. A small pillow was behind his head, a blanket across his lap and his book there, too. A sleep mask evidently helped him sleep. The old man obviously had this sort of trip down pat.

Sam glanced outside into the night darkness and hoped for daylight to break. He hated the night. It was so dark. You couldn't see anything. Things happened in the dark and you couldn't see them until it was too late. Of course, he knew from personal experience that evil didn't need the blanket of night to prosper. It just made things easier to do so.

He stood up and began walking down the aisle, back and forth, to get circulation moving in his body. If he could keep his core from hurting, it would take the edge off the pain in his leg.

Of course, the pain in his leg wasn't the only thing bothering him. How on earth could his parents have lied to him and told him that his other niece had been stillborn? How? If there had been four persons in his life that he could count on to do right by him, to stand by him always, and to always be honest with him, it would be his parents, his sister Livie, and Elsa. As far as he was concerned, his parents just moved down a notch in his praise. Why all the damned lies and secrets? Kate was right. He saw that now.

How could he stick up for his parents now? How could he justify their actions? Of course, his beliefs had begun to change away from his father's influence, away from his mother's when he went away to West Point in 'eighty-four. Not soon enough, though. Sure, he faced some racism, but overall, there he was a cadet, a future army officer, and one of them. He belonged to a group that wanted him. At West Point, things were no longer just Black and White. West Point had changed him and turned him into a better person.

The death of his sister had changed him too. When he lost her, he had lost a part of himself and faced the realization that maybe his parents didn't know it all. That he didn't either. Maybe, they were all wrong. Of course, it didn't help that, on top of everything, he had lost his best friend. Jackson Thayer V, better known as Jax, was the older brother he never had and wished he did. He should have been happy when Jax and Livie married. He should have offered his support and his hand to Jax, but he didn't. Jax was White, Livie was Black, and that was all he saw, then. He didn't realize how much he had hurt them back then by rejecting them and their decision, especially after Livie had shared with him her happy news. She was going to have a baby and make him an uncle.

He didn't want to be an uncle to mixed race baby, not even in nineteen-hundred-and-eighty-five. Now, he knew better. It was too late for him to be there for Livie and Jax, but not too late for Kate, and the other.

The other. Imagine that, his sister's little babies were both alive and all grown up. If only Livie and Jax were here now and could see them. If only…

He walked out of his car and out to head up to the upper level. Upstairs, he walked toward Kate's cabin and stopped. Was she asleep? He hoped so. She needed it.

He sensed she'd need a great deal of it, along with fortitude and patience, and he could see that, as angry as she justifiably was, she had both. Evidently, she had inherited that from his mama, Livie, and Jax because his daddy possessed neither.

"Can I help you, sir?" Sam recognized the voice from behind.

Sam faced him in the darkened passageway, now lighted with dim lighting. "George?"

"Yes, sir. It's me. Do you need something?" George asked.

"No. Just wanted to make sure my niece is safe," Sam said.

"I'm sure she is. She hasn't been out, and she hasn't called for anyone," George said.

"Thank you. What happened to…"

"Henry? He told me what happened and I moved him out.

Reprimanded him. I'm his supervisor. I apologize for him. He's a good worker, but forgets his place sometimes."

"I dealt with it. You're not going to fire him?" Sam said.

"No, but he will face a few unpaid days. We don't tolerate behavior like that. He was wrong. It would have been worse had he not come forward on his own. Of course, if you want to make it official, he will be fired."

"No, that won't be necessary. I don't think he'll be doing that again," Sam said.

"No, I don't think so either. Are you sure?" George said. "It is your right."

"No, I'm sure. Thank you." Sam listened at the door. Nothing. *Good. She's sleeping.* He went to move on.

"Oh, Mr. Johnson, I forgot—Henry did check on sleeper accommodations for you to New York. You're all set with a roomette. You won't have a private bath, but you won't have to sit up all the way to NY either."

"Well, thank you, George."

"You welcome, sir, but again it wasn't me."

"Oh?"

"Your niece, Doctor Thayer, called on ahead and made the reservations," George said. "She's a mighty efficient young woman. She doesn't know somebody on the line, does she?"

"Got me. Good question though," Sam said and moved to leave.

"Have a good night, sir. You might want to try and get some shut eye. We still have four hours until breakfast time and we don't pull into Chicago until nine."

"Thank you, George. I'll try."

Sam moved back the way he came and George went the other way. So Kate took care of things for him again. He shouldn't be surprised with that, but he was.

Her grandmother, Katherine Thayer, the toughest woman he had ever come across, trusted her enough to put her in charge of Magnolia Lane Farm at twenty-seven of five thousand acres of prime pasture in the county. Nope, he shouldn't be surprised by anything Kate did.

As much as he hated to admit it, she was a lot like her grandmother Katherine, strong, solid, and dependable. Had Katherine Thayer been a soldier, he'd want her on his side. And woe onto the enemy. No one could make those two women do anything they didn't want to do, and that he couldn't help but admire. If only his mama had been that way too.

ᥱᢇᐁᢇᐁ

Kate lay awake in her berth converted from a sofa out to a bed. She tossed to her left. She tossed to her right. She flopped onto her stomach. She tossed onto her back, placed her hands behind her head, and stared at the ceiling. She brought up her hands and covered her eyes, but sleep was far from within her reach. Why, oh why, did she always have trouble sleeping when things bothered her? Why couldn't she be more like her grandfather, Jackson? That man could sleep through a tornado tearing through the house.

Of course, she barely knew the man. He was rarely home, always traveling, always away as if he was running away from something. Evidently, he was, she realized. He was running away from her, her secret parentage, and the choices he made about it. What a foolish old man he was. No wonder he never spent any time with her. He loved horses and riding, but he never spent any time with her doing so. Katherine had been the one to put her on a horse. Katherine rode with her and instilled the love of riding. Katherine encouraged her interest in horse shows and the pursuit of ribbons. Katherine was the one who loved her and showed her so. Obviously, it too was Katherine, and not Jackson, who wanted her and kept her. It was Katherine who loved her, of that Kate had no doubt, but the lies, the secrets…

She sat up, buried her face in her hands, and took a deep breath. It released some of the anger, just some. Katherine? The woman regularly had roamed the halls of the house at night because she couldn't sleep. Often she checked on Kate, for the younger woman heard the creaking of the floor and would feign sleep. Her grandmother would come in and check on her, stop in and watch her, and then leave. But always Katherine waited outside the door for a few moments before she went back to walking or to her room, as if she was waiting for something to happen. Now, Kate knew why her grandmother couldn't sleep. Something was wrong—guilt, pain, sorrow? Only her grandmother knew which.

She should have taken a sleeping pill, Kate chastised herself, but she didn't want to go down that road again. Even with over the counter stuff, there was still a chance for dependency and she had no desire to go through that again. Once was enough for her.

She sat up, got to her feet, stared out the large window, and watched as the darkness passed by. Every now and then, she saw a flicker of light, from a nearby town, she guessed. When they had stopped in Memphis earlier, there was lots of lights and life. Now, as they passed through the rural areas, the country, there was nothing but blackness and the slight jerking motion of the train that made her a bit uneasy on her feet. She didn't really notice the motion until now. Probably because it was the middle of the night and here she stood, awake. She wondered if this was what an earthquake would feel like and discarded the thought. Tornadoes were a terrifying prospect back home as it was, though it was nothing compared to the tornado that her stomach was feeling right now. She should have eaten more than she did. She had a sour feeling in her mouth and heard her stomach rumble. In the morning, she'd try to eat something.

Chapter 12

At home, Lincoln sat in the overstuffed recliner near the unlit fireplace. He held a bottle of whiskey in his right hand. He wasn't normally a drinker but, tonight, it somehow seemed rather appropriate. Kate was gone from the manor house and, right now, it seemed that he was the only one who knew where she was or, at least, where she was headed. He hoped Katherine didn't call or show up. He didn't think he had the strength to lie to her again. He owed it to Kate not to say anything about her intentions. It was the least he could do for her.

Where did it all go wrong? Perhaps, if he was a stronger man, he wouldn't have done what Katherine and Jackson asked him to do back then. Of course, if he wasn't a strong man, he would have done exactly what they requested of him that night and, being a doctor, he couldn't have done that. Besides, those girls were his blood too. He just knew it. Though, there was a slight chance they weren't. He didn't believe that, though. Jackson traveled a great deal to promote Magnolia Lane Farm, even more so after his father, Jack, died and other women were his addiction. He knew Jackson as well as he knew himself. The other man was a good friend, but a terrible husband. It was no wonder Katherine sought him out. Oh, he'd heard the rumors about Katherine being with other men, aside from him, but he didn't believe them. He wouldn't believe them.

Ironic that he lied to Katherine yesterday, so that she didn't know he told Kate where her sister was, after having lied to Kate for thirty years about everything. He just couldn't tell Katherine that he'd told Kate what she wanted to know. He couldn't bring himself to tell her that he betrayed her. For try as he might, in the end, he couldn't deny Kate's request and told her everything she wanted to know.

After Betsy removed Astrid from the house that fated night

and sent her up north, via a social worker for the orphanage who waited outside the Thayer home, he requested the orphanage keep him abreast of the child. Over the years, he'd received a note or a call, informing him that she was all right and living in a foster home. He lost track of her after a couple of years, but then his sister Betsy followed up and kept the contact going. That is, until she died five years ago of breast cancer at sixty-five. Of course, Astrid was an adult by then at twenty-five and quite successful in art. Using the Internet, he was able to monitor her location. Betsy was right, though. He held a glass up to her framed photo that sat on his mantel piece along with other family photos.

"You were right, sis. You told me to keep tabs on the other one, just in case. Just in case the grandparents came to their senses, the parents wanted to take them away, or when Kate might want to find her sister someday." He took a swallow from the bottle. "You were right. You told me so and followed my wishes, anyway. You're the best sister a man could hope for." He burped and took another swallow. "I fell in love with another man's wife, my best friend's wife. If I had guts, I would have fought for her. If I had guts, I should be up at the manor house now with Katherine, shouldn't I? But she hates drunks, so here I sit, all alone, just like I should. I loved her, you know, Betsy. You always knew and never called your big brother a fool, even though I was. I loved Katherine. I love her still. Do you think God punished us for what we did, our part in it? You're dead, and you didn't go quickly." The bottle fell from his hand and he drifted off to sleep, alone in the world he created for himself.

ფოთ

The next morning, at fifteen minutes after nine, the train pulled into the Chicago Union Station. Sam and Kate were ones of the first to disembark and exit the station into the lounge area. They moved out of the way of the other passengers to a seating area just inside where the trains loaded off and on.

"If it's all right with you," Sam began. "I'm going to visit a few stores and see if I can get some things I'll need for this trip."

"I was wondering what you were going to do since all you came with was yourself," Kate said.

"A good soldier always fulfills the mission first, then worries about trivial things later," he said.

She nodded. "Well go on, then." She eyed her watch. "We have about twelve hours until we board our train to New York."

He eyed her. "That long?"

She nodded again. "Even with being a few minutes late in arriving, yes."

By the expression on his face, she knew that was not what he wanted to hear. She didn't either, but those were the facts.

He glanced to the side. "I'll be right back. Stay here," he said. And he moved away from her.

It sounded too much like an order so she glanced in the direction he had, knew why, and followed.

Sam moved to pick up the two elderly ladies cases when they stopped him in unison, "Sam Johnson, you don't have to do that."

He stood up and grinned. "Sorry, ladies. Reflex action. Do you have someone to help you?"

"We sent for a porter," Betty, the elderly White lady, said.

"He'll be along any minute," Rosie, the elderly Black lady, said. "He went to get a cart for our luggage."

"And here he is now," Betty said.

"Such a sweet young man," Rosie said.

"And so nice to see you again, Miss Kate Thayer," they both said.

The porter, an older White man about sixty, moved to pick up the four suitcases. Sam gave him a hand by picking up the larger ones and setting them on the trolley.

"Are you meeting someone here or are you taking a taxi?" Kate asked.

"Heavens no, honey. No one is meeting us," Betty said.

"Our children all live someplace else," Rosie said. "We'll have to make do with a taxi."

The porter had the bags all loaded up and thanked Sam for his help. Kate reached into her front slack pocket where she kept a small amount of cash, sixty dollars today. She surreptitiously pulled the money out in her clenched hand and walked over to the porter. She extended her clenched fist to him. "Please see these two ladies get a cab and the driver helps them with their bags at their destination."

He shook her hand and, from his eyes, she knew he understood her intentions. She certainly hoped so.

"Yes, miss. I will. Thank you, miss." He turned to the women. "Ready when you are, ladies."

The two women smiled and took turns shaking Sam's large hand and each gave a gentle kiss to Kate's cheek, which caught her off guard.

"You remember what we said," Rosie said with a winsome smile.

"Be good to one another and have no regrets," Betty added.

And then the two women were off, each waving to them as they followed the porter with their luggage.

Kate stood there in amazement, holding a hand to her cheek where they, two total strangers, had kissed her without reserve.

Sam walked over and rejoined her. "I admire those two women. They can run circles around me," he said.

"That was very nice of you, Sam," she told him.

"Reflex. I see someone in need and I help. You didn't have to do what you did," he said.

"Do what, Sam?" she said, turned away, and headed back to the sitting area where it would be a good place to set their base.

He followed her. "So, I guess I'll go do my shopping. You'll be here, then?"

"Yes, but maybe not exactly here. I may wander around when you're gone."

His eyes narrowed at her.

"I'm more than capable of taking care of myself, Sam."

"I know that." He brought up a large hand and scratched the back of his neck. "Just the concerned uncle that's all. So, you'll be here then?"

"Sam Johnson, I'm trying really hard not to be angry. Don't get me started, please. I'll be here, reading, or in that bookstore over there. Or I may go get something to drink, but I'll be back and sitting here when it's time for our train to board. Is that all right with you, *Uncle*?"

He sighed and coughed. "Okay, I had that coming. I'll be back."

"Fine. Go on. Have fun. Later on, we'll have some lunch."

"Okay. I'll be back. You'll be here?"

"Would you like me to come with you?" Kate said.

"No. That won't be necessary," he said, stunned.

She saw embarrassment of his face. "Then go on."

He hesitated and, after a few moments of thinking about it, he moved away and went to do his chores.

Kate shook her head. Was that what it was like to have an uncle? Well then, he was always there anyway, always in the background when he was home from leave and after, when he had retired two years before. Now she knew why he was always there for her, loitering, always watching out for her. If only she had known, things could have been so different. If only they had told her. If only…

Have no regrets, the two elderly women had said, not once but twice. Until the last couple of days, she had none. Be good to one another, they also had said. She had no problem with that. She always tried to do that with others. "Do unto others as you would want them to do unto you," was one of her favorite Bible phrases. "Love one another as I have loved you," was another. Question was, how could two God-fearing women, two Christian women such as her grandmothers, have ignored those teachings to the detriment of their own children and grandchildren? Answer was, she didn't know.

She still had so many questions, but she sensed that Sam would only be able to answer some of them. For the others, she would have to go to the source and, right now, she didn't have the time or the patience. And the questions she had for Sam could wait until they were alone again on the train. Discussing private family matters in a train station was just not a good idea.

She reached into the zippered pocket of her small suitcase and pulled out a novel and two newspapers. Which should she read now? She could play a game on her phone, but she wasn't into video games. Reality was much more favorable, though now she wasn't too sure about that. The new reality was a bit too much to bear, right now.

A voice cut into her thoughts. "Excuse me, miss." It was a young man with a loop ring through his nose, purple hair, and a green face—makeup, no doubt. "Is this seat taken?"

"I'm sorry, yes. I'm saving it for my uncle," she said.

He nodded and moved on.

My uncle? It sounded so foreign. She never had an uncle before and here she was saying it again in reflex and it sounded good, so natural.

My uncle. How many times had she said that without meaning to since she had learned the truth? It amazed her. Uncle Sam? How appropriate was that, in the fact that her uncle had been an army officer and Uncle Sam was a symbol of their country?

She decided on reading the papers first, but only after a phone call. She retrieved her cell phone, turned it on, and pressed a number from her directory.

"Shayla Williams's office, May I help you?" the secretary answered.

"Hello again, Tara. This is Kate Thayer. Is she available?"

All her friends from college and vet school knew her as Kate Thayer and not Kate Logan. It was the same back home. It just made things easier to just go by Thayer and Adam never minded. In private and among friends, she was Mrs. Adam Logan and that was all that mattered to him.

"Of course, Doctor Thayer. Always for you. Hold on."

The phone went silent for three seconds, accompanied by clicking, and then she heard the familiar energetic voice and east coast accent. "Hello again, Kate. I don't hear from you in six months and now I hear from you...what?...three times in two days? What can I do for you?"

"I'm sorry, Shayla. I didn't mean to bother you again. I need another favor and I don't mean to impose—"

"Oh, girlfriend, impose. You know me. I'm just harassing you. I owe you. You got me through vet school when I didn't stand a chance. Funny thing is, here I am at Daddy's office working with trains instead of animals, though sometimes they can be one and the same." She laughed. "Did you get the sleeper room for your uncle?"

"That's the problem. They only had a roomette, which is way too small and uncomfortable for him. He has a bad leg."

"Say no more. I'll see what I can do. Hold on, will you, honey? You want anything done, you have to do it yourself. And whatever you do, don't leave it to a man to do it, unless he's a good one."

Kate grinned and heard the punching of computer keys while Shayla mumbled to herself off the phone. A few moments later, she was back on the phone. "No problem now, Kate. It's done. In fact, I put him in a sleeper room next door to you. Is that okay, or too close for comfort? Now I have two uncles I told you about—one I wouldn't mind, but the other...well, I'd want him on another train."

Kate laughed with her. "No, that's fine Shayla. I appreciate it. Anything I can do for you, please let me know."

"It's always so good to hear from you. You keep those emails coming. We're all so busy now that we're all grown up, aren't we?"

"Is that what they call it?"

"Know what you mean, girlfriend. Next time you're back up north, come by DC way and we'll do the town. Okay?"

"I'll do that, Shayla. Promise. Keep in touch."

"You too. Good friends are hard to come by."

"Amen to that. Thank you, Shayla, for everything."

"Thank you. And you're welcome, too. Gotta go. Have a train company to run. Take care, girlfriend. Miss you."

The phone went silent. Kate ended the call, shut off the phone, and put it back into her purse.

"I was wrong," Sam said as he joined her. "No shops here."

She stood up. "That's all right. We can get a taxi to where some are and you can get what you need."

"You don't have to come with me."

"I don't mind. There's a museum or two nearby I'd like to see. One is a blues museum," she said as she gathered up her belongings. "It'll be better than just sitting here."

"You like blues?" he asked.

"Sam, I was born in the heart of blues country. Of course, I love blues."

He went to take her small suitcase from her but she shook her head. "Let's go shopping."

೬∕ꝝ೬∕ꝝ

Kate stared out the large picture window later on and watched the world go by. For each mile the train traveled onward, she moved one mile farther away from her home. Home? Where exactly was that now? Was Mississippi and Magnolia Lane Farm ever really her home? Would it ever be again?

Evidently, her grandfather Jackson didn't think so. Jackson Thayer the IV was just a man who occasionally lived in the house. Of course, she now knew why. It certainly explained his attitude toward her. He wanted no part of her. Katherine had accepted her because she was half-White, and looked it. But Jackson, George, or Maddy wanted no part of a mixed-race baby at all. And no one wanted her sister because she was a mixed-race baby that looked Black.

She wondered what it was like for her parents to be living under the same roof with Katherine and Jackson. It certainly couldn't have been easy. Her mother's journal said how intolerable it was, but reading about it and actually living through it were two different things. It made her realize just how very strong and independent they must have been and that explained her own strength. So many questions began to form and Kate guessed she might never learn all the answers. What was it like for her parents to have their own parents hate their spouse, their marriage, and their unborn child? Did they know what their parents had in mind for their unborn child? Why didn't they leave and live somewhere else? Why did they stay? Why did her mother endure the pregnancy when Lincoln had told her it might be dangerous for her? She must have loved Kate's father a great deal. Why did her father kill himself? He must have loved her mother terribly.

She knew what it was like to lose a spouse. It nearly killed her when Adam died. It would have killed her, too, had it not been for her grandmother's intervention. Her grandmother? Katherine was the greatest woman she ever knew. While young, Kate attended the local private school. Katherine did, too, and earned a degree in agribusiness. While Jackson traveled on business and after his death, Katherine ran the farm single-handedly, except for a few hands that were there since or almost at the beginning. Kate couldn't help but admire her. She taught Kate about life and how to survive in a man's world. Her entire life had revolved around her, and Kate had no doubt the other woman loved her, but the lies and the secrets were too much to handle.

And Maddy, another woman Kate had long admired. After the loss of her husband, George, Kate's other grandfather, it seemed, Maddy had gone back to school full time and, in six years, obtained a Master's degree and entered teaching at the Thayersville high school. She loved teaching so much that she only retired two years before at sixty-eight. She also loved to read. Both grandmothers did, Kate realized. No wonder the desire to do so was so strong within her.

Like it or not, she descended from strong women on both sides of her family. Like it or not, right or wrong, good and bad, they were her family. She leaned back in the chair and stared out the window. Her thoughts were interrupted by the touch of Sam's hand on hers.

"You all right, kiddo?" he asked.

She studied him. He was strong, handsome, gregarious, and

confident. He was a war hero. Most importantly, he was her uncle.

"You seem to be somewhere else. Not here," he said.

"I was just thinking…"

"Oh? Do I dare ask?"

"You didn't really hate my father because he was White, did you? I mean, I know what you said, Maddy's affair with Jackson, but I want to know. I need to know." She loved Sam. She wanted to keep liking him, too.

"No. You never let me finish. Back then, I was racist, just like my daddy."

"So you wouldn't have been my uncle then?"

"No, I guess not, but that's not what I meant."

"Explain it then. What happened? What changed? Your wife is White?"

"Half-White."

"Excuse me?"

"Her mother is White, German. Her father is Black, retired army officer, like me."

Kate covered her face with her hands. This was way too much for her.

"I'm sorry. I thought you knew."

"How could I possibly know that?"

"Katherine knew. Elsa told her straight off the bat when she hired her. I don't know why, except…"

"Except?"

"Elsa hates secrets. She wanted your grandmother to know. That's the way she is."

"And she didn't know about me, my parents?"

"No, I never told her. She knew I had a sister and she died in childbirth, but not the rest. I swore never to tell anyone. Mama and Daddy made me swear."

"But Katherine knows she's mixed-race?"

"Yes."

"And she accepted her?"

"She's crazy about her. You see that."

She stood up. "Sam, I know you were lied to also, but I'm tired and I can't discuss this anymore tonight. Do you mind?" The knot returned to her stomach and tightened up. She also felt a faint taste of bile rising in the back of her throat.

"Before I go—" Sam pulled out his wallet and handed her a

photo. "I want you to have this. It's your mama. You should have this. It's rightfully yours."

She stared at it and slowly took it into her hand. "My mama?" She tasted the saltiness of tears.

"Yes."

"She's beautiful." She was even more beautiful than Kate could imagine. Her skin was perfect with full lips and bright eyes. Kate was elated to stare face to face with her, so to speak. "My mama."

"Yes, she was, inside and out, just like you."

"I—never" she swallowed deeply, but tears filled the back of her throat. "Except for the night at Maddy's, I never saw any photos of her. I don't have any."

"You do now and Mama has lots. When we go home, you need to see them."

She nodded. She carefully ran her fingers over the pristine color photo. He obviously treasured it. She held it carefully, afraid to rip or lose it forever. This was her mama. *My mama.* Along the edge, there was a strip of white showing, a crease in the photo. She pulled at the edge of it. In the other half of the photo was her handsome father looking up at her. Her heart stopped for a long moment. These were her parents together in a photo she never saw before, when they were happy and had their entire lives before them. She ran her fingers over both their smiling faces. Their mouths showed full white teeth and their eyes were bright and wide. There was no doubt how happy they were. Mama was jutted right up to Jax. His arm was around her. Her hand in his other one rested on her lap. They were very clearly in love. Tears began to fall from her eyes.

"Your daddy. That photo was taken a week before they ran away and got married. We were all home for summer break. I left for West Point the next day after I took this photo of them. I wasn't there when they married. I guess I didn't want to see your daddy, but I couldn't rip him out of it either. We were friends." He reached out and placed his hand on hers. "I'm sorry, Kate. I know you're probably tired of hearing that, but I don't know what else to say."

She shook her head. "It's fine. Thank you for the photo." She placed the small photo on her lap, held it there, and stared down at it. Her throat suddenly became dry and she had difficulty swallowing.

He stood up. "Well, I'm going to let you try and get some sleep. You know where I am, if you need me."

All she could do was nod.

He moved to the door, stepped out, and waited for her. "Kate, you need to lock this door."

She stood up in reflex as if on automatic, went to the door, and locked it behind him while gripping the photo.

She went to her berth and sat down with the photo in her hand. *My mama, my parents together in a photo.* It was all so overwhelming. She let out a breath. There they were when they were younger than she was now. How could their parents have been so mean to them? So unkind? *Look how happy they are. How on earth were they rejected by those that loved them?*

She shook her head at the latest information she'd learned. It seemed the more she asked about her family, the more she learned and wasn't sure she wanted to know more. But she had to. She needed to. Her grandmother, Katherine, accepted Elsa, but rejected Kate's sister and her own son and his wife. Kate let out a short laugh at the irony. Katherine liked Elsa, immediately. *So, I was right about her when I surmised all her charity work to help the poor and underprivileged, mostly Colored children and families was to cover for her guilt for what she did.* Her grandmother rejected her son, her daughter-in-law, and her grandchildren because of race, mixed race, but then accepted a total stranger, Elsa, a woman of mixed race. No wonder she never told Kate. Of course, Kate wouldn't have known about the connection anyway. Wow! It was all too incredible. Talk about hitting the nail on the head. And Maddy too, it seemed, accepted Elsa, years after she rejected her daughter, her son-in-law, and her grandchildren. All for the same reason. Kate really didn't even know either one of them, did she? What else didn't she know about them, about everything else? The fear and uncertainty of that frightened her, but she had to know if there was more. Back then, Sam said. Back then...

She sighed, brought up a hand, and covered her mouth. She closed her eyes for a moment, leaned over, and placed the photo into the journal. Shaking her head, she reached down into her case and pulled out the small bottle of sleeping pills.

Should I or shouldn't I? I really need to sleep, but I really need to eat and drink too rather than just pick.

She had no appetite and just couldn't conjure one up. And

why was her back hurting? Was it the sleeping accommodations?

She decided that sleep was more important tonight and took one sleeping pill instead of the directed two. She placed her head on the pillow and shut her eyes.

Chapter 13

Kate tossed and turned. The voices were louder than ever. There was a light and that startled her. Where was she? What was happening? The voices were angry and she didn't recognize them. Stop the yelling. What was that loud noise? Stop it. Stop it! *Stop it*!

"Stop it! Just stop it!" she yelled in her sleep. "Enough! I've had enough!"

There was a banging noise on top of the other noises, the other sounds. There was a crashing sound. Where was it coming from? She didn't recognize any of it. What was going on? She heard another voice now, one she recognized. It was closer to her. It was urgent.

"Kate, are you all right. Answer me?"

"Sam?" She blinked in order to see him clearly and glanced around. "What's wrong? What are you doing here?" The cabin lights were on and the sudden brightness temporarily blinded her.

His hands were on her shoulders in a firm grip. "You were screaming so loud I could hear it next door," he said, his eyes wide and his voice deeper than usual.

"I'm sorry. It must have been a nightmare." Was that what it was?

"Want to talk about it?" he asked and relaxed as he went slowly down onto his good knee.

"I don't remember it. It was so real, but I don't remember," she said. What was it about?

"Is everything all right in here?" An elderly White couple stuck their heads in cautiously, concern evident on their faces. "Should we call someone?"

The woman clung onto her husband. They were both dressed in striped pajamas, long flannel robes and slippers.

Kate stood up. "I'm fine. Thank you. I'm sorry to disturb

you." Good thing she chose pajamas for the trip. "It was a night-mare. I'm fine now. I'm sorry."

"Are you sure?" the elderly lady asked, eyeing Sam.

Kate waved at them. "Fine. This is my uncle. You can go. Sorry again."

They backed out and he attempted to close the sliding door, but couldn't get it to cooperate. "I'm sorry," the man said. "I can close it but I can't seem to lock it. I think it's broken."

"That's fine," Kate said. "We'll take care of it." She sat back down on the lower berth.

The couple left and went on their way.

"What happened to the lock?" she asked when they were gone.

"I did. I heard you screaming," he said. "I thought someone was attacking you. I'll pay for it. You send me the bill."

"Thank you, Sam. I didn't mean to worry you. And I'll take care of it."

"No," he said. "I will. I don't accept charity."

"It's not charity, Sam. We're family right?"

She knew she had him, but he was still stubborn. "Yes, we are, but I'm still paying for it." He raised a hand. "No argument, Miss Kate—kiddo. I'll pay for it."

"Okay. Well, you better get back to bed then," she said, though she'd never give him the bill even if he did ask for it. And after that nightmare, she wasn't sure she could go back to sleep.

Sam got up slowly with effort. "About that—you should get your things together."

"I beg your pardon," she said.

"You can't sleep in here tonight. Not with a broken lock."

"Don't be silly. I'll be fine," she said. "Sam, what do you think can possibly happen?"

"These days? Anything. I won't leave you in here alone."

His concern touched her. "Sam, if I get up now and move about, I won't be able to go back to sleep at all."

He bought up his hand and scratched the back of his neck. "I'll be right back." He disappeared.

While he was gone, the male porter knocked on the wall and stuck his head in. "Is everything all right, Doctor Thayer? What happened to your door?"

"A misunderstanding, that's all. I'll take care of fixing it. Please send me a bill," she told him.

He looked at the door, up and down. "I'm not sure how to report this, miss, but I will. Would you like another room?"

"That won't be necessary," she said.

"She'll be safe and sound," Sam said from behind him and stepped inside. "I assure you."

The porter nodded. "As you say, Mr. Johnson, Doctor Thayer. Please call me if you need anything else." He stepped out, gave a last perusal of the door lock, and let loose a low whistle. "Wow! However did you manage to break this lock?"

"I kicked it," Sam said. "Good night, Jack." Sam closed the door and put her case and his bag in front of it. He faced her. "With my good leg, of course."

"Now what are you doing?" she said, puzzled by his movements.

"Getting back to sleep." He walked over to the easy recliner chair and sat down. "And so should you."

"You're not staying in here?" she asked.

"Normally, no, but you have no lock. I said I'm not leaving you alone."

His concern touched her, but… "Sam, I won't be able to sleep with you staring at me all night."

"I won't be staring. I'll be trying to sleep, and so should you," he said and leaned his head back in the chair and shut his eyes.

She sighed. He was incredible. Too much, and she didn't know what to say, except, "All right, Sam. But you won't be comfortable sitting up all night again. And what about your leg? It must hurt."

"I'm fine. My leg is fine. Hush now, kiddo, and sleep."

"Is that an order?"

He looked up and forced a grin. "No way. I know better than that."

She grinned back. "Good night, Sam. Thank you."

"You don't have to thank family," Sam said.

"I do. I was raised right," she said.

"Yes, you were." His eyes gleamed under the table light. "You get the light, kiddo. I just got comfortable."

"I prefer being called kiddo over Miss Kate."

"I like it better, too, but it'll take getting used to."

She reached above her berth and shut the light off, but not before glancing at her watch to check the time. It was nearly two. "Good night, Sam."

"Oh, Kate, do you snore?" he asked in the darkness.

"What," she asked as she lay her head down on the pillow.

"Do you snore?" he said.

"No, I don't think so. Why?"

"Well, I do. Sometimes. Sometimes, Elsa says it's soothing. Other times, she says it's like a train roaring into the station. If I get too loud, just tell me to shut up."

"Uh-huh. I'll do that. Good night, Sam."

"Good night, kiddo. Sweet dreams."

She hoped so. In a few seconds, he was snoring real low. Whether it was because he was there and cared, or because his presence, accompanied by the slight jerking of the train, soothed her, after about twenty minutes of thoughts about family, she drifted back to sleep, free of any more nightmares that night.

☙☙☙

It was daylight and bright in the room when Kate awoke to find she was alone. Sam was evidently already gone. He was definitely a morning person. Must be a leftover of his army days.

She was also an early starter, though not from the army. Growing up on a horse farm, running it made her one.

Katherine believed that going to bed early and rising early made a woman wise and prosperous. How could Kate argue with that when it proved to be true? How could she sleep in late when her grandmother, a woman forty years her senior and still sprightly as ever, was not afraid to be out in the pasture, often before the sun came up. Answer? She couldn't.

She sat up to see a piece of paper standing upright on the table held up by two water bottles. She got up and read it.

I'm in my room, kiddo, when you're ready to get some breakfast. I hope you eat more today than you did yesterday. You need to eat or you'll get sick. Sam. P.S. You don't snore.

She laughed at his postscript. Eat more? She had tried to eat more at lunch and dinner the night before, but she just wasn't that hungry.

Other things more pressing took precedence. Not to mention that dull abdominal cramps plagued her, accompanied by a dull headache, and she attributed it to the stress of it all. She certainly had plenty of that.

e⁄ჳe⁄ჳ

Evening came slowly on a train ride as anxiety settled in. There was nothing much to do on a train, except talk, walk, eat, sleep, or read and she had done plenty of the first over the last two days. Time was now growing short. She stared out the window as the train made its entry toward New York City's Penn Station. Penn Station was underground. Only now did butterflies fill her stomach and she wasn't even at her destination, yet, just in the city where she had to go.

Artificial light filled the car and replaced the natural light that no longer shone through from the outside. The artificial light was bright and intrusive and she found she had to blink a few times in order to have her eyes adjust.

The lights of the metropolis were amazing and quite different from home. Even the bright lights of Mississippi's state capitol of Jackson couldn't match the majesty of a New York skyline at night. That was something she had admired in photos she had viewed growing up and in her last visit here.

Sam snapped his fingers. "Kate? Kiddo?" he said.

She faced him. He didn't seem as uncomfortable as he had been earlier around her. He seemed more relaxed, at ease, and so was she. Had it been each other's vibes that pushed them forward? Or was it merely wishful thinking?

"I'm as ready as I'll ever be," she answered and willed it to be so. She was here to do the right thing, the honorable thing, and she would see it through.

She had never been so angry before in her entire life until she dug up the secrets that had been hidden away by those she had trusted and loved. There was no such thing as a secret, Katherine had been fond of saying, as long as one person knew about it. Talk about irony. How many persons knew about the secret? Maddy, Katherine, Jackson, George, Lincoln, and Betsy were there the night the babies were born. Did she leave anyone out? Did anyone else know? Sam learned about most of it later on. Her grandmother had been right. There was no such thing as a secret. Secrets always came out, always. Did they all think that they could actually keep such a secret about her from her forever? That she would never find out?

She glanced at him. Sam flinched and shifted in his seat.

"Are you all right, Sam?" she asked.

"Sure, kiddo. No worries about me."

She noticed him blink and the muscles in his neck twitched.

"It's your leg, isn't it?"

He stretched it straight out before him and massaged the knee. "It's fine. Just a little stiff."

"No more lies, Sam, about anything. You're obviously in pain."

He nodded. "Okay, it twinges. It flares up when I stand up for too long, or when there's a change of weather in the air."

"It probably didn't help when my grandmother hit you the other night, and sitting up the last two nights certainly didn't help either."

"No. I guess not."

"I'm sorry about that," she said.

"It wasn't your fault."

"Why did you let her hit you?"

"She's your grandmother and I don't hit women," he said. "Especially women the same age as my mama."

"I'm sorry, Sam. Really sorry." It was nice to see a gentleman, when that was such a rarity in the world.

He looked at her, into her. "You have nothing to be sorry about. We do."

She moved to get up. "I'm going to get you some aspirin for that."

"No. I'll be fine," he said, waving a hand at her. "It's not too bad. I've had bad before and this isn't it."

"Are you sure? I can ask the porter if there is a doctor on board," Kate said.

"I'm with one now," he said and forced a grin.

"I'm not that kind of doctor, and I don't want you suffering."

"I'm not. Stupid leg. It doesn't work right but can hurt like the dickens," he said. "I didn't want them to amputate, but every now and then I wonder if I should have just let them."

"Did it hurt? When it happened? The roadside bomb? I'm sorry. You probably don't want to bring that up. And it's a stupid question. Of course, it hurt. I don't know what I'm thinking anymore. Forgive me." Suddenly, she felt stupid.

"Your mind is a jumble of things," he said. "I understand. And, yes, it hurt. It was broken in three places and if they couldn't have gotten the infection under control, they would have cut it off, no matter what I said. I chose not to and now it's as useful as a piece of deadwood, but it's my leg, stupid as it sounds. I saw worse with my soldiers. I was lucky."

"It's not stupid to want to hold onto your leg. What was stupid and, I'm sorry, Sam, because I know you believe in what you did, but both those wars were a waste of time, effort, money, and loss of limbs and lives. We shouldn't have been there. There, I said it. You can lecture me now, if you like."

"No. Elsa would agree with you and so does Mama. So does your grandmother. As for me, the army officer says we did the right thing. The civilian says we should be home from both the wars, not just Iraq. We should plan our battles more carefully from now on and stop trying to save the world. Too many lives were wasted. We need to protect our own, first and foremost." He slowly bent his leg. "See. It's calming down now."

"I'm glad. I wish I could do something for you to help you with it." His pouring out of his heart to her touched her especially since they thought alike in one subject.

"There's nothing to be done. Of course, that doesn't stop Elsa from trying. Sometimes having a nurse for a wife can be...interesting."

Kate laughed. "I'm sure. She loves you and worries about you. Anyone can see that."

He laughed too. "You're right. She does and I see it every day. Sometimes I see your mother in her too. The way she fusses or scolds me and looks after me. Your mama did that with me, her baby brother. I guess I was blessed with Elsa just like your mama was blessed with your daddy. I'm sorry I said some things about Jax being White. Back then—"

"I know. Forget it. We move forward now and take care of the present. I'll try not to be angry with you and you be honest with me. Agreed?"

He nodded.

♥❧♥❧

When the time the train pulled into the station, stopped, and the doors opened ten minutes later, Sam grabbed her small case and his duffel bag and headed to the cabin door.

She shook her head at him and he replied with, "Uncle's prerogative. Complain to my union."

"Thank you, Sam," she replied instead.

The more time she spent with him, the more she liked and admired him. She wished she'd known him earlier.

Sam led the way out and played interference for Kate to exit the train. The porter said goodbye to everyone, wished them a safe journey, and said thank you for riding with them.

On their way past him, Kate reached into her pocket and shook his hand, releasing the cash into it. "Thank you," she told him. "Have a great night."

The porter beamed. "You too, Doctor Thayer, Mister Johnson. Thanks for riding with us. Hope to see you again soon. Go straight upstairs and you can get a taxi or bus. Or you can rent a car."

"Thank you," Sam said and followed Kate as she made her way up the stairs through the other passengers.

They climbed the stairs and exited outside the station onto the crowded and busy streets of New York City, Thirty-Fourth Street to be exact, Pennsylvania station. Good thing it was May or darkness would have greeted them instead of light.

"The weather isn't too bad," Sam remarked. "Little colder than back home."

She felt it too. There was a chill in the air. "I hear they can get cold fronts this late, sometimes."

"Let's hope not too cold. Don't know if these old bones could handle it."

"You're not old, Sam," she said.

"Tell that to my body." He shifted on his leg. "I forgot how loud and busy it is here."

"It is definitely different than back home," Kate said.

"Haven't been here since I spent a tour at Fort Hamilton," he said. "Elsa loved going to the theater and opera. I loved the food."

"Me too," she said. "We need to get a taxi to the hotel."

"I'll get one." He stepped just off the curb, waved his hand, and, with the other, blew a whistle between his fingers. A few cabs passed them by, but when one stopped just near them, it nearly ran into Sam. Sam just made it back onto the sidewalk before the yellow car rolled into the spot he had been standing in.

"Guess I'm not as fast and limber as I was last time I was here," he commented to her as he picked up her suitcase.

She moved to object but he wouldn't have it. He held a small duffel bag over his shoulder that he'd picked up in Chicago.

There, he bought the bag and the necessities he'd need while away from home for a few days. Good thing he had been a soldier. He'd learned how to travel light.

The cab driver got out, came around, and put the small suitcase in the trunk. Sam held onto his bag. He opened the back door and let Kate enter first then followed her in and sat down next to her.

The cab driver got back in the front seat. "Destination?" he asked, without looking back.

Kate noticed he had an accent, though she didn't recognize it. He had short black curly hair and light brown skin.

"Hotel Mark on Madison and—" she began.

"Seventy-Seventh Street. Got it," the driver said.

He started the meter and pulled from the curb.

"Makes you think of Mister Toad's wild ride in Disney World, doesn't it?" Sam asked.

She laughed. "Yes, it does."

She glanced out the windows as the car sped by a section of buildings and slowed down for traffic lights. In between, the cab stopped for red lights.

Another yellow taxi cut in front of them and their driver yelled an obscenity but she couldn't make it out.

"Stupid people!" he yelled out the window. "Go back to where you came from! If you can't drive, get off the street!"

Kate laughed. Visiting New York City was never dull. That was for sure. In a way, she sort of missed it. The constant buzzing and charge of this electric city and all the amenities it offered.

"Very different from home, huh, Sam?"

"Undeniably," he replied. "How long did you spend here when you interned at the vet hospital?

"Nine months. I liked it. It was different."

"To be sure. I'm surprised Miss Katherine let you go, leave Mississippi, that is. However did you manage that?"

"I told her I wanted to. Simple as that. That it would be a good experience to intern at a small animal hospital before settling down back home. Besides, I was married then. She had no choice. No big deal, Sam."

"Your grandmother worries about you. I'm surprised she didn't follow you out here."

"Oh, she did. Once a month for a weekend she flew up and stayed with us. We did the sights. I loved it. Good thing for the farm, or she would have moved up here until we left. Of course, she did the same thing when we lived in England for almost a year that I interned there at another vet hospital, large animals that time. Adam had a fellowship at Oxford. We had fun there. Adam adored her. She ran circles around us in both places."

"We're here," the driver said.

He pulled the taxi just alongside the curb nice and easy. Sam opened the passenger side and held it open for her, extending his hand to her. She took it and stepped out onto the curb.

A doorman came to meet them and took her suitcase from Sam.

Kate was about to take money from her purse but Sam beat her to it. He took his wallet from his back pocket, paid the bill, and gave a ten-dollar tip on top.

Kate stepped onto the sidewalk and went through the front door. She heard her footsteps from her boots across the black and white tiled floor. She was followed by the doorman and Sam.

Sam stepped up alongside her and whispered, "A bit pricey for this place, Kate."

"But convenient and Gran won't look for me here."

The doorman set her case by the counter while a woman behind greeted her. "Good evening," the slender Black woman said. "May I help you?"

"I have a reservation for Kate Thayer. And I'd like to get a second room or adjoining suites for Sam Johnson, my uncle, please."

The woman lowered her brown eyes onto the computer screen before her. "Yes, I have your reservation, Doctor Thayer. We have you booked in one of our Courtyard One-Bedroom Suites. Let me see what I can find for you…yes, I can give you another suite on separate floors, but no adjoining suites, or two rooms on the same floor in our Madison rooms with a king. I can see what I can do for the rest of your stay."

"I don't need a suite, Miss Kate," Sam said.

"We'll take the two Madison rooms on the same floor for now, thank you," Kate said. "If anything else becomes available, I'd appreciate being notified." She took a credit card from her purse and handed it to the woman, who eyed both of them while running the card. "In town for business, Doctor Thayer?" the woman inquired. Her nametag identified her as Keisha and she was very attractive.

"No. I'm visiting family, actually," Kate said it before she realized she had. It seemed so natural to say.

"Welcome to New York," Keisha said. "I'm sure you'll find both your rooms to your satisfaction. If you require anything during your stay, please don't hesitate to contact the front desk or the concierge." She handed Kate back her credit card, a key card, and another key card to Sam.

"Thank you," Kate said. "Have a good night."

The woman smiled at the greeting. "And you too, Doctor Thayer. Thank you."

Sam took his. "Thank you, ma'am," he said.

A bellboy showed up next to him, picked up her bag, and led the way to the elevator.

Kate followed but then stopped just short of the doors.

The bellboy pushed the button and waited.

Sam moved to her side. "Kate, are you all right? What's wrong?"

She swallowed hard and stared straight ahead. "I'm sorry, Sam. I forgot. I hate elevators."

"It'll be okay. I'm here. Don't be scared," he said.

"I can't do it, Sam. Not now. I can't."

"Okay, fine. Wait here."

He went to the bellboy and she overheard Sam. "You think we can take the stairs? I hate elevators."

The bellboy stared at him for a long moment. "Yeah, sure. Okay, but you realize you're on the eighth floor?"

When she overheard that, she stepped forward when the doors opened and rushed inside. "We're fine. Let's go."

Sam eyed her. She saw the concern in his eyes and heard it when he said her name, "Kate."

"Let's just go up, please."

Sam got in and the bellboy copied them. He pushed eight. When the elevator doors began to close, Kate grabbed Sam's hand and clasped it tightly. She didn't look at him, but remained focused on the doors. Sam couldn't have been more proud than if she had won another blue ribbon on one of her prize horses. He suddenly stood ten feet tall.

The elevator sounded a chime when their floor was reached and she exited before the doorman took a step.

The bellboy stepped out, turned right, took them to the end of the hall, and went to her room first. "This is your room, Doctor

Thayer. Mister Johnson's room is just across the hall."

With the key card, he opened the door for her and they stepped in first. The bellboy moved to show her the amenities, but Sam showed him to the door, took the keys, gave him a tip from his pocket, said goodnight, and closed the door. They didn't need a tour.

Two things bothered him. "Kate, this is—" He looked around the room. "—too expensive. Your grandmother will be livid." With furnishings of ebony, sycamore, and nickel, fine Italian linens and bedding, the room was overwhelming.

"Serves her right."

"You don't mean that," he said.

"No. I guess I don't. But we can more than afford it."

He knew Kate hadn't gotten much sleep on the ride up here. He certainly hadn't. And if she was half as tired as he was, she had to be totally exhausted.

She stood in the middle of the room and didn't look at him. "Thank you, Sam. I'd like to freshen up and then go find her."

"You mean after a good night's sleep?" he said.

She turned and faced him. "No. Tonight. I want to find her."

He knew he couldn't talk her out of it if she'd already decided, but he had to try. "I don't think that's such a good idea tonight. We're both tired. Why not start fresh tomorrow?"

"I don't want to wait too long. I want to do it tonight."

"Kate, listen to reason. You're tired. I'm tired. We both had a very long train ride up here." He checked his watch. "It's nearly eight. You don't really want to try and find her now, do you?"

"I have her address. We can go see her now," she said.

He had to try reason. She valued logic. "Are you really up to it now? Did you sleep last night? The night before. Did you?"

She brought up a hand and rubbed her temples. "Some, but you're right. I don't want to do or say anything stupid because I'm tired."

He sighed with relief. "Good. I'll freshen up and then I'll call room service and order dinner. And tonight, you'll try and eat more. All right with you?"

She nodded. "You're right." She yawned and covered her mouth with her hand. "I am tired."

"I'll leave your key here on the desk and go freshen up. Then I'll come back," he said.

"All right, Colonel," she said.

"Now I know you're tired. You're not putting up a fight," he said, heading for the door. "You make sure you lock this behind me."

She followed him. "Yes, Colonel."

He stepped outside. "Just do it, please, Miss Kate. Kiddo. Old habits die hard, Kate."

He closed the door and she locked it. He tried to get in. When he couldn't, it was silent.

A quick peek through the peep hole and she saw him enter his room just across from hers and the door closed behind him.

Uncle. Uncle Sam. She'd never had an uncle. Rather, she did but didn't know it. It was a weird feeling, though it really shouldn't have been. She had known Sam her entire life. He was Maddy's son and Maddy Kate had known for as long. When he had retired from his career in the army, he had returned to Thayersville to be near his mama, and Kate too, it seemed.

She didn't mean to frighten any of them two years ago. She didn't. Things just spiraled out of control so quickly once the accident happened. Before she knew it, she found her life was in a total blur.

Chapter 14

Back in Mississippi, at the big house, Elsa found herself staring out the large picture window in the living room, or parlor, as she'd learned to call it. Parlor was Katherine's word, not hers. As she quickly learned upon her arrival here, Mrs. Katherine Thayer had her own way of doing things and, in this house, her word was law. For Sam, Elsa could live with that. It wasn't as if one of them needed to work here. Sam wanted to and she agreed. Now she knew why. And after the incident that occurred after Kate went into the attic, Elsa didn't want to do anything that would harm her husband again. Of course, learning that Kate was her niece was a pleasant, though shocking, surprise. One she welcomed wholeheartedly.

The cell phone rang and she couldn't pull it from her pocket quick enough, "Sam?" Elsa asked.

"It's me."

"Thank God! Where are you? Is Kate with you? How could you leave without telling me—"

"Calm down, woman, and let me speak. I'm fine. Kate's fine, but I can't tell you where we are. And you're not to tell anyone where we are."

"How can I tell anyone anything when I don't know? Are you all right? Are you sure? Sam, this isn't like you—"

"Elsa, I love you, honey, but you need to shut up and listen."

"I'm listening. Go on." She restrained her natural inclination to barrage him with more questions. If he had been here now, she'd probably strangle him for worrying her to death. She began tapping her right foot on the floor.

"How is Mama?" he asked.

"You left without a word. Kate is gone. How do you think she is?" she scolded. "She's beside herself. And Miss Katherine is acting weird, too."

"How can you tell?"

"Don't be flippant, Sam. I've been married to you for twenty years and worked for her for the last couple of those. I know how she is supposed to act. She asked where you were and when I couldn't tell her, she jumped up at me in my face!"

"Did she hit you?"

She wouldn't tell him that she wouldn't stand for that nonsense. "No. She didn't do anything. She just stared. Carol's worried about her too. Said she's never seen her this way, ever."

"Miss Katherine is a tough ole girl. Don't worry about her."

"What am I supposed to say to them when your mama and Katherine ask if you called and where you both are?"

"Tell them the truth. I called. We're fine, but I didn't tell you where we are."

"When are you coming home? Can you tell me that, at least?" Elsa asked.

"I don't know. Kate has something to do and I'm going to help her."

"But why? Sam, what is going on? Is this about her sister? Your mama told me. She said you didn't know."

She heard silence and then a sigh. "*Why*? Because she's my niece and I owe it to her. I love you, honey, but I have to go. Say nothing, please, baby. We're fine. Bye."

"Sam? Sam? Don't you hang up on me now. Sam? Oh Sam, you old fool you. I love you, too. Jesus, please keep them both safe. Please."

If she didn't love him so much, upon his safe return, she would strangle him.

It was only then that she noticed that the portrait of Kate's grandfather was absent from its spot of worship above the fireplace. What on earth? That painting had been there for as long as she remembered. Of course, she never saw it until two years before when Kate hired her, but she had heard about it from Sam. Mr. Jackson Thayer the IV had been a big man in life and an even bigger man after his death. His family helped build the city of Thayersville. Hence the naming of it after his family. What could have happened to the portrait and who moved it from its cherished spot? Of course, when it came down to it, she didn't really care about that. Her family, her Sam and her niece, was what mattered to her most of all. Now all she had to do was pass on the word and up the stairs she went.

Elsa knocked on the door to Katherine's room. She figured she'd take the offensive instead of waiting. She took a deep breath and entered.

She hadn't addressed the issue of Katherine striking Sam earlier because Sam made her promise not to interfere and, as much as she wanted to, she would hold fast to her word, as long as Katherine held her tongue. She entered when Katherine told her to.

Katherine came to her feet from her desk when she entered. "Has Sam called? Is it Kate? Is she all right? Where are they? Is he with her? Did he find her?"

"Easy, Miss Katherine. They're fine, he said. No worries." Whether that all was a lie or not, she didn't know, but it made her feel better to say it. It soothed her soul.

"Where are they?"

"I don't know. He didn't say that."

"Where are they, Elsa? I demand you tell me."

"I don't know, Miss Katherine. He said he wouldn't tell me, but that they were fine. I swear."

"Why? Why wouldn't he say?"

"I don't know. He didn't say." Elsa said, trying very hard to hold her tongue. This was the first time the other woman was so abrupt with her.

"Fine. You can go now," Katherine snapped. She turned away and leaned on the desk.

Elsa couldn't help feeling for her and reached out to touch her shoulder.

"Don't touch me!" Katherine snapped. "Just go. Let me know when Sam calls again."

Elsa had had enough. To hell with the promise, she wouldn't allow this. "Miss Katherine," she said firmly.

Katherine faced her.

"I know you're worried about Kate. We all are. I also know the truth about her. Everything. And if you ever, ever lay another hand on Sam, I will forget your age and knock you flat on your backside. Do you understand me?"

"How dare you?" Katherine glared. "Kate gave you a job here."

"And I'm grateful to her for it, but I came here for my husband. I came to work for you for Sam, for Maddy. But don't ever underestimate where my loyalty lies because of skin color." She headed toward the door. "I will keep you informed about Kate when he calls again."

Elsa walked out and slammed the door behind her. The next thing she had to do was let Maddy know the same thing. She couldn't handle any more emotions today and decided to call Maddy rather than return to the house. Besides, no matter how angry she was at Katherine this moment, Elsa had job duties to tend to here. She owed that to Kate. Niece or not, she still worked for her and she'd better get to it. At least her work would keep her mind off other things. And dusting a large house like this didn't get done on its own.

ల్యాల

Back in her room, Katherine lifted the stapler off the desk and threw it at the door. She liked Elsa, but she wouldn't allow anyone to speak to her that way. Frustration consumed her. Anger consumed her. There was only one way to relax after all this. She hadn't acted upon her desires yet, but now she would. She'd delayed long enough, hoping to hear from Kate. She deserved to indulge.

She walked over to the desk, lifted the phone from the receiver, and dialed.

A woman answered on the other end of the line. "Edmonton and Edmonton, attorneys at law. Can I help you?

"This is Katherine Thayer. Is Gary available?"

"One moment, Mrs. Thayer, if you'll hold." The line went momentarily silent then she heard the deep voice.

"Katherine, it is always good to hear from you. Is it for business or pleasure you are calling me?" he asked.

She heard the enthusiasm in his voice. "First things first," she said. "I want you to hire a private investigator, Gary, a very discreet one."

"What? What for?"

She began tapping her fingers on the desk. "Kate has left home without a word."

"So she finally flew the coop? About time—"

"Don't be flippant, Gary. It doesn't suit you, the time or the place either."

"All right. What for?"

"I want to make sure she's all right and know where she is."

"This is a big country, Katherine. I'll need specifics."

"I don't have any. If I had specifics, darling, I wouldn't need a private detective. She just left. Sam is with her. He called from his cell phone. I don't know where she has gone. That is why I want a private detective."

"Okay. I'll see what I can do. Is that it?"

"I expect discretion, Gary."

"Discretion is my middle name, you know that," he said.

"I want to see you tonight."

"My place or yours?"

"You can stay for the night if you wish," she said.

"Well, that would be a treat," he said. She heard papers shuffling in the background. "Give me two hours."

"Fine. I'll see you then."

His enthusiasm for everything attracted her. His vitality kept her interested. He was so much like his father in that respect. Yes, younger men definitely had their advantages, as long as they remembered their place.

She hung up the phone, stepped over to the bed, and lay back on top of it. She was just so tired. Tired of all the lies and deceit. Tired of everything. Tired of being alone. Tonight, she wouldn't be.

Katherine had no regrets in her life. As far as she was concerned, she did the right thing by Jax and Kate and—the other one. As far as she was concerned, she had put things right that had begun when Jax married Olivia. Of course, the sudden death of her son, his suicide, had changed her and not for the better. She grew more bitter and resentful and only having Kate around in her life kept her grounded and sane in an otherwise insane world. Kate had become her world. Kate was her future and she'd let no one change that. No one.

c✹ɔ

Night fell upon the city of New York and darkness surrounded it and the hotel that Kate visited. There was a knocking sound and she wasn't sure if it was coming from inside her head or outside. After all, there was a thumping inside her head by time she lay down across the bed after Sam left her alone. She closed her eyes and tried to will it away but the banging continued. She became aware of a voice that seemed muffled at first. The banging became louder, urgent and the voice equally urgent, louder and clearer.

"Kate, are you all right? You need to open this door!" It was Sam's urgent voice.

She dragged herself up to a sitting position then dragged herself to the door. *How could I possibly be so tired?* She went to the door and unlocked it.

He raced in. "Are you all right? Why didn't you answer?"

"I'm sorry, Sam. I must have fallen asleep." She closed the door and locked it.

"It's all right, Miss Kate. You just scared me. You were tired. I know I was," he said.

"Kate," she corrected. "Sit down, Sam, and relax. I'm fine. Just tired. I'm not a china doll, you know." He sat down on the sofa. She noticed his worsened limp. This was one stubborn man. Kate sat next to him. "It's okay, Sam. I don't bite you know. You can relax around me. You did on the train, eventually."

"I know. It's just…it's different."

"How so? You've known me for my whole life. You were always my uncle and I your niece. I just didn't know it. Now I do."

"I'm just really, really sorry." He averted his gaze. "I should have told you sooner."

"You should have. We agree on that. Now we have to move on. Do you agree on that?"

"Yes, I do. So what's your plan: to see your sister?"

"Plan?" She sighed. "I hadn't thought about it. I guess I should have one. I was going to go by her home tomorrow and…What do I say?"

"The truth always works."

"As if I handled the truth so good myself when you and Maddy told me."

"Considering we hid secrets from you and lied, you did." There was a knock at the door. He stood up. "That should be room service. I hope I picked what you want."

"You know pretty well by now what I like and don't like to eat," she said. "I'm sure Elsa told you."

A young woman pushed the cart into the room. She and Sam greeted each other and she handed him the bill. Sam signed it and closed the door behind her. "They don't exactly serve Southern food up here."

She joined him at the table. "It'll do. I'm sure. I'm probably too tired to eat anything anyway."

He pulled up a chair opposite her and sat down. "But you're going to try anyway."

Kate nodded. She eyed the plate of food before her and pushed it aside. "I'm sorry, Sam. I'm just not very hungry."

He studied her. "You said you'd try and eat something."

"I know. Maybe in a little while."

Sam pushed the cart to their side just within reach, but out of the way.

"You can go ahead and eat," she told him.

"No. I'll wait for you."

Kate pulled the small laminate card she had in her pocket since she began the trip. She held it in her hand and tried to remember to follow the words on it. Remember the five simple rules to be happy. 1) Free your heart from hatred. 2) Free your mind from worries. 3) Live Simply. 4) Give more. 5) Expect Less.

She turned it over and read the rest.

"What's that you have there, Kate?" Sam asked.

She eyed the card and handed it over to him.

"Remember the five simple rules to be happy." He read them aloud.

"Turn it over," she said.

He did and read the title and words aloud of the serenity prayer. "I like this. Where did you get it?" he asked and handed it back to her.

"Fits the situation, doesn't it? Adam. He said I sometimes took some things too seriously and wanted to remind me that I couldn't control everything, no matter what I did, which is funny coming from him. He was serious about everything—becoming a doctor, University studies…"

"You," Sam finished.

"Yes, and me." She stopped, closed her eyes, and tried not to let it get to her. She had been doing okay with losing him until lately. Must be the added stress of the newly found secrets and lies. Of course, it was.

He reached out to her and grasped her hand. "I'm sorry, Kate. I didn't mean to bring up sad memories."

"No." She waved her other hand at him. "It's fine. I'm fine. I'm over it. It's done. It's in the past. I can't change it. I can't change anything." She stood up and walked away from him. "At least I had him in my life. We loved each other. We respected each other. We didn't have a great deal of time together, but we were happy."

"He was a good man, Kate. A fine young man. I liked him. I'm glad you had him in your life. I wish I knew him better. You deserved more time together. He loved you very much. Mama and I saw that, Elsa too."

"Thank you. I thought so too." She took a breath. "We met when I was at vet school. He was working on his master's in bio-chemistry. He wanted to be a doctor like his father. I miss him—" She choked out the last words. "He was a good man and I feel fortunate to have had a good man in my life. Not every woman can say that. Certainly, not Katherine." She walked back to the table and sat down. "I have only two distinct memories of Jackson Thayer. Do you want to know what they are?"

"If you want to tell me. If it'll make you feel better," Sam said.

"I don't think it'll me feel better, but Jackson—He always traveled. He was rarely home and, when he was, he paid no attention to me. None at all. I never understood it then. I remember when I was ten. We were eating dinner, grandmother and I. He came in late and just sat down, no greeting, nothing. I was so excited to have him home. It was my birthday. I had a party earlier with friends and grandmother.

"It was nineteen hundred and ninety five and I sat in the middle of the massive dining room table made of solid oak. It could seat sixteen comfortably but most of the time it seated just three. Grandmother—Katherine glared at him for being late. I really didn't pay any attention. I was so excited and wanted to thank him for my new present.

"'Thank you, Grandfather. The new horse you and Grandmother gave me is beautiful,' I said. 'I just love her.'

"He stared at me. "What new horse?" He glared at Grandmother. "Don't we already have enough horses? This is a horse farm!"

"'It was a present,' Katherine said. 'For Kate's tenth birthday.'

"He stood up, threw his napkin on the table, and stormed out of the room. Grandmother got up and passed me by. 'You finish your dinner, darling. I'll be right back.'

"She left the room to follow him. I didn't finish my dinner. I was curious about him and sneaked out to listen from just behind the doorway.

"'Jackson,' Katherine called.

"He stopped on the staircase and faced her.

"'Where do you think you are going?' she asked.

"'I'll eat in my room. Have a tray sent up for me,' he said.

"'Not tonight.'

"His face was rigid. I never saw him smile. I don't think he could. 'You wanted her. You have her. That doesn't mean I have to sit and watch or listen to her.'

"'Jackson! She's just a child, our grandchild. Today is her birthday and you weren't here.'

"'No, I wasn't,' he said. 'I don't need a reminder of the past and a countdown to the future.'

"'We had a deal,' she reminded him.

"He stepped down a few stairs to meet her. 'We did. You broke the first deal to send them away and kept her. I'm breaking this deal. This is my farm, my home. You are my wife and you will do as I say. Not the other way around. Not anymore!' He stepped away. 'I'll be upstairs.'

"'This is *our* house, Jackson.'

"He moved to raise his hand to her, but Grandmother stood her ground before him, her chin held high. 'Don't you even dare!' she warned.

"He lowered his hand and stormed up the stairs.

"I guess I wasn't hiding anymore because when Katherine turned around, she saw me and came over. 'Oh, darling, what are you doing here?' She caressed my face. 'Come with me.' She took my hand, led me back into the dining room, and stood behind me once I was seated back at the table. 'Eat now, darling. Everything will be fine.'

"I couldn't help it. I didn't understand what he said, but I began crying and she held me from behind and brushed my hair with her fingers. I never saw either of them so angry before. I had to ask, 'Why doesn't grandfather love me?'

"'Oh, he does, darling. He's just tired from all the traveling. That's all. Don't pay him any mind,' Katherine said.

"Later on that night, I figured I'd surprise him. I went to his room and knocked on the big wooden door and entered when he said, 'Come in.'

"I ran over to his big wooden bed with my favorite book. 'Grandfather, will you tuck me in? Will you read me a story?'

"I remember how excited I was. I wanted to make him happy and smile. I remember I was smiling my best smile.

"Instead, he said, 'I'm not interested. Go to bed. I don't have time.'

"I held out my book to him. 'It's a short story. It's about a horse and her baby.'

"He snapped to his feet. He was so tall. I remember I had to bend my neck all the way back to see his face. He said, 'I said, no. Go to your room and go to bed.'

"I turned around and went outside and closed the door and stood in front of it and cried.

"It wasn't long until I felt her hands on my shoulders. 'Darling, what are you doing here?' She went down on her knees and wiped my tears with her hand.

"I didn't look at her. I was scared. I told her, 'I just wanted him to tuck me in and read my favorite book, but he didn't want to.'

"She took my hand and led me into my room and tucked me into bed. 'I'll be back and I'll read to you. Will that be okay?'

"I nodded and watched her leave my room.

"A few moments later, I heard arguing and I knew it was my grandparents. I heard a door slam and then another door slam. I got down out of my bed and went across the hall and peeked into my grandmother's room. Grandmother sat on the edge of her bed with her face buried in her hands. I went in and sat down next to her. She looked at me and smiled. I reached out and took her hand into mine. I remember how strong and large her hand was and how warm she was too. I leaned against her and she held me. She smelled of flowers.

"I must have fallen asleep because I don't remember anything else from that night, except Grandmother holding me and telling me how much she loved me and that she would always take care of me, and that she was sorry. Sorry about Jackson's behavior that night or everything? I never knew or understood. Until now. Now, I understand everything.

"That was the last time that I ever saw Jackson or heard them fight. He died during the night. Uncle Lincoln said it must have been an aneurysm. It was sudden. That's the memories I have of that man, my grandfather Jackson. Now I know why he behaved so poorly. He didn't want me. He didn't want a mixed-race child in his home. Now I know why he paid no attention and traveled so much. He didn't want me. It was Katherine who did. And my other grandfather—George—I never knew him at all, did I? Died before I could talk or walk. That's the memories I have of my grandfathers."

"Kate, I don't know what to say," Sam said.

She faced him. "What is there to say, Sam? You know?" She sighed. "A baby doesn't ask to be born. It just is. And once we're born, our parents, grandparents, uncles, and aunts are supposed to be there for us and protect us, love us. We're not trash and we don't deserve to be treated as such. I was the lucky one, I guess. Katherine kept me, loved me, and took care of me. I must remember that or I'll hate her. My sister—no one kept her." She stood up, went to the window, and stared out onto the residential area below. She couldn't help but chuckle at the incredulity of it all. "I came from a family of bigots, except for my parents. How is that possible?"

Sam was silent for a moment. "Kate, I'm sorry."

She faced him and tried to keep the tears at bay. "Come on Sam, you know the truth. Lincoln told me. No one wanted a mixed-race baby. Not even you. You said so yourself."

He stood up and walked over to her. "Not true, kiddo, except for back then. Look, I can't answer that about Jackson," Sam said. "I can only say that, yes, my father, George was no better."

"Evidently," she said. "Since he didn't want either me or my sister."

"Kate, I didn't hate you father just because he was White."

"You told me. Because he was the son of the man your mother had an affair with."

He looked away and then turned back to her. "Look, kiddo, I don't have many regrets in my life, except for…" He sighed deeply and faced her. His lips were drawn and his eyes serious. "I regret turning my back on your parents. I regret letting my father influence me so much." He took her hands in his.

"Tell me this, Sam. What would you have done if your parents forbade you from marrying Elsa?" she asked.

He didn't even hesitate. "I would have run away and married her, anyway, just like your mother did with Jax. I'm sorry, Kate. Back then, I was a fool. I was. I know that. When I met Elsa in Germany, when I fell in love with her and married her, I knew exactly how your parents felt for one another. I understood why they went against all of us and society. I understood the guts it took for them to stand up against everyone, especially us. I didn't, back then." He placed a hand on her shoulder. "What I'm trying to say is that, back then I was a different person. I could say it was because I was just a dumb kid, but I was eighteen. I idolized my father and the ground he walked on. He heavily influenced my feelings—what I believed. I thought he knew everything. In our house, his word was law. Mama, she just went with the flow of things. I never understood why. Maybe, it was just easier for her. But people change, Kate, they grow, they learn from their mistakes. I know I've learned from mine. I know Mama has too. Yes, my daddy was racist. But Mama isn't, not anymore, and when it comes right down to it, I don't think Katherine is either." He held up a hand. "I'm not defending either of them. It's just a feeling. One, I know Mama. Maddy is a different person. She hated what she did. She regrets it all."

"Then why didn't she tell me this before? And you? Why keep silent all this time?"

"Fear that you would hate her. Fear that you would reject her. Fear that you wouldn't believe her. Most importantly, we didn't want to hurt you. We love you. You're family."

Family. Kate turned from him. "George worked for my grandfather, then my father." She faced him again. "He didn't mind working for White men?"

"He said it was different. They gave him a paycheck. He'd do whatever it took to take care of his family. I'm sorry, Kate. He was an idiot, a fool, a racist fool, but he did love his family."

"Some of them anyway, right?" she snapped.

"In the end, before he died, I think he realized what a mistake they made. I told you, he died six months after Livie did, after that night. They said it was a heart attack, but Mama thought it was guilt. Maybe it was. I don't know. I can't speak for Mama or Katherine, but I love you, very, very much. And if takes the rest of my life to prove it to you, I'm going to make it up to you. I swear." He cupped her chin into his hand. "You're just like her, you know, your mama, gentle and kind. Don't ever change. Don't let what we did change you."

She peered into his eyes. Could she ever believe him again? Would her mother? Her mother's journal revealed a great deal of information, more than her mother probably meant to. Family had meant a great deal to her. It certainly meant a great deal to Kate.

"I'm trying really hard not to hate you, Sam, all of you, for what you did and not be angry," she said. "All the lies. How do I trust any of you ever again?"

"I guess we have to earn it back, and you have to let us try," he said. He squeezed her shoulder. "I am so sorry, my dear, sweet niece. I'm sure I speak for all of us when I say you have a right to dish out whatever punishment you see fit to all of us. We were wrong. " He took her hand into his. He was warm and strong and she couldn't help but still admire this man she had admired for so long without knowing whom he really was. "Just know this old man here loves you. There isn't anything I wouldn't do for you. Anything, Kate. You just name it."

"You were wrong, all of you, but that's not my way. It's not who I am. I care about people, animals. I wish—I want to believe you, Sam. I really do."

"You will. You'll see. I'll show you. If it takes the rest of my life to prove it to you. I'm going to make it up to you. I swear, Katy."

"No one calls me Katy. Although…" She had a hazy memory of hearing it sometime before, a long, long time ago.

"No. I think I'm the only one. My first leave home after you were born, Miss Katherine—Katherine—let me put you on a horse. You were a natural. I called you Katy. Kate didn't suit you back then. It was too grown up for a little girl of just one. Now, it fits just fine. Every year I came home for leave, visited Mama and you, Katy, kiddo. I got away with it too, until you turned twelve and then you insisted on Kate, or Miss Kate, as we called you. That's when I brought Elsa home too, after we were married. Do you remember?"

"Yes, some. My grandmother—Katherine—let you see me? Be with me?" she asked.

"As long as we swore never to say anything. Besides, she loved Elsa. Took to her right away. Hates my guts and Maddy's, but took to Elsa. Elsa's my wife. Stands to reason Katherine would hate her too from the get-go, but she didn't. Makes one think, doesn't it? Like I said, she's changed too. Look how she took to Carol. I would have never seen that coming. No one in our town wanted to hire a murderer's daughter, but your grandmother did. She gave her a chance."

Kate nodded. It certainly made her think, more than she want-ed to, more than she expected to. "I see that. My grandparents rejected their children and their grandchildren, and yet, accepted Elsa and Carol, two total strangers. I understand."

He placed a hand on her shoulder and she didn't pull away. She didn't want to. He was right. They were family. "Kate, I'm sorry."

"No. It's fine. Okay. You're right. They have obviously changed, somewhat anyway. Otherwise, they wouldn't have wel-comed Elsa and Carol into their arms or their confidence. Better late than never, right?" She hated to be flippant, but she was only human. The knot began twisting in her stomach again.

"Kate, I don't know to say. I didn't realize. I just thought…I don't know what I thought."

"It is all so crazy, Sam. I don't know what to say myself." She turned from him and went back to the window, letting go a small laugh.

It made her think that this was getting to be more than she ev-er bargained for. The more she dug, the more she found. Was there ever going to be an end to it all? She was beginning to think that maybe she'd be drowned by all the things she discovered. Maybe she wouldn't surface from it at all. If she was another type of person, she would have just left it as it lay. But she wasn't someone else. She had to go on. She had to. The search for the truth consumed her. Besides, she owed it to someone else to find the truth, all of it, no matter how much it hurt. Thoughts of her sister and the life that belonged to her, should have belonged to her, obsessed her. Kate had to do right by her. She was obligated to. She couldn't see any other way. She couldn't see a way out of this except to do the right thing.

Evidently, there was more to Katherine's hatred of Maddy than the mere color of skin since she was so kind to Carol, or was it just wishful thinking and hope that her White grandmother, wasn't a bigot anymore? Katherine never hid her disdain for Maddy or Sam, but she did like Elsa, and she didn't argue when Kate hired either: Sam to be their new blacksmith and Elsa as the relief cook and housekeeper to help Carol out around the large house. As efficient and energetic as Carol was, there was just no way was she able to continue to keep up with it. And Katherine wouldn't hire just anyone to work inside her home. It was slowly starting to make sense.

Elsa was White, but she wasn't all White. In the end, she was just like Kate, and her sister. Were her grandmothers trying to make up for what they did by accepting Elsa? Were they trying to right a wrong with Elsa? If so, it was great that they accepted Elsa, but she wasn't the one wronged, or the one they owed anything to.

"Does Elsa know about me? The truth?" Kate finally asked.

"She does now, all of it. I never told her. I couldn't. She was angry when I did and had a right to be, but funny thing is, she understood. She couldn't have been more pleased than if we had a child of our own. I guess Europe is really different than the US when it comes to races."

"Why didn't you two have children of your own?" she asked

"Just never happened," he said. "I figured it was karma-payback, for what we all hid from you and your sister. And let happen to your sister. 'Vengeance is mine,' said the Lord. I believe it too. So does Mama. You know—we really need to eat something before everything gets cold."

She nodded and went over to the room service cart that had converted to a small round table. Sam pulled out a chair for her and she sat down. He sat down across from her.

Chapter 15

Later that evening, back at the big house in Mississippi, Carol entered the parlor in response to her employer's summons by phone. "You wanted to see me, Miss Katherine?"

"Yes, Carol. After you let in Mister Gary, you can take the rest of the night off. Go do something fun. Don't worry about being late tomorrow."

"Really?" Carol's eyes widened with excitement. It was evident in her voice. "Thank you, Miss Katherine. I know exactly what I want to do." She ran to the door and then turned around and came back. "The kitchen is all cleaned up. Everything is all locked up and set for the morning."

"Thank you, Carol. Go on now."

Carol nodded and moved to leave.

"Uh, Carol," Katherine called.

Carol stopped and faced her expectantly. "Yes, Miss Katherine?"

Katherine studied her. "Be sure that Miss Kate's cat is put out first thing in the morning."

"Yes, of course. I always do—" Carol stopped and pulled in her lower lip. "I'm sorry, Miss Katherine. Please don't be angry. She asked me to let him in at night. She didn't want him to get hurt. I couldn't say no to her. We always make sure he goes out first thing, though, just after he finishes eating."

Katherine eyed her. She had been right in her assumption. She couldn't be angry at Carol, not when she was being loyal to Kate, not when this issue was so minor in the scheme of things. "That's fine, Carol. Go on now and have fun."

"Miss Katherine, now that you know, can I still let him in at night? I promised I would."

"Far be it from me to have you break a promise to Kate. Yes, but first thing—"

"First thing in the morning, I'll put him outside. I promise," Carol said. She scurried on out and closed the doors behind her.

Katherine shook her head and went back to her paperwork, the farm's finances for the week. Carol was a gem. Katherine sighed. *Oh, Kate, darling, where are you and why haven't you called me back?* This was so unlike her granddaughter, but she wouldn't allow fear to grab hold of her.

ℰↈℰↈ

Carol scurried out of the room and moved to the kitchen. She picked up the phone, made a call, and hung up just in time to answer the door bell when it rang. She opened the door and closed it behind him when he came in. "Good evening, Mister Gary. Miss Katherine is waiting for you in the parlor."

"Thank you, Carol. Off somewhere?"

"Yes, I am. Going to catch a movie with some friends in town. A movie I've been dying to see. Have a good night." She scurried away down the hall behind the stairs.

He laughed a little and made his way across the hall. He slowly opened the door to the parlor and stepped inside, carefully easing it closed behind him.

Katherine sat at the desk. Her back was to him, her head lowered over her work. He put his briefcase near a table by the door and eased over to the desk.

"You're late, Gary," she said just as he neared her. "I'm not accustomed to being kept waiting."

"I know. Sorry. Last minute calls had to get done." He leaned over and kissed her softly on the neck. "I was very glad to hear from you today." He placed his hands on the back of her arms and ran them up onto her shoulders and the back of her neck. "Rough week? You're tense."

She leaned back against him. "You have no idea, darling. None at all."

"Want to talk about it, or would you rather hear how very excited I am to see you tonight?"

She leaned back into his arms and his lips found hers. His hands began to wander down her shoulders to her breasts until she caught both his hands in hers.

"First things first, darling," she told him and stood up. "We go upstairs."

She could see he was very excited to see her, but she'd make him wait.

"For once, can't we just stay down here? You said Kate wasn't home."

"She isn't."

"And I saw Carol go out."

"She did."

"Then—" He reached out and pulled her into his arms. "Just once, let me make love to you down here."

"No."

"Why not?"

She raised a hand and ran a finger along his lips. "Because, darling, this is my house and I don't want to." She removed his arms from around her waist and stepped away. "Now, darling, you can stay down here all by yourself, or you can come upstairs where things are infinitely more comfortable. The choice is yours. Choose wisely. I won't wait a second time," she said, moved to the door, and out she went.

"Oh shit," he said and rushed out the door and up the stairs. He dashed into her bedroom just as she shut the door and locked it.

"Happy now?" he asked.

She went to him, undid his tie, and pulled him to her, using the tie to do so. Her lips moved to his and she knew she had total control. She was once amazed how easy it was to manipulate a man and made her skills better through practice. As a result, there wasn't a man she knew and wanted to do her bidding that denied her anything.

His kisses scorched her skin across the side of her neck and, as his mouth enveloped each breast, she didn't dare gasp or she'd lose the upper hand. She told him how good he was and it energized him even more.

His hands groped for her dress. He lifted her off her feet and out of it and carried her to the bed. "I need you, Katherine," he said as he laid her down on the silk sheets. Katherine had turned the bed down earlier, just after her phone call to him, and it was waiting for them to sink into its recesses. "But you know that, don't you?" his voice became a husky whisper. "God, Katherine, you drive me insane."

His thrusts were desperate, quick, and filling. He never lasted long. She couldn't help smiling. She had that effect on men in her bed. They couldn't hold back, no matter how desperate they were to try. But while he did, it was satisfaction fulfilled. He drove her wild with desire, but she wouldn't let him know. Instead, she just urged him on toward the destination they both needed to find.

Sated, she lay back and put her head on the pillow so the curve of her neck nestled just so. Yes, the younger man of forty was a needed distraction tonight and every night she needed to be elsewhere in her thoughts or her desires.

He rolled over onto his back and let out a breath. "Here, I thought it was going to be just another dull late night at the office."

She rolled onto her side and ran her fingers along his muscled chest.

He caught her wandering hands. "I still can't believe you're a grandmother. You don't act like my grandmother ever did."

"Age is in the mind, Gary, darling." Why were people so consumed by age? Wasn't it more important how two people felt about one another?

He raised his hand and ran a finger along the nape of her neck. "Obviously, since you don't act anything like your age in bed."

"Oh? And how old should I act in bed?" she said.

He held his hands up above his head in mock surrender. "I apologize. So, do I really get to stay the night?" he asked.

She heard the hopefulness in his voice and wondered if she'd made an error in judgment. It certainly wouldn't be her first. "If you'd like," she said, "you may."

She sat up and put on the long silk robe that hung on the post of the headboard, went to her desk, and sat down. She took a cigarette case from out of her top draw and her matching gold lighter with it. She lighted the cigarette and returned both items to the drawer.

"I thought you gave that up," Gary said.

"I did."

"And?"

She took a puff of the cigarette and exhaled. "I found the sudden need to restart."

He sat up and leaned on one arm. "You're not going to work now and bury yourself in more charity work?"

"And what if I am?"

"Just asking. I'd really like you to come back to bed. I'm still very excited to be here tonight."

"Are you? Still?" she said, took another puff, and exhaled the smoke.

He lay back and put his arms behind his head. "Yes. Still."

She heard him yawn. It wasn't long until she heard him snore. That was way too easy, she thought. The younger man was just the distraction she needed. He kept her mind off wondering where Kate was and what she was up to, at least for a little while. All work and no play would make Katherine one very angry woman. She finished her cigarette and put it out in the glass ashtray. She went back over to the bed, debated whether to wake him up or not, and decided to let him sleep. She needed her rest. Removing the robe, she placed it back on the headboard post, crawled back into bed on her side, and hoped that she had let loose enough tension to sleep tonight.

$$\mathit{e\text{\sim}e\text{\sim}e}$$

Back in her New York hotel room, Kate eyed the plate of food before her and covered it with the cover. The meal was elegantly presented, smelled, and looked delicious, but a full appetite still eluded her. In fact, she noticed that Sam didn't eat much either. Kate caught him eyeing her. "Are you all right, Sam? You're staring at me."

"One, you barely touched anything. Two, I'm sorry. It's just..." He pushed his plated aside and covered it with the silver top.

"Just?" She folded her cloth napkin and placed it alongside the dinner plate.

"I didn't notice it until tonight sitting here with you. Not even last night or the night before. You look just like your mother, just as beautiful, and you have this glow and air about you—confidence, as if you could conquer the world. She had that same air about her. And you have your father's eyes." He stood up, walked to a window, and looked out. "I wish we had told you sooner. I wish—" He stopped.

She was at a loss as to what to say to any of that. She got up, walked over to him, and stood by his side.

"I miss her, Kate. I wish..." He sighed. "I wish I could go

back in time." He faced her. He looked exhausted and she knew it was more than just the long train ride that caused it. "What can I say? If I had to do it all over again—"

She took his large hand in hers and couldn't help staring, not only at the size difference but the difference in color. "I know now and that is all that matters. I want to move on from here. No more blame or shame. Okay? Agreed?"

He nodded, raised his other hand, and cupped hers in his. "Just like me and your mama. Our hands didn't match either."

"No, but our blood does. There's no color difference there," she said.

He grinned at her. "No doubt about that. Listen to me, Kate. I don't want you to ever be hurt by anyone ever again. God knows I'll never hurt you again, and I'll never let anyone hurt you. I promise."

"Who's going to hurt me?"

"Once you accept being Black, you will be."

"I am Black, Sam, just like my mother. Why the obsession with skin color? You and Katherine? I'm me. I'm no different than I was a few days ago. I'm the same person, Sam."

"The one drop rule." He placed a hand on her shoulder and grasped. "One drop of Black blood makes you Black."

"I am Black, and White. People can accept me or not. I don't care. Our president is mixed race. Times are changing. One day, I hope we'll have a woman president, an Asian one, or a Native American, or all three."

"You might care later on. And times are not changing fast enough. People can be set in their ways, their beliefs. Our president chose African American as his race on the census, instead of choosing both. Why do you think he did that?"

"I guess he needed to choose a side. I don't have to do that. I won't. I loved my parents, both of them—and my grandparents, whether they loved me or not and I don't care about skin color. I'm me, Sam. What you see is what you get. Others can take it or leave it."

"I take it as I see it," he said.

"Thank you, Sam." She walked over to the dresser, took the pill bottle in her hands, and retrieved two pills from it. She went back to the cart table and was just about to take them with a glass of water when Sam interrupted her.

"What's that you're taking?" he asked.

"Aspirin," she replied. "You want to see the bottle?"

"No. I just thought…I needed to know."

She heard the apprehension is his voice. "You needed to know that it was just aspirin?" she said.

He looked away. "Yes."

"You know about my problems from my surgery and losing Adam? Of course, how could you not?" She swallowed the aspirin and set the glass down. "I know Katherine didn't tell you."

"No. Katherine didn't say a word. Maddy and I wondered about the strange people staying in the house for two weeks. I checked around. We were worried about you."

"I'm sorry I worried you, then and now. I'm fine."

"That's good. Fine," he said and walked over to her. "So what is your plan for meeting your sister?"

"I figured I'd go to her home tomorrow morning, first thing."

"On a weekday. She may be working," he said.

"Good point. I hadn't thought of that. We can go in the evening then. See some sights tomorrow and kill some time. Sound good?"

"Sounds like a plan," he said.

"Sam?" This had been bothering her since she learned her true identity. "I have to ask. Did your retirement from the army have anything to do with me, the accident? It's no secret you retired at the same time I was hurt." She sat back down.

He copied her. Reaching out, he took her hand in his. He was warm and steady and had a powerful grip. His large brown eyes searched hers. "When Mama called and said what happened to you and Adam, when I heard the fear in her voice, when I heard that Adam was dead there was no other choice for me to make. I had to come home and stay. I love you. Mama loves you. And I can't believe I'm saying it, but Katherine loves you. I hope you believe that."

"I never doubted the love. Never. I never knew why—the real reason—the two of you cared about me as much as you did. That's also the reason you took the blacksmithing job too, isn't it? And Elsa helping out with cooking and cleaning? You're both way overqualified for menial tasks."

"Call me a concerned son and uncle. I needed to be near you and Mama and keep you safe. Duty, Honor, Country was the motto at West Point and one I followed. Family guides my actions now."

"I'm sorry, Sam. I had no idea."

He held up his other hand. "Now don't blame yourself. It's not your fault. It was my decision, mine and Elsa's, not yours. I needed to be where I belonged and now I am."

She reached out and placed her hand over his. She couldn't remain angry at this man. She just couldn't. "I never said it before. I never had a reason to, but I love you too, Sam, even before I knew who you actually were, and Maddy. I don't know how and I can't explain it but whenever I was around you two, I always felt there was something more to it, more than what I saw. I felt it with Grandmother too. Is that weird?"

"No. There's a lot we can't explain," he said.

She released her grip on him. "Like why computers crash and we created them."

He grinned. He looked quite debonair in his goatee beard and mustache, though she wasn't too sure of the shaved head—a remnant of military life? It made him look mean and there wasn't a mean bone in his body.

"Now that's a good one." He moved to get up. "It's getting late and if you're going to go through with this, we both need a good night's sleep without the ground shaking all around us."

She noticed his knee buckle under him and rushed to his side, grabbing his arm.

"Stop fussing, Kate. I'm not that old yet."

"There's no shame in accepting help, Uncle."

His eyes lit up. "I stand corrected, Kate. You're right. Thank you." She held onto him until he was fine on his own. He waved her back and moved to the door. "Get some sleep, kiddo. I'll call you in the morning."

"Unless I call on you first."

"You're talking to a career soldier."

"You're talking to a country girl and farm animal doctor."

"Touché, Katy. Good night."

She sighed deeply. It was very nice to have an uncle. Most definitely nice.

ℰ⁓ɔℰ⁓ɔ

Daylight arose over the Mississippi mansion the next morning. Katherine awoke with a start, as the light of the day ahead broke into the room, and found it to be later than she intended it to be. She sat up on the edge of the bed. She was very much in need of a shower, of washing off the remainder of the night before. She dashed into the marble shower and took a long leisurely one to start the day off proper.

She sat at her desk when she heard Gary stir an hour later. "You know," he said from behind. "I can call in sick and stay with you today."

Out of the corner of her eye, she saw him roll onto his side to face her. "Why would you do that?" she asked, turning in her chair to face him.

He slid his slim form to the end of the bed. "I thought I could help you relax some more."

He was a fine-looking man and he carried himself so well. "First things first, darling. I want to know what the private detective has found out."

"Now? I just hired him last night. What on earth do you think he could have possibly found out?"

"You won't know if you don't call him," she suggested.

He hung his long muscular legs over the side of the bed. "Will that make you happy? If I call him and see what he found out, even though he probably hasn't done anything yet?"

"Immensely happy," she said.

"All right." He came to his feet and walked over to her. His body was a work of art. He moved to kiss her on the mouth but she turned her cheek toward him. "What now?" he asked.

"Take a shower, darling," she told him. "You know how much I dislike perspiration and such."

"Fine, but I want to ask you something important first," Gary said.

"As long as you make that call," she said.

"Marry me."

"That's not a question."

"No, but why not? We have fun. We like each other's company. We care for each other. I know it can't be the age difference."

She couldn't help but laugh. "You're sweet, darling, but no. I've been married and I didn't like it much."

"So you gave up on marriage, just like that."

"No. I actually believe in marriage. I believe the institution works as long as it is with the right person. I don't get married for companionship. Now run along."

"Then afterward, can we say good morning properly? I'll stay the day."

"No," she said.

"No? Why not?" he asked, clearly startled by her refusal.

"A farm doesn't run itself, darling."

"You gave Kate the farm to run."

"And she isn't here," she reminded him.

"You can be frustrating at times, Katherine."

"It doesn't seem to hurt you any," she told him.

He grasped her in his arms. "You do make all the fuss worthwhile. I would like to come back again, later tonight?"

"If you want." She pulled away from him and walked to the door.

"I want," he said.

She opened the door and faced him. "Let me know what the detective says, anything he says."

He went to the floor to scoop up his clothes and headed out the door. She closed the door, glad to be free of him. She was very glad to be free of any man's hold on her. That was a mistake she'd never make again.

Chapter 16

Walking along the concrete sidewalks of the city of New York, that evening they stopped in front of one building down in the Greenwich Village section of the city. The history and art museums of Uptown were a nice way to spend the day. Along with lunch and dinner with Sam, it proved to be an enjoyable day spent together. It was a nice distraction to discuss art and history and New York rather than family matters. It gave her time to think about how to prepare for tonight. All day she thought about it and still it wasn't enough time.

"This is it. The address you're looking for," he announced.

She stopped and glanced, top to bottom, at the red brick building from a few blocks from Washington Square Park. Only three stories tall, the weathered building could have been one hundred stories, as imposing, as it seemed to her this moment. Her breath caught in her mouth. Had it been another time, another purpose for this visit, she could enjoy the architecture in front of her.

"Miss Kate—Kate, we're here," he announced. "This is the building."

Kate took a deep breath to calm herself and stared at the line of faded buildings butted up alongside each other before her.

He went to her side. "Are you all right, Kate?"

"I have to go in that building and tell a woman I've never seen before that she is my sister. Is that a good thing or a bad thing?" she replied.

"We can go. We can fetch a taxi, go back to the hotel, and leave for home tomorrow. Is that what you want?"

She looked at him. "No, I'm scared. That's all."

"We don't have to be here," he reminded her.

"I do." But a million thoughts were suddenly fluttering in her brain. She hadn't stopped to think about any of them until now. "What if she doesn't want to know? Would I want to know the truth? Am I doing this for her or myself? Maybe I shouldn't have come. What if I'm wrong? What if you're right? She has a right to know. Wouldn't you want to know?" She turned to Sam. "What would you do, Sam? Would you want to be told the truth?"

He raised a hand to scratch the back of his neck. "I think I wouldn't. I'd want to keep things as they are."

"Is that a true answer, or an answer for the easy way out?" she said.

He coughed. "The easy way out. It would be easier for all involved. I'm sorry, Kate. No more lies. I promise. And don't be scared. I'm here for you."

If only she could believe him, be able to trust him completely. Part of her wanted to, part of her kept her on guard. She took a step forward up the ten steps and stopped at the wooden door. She placed a hand on the doorknob and turned it. Nothing. It didn't open. "It's locked," she said.

"Maybe we need a code or something. There is still time to leave," Sam said.

A voice from behind joined them. "May I help you? Are you looking for someone?"

Kate faced the woman. She was light skinned and evidently a beauty in her youth. There was no doubt she was Black. She had short white hair cropped around her ears. Blue bell earrings hung from her ears.

"I—I'm looking for Astrid, Astrid Thomas," Kate said. Her throat suddenly felt as if it was full of marbles. Her brain turned to mush.

"Are you friend, family, or buyer?" the woman asked.

"Excuse me?" The words stunned her. She hadn't expected the question. "Friend…and buyer, I guess."

"I'll let you in then. She lives upstairs on the third floor, front apartment." The woman took her key in hand, set it in the lock, and opened the door. She indicated Kate and Sam should go first, but Kate and Sam declined.

"Please, ma'am, you first," Kate said.

The woman entered through the door. "Thank you, sweetie," she said.

Kate and Sam followed her in. The elderly woman moved to a door off the hallway. Kate moved past her toward the stairs and stopped.

"You go right up there and she's on the third floor, front apartment. 3A. Right there," the woman said.

Kate swallowed hard. "Thank you, ma'am."

The woman eyed her. "You're not from around here, are you, sweetie?"

"No, ma'am. The South."

"I knew it. Georgia? Alabama?" the woman asked.

"Mississippi."

The woman showed a mouth of full shiny teeth. "I knew from your accent. I moved here in the '60s from Savannah, during the civil rights movement."

"Yes, ma'am."

"Welcome to New York, sweetie!" the woman said.

"Thank you, ma'am."

"Up those stairs now. 3A," the woman reminded her.

Kate eyed her and hoped she wasn't staring, but she couldn't help it. Did her sister look anything like this woman? Maddy had said, "Black as I am," but Maddy wasn't that black. Her skin was more of a soft, beautiful sorrel. Maddy had a beautiful complexion. Kate never gave it any thought before.

"Sweetie," the woman said. "Whatever it is, it can't be all that bad."

The woman's comment startled her. Kate looked up. "Ma'am?" Did this woman see through her? Impossible, but her comment rattled her just the same.

"You're not a buyer, are you?" she asked.

Did her anxiety show? She didn't want it to. "I'm sorry. No. I don't understand."

"The first step is always the hardest, sweetie," she advised. "The rest move along just fine."

The old woman was right about that. "Yes, ma'am. Thank you, ma'am. "

The woman walked back to her door and waited, eyeing Kate expectantly.

Kate faced the staircase. In a glance, the stairs appeared to stretch out before her. She had to shake her head and blink her eyes a few times to clear the illusion. One step forward and that is all it would take. *Up you go, Kate. Just do it! One foot forward and the rest of the stairs were easy*. The momentum was addictive. She did fine until she hit the third floor and found the door marked *3A* in large gold tone letters. Sam stopped just beside her.

"This is it," he said. "Are you sure you want to go through with this? There is still time to head back home and forget all this."

"Uh-huh. Is that what you think I should do?" she asked.

"There's no going back after this. Things will change."

His words cut through her. "As they should. I have no intention of going back, Sam. And if you and Maddy and Katherine, my family, had behaved as a family, I wouldn't be here now," she scolded.

She raised a hand and knocked. The hall was silent and the sound echoed in her ears louder than it should have. Her mouth became dry and she found it difficult to swallow. She knocked again, half hoping someone would answer and half hoping no one was home. Scared to death was an understatement.

"Yes, who is it?" a female voice answered.

She licked her dry lips. "I—I'm looking for Astrid Thomas, please."

It took a few moments and various sounds of clicks and then the door opened. A young Black woman answered, about her age or a few years older, maybe. Was this Astrid? Was this her sister? Kate caught her breath. She could have sworn that her heart was trying to crawl out of her mouth. Suddenly, she couldn't remember what to say.

"Yes?" The woman was attractive. Smooth, shiny skin and black hair pulled back. Large gold hoop earrings hung from her ears. "Can I help you?"

"I—I'm looking for Astrid Thomas," Kate blurted out.

"Hold on, please." She opened the door. "Come in. I'll get her."

Kate couldn't feel her legs. They weren't listening. She felt a warm hand on her shoulder and glanced over to see Sam urging her onward with a nod of his head. She appreciated his presence.

Kate forced her legs into action and in they stepped inside, Sam following close behind.

"Please sit down," the woman said. She indicated an overstuffed sofa in front of them. It was a red sofa with lots of multicolored throw pillows on it. The woman stepped out of the room, giving Kate just a moment to take in some of it. The apartment was one massive room and sparsely furnished, rather attractive, in fact. Full of color, yet reserved at the same time, just the way she would have furnished an apartment of her own.

Kate heard two voices now, two women.

"Who is it?"

"A buyer, I guess. I didn't ask,"

"Incredible. Born and raised in New York City and you still just let someone in without asking?"

"She seemed harmless enough."

The two Black women came into the living area. "Yes, may I help you?" the one that hadn't answer the door asked. "I'm Astrid Thomas. How can I help you?"

Kate stood up and met her gaze. For a moment, their eyes met. She was also an attractive Black woman. High cheekbones complemented her face of light caramel colored skin.

"I'm Katherine." She swallowed. "I'm Kate Thayer from Mississippi. I came—"

"I know who you are," Astrid snapped. "You can go back to the South."

"I'm sorry. I don't understand," Kate said. "I'd like us to talk. I traveled all this way—"

Astrid turned to the other woman. "This is the one I told you about. The one those phone calls mentioned. This is supposedly my sister."

The other woman stared at Kate.

Astrid faced Kate. "You can go now. I have nothing to say to you. I don't know who you are, or what kind of game you are playing. I didn't find any of those calls amusing."

"This isn't a game," Kate said. "I don't know what you're talking about. I made no phone calls. I didn't even know where you were until a couple of days—"

Astrid cut her off. "I don't believe you. Now, if I were you, I'd leave here quickly."

"Maybe you should let her explain," her friend said.

"Stay out of this, Julia," Astrid barked. "Look at her. Do we look anything alike?"

"You don't have to be angry. Miss Kate came here to tell you the truth," Sam said.

"Miss Kate? Where you from old man?" Astrid snapped.

"Sam, let's go," Kate said. This was evidently not a good time for the meeting. Perhaps the entire idea was a bad one.

He held his chin up. "Mississippi. And don't you mock me, young lady."

"Well, you can both go back," Astrid said.

"You have no right to speak to her that way," Sam said. "She doesn't lie. She is your sister. I know, because your mother was my sister."

"Sam, let's go now," Kate repeated.

"Get out, now!" Astrid rushed across the room and picked up a phone. "Leave now."

"Sam," Kate said. "We're leaving now!" Sam backed away and joined her as she moved toward the door. "I'm sorry we bothered you," she said. "I did not mean to upset you."

Astrid moved to the door, slammed it shut behind them, and locked it.

"Maybe you should have heard her out," Julia suggested.

"Are you mad?"

Julia tilted her head.

"I'm sorry. I didn't mean—Oh shit. I don't know what I'm saying." Astrid brought her hands up to cover her face. "There is no way she is my sister. No way."

Julia went to her and grasped her hands in hers. "There is only one way to find out."

"No. No way." Astrid pulled away and stormed out of the living area.

⊱⊰

Outside, Kate led the way down the stairs. Sam moved to the curb but she didn't follow. Instead, she turned around and looked up at the third floor front windows. The sheer curtains were drawn and the shades were up.

Sam placed his hand on her shoulder. "We should go. She won't talk to us. I'll get us a taxi."

She would not let it end this way. Not like this, not yet. "No. We've come all this way. We're not leaving yet," she said.

"We'd be wasting our time," he said

"It's my time to waste." She faced him. "Did you call her?"

"No. How could I? I had no idea where she was," he said.

"Someone did. Are you sure you don't know who? Elsa?" she hinted.

He sighed. "No more lies. Maybe. She probably wanted to help. I'm guessing she went to see Doctor Linc on your behalf."

"But how? I only just found out—"

"Mama told her everything. Once she had a name, she just looked it up."

She moved to the curb. "Please get a taxi to take us to the hotel."

He moved to the curb beside her.

"Kate Thayer," a voice hollered from behind.

Kate stopped and turned around.

"I'd like to speak with you, if you have the time," Julia said. "There's a coffee shop just around the corner." She pointed north of them. "I can meet you there in a few minutes."

Kate considered it. "Fine. I'll be there." She waved at Sam to cancel the cab.

Julia nodded and ran back up the few stairs and into the building.

Sam walked up to her. "Kate?"

"Let's go find this coffee shop."

There it was. The sign read simply, *A Coffee Shop*. It couldn't have been plainer. It wasn't even a five minute walk away. Inside, they sat at a table across from one another. The place was desolate except for a couple seated at the other end of the place. It was plainly furnished. Coffee, tea, donuts, and bagels were the staples. It was a self-service place. There was no wait staff.

"What do you think she wants?" Sam asked.

"I don't know. But we traveled all this way. I'd like to find out."

"Then we can go home?"

"Sam, you can go home anytime you want. You don't have to be here."

Sam shook his head. "No, not without you. You don't have to be here, either."

"I thought I made myself clear. This is something I must do. Or I can't live with myself."

"Then we wait." He sighed. "She's a beautiful girl. From what I saw of her. Just like you. You both take after your mother. You both have her high cheekbones. Both are just as stubborn too. You're still angry with me?"

"Yes. I still am, but I am trying hard not to be. I told you that." She had to admire his tenacity. She wasn't making it easy for him and she had no plans to do so.

"I was wrong for keeping silent," he said. "I'm sorry. We—I thought Katherine and Maddy were right."

"They weren't. None of you were," she pointed out.

They were interrupted by the sound of someone breathing hard next to them. It was Julia. "T—thank you for w—waiting." Kate nodded. Julia spoke first. "I'm Julia Comedy." She extended her hand. "We weren't formally introduced."

Kate took her hand and signaled for her to sit. "Kate Thayer. This is Sam Johnson, my uncle."

It came out so easy, uncle, that it surprised her again. No matter how many times she'd said it in the last couple of days, it still surprised her, and yet it seemed natural at the same time. She couldn't deny that.

Julia nodded at him. She went to sit next to him when he stood up. "I'll let you ladies talk alone." He gestured at another table. "I'll just head back here and get a cup of coffee. You two ladies want anything?"

Kate shook her head. Julia copied her. He scooted away. Julia sat across from her. "Your uncle? Really?"

Kate nodded. "Our mother's brother."

"So you really are black?"

Kate should have expected that, but didn't.

"I'm sorry," Julia said, "It's just...I thought someone was playing a cruel joke on Astrid and now I see it, but I don't believe it. I mean, I didn't expect—"

"Seeing is believing, they say."

"Yes, they do," Julia said. "What I meant was you're not just passing for White. You are White?"

"Half, yes, technically."

"Which makes Astrid—"

"Half-White too. Yes," Kate said.

"Thank you for agreeing to talk with me," Julia said.

"For Astrid, I think I'd do anything," Kate said. Her sister deserved that.

Julia stared at her. "I believe you would. Astrid and I are friends. I didn't want you to leave like you did."

"She made her feelings known. There was no reason to stay."

"May I ask you something?" Julia asked.

"Yes," Kate said.

"Are you going to leave now? And leave things as they ended?"

"No. That is not my plan."

"Good, because she's not as tough as she seems." Julia

reached out to touch her cheek. Kate pulled back, startled by the movement. "I'm sorry," Julia said. "It's just...close up, you two do look alike. You have the same eyes."

"My eyes?"

"Yes, green as emeralds. Now I know why."

Kate shook her head. "I saw her. She doesn't have green eyes." They were brown. She was sure of that. It had happened so fast—the short visit—but she saw them.

Julia shook her head. "No. She wears contacts to blend in. She doesn't want to stand out. Be different."

"I had no idea." That explained it.

"How could you?"

"Our father had green eyes, as his mother does, our grandmother," Kate said. "They say green eyes are rare. Evidently not."

"Especially in Blacks. Is your father mixed race too?"

"No." Of course, the question was a logical one. A good guess. "He was White. Our mother was Black, but she looked White."

"I see. So she passed for White? I just assumed."

Kate could see Julia figure out some of it. "What did she mean by phone calls? What phone calls did she receive?" Kate asked.

"We don't know. It was a woman. She didn't give her name, just told Astrid that she had a sister and she might come to see her—a White sister. She had a weird accent, not southern, but some, mixed with European, German, I think," Julia said.

"I see. I didn't make them." It was Elsa. The mixed accent confirmed it. Question was why?

"I believe you," Julia said. "Why make them and then deny it? It just doesn't make sense. I must ask, though, why are you here? Really?"

"Exactly what I said—to get to know her. Talk to her," Kate asserted. "To make things right."

"Not for some ulterior motive?"

"No. Like what?" Kate said.

"Like cleaning your conscience. Relieving you of a burden to make yourself feel good," Julia said.

"No. I'm here to say I'm sorry. That is all. Had I known sooner, I would have been here sooner. I didn't."

Julia eyed her. "How long have you known? When did you find out?"

"A couple of days ago," Kate answered.

"A couple of days, and now you're here?" Julia said.

"I don't believe in putting things off until tomorrow if I can do them today."

"Obviously. You must be tired from your flight."

"I don't fly unless I really have to. I get terribly air sick," Kate said.

Julia grinned. "So does Astrid."

Kate grinned. They had similarities, after all. That had a strange, yet comforting feel to it all.

"Oh, you two are sisters all right. I see it," Julia said.

"I wish she would."

"Don't think harshly of her," Julia said. "She's had a rough life. And she always wanted to know about her family. Why they gave her up, where they were?"

"I didn't know. I should have."

"How could you? Do you know why they gave her up? Why aren't your parents here to apologize instead of you?" Julia interrogated.

Kate took a deep breath. "It's a long story, one I owe it to her to explain first."

"Of course, you should. I'm sorry. I didn't mean to intrude. I guess it's a curse of my career. Sometimes I push too hard."

Kate was intrigued by this woman. It was obvious that she cared about her sister or she wouldn't be here, prying for information. "What is it you do?"

"I'm a psychiatrist, but please don't run. I won't analyze you, at least not yet."

"I won't run. I'm sort of a doctor too," Kate said.

"Really? What kind?"

"I'm a vet, an animal doctor. I run our plantation. Our farm."

"Plantation? Sounds so Southern," Julia remarked.

Kate laughed. The moment of levity was very refreshing. "It is Southern, very Southern. We grow cotton and hay. We have horses and cattle." She had never given it much thought. Home was home. At least it had been for so long. Would it ever be again?

"You run it? I'm impressed. That's a lot of work," Julia remarked.

"It is, but it's home." Kate stopped. "It should have been Astrid's home as well."

"Come back with me to the apartment and tell her that," Julia said.

"Not now. Maybe later on."

"When? If you leave, you may not come back," Julia pointed out.

"You mean I may lose my courage?" Kate said.

"Something like that. Yes."

"You are a shrink," Kate blurted. "Sorry. I couldn't resist." She hoped she didn't insult the other woman who made an effort to seek her out.

"It's all right. I have been called worse." Julia sat back. Kate could only imagine what she was thinking. Julia glanced at Sam then back to her. "How is it you never knew about Astrid? No one ever told you? He never told you either?"

"No. No one. So much for family, huh?"

"But he's here with you?"

"I think he feels guilty for not telling me the truth," Kate said. "He's really a good man. I've known him my whole life. He pretended to be an employee to be near me."

"I don't know what to say."

"That makes two of us." Kate sat up straight. "Look, I appreciate you meeting with me. I really do, but she obviously doesn't want to see me now, or have anything to do with me. And I understand why. I'd like you to tell her that I'm sorry. Sorry for everything. Sorry for not finding out sooner."

"You have nothing to be sorry about. You didn't do anything wrong," Julia pointed out.

Kate held up a hand. "Please. Let me say this. Please tell her that if she ever needs anything, anything at all, I want her to contact me. Please, tell her that."

"You really need to tell her that yourself."

"I would, but—does she need anything? Money? I don't know...anything at all?"

Julia shook her head. "She doesn't need money. She's quite comfortable. She owns the flat and the building it's in. She is quite successful. You'd be proud of her. She's a sculptor, a very good one."

Kate grinned. "A sculptor? I'm impressed. Our mother studied art at the university. And I love art, too."

Julia's eyes brightened. "Come back to the apartment with me and tell her that. All of it."

"I can't. Not now. She doesn't want to see me," Kate said.

"She will. Talk to her like you just did with me. Give her another chance," Julia said.

"Why?"

"Because you both need to. That's obvious. Trust me," Julia said.

"I don't even know you."

"And I don't know you, but I'm willing to take a chance."

"Why?" Kate asked.

"Because." Julia touched her hand. "Dealing with people is what I do. Getting them to open up and fix their problems is my job. So is reading people. And I believe you mean what you say. And Astrid needs that now. She doesn't need material things, but she does need family. She needs a sister. She needs you."

Kate shook her head. "I just don't know."

"You asked if she needed anything. This is what she needs. Trust me, I'm a professional."

Chapter 17

Five minutes later, Kate and Sam walked back to the apartment building with Julia. Upstairs, Julia went in and indicated that Kate should sit down and wait. Sam had decided to wait downstairs while the women spoke. Kate heard Astrid and Julia argue in the kitchen.

Astrid was the first to speak, "Where have you been? It's been two hours. And what is she doing here?"

"I think the two of you should talk," Julia said.

Astrid hollered, "Never. You can tell her to leave."

Julia said calmly, "You don't want her here. You tell her to leave."

"Julia, sometimes you really need to mind your own business."

"You are my business."

Astrid entered the living room. Kate shot to her feet to meet her. She heard Astrid sigh in frustration.

"Why are you here?"

"I told you—" Kate began.

"And I'm just supposed to believe what you say? Someone I never met before?" Astrid snapped.

"No, but your friend Julia does. She suggested we talk."

"Just so you know, Julia, is my lover, not just my friend. I'm a lesbian," Astrid blurted.

Kate didn't expect that, but what could she say? It wasn't any of her business, as long as Astrid was happy. "That's nice. I like her. She seems like a very nice person."

"She is."

Kate couldn't help wondering if the other woman was testing her. "Is that supposed to shock me?"

"Maybe. Did it?" Astrid asked, placing her hands on her hips.

"No." Kate watched the other woman's eyes study her. She

could understand the need for the test. They didn't know each other. Of course, after all she'd discovered in a couple of days, Kate didn't think anything could shock her now. Nothing at all.

"Sit down," Astrid said and remained on her feet. "So, what do you think? Not exactly like looking into a mirror, is it?"

"No, but we are sisters," Kate said. "Twins, I've been told."

Astrid pulled back. "Yea, right. You're not serious. We look nothing alike."

"We do have our father's eyes," Kate asserted.

Astrid eyed her. "Do we?" She sat down. "You have green eyes. I don't."

"You would if you took out your contact lenses."

Astrid's glare softened. "H—how?" She pursed her lips. "Julia." She stood up and stepped away from her, her eyes never leaving her. "Why are you here? Really?"

"I told you, to see you," Kate said.

"For what reason?"

"To meet you. Know you."

Astrid stepped closer. "Why? We don't know each other."

"But we should have and it was taken away from us," Kate said.

Astrid seemed to study her then spoke. "How does it feel?"

"How does what feel?"

"Being Black."

Kate should have expected that, but didn't. "It doesn't bother me. I'm still the same person. I haven't changed. At least, I think I haven't. I'm not sure of anything anymore. But we're only half-Black."

Astrid crossed her arms across her chest. "Oh. What half?"

"Our mother. Our father was White."

Astrid eyed her up and down. "Obviously. And the Black man with you. He family, too?"

"Yes. He's our mother's brother, Sam Johnson." Kate leaned forward. "I understand your anxiety—"

"Do you?" Astrid growled.

"Yes. I don't want anything from you," Kate said. "That's not why I'm here. I just want to get to know you. That's all. I want nothing from you."

"And why should I believe you?" Astrid shot back.

"Well, here we are," Julia said as she entered the room with a tray. She set it down on the cocktail table before them. "I thought we'd need some refreshments." She picked up a coffee pot in one hand and a tea kettle in the other. "Coffee or tea? Which is your pleasure?"

Astrid's mouth dropped open. Kate was relieved by the interruption. She definitely liked this woman, her sister's lover. Her timing was perfect, twice. "Coffee please," Kate said.

"So what are we talking about?" Julia said. "Kate, why don't you tell us a little about yourself? Or maybe—" She looked at Astrid. "You want to tell her about yourself."

Astrid placed her hands on her hips. "I know exactly what you are doing, Julia, and I don't appreciate it."

Julia poured three cups of coffee. She placed two on her end of the table and one in front of Kate. "Cream or sugar?"

Kate placed her hand over the cup. "Nothing. Thank you. I like it black."

Julia faced Astrid. "What am I doing?"

"You know and you can stop it, right now!" Astrid said.

"Calm down and sit. You two have a great deal to talk about," Julia said, taking a seat on the sofa across from Kate.

"I'm not playing into your hands, Julia," Astrid said. "You don't know this...woman...any more than I do and you're trying to get me to open up. Spill my feelings. I'm not one of your patients!"

Julia took a sip of coffee from the cup. "Sit down, love, please. You're exciting yourself for no good reason. This woman traveled all the way by train from Mississippi to talk to you. Not by plane. You should listen." She turned to Kate. "So, Kate, tell us about yourself," she said, crossing one of her lean legs over the other.

Astrid glared at both of them. Kate appreciated Julia's intervention. It was clear that Astrid respected her.

"There's nothing to tell," Kate said.

Astrid moved to the couch and sat down next to Julia. "There must be something, like why are you really here?"

"I told you that."

Astrid leaned against the back of the couch. "Tell us again."

"To see you."

Astrid brought up her arms and folded them across her chest. "All right, you've seen me. Now what?"

"I thought we could talk."

"About what?"

"Tell her about yourself, Astrid. I'm sure she wants to hear," Julia advised.

"There's nothing to tell," Astrid snapped.

"You'll have to forgive, Astrid," Julia said. "She's a bit shy around new people."

"I am not!" Astrid retorted. "You'll have to forgive Julia. She is a shrink."

"She knows that," Julia said.

"You told her?"

"It's not a state secret."

"Are you married, Kate?" Julia asked.

Astrid stared at her hand. "You're married?"

Kate reached for her left hand in reflex. She turned the diamond encrusted gold wedding band with her right fingers. "I was." She still couldn't bear to part with it.

"I'm sorry," Julia said. "What happened?"

Kate heard concern in Julia's voice and appreciated it. She appreciated her intervention. "It was a while ago."

"What happened?" Astrid asked, her voice mocking. "A nasty divorce? Did he cheat on you or you him?"

"No. He died—a riding accident. It was a broken neck," Kate said. "He suffocated."

"Oh, God. I'm sorry," Astrid said. Kate noticed her face relax, her glare vanish. "I just assumed. Nowadays…"

"Thank you," Kate said. She could feel the tears flowing in the back of her throat and pushed them back. "No insult taken."

"How old were you when he died?" Astrid asked.

"Twenty eight. It happened two years ago," Kate said, trying not to choke up. Even now, she found it difficult to speak about and didn't realize it until she began recalling it over and over the last couple of days.

"It must have been difficult," Julia added. "Were you married long?"

"Two years," Kate said. "I'm over it now." She felt Julia's eyes scan her. Did the psychiatrist believe that? Probably not, since she didn't, really.

"Do you have a photo of him? Your husband?" Julia asked.

Kate took her wallet from out of her shoulder bag, opened it, and showed it to them.

Astrid took it. "He's handsome." She handed it to Julia.

"Very," Julia said. "He has gentle eyes. Strong chin."

"Thank you," Kate said as she took it and gave it a quick glance before returning it to her wallet and putting it back in her shoulder bag.

"I bet he's from the South," Astrid said accusingly.

"Actually, no. Philadelphia. He adopted Mississippi as his home."

"Really? So your in-laws are from the North?" Astrid remarked.

"My father-in-law is. A bonafide Yankee, yes, he is, and quite proud of it, too proud sometimes," Kate said and appreciated the brief moment of distraction in the conversation. "My mother-in-law is from Mississippi."

"Do you have any children?" Astrid asked.

"No. We both decided against it. With all the children in the system and all the things going on in the world, we thought it would be selfish—"

"To bring another child into the world," Astrid finished her thought. "Julia and I feel the exact same way about it."

"I know a lot of people don't agree, but to us—" Kate said, "it would have been a selfish thing to do, especially since we really didn't want children."

"Bravo," Julia said.

"Well said," Astrid agreed. "There are too many people out there that have children, but really don't want them. They shouldn't have them. They'd save a lot of people a lot of pain."

"I agree," Kate said.

"Mainly their children. Take our parents for instance. They didn't want me, right?" Astrid said.

Kate had hoped to avoid this subject until at least later on, after they had more time to mesh.

"Why don't you tell her about yourself?" Julia interrupted. "I told her that you sculpt. I bet she'd love to see the studio." She stood up. "She likes art."

Kate eyed her. "I'd love to see it. See your work. I like art. Our mother studied it at the university. Perhaps I can bring something back to Mississippi and impress some people."

Astrid glared at both of them. "Okay, it's obvious you don't want to discuss our parents. I'll let you slide, for now," she told Kate.

Julia moved to leave.

"Where are you going?" Astrid said.

"You two don't need me."

"You're not going anywhere, Doctor Know-It-All," Astrid ordered. "You started this. You're going to see it to the end."

Julia held up her hands to surrender. "All right, don't get so bossy."

Astrid led the way across the room through a doorway and stepped aside once inside. Windows ran across one wall from floor to ceiling and light from the streetlights from outside filled the room. Astrid hit a light switch along the doorway and fluorescent light replaced the outside meddling lights.

Kate took it all in. Sculptures of all sizes filled almost all corners of the room. Some were life size such as the one that looked like a man with no arms or mouth. Some were tiny and sat on shelves of clear glass that covered a wall across from the windows. One wall situated between the wall of windows and the wall of shelves was obviously the work area. There was a low table with a huge glob of clay on it and canvas cloths spread out on the floor.

Julia entered and stood alongside Astrid. Astrid leaned against the wall. She had one leg bent up backward with her foot up against it. Kate noticed Julia mouth to Astrid to be nice.

"Are you impressed," Julia asked.

What could Kate say but the truth? "Yes, very." She faced Astrid and their eyes met for a moment. "You're very talented."

"Thank you," Astrid said and was the first to turn away.

Kate walked around the room, looking at everything. She'd never been inside a home studio before, or any artist studio, for that matter.

She stopped at the life-sized sculpture of the man with no arms. It was unnerving to see close up. He had a life-sized body. He wore a three-piece suit sculpted into the clay. He had a face with a nose but no eyes, no mouth and no ears. He had legs but no feet and no arms.

"This piece is called, the sound of silence," Astrid said from behind. "It is my favorite. It is a metaphor of our world. Life around us. Can you see why?"

Kate looked it over. It seemed simple enough to her. "He can't see, speak, or hear, so he never reaches out. He never sees, speaks, or hears anything that goes on around him. As a result, he never reaches out for anything new. He is stuck where he is," Kate said.

Astrid's eyes brightened for a moment and then she nodded. "Exactly."

"I like it. Really," Kate said. "Sometimes, I wish I couldn't see, hear, or speak. It'd certainly make things easier."

"I know what you mean," Astrid said.

"Did it take you long to sculpt?" Kate asked. "Was it difficult to make?"

"No. It took me about three days. Sculpting is all about looking inside the clay, seeing what is inside and letting it out. The man was already there. I just let him out."

Astrid walked over to the shelves and pulled down from the top shelf a small figurine. She walked back and handed it to Kate. "What do you see here?"

Kate took it. She ran her fingers over the cool clay. The figurine was small, about six inches tall. There was nothing extraordinary about it. She felt Astrid's eyes watching her. Was this another test? She didn't want to fail. If this was what it took to connect to her sister, she'd do it. The figurine had hands, arms, feet, and legs. It had a face with a mouth, nose, and eyes, but no ears. She recognized his type immediately. It was her grandfather, Jackson Thayer IV and perhaps, George Johnson as well.

She felt for the spots where the ears should have been and found small indentations instead. "He can see, speak, and smell, obviously." Kate said. "He's normal in every way, except he doesn't hear a thing said to him. He's deaf, not physically deaf, but deaf to those around him."

"Yes," Astrid said, evidently impressed. "That's right. What is it you do for a living?"

"I'm a veterinarian," Kate said matter-of-factly.

"Uh-huh," Astrid said. "How do you know about art?"

"Took some art classes in college. I didn't take just science classes. May I see the rest?"

Astrid nodded.

"Maybe she'd like to go to the show," Julia suggested.

"Maybe she wouldn't," Astrid said.

"She knows art and understands yours."

"What show?" Kate asked.

"It's nothing," Astrid said.

"Tomorrow night," Julia said. "Her wares will be on display for sale at the Wells Gallery. All the press will be there. Free champagne and caviar to all comers."

"I'd like to see that. Yes, I would," Kate said. A night together away from discussing the inevitable would be nice.

"Good. Then it's a date," Julia said.

Kate glanced over and noticed that Julia grinned.

"I'll make sure they have two tickets for you and your uncle, okay?" Julia added.

"Thank you, yes," Kate said.

"You don't really want to go to a stuffy and boring art gallery for a show, do you?" Astrid said.

"No, not just any show. Yours? Yes. I really like your work."

"You're just saying that."

"No. I don't say anything I don't mean, and I mean everything I say. That's me. That's who I am," Kate said. "And I'd like to see your show, but first I'd like to see the rest of your work here."

Astrid took her around the room and showed her the pieces she had created and Kate correctly guessed their meanings. After a half an hour, they returned to the living room and sat down.

Julia had brought out some more coffee and cake to go with it. "I hope you like chocolate cake."

"I love chocolate cake," Kate and Astrid answered in unison.

Kate noticed Julia smile as she cut three slices from it, placed one slice on each plate, and handed one plate to each sister. She also gave them each a paper napkin and a plastic fork.

"Now that we've connected, so to speak," Astrid said. "I'd like to know why you're here and not our parents." She set her plate down on the table and leaned back against the sofa. She didn't even touch the cake.

"They couldn't," Kate began as she hoped to delay the subject as long as possible.

"Why couldn't they? They didn't want to? Are they cowards and couldn't face me, or did they just not care to come? Are you their emissary?"

"No. It's nothing like that," Kate said.

"Then what? Why aren't they here? You wouldn't happen to know why they gave me away and kept you. Do you?"

Kate glanced at Julia.

"Are you going to answer me? Or has the cat got your tongue?" Astrid pressed.

Kate felt her heart race. She could hear it pounding in her ears. She knew she had to focus to do this. This was why she came here—to tell her the truth. But intentions always seemed so much easier than actually setting them into play. She took a deep breath and set the plate and fork with the untouched cake back on the table. She couldn't eat. Hadn't been able to eat much over the last few days, if anything at all.

"Our parents—they couldn't come," Kate began again. "They—our parents—are—dead. I'm sorry."

Astrid stared at her. The stare became a glare. "Wh—what? What are you talking about? How? When? How old were they?"

Kate stood up. She couldn't do this now. She was tired. The train ride was catching up to her. All the secrets and lies were pulling at her from every which way. "Maybe we can do this tomorrow. I'll tell you everything you want to know tomorrow."

Astrid shot to her feet. "No! Not tomorrow! Now! I want to know! You owe me that!"

Julia stood up. "She's tired. It's getting late—"

"No. I don't care! I want to know!" Astrid demanded. "That's why you came here. You said so. Answer my questions, now, sister."

Kate brought her hands in front of her and clasped them across her chest. "I only know what they told me," she said.

"Who are they?"

"Our grandmothers. Our uncle."

"Grandmothers? As in?"

"Our father and our mother's mothers. They're still alive," Kate said.

"Our grandmothers are alive, but our parents aren't! How is that? Explain that to me. Please!" Astrid said.

Julia must have sensed what she was going to say because she went to Astrid's side.

Kate couldn't look at her now. "Our parents—they died the night we were born." Silence egged her forward. "Our mother died after I was born. She was bleeding and they couldn't save her." She swallowed hard. The lump she felt wouldn't go down. "Our father—he killed himself that same night. He—uh—he couldn't live without her. He shot himself."

She looked up to meet Astrid's stare. Her eyes shimmered under the halogen lamps spread around the room.

"Go on," Astrid said.

Julia had taken her hand into hers. She nodded at Kate.

"There isn't anything else to say."

"You forgot the most important part. If our parents died the night we were born, how was I sent away?"

Kate let out a slow breath to soothe the pain. "Our grandparents did that. Katherine and Jackson, Maddy and George. It was a secret. I just found out a couple of days ago."

"How? Why?" Astrid demanded.

Kate raised her hands and ran them through her hair. "I found an old journal our mother had kept. In it, she spoke about how much our grandmothers hated each other and our parents. Basically, our Black grandparents didn't want our mother anywhere near our father—"

"And our White grandparents didn't want our father with our mother?" Astrid finished.

"Yes."

"And me? Why was I sent away and you weren't?"

Kate looked at her. She had to face her when she told her. She owed her sister that. Astrid looked as if she was going to cry, but was doing a great job of not doing so. Kate knew exactly how she felt.

"Our mother had written down—Katherine and Jackson, George and Maddy, were talking about what if I—you. They weren't expecting twins. When the baby was born, they would send it away. Our mother wouldn't let that happen. She'd die first."

"But she did die. And he killed himself. And I was born Black, so they sent me away? All of them? Even our Black grandparents? Even they sent me away?" Astrid asked as she sank back down onto the sofa.

"Y—yes," Kate said. Her heart was aching for Astrid. Maybe this was wrong. Maybe she should have stayed away. Maybe she should have never said a thing. Maybe she should have never opened this Pandora's Box.

"Why did they keep you?" Astrid asked. "Because you were White? Who raised you?"

"I'm sorry, Astrid. Yes," Kate said. "And it was Katherine who kept me, and raised me. I didn't even know that Maddy or Sam were family. They worked on the farm to be near me."

"And they gave me away!" Astrid shot out.

"Yes. I'm sorry."

Astrid advanced on her with inches between them. "Sorry? Sorry? Do you think that helps me now? Do you think that makes it all better?" She glared at Kate. "Do you?" Julia grabbed her arm from behind.

"No. It doesn't help you," Kate said. "And I know it doesn't make you feel better. Nothing I can say or do can make things feel better for you. Or make things right for you. I'm sorry."

"Get out!" Astrid barked.

"Wh—What?"

"*Get out*!" Astrid said.

Kate stood her ground. "Astrid, I came here to tell you the truth. I felt you should know. It is your right to know."

"Get out! Now!"

"Please, let me stay and—"

"And what, Kate? What are you going to do? Huh? What are you going to say next? You've led a charmed life, haven't you?"

"No. I haven't," Kate said. She'd known Astrid would be upset, but she expected nothing like this.

"They *kept* you. You're White. They wanted you. Me? They threw me out with the trash."

"That's not true."

"No? You just told me so."

Kate grasped for the right words. "That's not what I said. Not what they did—"

"No? Our grandparents didn't want our parents together. Our White grandparents, Katherine and Jackson, didn't want a Black grandbaby. Our Black grandparents obviously didn't either, or they would have kept me, right?"

"Our Black grandparents didn't want me—"

"But the White ones did and they kept you! Not me! No one kept me! I grew up in group homes and foster homes. Twenty-one different ones in eighteen years. Do you know what it is like in a foster home? A group home? No, of course not. How would you know? Take your lily-white ass and get out of here! Now!"

"I'm sorry, Astrid, but I do know how you feel," Kate asserted.

"No, you don't. You grew up White. I grew up Black. You have no idea."

"But I am Black too," Kate reminded her.

"No, you're White. And until you live as a Black person you haven't a clue as to what I'm saying to you. How could you? You may be Black on the inside, but on the outside, you're White. And I don't want to know you."

"I'm sorry. I am sorry. I thought—I was wrong—I'm sorry—I just hoped—I thought—"

Astrid stormed to the door and opened it. "Just get out! And don't come back. Ever!"

Julia looked away. Kate turned away, picked up her purse, took a deep breath, and walked to the door. "I'm sorry," she said. "I really am. I didn't mean to hurt you, Astrid. You're right. I don't know what it is like to be Black. But I do know what it is like being lied to and being hurt by the one person that I loved and believed in. Our mother died giving birth to us, but specifically to me. Our father killed himself because he couldn't bear to be parted from her. Our grandparents couldn't stand that our parents loved one another and had us. They hated it. So they rewrote our lives and, for that, I'm truly sorry."

"Keep it," Astrid said.

Kate walked out and Astrid slammed the door. She stared at the steel door. She brought up her hands and placed them on it. Her hands almost matched the color of the beige paint, but darker. She couldn't hold back the tears that forced their way through and buried her face in her hands.

Julia walked over and placed her arms around her waist from behind. "Let it out!"

"They're dead. My parents are dead." The words came between the sobs. "All my life, I've hoped to somehow meet my real parents and hear them apologize and say it had all been a mistake. They didn't mean to send me away. All my life—I wanted to find my family—I hoped they'd find me. Now I know why they never found me. My parents are dead. And—" She sniffled, "—their parents—they never wanted me."

Julia leaned her head against Astrid's neck. Her lips rested in the curve there. "Let it out, baby. Let it out. It'll be all right. I promise. Let it out."

"It'll never be all right again. They—never—wanted me. My family didn't want me. They kept her instead. Why? It isn't fair. It isn't fair." Astrid couldn't hold on anymore. She let her body crumble down to the floor.

Julia sat down with her, took her into her arms, and held her close against her. She patted Astrid's head.

"I don't want to be here anymore. I don't want to live anymore."

Julia squeezed her close. "Don't say that. You don't mean it. I won't let you give up. I love you."

Astrid buried her head into the nape of Julia's neck and cried. She couldn't help it. The tears kept coming in waves, crashing against her one after the other.

Kate had understood her. She had understood her art. That was difficult to accept. Not many did. And she was her sister.

౿ᴈᏹᴈ

Outside their apartment door, Kate raised her hand and set it against the cool metal, palm to paint. She heard sobbing inside and wished she could say or do something for Astrid to stop it.

"I'm sorry," was all she could come up with in a whisper. She brought her hands to her face and wiped the tears that fell on her cheeks. She knew she had to leave. Get away now, for Astrid wouldn't speak to her. Kate's legs were rubbery, and she found herself stumbling down the stairs, as if she had a little bit too much to drink, which, of course, she hadn't. The handrail fit her hands as she made her way downstairs and out the front door.

Sam met her as she descended the few stairs down to the sidewalk. She could tell from the expression on his face that she looked as bad as she felt. "We're going. Get a taxi," she announced.

"Are you all right. Did she hurt you?"

"Hurt me? Of course not. If anything, I hurt her, terribly. Get a taxi. Tomorrow, we'll get ready to go home."

In the taxi, Sam placed a hand on hers. "I'm sorry. We all thought it was the right thing to do."

That set off Kate. She pulled away from him. "Right thing to do? There is a woman in that building who is my sister—should be my sister, and she doesn't want to see me! Right thing to do! Bullshit, Sam! You all did what was easy for all of you, then blamed Katherine for everything. Right thing to do? You did nothing but hide the truth. My truth! Her truth! The same as Katherine did. At least she was open about it. She was a racist, but she kept me. The rest of you—what was your excuse? No one kept my sister! No one! I don't ever want to see any of you again."

"Kate, you're upset—"

"Yes, I'm upset. I'll see that all of you are taken care of. But I want all of you out of my life as soon as we get home."

She leaned back in the seat and stared out the window. She had never been so full of anger in her life. It terrified her to be so full of fury like this.

Chapter 18

It took Julia two hours to calm Astrid down and get her into bed. Of course, one Valium pill didn't hurt. She'd stepped out of the bedroom for a few minutes to get a glass of water when she saw it. On the cocktail table near the paper plates and forks was a small blue book. It wasn't there earlier and it wasn't familiar. It had to belong to Kate. She picked it up, walked over to the trashcan to throw it away, and decided against it. It wasn't a book. There was nothing on the spine or covers. It had an old cloth cover with worn edges. The spine was torn as well. She opened it to find handwriting in script on the yellowed frayed pages. She returned to the bedroom with it in hand. She set the book on the nightstand next to her side of the bed and leaned over Astrid to check on her. The Valium had worked. Astrid was asleep.

Julia turned down the comforter on her side of the bed, got in, propped up her two pillows, and sat up. She opened the top draw of her nightstand, retrieved her reading glasses, and put them on. She took the book from the nightstand, opened the cover, and flipped to the first page where she noticed the handwriting began.

Entry Number 1:

I'm not much for writing, so I don't know how many pages I'll really write on in this, but I'm determined to try. Jax gave me this journal to write in so we'll see what I write. Today, Jax told me three times that he loved me and I never get tired of hearing it.

He is such a beautiful man. Not in a girly way. I mean that he is a good person and I love him to death. I only wish Mama and Daddy felt the same way about him. I guess that's the way it's going to be since Jax's mama and daddy can't stand me either. But we love each other and that's all that counts. Both his mama and daddy and my mama and daddy can do whatever they want to do, but Jax and I are determined to make our marriage work. He's going to go back to school to finish his last year at Ole Miss and I'm going back too. At least away at college, we don't have to be near either his mama and daddy or mine. Why can't they understand that we love each other? Really love each other and we completely understand what we are doing. We're not children, though they keep trying to treat us as such.

Today, Jax stood up to his mama and daddy and I thought Katherine and Jackson were going to have a heart attack on the spot. He told them that if they didn't let him live his life that we would leave here and go live in Europe. I think I'd like to live in Paris. People aren't racist there. They don't care what color your skin is. Of course, we'd have to figure out a way to get me there since I get so sick when I fly, just like my daddy. I was proud of Jax. I know how hard it was to stand up to them. He loves them so much. My parents were just as bad. I had to stand up to my mama and daddy when they tried to break us up and keep me away from Jax. We fixed them. We fixed them all. We ran away and got married. They weren't very happy about it but, oh well, it's done now. I am officially, as of today, Mrs. Jackson Atticus Thayer the V for exactly one month.

That was the end of that entry. She went to the next page.

Entry Number 2:

I haven't been feeling well the last month or so. I've been throwing up. Jax took me to see the doctor, Doctor Lincoln Castle. Jax calls him Uncle Linc because he's a close family friend. He seems nice enough and nice to me. He doesn't fuss about Jax and I being married. I'm going to have a baby. We sat down tonight and had a family dinner here at the big house—my mama and daddy and Jax's mama and daddy. We told them. We hoped they'd be happy, but they weren't. My daddy jumped all over Jax. Jackson jumped all over my daddy and then Jackson jumped all over Jax. Jax didn't back down and repeated his threat of moving to Europe. I stood up for Jax, but he told me I didn't have to. I was his wife and his life and if our parents didn't like it, to hell with them all. He was right. We're going to have this baby and prove them all wrong. I wonder if it is going to be a boy or a girl. Our parents are worried about what "it" will look like and suggested we get an abortion. Jax was livid and told them to stay out of our lives. Jax and I don't care. We'll love him or her with all the love we can give him or her. Uncle Linc said I can do an ultrasound to find out whether it is a boy or girl, but Jax and I want to wait and let it be a surprise. I can't wait. Uncle Linc says I'm nine weeks pregnant, so it won't be too long. Jax and I discussed college again and decided to wait until the baby is born before we go back to Ole Miss. We haven't decided what to do with our baby then, take him/her with us, or leave the baby here during the week and come home on weekends. The way our parents are carrying on, worrying about what our baby will look like, we'll probably take our baby with us. They say we have no idea about the real world and that we live in a fantasy world. Well, we don't. We just love each other and our baby.

I've tried to like Katherine. I've tried to be nice to her, help her around the farm, but she hates me, really hates me. She doesn't come right out and say it, but her behavior says a lot and I don't know why. And Mama and Daddy really hate Jax, too. I don't get any of it. Sam wasn't too crazy about me marrying Jax either and I don't get it. They're friends. We all grew up together. Good thing Sam is away at West Point or we'd have to deal with him too. Sam was never that way before. I love Sam and I'm proud of him, but Jax is my husband and I'll stand by him just like he stands by me. Strange how people change. Strange how people don't get along. Strange how people are so judgmental about each other. I hope when our baby is born, it helps bring everyone to their senses and together as a family. I pray that it is so.

I love Jax and Jax loves me. That is all I care about. That and our baby. I guess we'll have to start thinking about names. If it's a girl, maybe I'll name her after Jax's mother and maybe, just maybe, she'll feel differently toward me. I wish I knew why she hates me so much. Every time she looks at me, she makes me shiver. I wouldn't live in this big house, except its Jax's home and one day he'll inherit it and will get to run it the way he wants. I don't want to take that away from him. We did start inquiring about college and apartments in Paris and London, just in case our parents continue to harass us. Jax has had enough. He told me that when I've had enough, we are leaving. I have, but I don't want to take him away from here. I don't want to leave my family either, though they're just as bad toward Jax. I'd like our children to have grandparents in their lives. I want our children to know they are loved. I want our children to treasure the world we give them. One day, this big house and the horses and the land will be his or hers. And I want them to have that.

I hear Jax coming up the stairs so I'm going to end here tonight. Good night, diary."

That was the end of that page. Julia turned to another…

Uncle Linc is worried about me. I don't know why. I feel fine. He says that I'm run down and am showing signs of anemia. He keeps asking if I'm tired. I am a little bit, but I am pregnant. Jax wants me to stay off my feet. He's being a worry wart, but he loves me. I love him too. Every time he looks at me with those bright green eyes, I melt, and when he takes me into his strong arms, I can refuse him nothing. I'm a part of him and he is a part of me. He's so worried about me too. He's always asking me, "How are you feeling? Are you okay?" He is so sweet. I hope, if we have a son that he is just like his daddy. Jax is so busy working on the farm. He broke two horses in the last month and boy did his butt hurt. Poor baby. I massaged it and tried to make it all better. He said that making love to me every night made it all better. Of course, these last couple of months, I haven't really felt up to it. I feel like a big whale. He says I'm beautiful. He hopes we have a girl and that she is as beautiful and smart as I am. I think he's being sweet because I'm sure he really wants a son. He said he didn't care what we had, boy or girl, as long as it was healthy and safe. Jax is going to be a great father. He's strong like his father, smart too. But he's nicer. I can't explain it. His father Jackson sometimes seems so controlling just like Katherine, but Jax isn't like that. Katherine still hates my guts. My daddy won't even speak to Jax except to take orders. Our parents still want us to get an abortion.

The other night I overheard Katherine and Jackson talking about our baby, what to do when it is born, just in case, as if it is up to them. I haven't told Jax yet. I don't want him and his parents to get into another big fight. I figured I'd wait until the baby is born and if they try to pressure us one way or the other, we'll leave.

Another day. Another entry. Good night diary."

She flipped another page and read the final two pages written on a Friday night which made it all come to reason. It all made sense now. Astrid had to read this. All of it.

Julia flipped through the rest of the pages after it, but that was it. And no pages had been torn from it. It would be noticeable. That was fine, though. She couldn't read anymore. This woman, Astrid's mother, put the contents of her heart and soul onto paper. Then, in the middle of the book, she found the small color photo of a young couple. She read the back of it and sighed. She closed the small book and set in in her nightstand drawer with her glasses. Leaning back against her pillows, she took a deep breath.

She looked over at Astrid. She was still asleep and breathing normally. Astrid had to read this. If nothing else, it would assure her that her parents wanted her and loved her. No wonder Kate left it behind. It was no accident that she had done that. At least Julia had been right about her. Poor Astrid. Julia leaned over and kissed her gently on the forehead. Reaching out, she brushed her hair with her fingers and down the nape of her neck.

"Sleep now, love," she said. "It's going to be all right."

She couldn't stay awake anymore, so she shut off the light, and lay back onto her side. She snuggled against Astrid's warm skin, wrapped her arms around Astrid, and fell asleep.

ოოო

Filtered blue light of the early morning shone through the lace curtains that hung in the two oversized windows of the room. In all the upset last night, Kate had forgotten to close the drapes and shut out the buzzing of the city below. If not for the sleeping pills she took last night, she wouldn't have been able to sleep at all. She didn't mean to snap at Sam, but she couldn't help it. He was part of the cause, part of the reason that this visit was necessary, and the reason why Astrid was so angry. Who could blame her? Certainly not Kate. She'd had no idea Astrid grew up in the way she had. That shouldn't have happened to her. Kate couldn't swallow the guilt she felt, or the anger that started to well up inside her again. Not when she was trying so hard to push the anger aside and move on from here.

She tried to turn her head to check what time it was on the clock that sat on the nightstand, but she had a stiff neck and a sore back. She tried to break the stiffness by moving her head side to side, but it didn't work and, instead, increased the severity of the pain. She moved to sit up and became extremely dizzy. That told her something wasn't right, but not what that something was.

She sat there and collected herself. Slowly she got up and made her way to the bathroom on shaky feet. Once there, she turned on the ceiling light and stared at herself in the mirror, leaning on the sink to steady her. She appeared fine, but the reality was she wasn't a human doctor. She could guess and guessed it was just stress and lack of sleep. She certainly had more of one and less of the other over the last few days. It didn't help that she wasn't eating much either. She touched her forehead. Why was she so hot to her touch? Could it just be her imagination?

Of course, it would be wiser to be safe than sorry, especially with the tests Lincoln was concerned about. She picked up her cell phone from the nightstand as she passed it and walked to the front door to go get Sam. Another dizzy spell hit her so hard, her legs buckled beneath her and she fell to the floor on her back just short of the door. She could hear her heartbeat pounding in her ears, incredibly loudly. It was rapid and deafening. With the cell phone still in her hand, she immediately dialed 911.

The call was answered with a woman's voice, "Nine-one-one Emergency. What is your emergency?"

"I've—collapsed in a hotel," Kate said.

"Where is your location?"

"Hotel Mark. Madison and Seventy-Seventh. Hotel—Mark—New York."

"Hold on ma'am, I'm dispatching an ambulance now. Ma'am? Ma'am, are you there? Ma'am…"

Kate felt herself losing her sense of being, of where she was. She lost the strength in her hand and the phone fell from it.

She heard banging and had to focus. She heard voices…a man…two…Sam? Her head hurt. She was so thirsty. Her abdomen hurt too. She was getting cold. She couldn't move her legs. She heard the door open, saw blurs moving toward her.

"Kate? My God!" Sam ran to her. "Get an ambulance!" he told someone she couldn't quite make out. She felt Sam kneel beside her and lift her up to him. She heard his voice. "Kate, what happened? What's wrong?"

She tried to reach out to him but couldn't move her hands. "Shock—I think—I'm going into shock—cold. I'm so cold. Get me to a hospital. Check my blood work—my kidneys—check my kidneys, Sam—"

He took off his blazer and wrapped her in it. "Kate, you hold on now. You hear me? Hold on, kiddo," he ordered.

She could barely make him out. She was losing all sense of reality. "I—can't—think—trouble focusing—breathing, talking," she said.

"Don't talk. I'll talk. You hold on for me. You hold on."

"I'm scared, Sam."

"Don't be. I'm here and I'm not going anywhere without you." He held her against him and she felt the tears from him fall. "I'm here and I'm not leaving you."

The hotel concierge led in the two EMTs who rushed to her side and immediately went to work on her. The woman took vitals while the man hooked her up to a portable IV bottle. Through blurry vision, Kate watched them tend to her. She heard them speak.

"Is she on any medication, sir?" the woman asked.

Sam didn't hear her.

"Sir?" the EMT repeated. "Any medications?"

"No. She was on the floor when I found her. She thinks she's going into shock," Sam said. "That's what she said," he said, stronger, regaining his composure. "She said to check her kidneys."

The EMTs conferred with someone by radio via Blue Tooth headset and then, in two quick moves, lifted her off the floor and onto the gurney. "We're taking her to the hospital," they ordered and wheeled her out of the room with Sam right alongside her.

👁👁👁

Downstairs, outside at the curb, they put her into the back of the ambulance and Sam moved to get in with her. The doorman stood aside and held the ambulance door open for them.

"Sorry, sir. You can't go," the male said.

"Like hell, I'm not. That's my niece," Sam said. "You're not taking her without me." He wasn't about to be separated from her now.

"Get in, sir," the woman said. "We don't have time to argue."

Sam got in and squeezed himself in between the shelf and the gurney, holding onto Kate's hand. She was going in and out of consciousness. He'd seen that look too many times. The man closed the door, got into the front to drive, and, within moments, Sam felt the vehicle on its way. He took her free hand and held it.

"Sam," Kate said, her voice a whisper.

"Don't talk now," Sam said. "Save your strength."

"If something—happens to me—"

"Nothing is going to happen to you." He wouldn't allow it to.

"If it does," Kate said. "Take me home. Don't leave me here. Bring me home—to my mama and daddy. Put my ashes—with theirs."

"I will."

Sam overheard the EMTs talking on the radio. "White female. Uncle says she was on the floor when he found her. BP is one hundred over sixty. Temp is 104.1. No sign of injuries. Administering protocol for shock."

"Promise." Kate grabbed onto his shirt collar. "You owe me. Reach out to Astrid like you did for me," she said. "Let her know you're there for her. Promise me."

"I promise, Katy, but nothing's going to happen to you."

"What's your name, miss?" the woman EMT asked while monitoring her and relaying information via Bluetooth headset.

Sam could see Kate didn't hear the words. He saw her mouth open but she couldn't say anything.

"Kate Thayer," Sam said. "She's thirty years old and in excellent health. Look, can't you do something for her?"

"We're doing what we can, sir. We're treating her for shock. Was she in an accident recently?" the EMT said.

"Accident? Two years ago," Sam said.

"No. Now. Any reason for her to collapse?"

"No," Sam said. "No reason. No accident."

"Uncle says no accident. No medications," the EMT said into the headset. "She's lost consciousness."

At the hospital, the ambulance shot into a parking spot just outside the emergency room doors. The driver came back and joined Sam and the other EMT as they removed the gurney, popped down the legs, and wheeled her toward the door. A young man in white coat and stethoscope about his neck met them at the open doors and identified himself as the ER doctor.

The EMT relayed information he had to him.

The doctor checked her eyes with a penlight he pulled from his shirt pocket and yelled, "Get her to the ER. STAT."

They wheeled her down the hall and into an ER room. Sam stayed by her side and moved to follow. A nurse blocked him, but Sam wouldn't be deterred.

"She is my niece and I'm going in. You want me out, call the police and I still won't leave. We're not even from here and I'm not letting her go in there alone. Please." He'd led combat missions and he wasn't afraid of anything as he was right now about Kate.

The doctor nodded. "Tell me her medical history," he asked while beginning to examine her.

"Her medical history?" Sam declared and stepped inside. What did he know about her medical history? "She doesn't have one. She's in perfect health. She said to check her blood tests. Something with her kidneys."

"What about her kidneys? Do you know her medical history or not?" the doctor repeated.

"Look, she's an animal doctor. She knows something about medicine. She said to do some blood work. Can't you at least do that?"

The doctor nodded at the nurse near the door. "Do you know her medical history, sir?" she asked.

"I just told you. Aren't you listening?" Sam repeated. "What the hell is going on here?"

"I'm afraid you'll have to wait outside," she told him.

"Like hell I will! That is my niece! Check her kidneys, damn it!" Sam tried to restrain his temper, but they weren't helping him, or her.

"Sir!" the doctor yelled. "She is in bad shape, so unless you can help me, you have to leave."

"Please sir, you can wait just outside." The nurse moved to lead him out. "Please, sir, she's in good hands."

Sam forced himself to calm down. "She's my niece. My sister's daughter. I can't just leave her. Please don't make me leave."

"Nurse, I need you here! Now!" the doctor said.

She pointed outside for Sam and then went to help the doctor tend to Kate.

"BP is still low, Doctor, ninety over sixty," another nurse said. "Heartbeat is erratic. Body temp is 104.3"

"Get her blood work done STAT! Increase ringer's solution. She is badly dehydrated. Run kidney function tests. Let's see how her kidneys are working," the doctor said. "Keep treating for shock."

Sam waited by the doorway, out of the way, hoping they'd ignore him and let him stay. They were so busy that they didn't pay him any mind, but he overheard everything.

"She's still non-responsive, doctor. BP is ninety over sixty and steady," the same nurse said.

"She's badly dehydrated. Let's continue on fluids and antibiotics. Continue as is. Temp is still high. I'm guessing infection. Get me the kidney tests, CBC, ASAP." He moved to the doors and stopped when he saw Sam. He pointed and led Sam outside into the hall. "We're doing all we can to stabilize your..."

"Niece. My niece. My sister's girl," Sam said.

"She is in shock. I'm just an ER doctor, so I can't get into specifics without going over her blood work and ordering some more tests. You mentioned her kidneys, why?" the doctor asked.

"I found her on the floor of her hotel room. She told me to get her to a hospital, to ask for lab work, and to check her kidneys. I don't know why," Sam said.

"Do you know her medical history?"

"I told you. She's in perfect health."

"Evidently, she isn't, sir," the doctor pointed out. "Or she wouldn't be here. She is badly dehydrated, which we can take care of. Her blood pressure is dangerously low, and there are no apparent injuries. Her heartbeat is erratic. Has she complained of any symptoms?"

"Doctor, she's my niece, but we've been out of touch for a while. She did—she was really tired, but we just came up here by train, which took two days. She did mention having a headache, but that's it. And she ate very little when she ate."

"Does she have any other family? Is her mother alive? Her father? Siblings? Someone who could give me a better idea of her medical history?" the doctor asked.

"Her parents are dead."

"May I ask the causes," the doctor said.

"Her father killed himself. Her mother—my sister—died in childbirth," Sam said.

"Cause?"

"Hemorrhaging. They couldn't stop the bleeding. Her grandmother—grandmothers—are still alive."

"Good. If you can contact them, get her medical history. Does she have a family doctor?"

"Yes," Sam said.

"I'd like to speak with him, too. If you can get me that info, it would make a difference."

"I can do that," Sam said.

"Good, when you have it, give it to one of my nurses." The doctor moved to leave.

"Wait a minute, what is wrong with her? What happened?"

"I don't want to say anything until I gather all the tests and go over her history, so the sooner you can get back to me the better. In the meantime, we'll work on getting her rehydrated and stabilizing her blood pressure. Is she on any medications? Does she have any allergies that you are aware of?"

Sam had to think again. He never saw her take anything, except... "No. Nothing, but I'm not one hundred percent sure. Just aspirin for a headache. That's all I saw her taking."

"I need to know all that also." The doctor started to walk away.

"Doctor," Sam called. He grasped for straws. The doctor

faced him with expectance. "She was in a bad accident a couple of years ago. Could that somehow be related at all to this? "

"Good question. I highly doubt that, but I'll pass it on. It could. We'll see," the doctor said as he walked away back into the exam room through the double doors.

Sam saw him through the window, checking over Kate again as a nurse assisted him. The doctor spoke to the nurse then moved onto another room. The nurse remained behind and monitored Kate.

Sam didn't want to leave her, but he knew what he had to do next. He raised a hand to touch the cool wooden door. He'd do anything, anything, to keep Kate safe.

A woman came up alongside him. "Did you just come in with the young woman by ambulance? The woman in this room?"

"Yes, she's my niece," Sam said.

"I'll need to get some information from you, sir."

"I already gave some information to the doctor," he said.

"I need to know about insurance, name, address and such."

"And such? They can't tell me what's wrong with her and you're worried about insurance? You've got to be kidding."

"I'm sorry, sir. It's policy," the woman said.

"I'll give you all that information *after* I let my family know she's in the hospital. All right with you?"

The woman seemed taken aback, but didn't push it. Maybe the crazed look of a Black man who stood six feet, four inches tall scared her. He could only hope so, though that was the last thing he meant to do. Kate was the only thing on his mind right now. He didn't mean to scare anyone.

He walked down the hall, outside to the front of the hospital, and took out his cell phone. It wasn't even five in the morning yet back home. He dialed Elsa. After a few rings, she picked up with her usual barrage of questions.

"Sam, thank God. Is everything all right? Your mama says she feels something isn't right. Are you okay? Is Kate okay? Where are you?"

"Elsa honey, shut up for one minute. Please," he said. "I'm in a hospital in New York. I'll give you all the details in a minute. Where are you?"

"I'm home. Why?"

"Where's Mama? Is she sleeping?"

"I told you. She's worried. Says she has a bad feeling. She hasn't been herself since you left."

He sighed. Mama and her feelings. "Listen, honey, Kate is sick. She's in the hospital. The doctor needs to know her medical history. Everything. We're going to have to tell Mama and Katherine…just in case."

"How bad is it? What's wrong with her? What happened, Sam?"

"Is that Sam? Is everything all right?" Maddy asked, over-hearing Elsa on the phone.

Elsa turned around. Maddy was in the doorway. She didn't look any better than she had over the last few days.

Sam heard his mother's voice. "Tell her what I told you. The doctor didn't say it, but he's concerned too and I don't think he knows what's really wrong with her."

"Do you want me to tell Miss Katherine?" Elsa asked.

"No," Maddy said. "I'll tell her after I speak with Sam." She held out her hand. Elsa gave her the phone. "Son, where are you and what has happened? Are you and Kate all right?"

"I'm fine, Mama," he said. "We're in New York city."

The silence spoke more than she wanted to know. "What has happened to Kate? Tell me."

"I don't know, Mama. I don't think the doctor does, either. Kate said something about her kidneys. But they need to know her medical history, allergies, and if she's taking any medication. Mama, I don't know that stuff." Maddy heard him take a breath. "She's unconscious, Mama."

Maddy took a deep breath and said a quick prayer. "Katherine will. I'll talk to her. I'll get the first flight out there I can. Sam, take care of yourself and keep us posted. I love you, son."

"Mama, you don't have to come up here—"

"Yes, I do. My grandchild needs me. We'll call as soon as we make the reservations. Elsa, you talk to him then call the airlines for a flight to…wherever they are."

Maddy handed her back the cell phone and moved to the front door.

"Mama, where are you going?" she asked.

"To tell Miss Katherine what has happened. You find out the rest Sam has to say then make those flight reservations. Go on. Get to it, girl."

With that, Maddy was gone.

"Your mama is going to the big house. Do you want me to go with her, Sam?" Elsa asked.

"No, I need you to get a hold of Doctor Lincoln and tell him what has happened to Kate. The doctor here wants to speak with him. Then you get ready to come out here with mama. I'm going to go back and check on Kate. I'll call every few hours when I know something. Don't call me. I'm in the hospital. I love you, honey."

"I love you, too. Be safe."

He hung up and released a breath he hadn't even known he was holding. He wiped a tear from his cheek with the back of his hand. Mama was going to see Katherine? For any other reason, he would love to see that. He replaced his cell phone in his back pocket and returned inside.

Chapter 19

Maddy hadn't been up to the manor house in years. Many years. Not since she and Katherine were friends, fifty odd years earlier. Of course, all that changed all those years ago, as times and people so often do. Katherine changed. Maddy changed. Everything changed.

Maddy didn't even notice the time until she stopped outside the massive oak door. She used the heavy doorknocker rather than the doorbell. She hated modern contrivances and the annoyances they caused. No answer. Then she pressed the doorbell three times in a row.

She half-hoped Carol would answer the door. The other half of her hoped it would be Katherine.

The door swung open and she got her wish. "We need to talk," she said as she brushed past a startled Katherine and went into the parlor.

Katherine slammed the door and followed her. "What the hell are you doing here? You know you are not allowed up here!"

"Shut up, Katherine," Maddy announced. "Sam just called. Kate is in the hospital in New York city."

Katherine sank down into the chair. "What happened? Is she all right?"

"Sam doesn't think the doctors know, but they want to speak with Doctor Lincoln about any medications and her history."

"She's not taking any medications and she's in perfect health. You know that."

"Then what happened to her?" Maddy asked.

"I don't know," Katherine snapped.

"I'm flying out there as soon as I can. I thought we should put our differences aside until we find out what happened to her. Can you do that?"

"Can you?"

"We were wrong, Katherine, all of us. I see that. I saw that as soon as we gave that baby away. I shouldn't have listened to you and Jackson."

Katherine shot to her feet. "Then why did you? For the same reasons we did. Our children made a huge mistake. We knew their marriage was wrong. I don't regret anything I did," Katherine said. "But I will be there for Kate." She brushed past Maddy and went to the desk. "Where is Kate? What hospital?"

Maddy went to the desk, took a pen, and wrote down the information she knew. "Elsa is getting the rest of the information. You can come to the house and get it, or call Sam on his cell. Elsa will be getting plane reservations for the first flight to New York City. Do you want her to get one for you?"

"Now why would I want her to do that? I'll make my own reservations, thank you. Do you really think I want to go anywhere with you?"

"Fine, Katherine. Suit yourself. I thought we could be civil, at least for a short time for Kate, but you can't do that, can you? Not two years ago and not now. Still bitter after all these years?"

"No less than you are, Maddy. Now get your Black ass out of my house!" Katherine told her.

Maddy stepped up to her. "If it wasn't for Kate, I'd slap you silly."

"If it wasn't for Kate, you could try. Of course, you wouldn't be anywhere near this house if not for her. Now get out!"

"Gladly," Maddy shot back and moved to leave.

"Katherine, what the hell is going on?" It was a man's voice. "Where are you?" Gary entered the parlor.

When Maddy saw him, she did a double take. The younger man was dressed simply in a short robe. He didn't even wear socks or shoes.

Ooookay, she thought. Evidently, she had interrupted something here. "And here I thought you were worried about Kate," Maddy said.

"Don't ever accuse me of not loving my granddaughter! You know nothing, Maddy," Katherine spat.

"Don't you ever get tired of playing lady of the manor?"

"No. Now get out!" Katherine pointed to the door.

"Gladly!" Maddy repeated and stormed out past her, nearly knocking Katherine off her feet.

"I—I'm sorry," Gary said. "I didn't mean to interrupt—"

"You didn't." She picked up the phone receiver. "Get dressed. You're leaving."

"Wh—what? It's not even light out yet. What time is it?"

She ignored his pout. "It doesn't matter, and I don't have time for you to have a tantrum. Do as I ask." She picked up the phone and dialed, tapping her foot on the hardwood floor as she waited.

Gary walked over and kissed her on the nape of her neck. "You'll call me when you need me again?"

She nodded and waved him away when a voice answered on the other end. "Tessa, I need you to book me two tickets on the first flight out to New York City and be sure to have a car waiting. I'll get you the rest of the details shortly. Call this cell number." She flipped open her rolodex for Sam's cell number. "Call Sam Johnson for the rest of the details." She hung up and then dialed another number from memory.

Gary waited, but when she ignored him, he left the room.

"H—hello? Who is it?" Lincoln said into the phone. "Katherine?"

"Linc, darling, something terrible has happened to Kate. She's in a hospital in New York City. I'm going out there as soon as possible."

"I know," Lincoln said. "Elsa just phoned me. What happened? She was rambling."

"I don't know and I'm not waiting around here to find out," Katherine said. Did he just slur a word, or was she imagining it?

"You better book two tickets then."

"I already have."

"Which airport are we flying out of?" Lincoln asked.

"I don't know yet."

"Call me when you do. I'll come by and pick you up."

"Fine." She hung up the phone and rested her hand on it for a moment. She pressed the button to summon Carol and spoke into the intercom. "Carol, pack me a bag. I'm flying to New York City."

"For how long?"

"A week or two should do. I'm leaving immediately."

"Yes, Miss Katherine," Carol said.

"No one is to know where I'm going or why. Tell Carl he is in charge until we return. Thank you, Carol."

"Yes, Miss Katherine."

Katherine leaned against the table. She waited until she heard the door close and sank into the Queen Anne chair by the phone. The fine furnishings that surrounded her couldn't help Kate. *Oh God, this can't be happening. Not again.* It wasn't possible. Not after all they went through two years before. Not when everything was finally back to normal.

First, the accident occurred and then nearly three months of recovery. After two weeks in the hospital, Katherine brought Kate back home. Kate didn't eat or interact and remained in bed. After a few days, Katherine had had enough. She refused to let Kate consume herself with grief anymore. The riding accident wasn't her fault. It was over and done with. Kate was unresponsive to everyone around her, except her grandmother. After not eating anything for a fourth day, Katherine shook Kate and slapped her. The slap brought Kate back to reality and she broke down in Katherine's arms about losing Adam, the accident, and the baby. Katherine held onto her and comforted her until Kate calmed down and fell asleep. After all, she knew exactly how her granddaughter felt—exactly.

After a few days, and with her grandmother's support, Kate began to eat and interact. She was in bed for eight weeks until she physically healed, followed by six weeks of intensive in-home physical therapy. Finally, she was able to get back to work. Slowly, she returned to running the farm and her activities and Katherine couldn't have been more pleased.

Of course, the battle wasn't over yet. Katherine found the pills and called Lincoln and Doctor Hammond Curtis, a younger doctor and family friend, about it. She didn't like the answer either gave her. She confronted Kate at breakfast about them the very next day. Katherine recalled the incident verbatim, as if it just occurred yesterday...

☙❦❧

"Darling, we need to talk about these," Katherine began and produced the two bottles of prescription medicine.

Kate glared at her as she sat down next to her at one end of the dining room table. "You went into my room, into my bathroom, into my cabinet?"

"Yes, darling, I did."

"How dare you? Who are you? Why would you do that?"

"I'm your grandmother and I love you very much. I know you

*don't believe that right now but I do. You have a problem. I want
to help you."*

Kate shot to her feet and her eyes blazed. *"I don't have a
problem. Maybe you do."*

*"Then show me, darling. It's been five months since you've
been home. You should be off these by now."*

"Says who?"

Katherine ignored her. This wasn't a debate. *"Don't take
these for a week, and I'll give them back to you."*

"I can do that."

"Then do it."

Carol came in. *"I have your breakfast, Miss Kate."*

"Take it away! I'm not hungry!" Kate snapped and faced
Katherine. *"You're not my mother to dictate anything to me. And
even if you were, I'm old enough not to listen."* She stormed from
the room.

*"It's all right, Carol. She won't be eating this morning. You
can take it away."* Carol left. Katherine sighed. This is exactly
what Lincoln and the drug counselors warned her was one of the
signs of addiction: drastic personality changes. She wouldn't
ignore this problem.

She stood up and leaned on the edge of the table then started
to go upstairs to see Kate, but she needn't have bothered. Kate
was standing inside and leaning against the front door with her
head lowered.

Katherine couldn't handle seeing Kate in this state. She went
up to her and stroked Kate's hair with her fingers. Katherine
heard her sniffle.

"I'm sorry, Grandmother," Kate said. *"I can't do anything
without the drugs. I can't get up in the morning without the pain
pills, and I can't sleep without the sleeping pills. I have tried. I
just can't. I'm sorry. I didn't mean to disappoint you."*

Katherine placed her hand on Kate's shoulder and felt her
trembling. *"Darling, you have never disappointed me. This is
merely a setback. We'll get through this. I promise."* She reached
out her hand to touch Kate's cheek. *"Darling, look at me. Turn
around and look at me."*

Kate slowly turned, but didn't look up at her. Katherine lifted
her chin so their eyes would meet, but still Kate wouldn't look at
her. *"Katherine Caroline, look at me, please, darling."*

Kate slowly raised her eyes and Katherine saw the tortured

look of pain and anguish. It nearly broke her heart. She had to help Kate, no matter what it took. "I won't let you hurt yourself anymore. I won't lose you. Darling, what would Adam say?"

That was all it took. Kate started to cry uncontrollably and Katherine took her into her embrace and brushed her hair as Kate said through sobs, "Oh—Gran—I—miss—him—so—much. I want him back."

"I know, darling. I know." *Katherine wanted to make all the pain go away for her.* "I know, darling. He's gone, but you're here and that's all that matters." *Kate wrapped her arms around her grandmother's waist and held on tight.* "You have a problem," *Katherine continued.* "And I'm going to fix this. I'm not sending you away to some rehabilitation center. I've sent for one of the finest team of private drug counselors to help you here at home, all very discreetly and privately. All you have to do is let them help you. We'll get through this together. I promise. You're not alone, darling. You must let me help you. All right?"

Kate nodded. It took nearly a week for the in-home counselors to get Kate off the prescription medications using sleep therapy, but it had worked. Kate was back to herself and had moved on with her life. Everything was as it should be.

⟡⟡⟡

And now this? She steeled herself to be strong this time just as she did then. She had to be there for Kate.

Oh my God. What has happened? She brought her hands up to her face. *What has happened to my darling baby this time? Kate, why couldn't you just leave things alone?*

⟡⟡⟡

Sam ended the call and went back inside. He looked for the check-in counter and found the lady who had already questioned him. The small cubicle she worked in was free. He approached it and sat down. "I'm sorry I lost my temper with you earlier, ma'am."

She looked up from the computer screen. "I'm sorry too, sir. We tend to forget that our patients are people, and then someone comes along and reminds us." She took out a clipboard and placed it in front of him. "If you can fill this form out, it would be appreciated." She handed him a pen.

He glanced at it. "I may not know some of this information."

"You can come back and fill out the rest later on. We need the basic information—name, address, emergency contact, and insurance coverage."

"I'll have to get her insurance card from the hotel. She has insurance. I just don't have it." He reached into his wallet and handed her a card. "I can give you my American Express Card to put her bill on."

"You can bring her insurance card in later on. That'll be fine," she said.

"Well, you take this and we'll go from there. We're good for it." He didn't want Kate's care jeopardized in any way.

She took the card and smiled. "I'm sure you are, sir." She took the information and handed it back to him. "I'll process this form and we'll have most of what we need."

"Can I go back and see her?" he asked.

"You'll have to speak with the nurse. I'm sure that won't be a problem," she replied.

"Of course." He stood up. "The nurse. What was I thinking?"

"Sir," she said with deep concern. "I'm sure your niece will be just fine."

He appreciated the perfunctory gesture. "Thank you, ma'am." He made his way back down the same hall and stopped at the nurses' station. The young Black woman behind looked up and greeted him. "Can I help you?"

"Sam Johnson. I'd like to go back and see my niece, Kate Thayer."

She viewed some notes on the computer. "One moment and I'll get the doctor."

"I just want to go back." He noticed a look of concern wash over her face. "Is something wrong?"

"I'll get the doctor for you. If you wait over there." She got up from behind the counter and moved down the hall, out of his sight.

Sam walked over to the waiting room and sat down in one of a dozen or so wooden chairs that were laid out. A small table stood next to his chair had some magazines on it, but nothing interested him. Not that he could concentrate enough to read anything right now, anyway. Worry about Kate consumed him. His niece. It felt so good to finally be able to say that out loud, and now this. What had happened to her? He had seen no indication of her being ill, none at all. She was a healthy person, an active one. She swam. She rode. She hiked. She never spent any time in a hospital, except for two years ago. Fear slammed into him alongside the worry.

He served twenty-five years in the army and traveled the world, and not always in the best of places. While a captain, he spent a tour in the first Gulf War, which fortunately didn't last too long. As a colonel, he commanded a battalion in Kosovo, in the second Gulf war, and in Afghanistan. He witnessed men and woman under his command blown to bits, or left maimed, and yet he wasn't as scared then, through all that death, as he was right now, here in the hospital, waiting to hear about Kate. Not even the loss of the use of his right leg that left him with a limp had scared him so. The bomb blast under his Humvee in Kabul had been sudden. Surgeons had worked feverishly to save his leg, which they did, though it would never be the same. Nothing was the same again.

He turned down a presidential post in the cabinet to go back home to Mississippi and be near his mama and niece, even though Kate didn't know his real identity. To him, it just made sense. Family was family. He wished he had felt that way when he was younger.

Things could have been different. Perhaps, his sister would still be alive. Jax would be too and their children around them, as it should have been. They had been close to telling Kate the truth back then, but couldn't. She had already been through so much then. Perhaps, they should have. Perhaps. Would it have changed anything that happened now?

All he wanted to do when he retired two years before, and after what he had seen in battle, was to settle down and be near his family. Now, she did know, and he was scared to death about what was wrong with her. What if something was very wrong? Could he lose her this time? No. He wouldn't go there. He couldn't face that.

"Mr. Johnson?"

Sam looked up to find the same ER doctor, who had first worked on Kate staring at him. He hadn't noticed then how young the doctor was. He guessed the other man was Kate's age or a year or two older or younger.

Sam came to his feet. "The nurse said I had to speak with you before I went back there. Is she all right?"

"We have received some of her lab tests back. As she suspected, there is an irregularity with her kidneys, and her white blood cell count is elevated, which would indicate an infection. We're moving her into a room upstairs to be on the safe side and keeping her overnight, at least."

Sam swallowed hard. "I see," was all he could say. "Can I go into see her?" It was two years ago all over again. Again, he was at a loss as to what to do, he never felt so useless.

"I'll have a nurse come and get you and bring you up. I'm sorry I can't offer you more right now."

It wasn't five minutes later when a young blonde nurse came out to meet him and took him up in the elevator to the second floor nurse's station. After checking in with another nurse, she walked him down a hall to a room. "You can go in now, Mr. Johnson."

He hesitated. "I—I have more family flying out. How can I let them know where we are?"

"Don't worry about that. As soon as they ask about her, they'll be directed here."

"Thank you," he said and walked into the room. It was a private room and the door was open.

There she lay in a single-sized hospital bed. The side rails were up and Kate had tubes running from her nose, fingers, and hand to various monitors and an IV bag. He stepped over to the bed. The room was white with a few bland paintings of flowers scattered on the walls, which did nothing to offer any solace. He neared the bed and leaned one arm on the railing.

He looked down at her. She was paler than her normally white skin should be. Her long hair was damp and plastered against the pillow. He reached for her hand. The right hand didn't have an IV connected to it. Instead, it had a clip over one finger.

He placed his large hand over her small one and grasped it. She was so hot under his touch.

"I'm here, Katy. You're not alone, kiddo. I'm sure you're scared, but I'm not leaving you." He leaned in closer to her ear. "I don't know if you can hear me, but your grandmothers, both of them are on their way here. That, I would like to see. We'll all be here for you soon, Katy. Don't be scared."

He looked around, pulled the chair away from the wall next to the bed, and sat down. He released her hand, retook it through the rail this time, and held it.

"You rest now. I'll be here when you wake up."

She didn't respond. All he heard was the sound of the monitors bleeping, buzzing, and chirping. Every several minutes, the blood pressure monitor made a hissing sound. The cuff around her forearm inflated and then released the sound of air escaping as it deflated. He didn't need the doctor to tell him how to read the blood pressure and hers was still lower than normal, her temperature still high.

He shook his head as he watched her and couldn't help thinking about life and death. Of the ones he saw and lost. Holding Kate's hand in the ambulance and seeing her lose consciousness brought back a flood of memories he'd tried very hard to suppress.

How many hands of young men and women in his battalions the same age as Kate and way younger did he hold onto and lied to them by telling them that they'd be all right? Yes, some had survived. Others didn't. Some ended up worse than dead. Kate was right. Lives were wasted in the wars that had nothing to do with protecting America. It was all crap, all propaganda started with a gung-ho, war happy, cowboy president, and continued with a president that hadn't a clue as to how to properly run the country. As a Black man, when he first heard that the first African-American was going to run for president back in 2007, Sam couldn't have been more pleased. He knew exactly who he would vote for. No questions asked. There was some doubt in the back of his mind and concern that Obama wasn't a veteran and had no leadership experience. However, like other African-Americans, he had hope and promise in this man, especially when he learned that the man was of mixed race. For Sam and Maddy, that was a plus.

Sadly, it turned out that Obama was no different from his White male predecessors. And Sam's fears were warranted. Things became worse and no one wanted to admit it. The leaders just couldn't seem to get along and, worse, they didn't care whether they did or didn't. No matter that the United States was going to ruin. As Doctor King once said on the steps in Washington, DC, instead of the leaders honoring their obligation to the American people, they presented America with a bad check, a check that came back marked "insufficient funds." Maybe, it was time for a woman to run things. A woman such as Kate, or even her grandmother Katherine could only run things better. Look at Magnolia Lane Farm. It thrived under their charge. And even though, he didn't get along with Katherine, he respected her fortitude. That woman had nerves of steel. Until that night of the incident, she had never struck him before. And as much as he resented her for it, he understood the fear that drove her to do it. His wife Elsa would be another contender. No holds barred. If they ran for president, or a woman just like them, she'd have his vote. Maddy and Elsa's too.

Of course, it didn't endear Sam any closer to the president when it came time to fill out the 2010 census and instead of choosing mixed race, Obama chose just African-American. To Sam and Maddy, that was a cop out, a slap in the face, an insult to all those born of mixed race like his niece, and his wife, a woman who was quite proud of her mixed heritage. And so, it seemed, was Kate. He was proud of her. Kate was like the two elderly women they met on the train who didn't care about skin color.

She was the future of this country. She was rational, realistic, and, most importantly, not the slightest bit racist. She was fair and tough, when necessary, to everyone. She was what Doctor Martin Luther King imagined, spoke about, and meant. Sam was proud to know her, have her in his life.

Family was what was important now. Family was the only thing that mattered to him now, and should have mattered to him back then. The hell with the world and the country. He did his service. He gave his all for king and country. He gave his leg and his freedom and his ability to have children. No, he could never father a child. The bombing saw to that. Of course, he was lucky to have lost the use of just one leg. Only Elsa knew the extent of the real damage done to his body.

He was too embarrassed to tell anyone else, certainly not his mama. As it was, he almost pushed Elsa away when it happened four years before, but his beautiful wife proved to be more stubborn than he was.

She wouldn't leave him and she wouldn't let him give up. She was still a nurse then in the army hospital back in Germany and she personally saw to his recovery. He was given his battalion back until he retired.

No, he owed the government nothing. But his family, his mama, his wife, his nieces, he owed them his everything. He'd die for them if that was what it took.

He lay back his head and shut his eyes, only meaning to do so for a few minutes.

Chapter 20

Astrid opened her eyes slowly to avoid being shocked awake from the bright light of the eastern sunlight shining in through their picture window. The light was a wonderful thing when she sculpted, but not so nice when she first woke up on a bad morning. Slowly, she brought herself up to a sitting position and hung her legs over the side of the bed.

"Good morning, sleepy head," Julia said as she walked into the bedroom with a tray in her hands. She carried it to the nightstand on Astrid's side of the bed and set it down. "I made you breakfast and I want you to eat something. Eggs, bacon, toast, freshly sliced apples in cream. Your choice."

"I'm not very hungry," Astrid said, though it did all smell good, despite a slightly stuffed-up nose.

"Nevertheless, you're going to try, for me," Julia said. "Afterward, I have something for you."

"What? A lecture?" Astrid brought a hand to her forehead. "Did you slip me a Valium?"

"Yes. You needed to sleep," Julia said.

"You know how I hate when you do that to me."

"So shoot me for caring about you. Eat something. Now."

Astrid picked up the plate and reluctantly munched on a piece of bacon. It tasted so good, she ate the rest. She finished the scrambled eggs and toast and downed the apples in cream. She washed it all down with a glass of orange juice and then took a sip of the hot coffee.

Julia walked over and inspected the tray. "Well done. See? You were hungry."

"What are you doing home today?" Astrid asked.

"I took the day off. I thought you might need me," Julia replied.

"Last night wasn't a bad dream then? Do I look as bad as I

feel?" No wonder her nose was stuffed-up—from all the crying, obviously.

Julia sat down next to her, placed her arm around her, and kissed her on the forehead. "You're beautiful and I love you."

"You didn't answer the question," Astrid said. Julia was really an expert at evading questions, but it didn't usually work on her.

"You look better now than you did last night." Julia brought her arm from behind her back and handed Astrid the journal.

Astrid eyed it. "What's this?"

"A journal."

"You're keeping a journal? Where did you find it? It looks ancient."

"It is, but it isn't mine." Julia took Astrid's hands in hers, placed the small book in them, and held her own hands over them. "Take it. Read it."

"Why?"

"You need to."

"Whose is it?"

"Your mother's."

Astrid swallowed hard. "My mother is dead. Kate said so."

"Yes, I know, but she wrote this and you need to read it. Now. Take it. You were never thrown away by your parents. They loved you very much."

"How—do you know that?" Astrid said. Dead people told no tales.

"It says so in here. Your mother said so. She wanted you to know. Read it, love. You need to know."

Astrid stared at it. "I can't."

"Yes, you can and you should. It isn't very long, but it says a great deal."

Astrid took it and placed it on her lap. The little blue book had a cloth cover and was badly worn around its edges. Did her mother really write in this? Had her mother actually held it in her hands? She brought it up to her nose and sniffed it for a clue. All she inhaled was dust and a stale scent, and she sneezed in reflex. She looked at Julia, who just waited nearby watching her. Julia offered her a tissue, but Astrid declined.

She swallowed hard and slowly, carefully opened the cover, afraid to break it, as much as she was afraid of what she would find inside the book.

The inside cover had cursive handwriting, which said simply,

To my beautiful, beautiful wife, Olivia Thayer. With all my love, always, your adoring and very handsome husband Jackson, better known as Jax. I love you. Now and forever.

She brought up one hand and ran her fingers across the hand-writing. *My father wrote this? He gave my mother this journal. He loved her. Father? Dad? What happened to you? Why did you leave us?*

She carefully turned the first blank page and another until she found more writing. This writing was different, was more elegant and with light strokes of a pen, whereas her father's handwriting was heavier and darker.

> *Entry Number 1:*
> *I'm not much for writing, so I don't know how many pages I'll really write on in this, but I'm determined to try. Jax gave me this journal to write in so we'll see what I write. Today, Jax told me three times that he loved me and I never get tired of hearing it.*

She ran her hand along each page trying to take the words into her hand and absorb part of the woman who wrote the words. When she got to the final two pages, she read them over three times.

> *Friday night:*
> *A lady in town said that the way I was carrying the baby that I was going to have a girl. She swore by it. I hope so. I'd love to dress her up in all the frilly little dresses I could find. Jax could put her on his shoulders and carry her around like my daddy used to do with me. She even said it might it be twins. I laughed at her because no one in my family ever had twins. I don't think Jax's family has either. I wonder what that would be like, especially if it was two little girls. Sisters. That would be wonderful for them. They'd have someone to play with and huddle with when they're afraid. They'd be able to share secrets. I'd like that. And if it was a boy and a girl, I'd like that too—a girl for me and a boy for Jax would be perfect. I guess we'll just have to wait and see.*
> *It won't be too long now. And I can't wait. It's very*

difficult to get in and out of bed and a chair when you're as big as a house. Jax still says I'm beautiful. Every night we go to bed, I curl up against his warm naked body. He holds me from behind and we fall asleep. He says he'd never be able to sleep again without me by his side. I feel the same way. We've only been married now for nine months and I couldn't imagine my life without him. He told me last night, as we lay together that if anything ever happened to me, he couldn't go on. He'd rather be dead than live without me. I told him he was being foolish. I'm only twenty. What is going to happen? He just wanted me to know how much he loved me. Funny thing is that I feel the same way. I couldn't live without him either. He's so good to me. He always has been, even when we were children. He was always the perfect Southern gentleman. He never cared about what I looked like. He always cared about what I was like inside. He says I have a good soul. He does too. I thank God and Jesus for Jax every day. They brought us together. How can I not thank them? I pray every night that our baby is born safe and healthy. I don't care what it is, as long as it is safe and healthy. I told Jax that I'm trying to write in this journal he gave me. He liked the idea. He said that we could write it now and give it to our baby when he/she is old enough to read it. So, hello little baby, Jax says, your daddy says, that he loves you very much and, after you are born, he'll even write a few pages in here every now and then and tell you so himself. Won't that be nice? Anyway, there is only one month left to go until you are born and we can't wait. In exactly twenty eight days, you are scheduled to come into the world and into our lives. Of course, a baby never comes on schedule, so we'll see. Your daddy is climbing the walls, waiting for you to be born. He fixed up the spare bedroom next to ours into a nursery with ponies and lambs and cows on the walls. He's even going to buy you a pony. You, my precious little angel are going to be a very lucky little girl or boy because your mama and daddy, Jax and I, love you very, very much and you aren't even born yet. I feel you kicking every

> *now and then. I touch my stomach and you kick back.*
> *Do you feel me touching you? I hope so. I love you, lit-*
> *tle one.*
>
> *We'll get to meet soon. You're going to love your*
> *daddy. He is such a special man. I'll write again when*
> *I get a chance. I love you. Your daddy loves you. No*
> *matter what happens in this big old world, don't you*
> *ever forget that we love you very, very much. We can't*
> *wait to hold you in our arms and cherish you. You are*
> *cherished already and you're not even born. Love,*
> *your mama and daddy. Forever and always. Hugs and*
> *kisses.*

The tears fell on her cheeks and Astrid couldn't move to wipe them away. She was lost in the moment—the moment in time that she didn't even know about. The moment in time when she was tucked safely away in the warm recesses of her mother's womb along with a sister she had never known about.

For a long moment, all she could do was stare at the last words of her mother's handwriting. *Don't you ever forget that we love you very, very much. Love, your mama and daddy. Forever and always. Hugs and kisses.* Astrid closed her eyes but it was no good. The tears kept coming.

Julia wiped the tears from Astrid's cheeks and held her face in her hands. "They loved you. They didn't send you away. They wanted you very much, both of you." Julia placed her hands over her lover's. "Now you know what happened." She flipped to the middle, took out the photo, and handed it to her.

Astrid took it and stared at the handsome couple smiling up at her. She turned it over and read the perfect script letters, "Our parents, summer 1984. Olivia and Jackson the week before they married."

"My parents?" Astrid said. "She's so beautiful and...so White. Where—where did this come from?" Astrid choked out. Tears backed up into her throat.

"Kate left it. First, I thought by accident, and then I read it. She wanted you to know. Don't you see? That's why she came here, all this way. She wanted you to know the truth, just as she said."

"To tell me? I was horrible to her last night. I blamed her. I was wrong, wasn't I?" Astrid said.

Julia cupped her chin in her hand. "She understood."

"Do you think so?"

"Yes, I do," Julia said.

"I should apologize. I should talk with her. I should listen too. Do you think it's too late?" Astrid asked.

"It's never too late to apologize. It's never too late to talk and listen."

"What time is it anyway?"

"Noonish," Julia said.

"She probably left. She's probably on her way back to Mississippi and who could blame her after last night?"

Julia caressed Astrid's cheek. "Nope. She's still registered at the hotel. I checked."

"How? What hotel?"

"She left her contact info as a bookmark in the journal." Julia pulled out a business card from the hotel with her info scribbled out on the reverse. The writing was nearly identical to her mother's.

"I guess I should go see her," Astrid said. "I'm going to take a shower."

She leaned over and kissed Julia fully on the lips. Julia held her then released her.

❧❦❧

Katherine strolled into the first-class airport lounge at Jackson International Airport in Jackson, Mississippi. Lincoln dutifully followed her. Rather than take a seat, she paced the lounge and stared out the window. When they called to seat the first-class passengers a few minutes later, Katherine and Lincoln were the first two to board.

The female flight attendant showed them their seats. Lincoln helped Katherine off with the knee-length mink coat. She waited for him to fold it and place it gently overhead. He declined assistance from the flight attendant.

Another flight attendant turned to assist two other passengers. "Yes, your seats are right back here."

Katherine stood tall when she saw Maddy and Elsa board and head for their seats just across from and behind Katherine.

"Ladies," Lincoln acknowledged and nodded in their direction.

"So good to see you again, Doctor Lincoln," Maddy said. "I'm glad you're coming out as well."

"Me too. I just wish it was under different circumstances—"

"Excuse me," the first flight attendant interrupted. "If you all know each other and would like to sit together, I could check with the other first class passengers to see if they wouldn't mind moving?"

Katherine waved a hand. "That won't be necessary. Thank you." She took her seat at the window while Lincoln nodded at the three women and walked away for a moment.

Katherine pulled a gold cigarette case from her leather purse. She took out a cigarette, but before she could light it, the flight attendant came by, "I'm sorry, Mrs. Thayer, but there's no smoking."

"You've got to be kidding," Katherine snarled. "This is ridiculous!"

"I'm sorry. No smoking. Can I get you something to drink, instead?" the attendant asked.

"Yes, two soft drinks," Lincoln said as he returned to his aisle seat.

Katherine returned her cigarette case to her purse. "I'll have an old fashioned," she said. "He'll take the soft drink. Thank you."

The attendant eyes widened but she took the order and left.

Lincoln studied her. "Alcohol this early in the morning? Really, Katherine."

She ignored him. "I'm old enough, thank you."

"And I thought I told you about the dangers of smoking."

"I'm seventy, Lincoln. Tell me again when I'm eighty."

"I mean it. I told you to give that up."

"Lincoln, since when have I ever listened to anything you told me to do?"

"Does Kate know?"

"No, and she's not going to, now is she?"

Lincoln sighed and turned away. He took a magazine out of the seat pocket and flipped through the pages.

Katherine eyed Maddy, watching from across the aisle, and then turned away, looking out the window. If time wasn't of the essence, Katherine would have taken another flight.

∽∾∽

Across the other side of the plane, Maddy thanked the stewardess and took her seat by the window. Elsa sat down next to her.

"You have to admit, Katherine does put on a show," Maddy said.

Elsa dared to ask. "Why is she so dramatic?"

Maddy laughed. She loved her daughter-in-law. She had a way with words and didn't fear using them. It drove Katherine crazy—and her son Sam, too, to an extent. But Maddy admired Elsa's fire. She was a strong woman and her son needed that. Every man did. Maddy wished she had known that when she was married.

"Practice, child. Much practice." Maddy snickered. "You have to say one thing about her. Either you like her, or you don't. There is no in between."

"I guess. I liked her until she hit Sam."

Maddy placed her hand over Elsa's that rested on the armrest.

It was hard to believe that at one time, long ago Maddy and Katherine had been friends. For now, they were anything but. Maddy admired Katherine's strength, though, and her tenacity in the face of adversity. She had a strong feeling that the two of them would need an endless supply of both in the days ahead.

❧❧❧

When the plane landed in Atlanta for the change of planes nearly an hour and a half later, Katherine and Lincoln were the first off the plane, but Maddy and Elsa weren't far behind. They walked in the same direction to the same connecting plane and waited in the same line to board with other first-class passengers.

"If we're all on the same flight again?" Elsa asked. "Why didn't we just all fly out together?"

"Katherine didn't want to. Would you like to ask her why?" One day soon, Maddy would have to tell her daughter-in-law and son about her history with Katherine, but not now.

"No. I think I've had enough of her dramatics to last me for a while."

Maddy patted her arm. "Wise choice, child. And in case I ever forgot to tell you, thank you."

"For what, Mama?"

"For being you. For being with Sam. With me now."

Elsa waved a hand at her. "Oh, Mama, stop it."

"Let me finish. For also going to work for Katherine and agreeing to settle in the states, in Mississippi. And never demanding to know why I wanted you and Sam to do that or to live here."

"I asked. He said family. That was enough for me. Besides, we had a deal. We settle in Mississippi when we both retired from the army, as long as we can go visit my parents whenever I want, or whenever they wish to visit us here."

"You're a wise woman, Elsa."

"Thank you, Mama. I try to be."

Maddy sighed. She didn't deserve Elsa, certainly not after— she missed her Livie so much. Still, after all these years.

"Kate will be fine, Mama. Besides, we'll be there soon."

"I know, child. I know." But that didn't do anything to calm her down. What kept her calm was her determination not to upset Elsa. That kept her calm, that and Elsa's company.

On this connection to New York City, Katherine and Lincoln sat up front again, with Maddy and Elsa two rows behind them.

¢⁄ᴈ¢⁄ᴈ

A four-door car and chauffeur picked up Katherine and Lincoln at LaGuardia Airport and drove them from Queens Island to the Island of Manhattan and the hospital without delay. Maddy and Elsa arrived a few minutes later in another hired car. It was a little before three in the afternoon when they all arrived.

Katherine was the first to show up at the nurses' station. She didn't even wait for Lincoln to catch up to her. There was only one thing on her mind. She tapped her fingers on the counter.

"I'm Katherine Thayer. I'm here to see my granddaughter, Katherine Thayer."

The nurse looked it up on the computer. "I have a Kate Thayer."

"Yes, we call her Kate. I'd like to see her and her doctor, please," Katherine said. "Right away." She glanced around at the austerity of the place. She hated hospitals and the reason they existed.

"One moment. I'll page him."

At the counter, Maddy and Elsa arrived just next to them. "I'd like to see Kate Thayer."

The same nurse looked up. "Are you a relative?"

"I'm her grandmother, Maddy Johnson."

She eyed both of them carefully and her eyebrows rose. "You're both her grandmothers?"

"Yes, is there a problem?" Katherine asked, knowing, yet not caring, what the other woman thought. She didn't even glance Maddy's way.

"No," the nurse said. "No problem. If you take a seat in the waiting area through that door, I'll get the doctor for you." She pointed away from the counter toward an open doorway.

Katherine took the lead. Maddy moved alongside her. "You know we could have come here together."

"I'll deal with you here for Kate, but I won't travel anywhere with you," Katherine snapped and rushed on ahead to take a seat.

Lincoln entered behind just as the three women headed into the waiting room and he followed.

A young man in a white coat entered and scanned the room. A minute later, the nurse came in and pointed to the two women. He walked over to them.

"I'm Doctor Jeremy Patel. I'm a staff doctor tending to your granddaughter, Kate Thayer."

"Yes, I'm her grandmother," Katherine said with Lincoln seated next to her.

"As am I," Maddy added with Elsa seated near her.

He sat down just across from them and began, "As near as I can figure, your granddaughter has—"

"As near as you can figure," Katherine asked. "Are you a doctor?"

"Yes, madam, I am."

"Please go on," Maddy said.

"Her tests show some irregularities with her kidneys," he said. "And I've called in a specialist to address it."

"Kidneys? What is wrong with her kidneys? My granddaughter is in perfect health. You've made a mistake," Katherine barked.

"I assure you, madam, I haven't—" he tried to protest.

"Lincoln, are you just going to sit there and say nothing?" Katherine demanded.

Lincoln stood up. "Doctor, may I speak with you?" He moved to step away. He hadn't intended to butt in until he needed to, which obviously was now.

The doctor stood up and followed him. They stepped outside the waiting room into the hall out of the way.

Lincoln extended his hand. "Doctor Lincoln Castle, GP. For the last two years, my practice has been limited to caring for Kate and her grandmother. If you tell me what you've found, I can tell them."

The young man looked quite relieved. "Thank you. That would do nicely. Mind you, I'm just on staff here. My specialty is more in the area of car accidents, stabbings, and broken limbs from time to time."

"That makes two of us. I'm just an old country doctor," Lincoln said.

"Is Miss Thayer on any medications? Any allergies that you are aware of?" Patel asked.

"No. Nothing. She's in excellent health. What have you found wrong with her kidneys?"

"I'm not a specialist, but I've sent for one on staff and he's reviewing her tests now. As near as I can figure, she has a severe kidney infection. She arrived badly dehydrated. We are treating her for shock and the infection. As I said, this isn't my specialty and I don't want to do anything that might harm her further. I've started her on antibiotics and IV fluids. Her temperature is dangerously elevated, and her blood pressure is low. We did manage to rehydrate her. I'd appreciate if any tests you may have done could be forwarded here. She's not responding to standard treatment for shock so I'm at a loss. As a result, we moved her up to ICU."

Lincoln wasn't going to show it, but this news scared the crap out of him. He knew it was something, just nothing like this. "I'll call my nurse to fax you her latest tests. I did find irregularities with her kidney function test I did a week ago, as well. I will pass this on to her family. Please don't think too harshly of her grandmother. She raised Kate when her parents died as a baby."

"Yes, I did see that in her file." He removed a business card from the inner pocket of his jacket and handed it to Lincoln. "You can fax the info to his number. I'll have someone come and take you all up to ICU to see her." He extended his hand to the older man. "Thank you, Doctor, for your time and assistance. If I can be of any further assistance, please don't hesitate to have a nurse page me."

Lincoln pulled out his cell phone from inside his sport coat and walked toward the door. When he was away from the crowds of family members and friends of other patients, he stepped outside. He dialed his home office and when his secretary answered, he said, "Dinah, this is Lincoln. I'm at the hospital here in New York City. Please fax Kate's file to this number—212-555-7500. Everything in the file, especially her latest lab tests. Stay near your cell in case I need anything else. Otherwise, you can go home. I'll call if I need anything else."

"How is Miss Kate?"

"Not too good." He scanned the building. "Worse than I imagined. But I get the impression that, so far, she is in good hands. Yankee hands, of course, but we'll see. Did she ever follow up with you to make an appointment with the specialist?"

"No. I left her three messages on her voice mail but she never returned my calls."

He already knew the answer, but he'd had to know for sure. And now he did. "Stubborn girl," he mumbled. "Just like your grandmother." *I should have taken her to Jackson or Madison myself.*

He ended the call and replaced the phone in the inner pocket of his sport coat and went back inside. He dreaded what he had to do next. No matter how many times he relayed bad news, it never got any easier. Sometimes, he didn't like being a physician. This was one of those times. Here he finally told Kate that he was her grandfather and now—

No, he wouldn't go there, not yet anyway. As a physician, he knew that sometimes things happened without a clue as to how or why, and patients could make a quick recovery for the same reasons. Medicine was a science, supposedly an exact science, but he didn't agree. No matter how much technology they had at their disposal, physicians were still limited by education, experience and available technology.

When it came to cancer and other deadly diseases, physicians only knew one percent out of one hundred, which wasn't very good odds at all.

He took a deep breath, stepped inside the waiting room, sat down, and explained it all to them.

"Intensive Care?" Katherine was the first to speak and brought her hand to her chest. "Why is she in intensive care? What has happened, Lincoln?"

Maddy copied her when he relayed to them what he learned.

Instead of waiting for someone to come get them, they rushed upstairs to ICU with Katherine in the lead. Once up there, both grandmothers wanted to go into the room to see Kate first and they wouldn't be deterred.

"I'd like to see her first," Katherine said. "I'll let you see her, but I want to see her first."

Maddy relented and allowed Katherine to go in. Maddy waited. Lincoln offered her a seat next to him and she took it.

Elsa sat down on the other side and glanced around. "Where's Sam?"

Katherine walked up to the large private room and looked in through the glass. She took a deep breath, pushed open the door, and let it close behind her. All she heard was the swoosh sound of it closing and the sounds of monitors surrounding Kate.

She gasped and brought her hand to her mouth. Fear pervaded her soul. It was two years ago all over again...

e/ɔe/ɔ

Kate lay motionless and helpless—tubes leading into and out of her to machines. Katherine had waited for four hours that day as they took Kate into emergency surgery after they examined her.

It was all so sudden and quick then. Kate and Adam went riding together as they always did Saturday mornings, before he went to work part time at the local hospital. Kate's horse returned to the barn without her. Katherine called Lincoln and initiated a search of the farm. An aerial search was initiated by the local sheriff. Carl and Katherine and two hands with them found them first. One of the hands checked Adam. He was dead.

Kate suffered a concussion on top of everything else and stayed in a coma for five days before waking up. Then just when she thought it couldn't get any worse than it already was, Doctor Hammond Curtis, a family friend relayed more bad news.

"I'm sorry, Katherine. I should have recognized Kate. She is alive. We had to remove her uterus. She was hemorrhaging internally with several broken bones."

Katherine tried not to react.

"We couldn't save the baby," he said.

"Baby?" Katherine said, trying to conceal her shock. "W—what baby?"

"She was nine weeks pregnant. I don't think she even knew," he said. *"I'm sorry I couldn't do more."*

Katherine was shattered but wouldn't show it. Not here. Not now. This was all too familiar to her.

"What matters is that she is all right. I want to see her."

"She's heavily sedated. She won't even know you're there," the doctor said.

"Nevertheless, I want to see her."

"I'll have a nurse bring you back when we get her settled into a room," he said and placed a hand on her shoulder. *"I'm sorry, Katherine."*

☙❧☙

Quickly, Katherine pushed that memory aside. The pain was too much to bear. It was twofold. With a sideways glance, she found Sam next to the bed. He was obviously asleep as his head was down with his chin tucked in against his chest. She sighed. She hadn't meant to be harsh with him the other day. The last thing in the world she wanted to do was hurt him, but he had infuriated her. They all did. They'd sworn an oath. All of them did, and to break it, meant betrayal. Evidently, Sam was with Kate since the wee hours of the morning when Maddy came up to the house to notify her. He was a good man. He loved Kate. She couldn't deny that.

Slowly, she made her way over to the bed that held her granddaughter. Kate didn't move or make a sound. She lay as still as she had two years ago, though under different circumstances. Yet, the situation was the same. Kate was unconscious and in danger.

Katherine placed a hand on Sam's shoulder and whispered, "Sam. Sam," she repeated a bit louder and shook his shoulder. "Sam," she repeated a third time, this time a bit louder and with a rougher shake to his shoulder.

He shot to his feet. "Yes? What is it? Kate?"

"No, Sam," she replied.

He faced her and she noticed from his expression, she'd startled him, even shocked him. "Miss Katherine?"

"Yes, Sam. Your mother and Elsa are outside. I'd like to be with Kate alone."

"Of course." He moved to leave.

"Sam," she called.

He stopped. "How long were you with her? Where was she?"

"Since she left home the other day. I found her at the train station in Yazoo," he said.

She nodded and turned back to Kate. Katherine coughed, swallowed hard, and said a quick silent prayer. She aimed to be strong again for Kate. She was strong two years ago. She could be strong now, no matter what it took.

At the headboard, Katherine reached out a shaky hand, ran it over Kate's forehead, down her right cheek, and rested her fingers on her granddaughter's lips. They were dry and pale like the rest of her. Her skin was clammy, but hot to the touch.

Katherine eyed her own hand surprised by the trembling of it. She brought her hand to her mouth and held it there for a moment, as she eyed her granddaughter's helpless body. Katherine couldn't breathe. She swore her heart had stopped. She took a deep slow breath to calm herself. This was worse, more serious than the accident two years ago. She could feel it in her bones.

"Grandmother is here, darling," she said and hoped her voice didn't waver. "Don't be afraid. I'm going to take care of everything. I promise. Everything will be all right. You just rest and get strong and stay with me."

There was a chair next to the bed and she sank down onto it. She reached through the bed rail and placed her hand over Kate's. Kate's hand felt as if it were on fire.

"Please don't take her away from me, God. I know I haven't always done the right thing, but please don't let Kate—please don't take her away from me." It was more of an order than a plea. "I loved this child as I loved my own and only did what I could to protect her. If you must punish someone, make it me. This child did nothing to warrant all she has gone through in her short life. Hasn't she been through enough?"

Katherine stopped when she heard the door open. With a sideways glance, she saw Maddy walk in and stop just inside the door. From her peripheral vision, Katherine saw Maddy bring up her hands and hold them over her mouth and heard her gasp.

Cautiously, Maddy walked toward the bed and stopped. For a few minutes, she just stood there staring down at Kate, her hands in prayer just over her mouth. Maddy closed her eyes for a moment, then walked over to the other side of the bed opposite Katherine, and leaned over. She reached out a hand and brushed

Kate's hair, removing the stray strands away from her face.

"She's so warm," Maddy said.

"This is all your fault," Katherine whispered to her.

"I won't argue with you. Katherine. Not here, not now," Maddy whispered in return.

"All you had to do was keep your mouth shut. She wouldn't be here now if not for you," Katherine said.

"She's barely breathing," Maddy said. "And she's so warm. Is that her temperature?" she asked, indicating the one monitor that read 103.6.

"Don't change the subject."

"Kate is the subject," Maddy retorted. "She always has been."

"Kate will be fine."

"What makes you so sure?"

"I wouldn't contemplate otherwise."

"It must be nice to live in your world, Katherine, but this time you don't get to play God. None of us do."

Anger and worry consumed Katherine. She shot to her feet and stormed from the room. She wouldn't argue in Kate's room. She just wouldn't.

Maddy ignored her and focused on Kate. Her granddaughter needed her and that was all that mattered. She couldn't save Olivia thirty years ago. There was nothing anyone could have done. But she'd be damned if she'd lose Kate too, especially after nearly losing her two years before. At least this time, things were out in the open. Maddy and Sam could be with Kate, as family should, unlike two years earlier where Maddy and Sam hid in the background and gathered news second hand, as pretend neighbors and employees. Kate's in-laws were allowed to see Kate then, but they weren't. Of course, it was their fault for not speaking up then.

She sat down in the other nearby chair, reached through the railing, and took Kate's hand in hers. "It's hard to believe your grandmother and I used to be good friends. Of course, you never knew that. You never saw that side of us. Oh, my darling child, I wish…Oh God only knows how truly sorry I am. I'm so sorry, child. We shouldn't have kept anything from you. We shouldn't have lied. We shouldn't have played God. There's only one God and he's showing us again because we didn't listen when he spoke to us two years ago." She sighed deeply and caught her breath. "I guess that was a warning, a chance to make things right then and we didn't listen. I'm listening now, God. Please don't take this child away from us, from me. Please, God, hear my prayers. She did nothing wrong. She's innocent. We're the sinners. Please don't take her. You already have my baby Livie and this child's daddy. And only you know whatever happened to Livie's other girl. Please keep her safe too wherever she is."

Maddy felt the strong hands of her son on her shoulders. "Mama, you and Elsa had a long day. Why don't you go to the hotel and I'll stay with Kate?" he said. "Get something to eat. Freshen up. You both must be tired. You can always come back."

Maddy didn't have to look at her son to know he was tired. She heard it in his voice. And she knew Elsa would never say how tired she was.

"I'll be fine, Sam. You've been with her all day. You and Elsa go to the hotel, and I'll stay. You're tired."

"Mama, I'm fine."

"Is that why you're limping so badly today?" she said.

She heard him sigh. Her son knew there was no arguing with her, not since George died. She never argued with her husband when he was alive. She had never disagreed with him, on anything, and the price she paid for her silence was exorbitant. Katherine was right about everything. Maddy should have said something back then. Instead, she let George say everything. She let him, Katherine, and Jackson decide what was best for their children. Yes, back then, she agreed with them, but not after. Not after the death of her Livie. No.

She still didn't argue, but this time it was because she didn't unless there was something to argue about. Now, she didn't let a man lead her where he wanted her to go. Now, she stood up for what mattered to her. *Fool me once, shame on you. Fool me twice shame on me.* There wouldn't be a third time. She heard God speaking this time loud and clear. And this time, she would heed his words.

"We'll wait to see what this specialist has to say and then we'll decide," she told him.

The door opened and it was Katherine returning. The love they shared for Kate could not be disputed or put aside. That was the only thing the two women had in common. Too bad Katherine was still so blind to see that.

Katherine walked back to the bed and sat back down in the chair that she had vacated earlier. She didn't even look Maddy's way and that was fine. Katherine loved Kate. Maddy never doubted that for a second. Kate loved Katherine. Kate turned out to a better person, a better woman than the two of them together, which meant that Katherine did something right with raising her. Or was it because Kate was the product of two extraordinary people? Like her parents before her, Kate wasn't a bigot. She respected everyone. She was so unlike her grandparents. She deserved so much better in life than losing her husband, her parents, and being lied to by her grandparents. They both did.

The both of them. Whatever became of the other baby, of Livie's other little girl? Perhaps, when all of this was over and Kate was back on her feet, Maddy would try to look for her. Maybe Kate would like to help her. Maybe was such a non-committal word.

Chapter 21

The yellow taxi pulled up to the curb of the luxury hotel. The doorman on duty came over and opened the back passenger door. Julia and Astrid stepped out and headed through the glass doors into the lobby. The black-haired woman behind the desk greeted them both with a smile. "Can I help you?"

"I'm looking for Kate Thayer. I don't know her room," Astrid said.

"Yes, I know Doctor Thayer. She isn't in right now," the desk clerk replied.

"I'd like to leave a message, please," Astrid said.

"I don't know when I'd be able to give it to her, though if you'd like, I can give it to her uncle, Mister Johnson."

"Has she left?" Julia asked.

"No. She was taken away ill in an ambulance early this morning."

"Ambulance? What happened? Do you know? To what hospital?" Astrid asked. Millions of things went through her mind as to what happened to Kate.

"I don't know and I don't know what hospital, though our doorman might know. He was on duty."

"Thank you," Astrid said. She exchanged a glance with Julia and went back outside to speak with the doorman.

"Hello, ladies," he said as he tipped his top hat. He stood about six feet tall and had bright brown eyes. "Can I help you?"

"I understand Doctor Kate Thayer was taken to a hospital by ambulance. Do you know what hospital?"

"Saint Mary's University Hospital," he said. "Would you like me to call a taxi to take you there?

"Yes, please," Astrid answered. "Thank you." She wished she could blink herself there, but she'd settle for a taxi.

He went to the curb and withdrew a whistle from his jacket pocket. He gave it two quick blows. A yellow taxi, that was about to drive past, turned toward them and came to a screeching halt.

The doorman opened the passenger door and closed it behind them once they were in. He told the driver the destination then stepped back to his post. Astrid offered a tip, but he refused with a wave of his hand. His grin was warm and reassuring to her and, right now, she needed that.

℘℘℘

At the hospital ten minutes later, Astrid was the first to exit the cab as it pulled to the front door. She slammed the door open and shut and rushed into the front lobby and to a visitor desk just inside. Julia paid the fare and followed her. Inside, two elderly ladies, one White and one Black, manned it. One was on the phone. The White one greeted them. "Can I help you?" she asked.

"I'm here to see a patient. Kate Thayer," Astrid said and tapped her fingers on the counter.

The woman looked at a computer screen. "Yes, she is in our ICU unit on the sixth floor." She pointed across from her counter. "You can take an elevator there. Just go to the nurses' station upstairs and they'll direct you to her room."

Astrid rushed off. "Thank you," Julia said as she followed Astrid to the elevators.

℘℘℘

Upstairs, they exited and met with a nurse at the counter set in the middle of the large hall. Rooms were set off to each side. By her count, Astrid saw eight rooms. The Intensive Care Unit here was evidently set up for the comfort of the patients and family and friends who visited. Each ICU room had its own private waiting room for family members and friends.

"Can I help you?" asked the nurse.

"I'm looking for Kate Thayer. I was told she was up here," Astrid said.

The middle-aged woman checked the screen over her shoulder. "Yes. However, we're only allowing family into see her."

Astrid swallowed hard. "I—I am f—family," she whispered at first, coughed, and then added volume. "I am family. She's my sister. Can I see her, please?"

The nurse studied her. Astrid knew what she was thinking—they couldn't possibly be.

"She is my sister. Our mother was Colored. Look—Please—I have to see her." Why did she just say that? She didn't have to justify herself, yet it had just come out. All of it did, it was more of a reflex than anything else. "We haven't seen each other for—for a long time. Please...."

The nurse nodded, led her to room number six, and then left them. Astrid stopped dead in her tracks when she saw Kate through the glass walls. There she lay on a metal bed in the white room with tubes connected to her, in her hand, and through her nose. Even this total stranger to her deserved better than these surroundings. Total stranger? She wasn't that after all, though, was she?

Julia came up beside her.

"I hate hospitals," Astrid said.

"I know," Julia said as she reached out and grasped her hand.

"I—I can't do this. Not now." Astrid had to catch her breath. "I don't even know her."

"Let's go sit down. You can always come back."

"Where's her family?" Astrid asked, noting Kate alone in the room. "Why is she alone? Didn't they say at the hotel she was brought in early this morning?"

"Maybe they're on their way. Let's go sit down."

Astrid nodded. Just as they headed into the waiting room, they heard raised voices. Shouting. There was a tall, white-haired White man trying to calm an older White woman down without any success.

ꕥ

Katherine yelled at Lincoln and tried to slap him. "You knew? You knew she was ill and you didn't tell me. You betrayed me, Lincoln!"

"I promised her," he said, holding onto her flailing arms.

"You promised me too. How could you let her travel out here when you knew she was ill? How could you? If she dies, Linc, I swear—"

"I didn't know how sick. I'm no specialist, Katherine. I'm retired," Lincoln replied. "She was fine."

"What did you know?" Astrid demanded as she stepped toward the fray. "Who the hell are you people? Are you Kate Thayer's family?" Saying those words tossed her stomach.

Everything stopped. Total silence replaced the chaos. "Who are you?" Katherine asked and turned to face her.

Astrid stepped forward. "Who are you?"

"I'm her grandmother."

"Katherine?" Astrid could see the other woman didn't have the slightest clue whom she was. "I'm her sister, *Grandmother.*"

Katherine brought a hand to her chest and nearly collapsed on the floor. Fortunately, Lincoln was close enough to catch her and led her to a chair while she stared back. "It can't be. This isn't possible. You're—" She stopped.

Astrid stepped toward her and relished the look of astonishment on the older woman's face. "What, *Grandmother*? Dead? Sent away? Sent away thanks to you." She looked around. "All of you, actually, right? The family secret?"

Julia caught her arm. "Don't lose your temper. Not here. Not now."

Astrid wouldn't be deterred. "Why not? Here is as good as any place, right, *Grandmother*? We're all here, right? Family reunion?"

"Astrid, don't do this. Don't upset yourself," Julia whispered into her ear.

She ignored Julia. "Who are you?" she asked Lincoln.

Lincoln faced her. He paled under his white skin. "I'm Kate's doctor."

Astrid moved closer to him. "Her doctor? What are you, a hundred? You knew she was sick? What's wrong with her?"

He sank into a chair next to Katherine. "Kidney infection, they're saying." He nodded slowly. "I told her. I referred her to a specialist."

"When? Why did you let her travel?" Astrid asked.

"Let her? I didn't let her do anything. I couldn't change her mind. It was more important to her to find you. And bring you home. That is all she cared about, once she knew." He swallowed hard. "I am sorry."

Astrid stepped back. Julia was there to catch her. "And now what? What are they going to do for her?"

"A specialist is reviewing her tests," Lincoln said.

"And? This is how you all handle it? She is in intensive care and you fight? What kind of people are you? You're all incredible!"

Maddy moved toward her. "Don't be upset, child."

"Don't even try to touch me!" Astrid shot up a hand in defense. "And who are you? My other grandmother? My Black one?"

"Yes, I am."

"Kate told me about my parents—everything. I know how you all sent me away. I know how you hated my parents loving one another! You need to look at yourselves. You're a joke. All of you. You all belong together. All of you. Black and White, White and Black. You're all the same. Look at each other. Liars! You all make me sick! Stay away from me! Stay away from Kate! You've all done enough!"

Astrid spun on her heel and left followed by Julia close behind.

For a moment, Katherine glared at Maddy and Lincoln.

Maddy spoke first. "Don't glare at me. You caused this."

"No, you did," Katherine snapped. "You should have kept that slut away from my son."

"Slut? Livie was a lady right up until she married your son. If she didn't marry him, she'd be alive today, but he loved her and that tore you up. They loved each other, but you couldn't see that. You're a blind, bitter old woman and now you're all alone, just as you deserve. You destroyed our children and now you destroyed our granddaughters."

"Don't you preach to me, you damn Black fool! You self-righteous nigger! You and George were against their marriage as much as Jackson and I were, and don't you forget it, and for the same reasons!"

Maddy didn't mean to lose it here. She didn't want to but she clenched her fists into balls.

"You knew what was going on," Katherine went on. "You knew how we felt. You and George felt the same way. You knew what we would do. We all agreed. You didn't step forward once, not once, to ever stand and say different. I kept Kate, but you chose not to keep the other one. You knew we were right. That is why you let it all happen. You knew, as we did, that Jax and your daughter did not belong together. It wasn't natural. You fool.

You couldn't just leave things alone. Kate was happy. She didn't need to know the dirty truth because you couldn't handle the guilt anymore. You dumb foolish nigger. I hate you. It is all your fault and that slut you raised! "

Maddy slapped her and Katherine slapped back. Then they pulled on each other's hair. Lincoln, Sam, and Elsa jumped to their feet, grabbed each woman, and barely managed to pull them back from each other. Lincoln held onto Katherine as she struggled to break of his grip.

"Let go of me!" she ordered.

Sam held onto his mother as she flailed about her arms.

"Let go, Sam!"

"Stop it! Both of you! Stop it!" Sam yelled. "Enough!"

Elsa held onto Maddy's arm. "Sam is right! Stop it! You're behaving like children! Kate needs us now! All of us."

Katherine pulled free and faced them. "Kate needs none of you and nothing from you! You can go home! All of you! I don't want you here!"

Maddy pulled away from her son and met the other woman head on. "Not a chance. We stay here until Kate goes home. I won't make the same mistake again! She is my granddaughter too, and don't you damn well forget it!"

Katherine glared. "How can I when I have to look at your ugly Black face?"

Sam took a step in between them and leaned toward Katherine. "Enough out of you. I mean it. The only reason I let you get away with so much of your bullshit is because of that niece of mine and now she is in there fighting for her life. So shut up now or I swear I will slap you!"

"How dare you?" Katherine spat.

"Enough, all of you!" Lincoln hollered. "This isn't the time or place for this. Sam, you sit down and mind your manners. All of you, do the same. Remember where you are. Remember why you're here."

"You're right," Sam said. "Doctor Lincoln, I'm sorry."

Katherine relented, slowly backed up, and sat down. Lincoln shook his head and sat down next to her. He moved to take her hand but she pulled away from him.

"Don't touch me!"

Maddy nodded, moved to a seat across the room, and sat down. She remembered the last time Kate was in the hospital all too well. Maddy was relegated to the waiting room like one of the farm employees when she should have been in the room with Kate, like Katherine was. But she didn't speak up then. She kept the secret close to her heart, though, as she was terrified of losing Kate. So even when Kate's in-laws were allowed to visit with an unconscious Kate over those first few days after the riding accident, Maddy had to settle for news about her secondhand from Carol, Lincoln, or Kate's father-in-law Doctor Perry Logan. Thank God, Lincoln and Perry were good men. Though, Perry was clearly devastated by the loss of his son, his grandchild, and deathly worried about Kate, unlike both his wife and Katherine, he was able to talk about it and let her know. He somehow knew how concerned Maddy was and kept her informed. At least this time, she was where she belonged, where she needed to be, and no one was going to change that. No one.

Sam sat down next to her and Elsa sat next to him. Where would she be without them? Maddy hadn't been so scared in her life, except for a few times—the accident two years ago with Kate, losing her daughter Olivia years before, and now this with Kate.

There was only one time in her life she ever remembered feeling really safe and secure, and that was so very long ago. It pained her to think of it now.

☙❧☙

Astrid stormed from the waiting room and made her way to stop outside of Kate's room. She looked through the clear glass and watched Kate. "So," she began. "That's the family that sent me away. I don't know whether to thank them or curse them."

"I'm proud of you," Julia said, taking a few steps to stand alongside her.

"For losing my temper?" Astrid asked.

"No. For saying what you felt. You held that back for a very long time. I know it wasn't easy."

"Did I actually tell them to stay away from Kate?" Astrid said.

"Yes, you did," Julia said.

"Why did I do that? I don't even know her. She's nothing to me." So why did she feel so protective of her?

"Why are you here?"

"Julia, I'm not one of your patients. Stop analyzing me."

"I'm not. Answer the question."

Astrid sighed. "I don't know."

"Yes, you do. You've been wondering your entire life about your family. You met them and they're not what you expected, right?"

"Wrong, Doctor. They're exactly as I pictured them. They are." She glanced back at the glass. "Except for Kate. I didn't picture a sister. I certainly didn't picture her. She came out here to see me, to tell me the truth she just found out herself and when she was sick, on top of it. Who does that?"

"You would," Julia said. "You would."

"I need to know what is really wrong with her. What happened?"

☙❧☙

It seemed like forever when the specialist they all waited on summoned them, when, in fact, only an hour had passed. Katherine glanced toward the hall and saw a man in a white shirt and black tie step inside the waiting room.

"I'd like to speak with the family of Katherine Thayer," he announced.

"Here," Katherine said, as she came to her feet.

"Right here," Maddy said, copying her.

Katherine didn't even look in her direction. That would be acknowledging her.

"I understand her sister is here, too."

Sam stood up. "She's around here somewhere. I'll find her."

"Fine," the doctor said. "When you return, let the nurse know and she'll take you back." He turned his attention to the two older women when Sam and Elsa left.

"May I ask your relation to Miss Thayer?" he asked as he led them down a hallway.

"I'm her grandmother," Katherine said.

"I'm her grandmother, also," Maddy added.

The doctor nodded in acknowledgement, but Katherine knew what he was thinking, or so she thought, and she didn't care. She didn't care what anyone thought, except for Kate.

They came to a pale wooden door. He opened it and let them enter first. He went behind a massive wooden desk and indicated that they should all sit in the four chairs set before his desk, opposite him.

"I'm Frank Stanley. I'm a nephrologist who will be taking care of your granddaughter Kate," he said. "I'm sorry for the delay in seeing you, but I wanted to review her tests. Thank you, Doctor Castle for forwarding what you had."

Lincoln nodded in acknowledgement.

Katherine studied him. He wasn't that old. He couldn't be more than thirty-five, forty at most. That concerned her. "Yes, Doctor. Please go on," she said. Of course, if he was as smart and efficient as Kate was, there'd be no problem, but she didn't know the slightest thing about him.

"I'd like to have her sister here too, if I may," he said.

"We can wait, can't we, Katherine?" Maddy said.

She knew what Maddy was doing, but Katherine wasn't sure if she should be annoyed or relieved. Putting up a unified front for a stranger was one thing. She didn't like the other woman being so familiar with her by using her first name, as if they were dear old friends. That gate was closed years ago.

"I can start with the basics while we wait." He opened a manila folder that was on his desk. "I have reviewed all your granddaughter's tests we have run since she arrived here earlier today. Your granddaughter came in badly dehydrated with a high fever, which by all accounts was caused by a kidney infection. Her blood pressure was extremely low and she went into shock. We have her on IV fluids to rehydrate her. Our main concerns right now are to treat the infection and keep her hydrated and, of course, locate the underlying cause of the blockage."

Just then, there was a knock on the door and it swung open. It was Astrid and Julia along with Sam and Elsa. Katherine noticed he tried not to stare, but it was obvious he wasn't prepared for Astrid any more than he was prepared for her and Maddy. He gestured at the empty remaining chair in front of his desk, or the four empty chairs along the wall for them to sit.

Julia stepped forward with an extended hand to him and he stood up to meet her. "I'm Julia Comedy. I'm on staff at St. Michael's. Psychiatry."

"I'd like her to stay," Astrid said. "She can explain the medical stuff to me later on." She stared at the empty chair in between the two grandmothers and the elderly doctor. She instead chose to sit along the wall. Sam and Elsa copied her, as did Julia.

The doctor nodded. "Of course. No problem here. As I just told your grandmothers, I've reviewed your sister's file." He closed the folder and clasped his hands on top of it. He picked up a pen to write on a yellow pad. "I would like to get some information and answers to some questions. Some of these you may find personal, but it is very important I know Kate's entire medical history."

"Please, go ahead," Katherine said. "My granddaughter's wellbeing is my first and only priority."

"We have no secrets," Maddy said.

From the corner of her eye, Astrid noticed Sam and Elsa eye each other. She couldn't help but laugh inside at the incredulousness of it all. *No secrets? Really? How about me?*

"Fine," he said. "Please answer honestly. We must look at what is causing the blockage of the left kidney. It can be any number of things, stones, injury, or a birth defect can be a preceptor in all of this."

"Cancer?" Katherine asked.

Astrid thought she heard a waver in the older woman's voice but couldn't be sure. After all, what did she know about this woman, except that she didn't want her granddaughters born?

"We won't look at that just yet, as there are a number of things it can be, but yes, that, is always a possibility," he replied. He made some notes on the pad then looked up. "Tell me, has Kate ever been in any kind of serious accident? What kind of physical activities does she engage in? Any prior surgeries?"

"Surgeries?" Katherine took a deep breath and released it. "She had a horseback riding accident a couple of years ago. We raise horses. Her husband Adam died in the accident. They were riding on the north pasture—"

Lincoln took over. "They didn't see the snakes in a gully. They were both thrown from their horses."

"How bad was it?" the doctor asked. "Any internal injuries?"

"Her husband suffered a broken neck," Katherine said. "Kate had a concussion. Some bones were broken, yes." She took a deep breath. "We almost lost her."

Lincoln placed his hand on her shoulder. She didn't resist. Astrid couldn't help wondering what exactly their relationship to one another was.

"Kate did suffer several broken bones, her ribs, some vertebrae, and pelvic injuries. There was internal bleeding and damage that necessitated the removal of her uterus. She underwent a sub-total hysterectomy," Lincoln said. "She was in a lot of pain afterward, emotionally and physically. She had trouble sleeping. She developed an addiction to the pain pills she was on. Could this be related?"

The doctor eyed him. "Opiates?"

"Yes," Lincoln replied. "But she's fine now for the last year."

"I see," the doctor said. "There is no evidence of any opiates in her system, which is good. It is possible that the injury may be related to the underlying problem at hand, as a precursor. I'm going to consult with the urologist to be sure." He made some notes and looked up. "Does anyone in your family on either side suffer from any form of kidney disease? Any history of high blood pressure?" he asked.

"No. No kidney disease," Maddy replied. "I do take medicine for high blood pressure and so does my son."

He looked at Katherine. She hesitated. "My—my husband died of a stroke when he was fifty-four. That was twenty years ago, but I don't think he ever had kidney disease. It was an aneurysm, I think. I think his father also died from an aneurysm around the same age. But no one in my family or his has kidney disease. I also take pills for high blood pressure."

"I see." He made some notes on the yellow pad that sat next to the folder.

Astrid noticed him going over something in his mind. He opened the folder and flipped through some pages then closed it. He clasped his hands on top of the folder. "That falls in line with the images we took."

He stood up and went to a box hanging on the wall. He flipped a switch and it lighted up a white screen. On one side, there were radiographic pictures.

"Has your granddaughter ever had a history of kidney disease, urinary tract infections?

"No, why?" Katherine said. "Maybe once as a child, urinary tract infection."

"Has she ever complained of back pain, itchy skin, headaches, fatigue? Any form of discomfort?"

"She's had some headaches on and off for the last month and some stomach cramping, but that is all," Katherine said.

"What is all of this about?" Astrid asked. It was frightening to her and she had to know more.

"I'm pretty sure Kate has what we call polycystic kidney disease."

"Polycystic what?" Katherine asked.

"Is that what is causing the infection? Because that is what the staff doctor said was wrong," Maddy asked. "Or was he wrong?"

"No. It's not the same thing. And he wasn't wrong. The cause of the kidney infection is unknown. We found the cystic kidneys by accident during the tests."

"Are you saying there's more wrong with her kidneys than an infection?" Maddy asked.

"Yes. Let me show you." He turned sideways. From a group of images on the left side of the white illuminated screen, he took one and placed it on the other side of the screen by itself. "This is a Cat Scan image of Kate's kidneys. It's not the best imaging for this, but this is how we found it. We also confirmed it on the ultrasound and MRI I ordered. These are her kidneys." He ran a pencil over the black and white radiographic images and outlined the image from one end to the other. "The right one is normal in size for now."

"What do you mean, for now?" Katherine asked.

Lincoln squeezed her shoulder. "Go ahead, Doctor."

"Doctor, please just say it. What is wrong with Kate?" Astrid said. "And why is she unconscious?"

He faced her. "Your sister is unconscious from shock due to dehydration and the kidney infection. I've already conferred with an urologist and he can do the surgery, should we have to, as soon as she is stabilized."

"Surgery? What surgery?" Katherine was the first to speak. "No one mentioned any surgery."

"To remove the cystic kidney," he said. "If this is what is causing the blockage, it will have to be removed."

"What cystic kidney?" Astrid asked. "You said she has an infection and some cysts and she's on antibiotics. That's it, right?"

"No. These little spots you see on her kidneys are cysts," he said. "A few simple cysts on a person's kidneys are no big deal. Some people develop them as they age and they are of no concern. They're nothing to worry about. Your sister, however, has half a dozen on her right kidney." He pointed each one out with a pencil. "There are over twelve on her left kidney." He pointed each one out with a pencil. "The left kidney is our major concern right now. It is not functioning at all. As you can see, it is larger than the other. This isn't normal. I believe it may be filled with fluid that's not going anywhere. It is a likely the cause of the infection and blockage. We'll know if she continues not to respond to standard treatment and her temperature continues to elevate. In that case, the kidney will have to be removed."

"Can she survive with one kidney?" Sam asked.

"Many people do, without issue. However, with poly cystic kidneys—" He sighed. "I suggest we be optimistic and not go there yet."

Katherine pushed Lincoln's hand aside and stood up. "Doctor, what exactly is wrong with Kate and what is the final outcome of all of this? Will she recover or not?"

"One of two things can happen. She can fully recover from the infection, go home, and move on with her life," he said. "Without any residual effects, for now. We'll schedule regular monitoring of her blood pressure and viewing of her kidneys. We'll put her on medicine for her hypertension and that will be it."

"Or?" Astrid asked.

"Kate has what is called adult-onset polycystic kidney disease. It is inherited as an autosomal dominant disease," he said. "Autosomal dominant means you only need to get the abnormal gene from one parent, in order for you to inherit the disease. One of the parents may often have the disease and the abnormal gene dominates."

"Inherited? That is why you asked about family history?" Maddy asked.

"Yes. Either one of her parents could have passed it on. Years ago, we didn't know much about it. If there is a pattern of family members that died of aneurysms, there is a good chance it was because of polycystic kidneys and we didn't know until an autopsy was done. From the history of your husband's side of the family dying in their fifties of aneurysms, Mrs. Thayer, it is a good chance that is the line it passed down from."

Astrid could have sworn she saw Katherine flinch.

"And?" Katherine said. "Doctor, just be up front with us, please."

"The infection can spread. Acute kidney failure will occur and that failure could be permanent. In which case, she will require dialysis or a kidney transplant." He walked around back to his desk. "As I said, we don't want to go there just yet."

"But we may have to," Astrid said. "So finish, please, what you were saying. Dialysis or a transplant? What else can you do for her?"

"There must be something else," Elsa said.

"There are tests and trials going on," the doctor said. "But as of now, there is no effective treatment for preserving kidney function in polycystic kidney disease."

"Let me get this straight," Astrid said. "Are you saying that Kate—" She swallowed hard. "She could d—die from this?"

"That's rushing things ahead where we don't want to go," he warned.

"But that is what you are saying?" Astrid said. She felt Julia place her hand on her arm. This was all so wrong and unbelievable. Not when they'd just found each other.

"Yes. It is possible but dialysis is quite effective."

"You mean being hooked up to a machine for how many hours for how many days a week?" Astrid said. "What kind of treatment is that? And what are the side effects to that I wonder? Certainly not good ones."

"There is no cure all. I wish there was. We can only work from what we have," Doctor Stanley said.

"I don't like the options," Katherine said.

Astrid eyed her and agreed. Their eyes met and Astrid had to turn away.

"This is why I suggest we concentrate on treating the disorders we have in front of us that we can treat," the doctor said.

"May I ask how long you've been doing this?" Katherine said. "And what are your credentials?"

"I understand your concern, Mrs. Thayer. I'm a graduate of Harvard and Columbia Medical School. My specialty is the diagnosis and treatment of kidney disorders. That is all I deal with. I've been doing this for twenty-six years."

"And how many of your patients with this kidney disease needed dialysis and transplant?" Katherine asked.

"Mrs. Thayer, each patient is an individual. It is not worthwhile to think that, because one patient fared one way, your granddaughter will too," he answered.

"Can you answer the question or not, doctor?" Maddy added.

"Some of my patients never needed either. Since her grandfather and his father needed neither, there is a good chance she may not."

"And a good chance she might have an aneurysm instead like they did?" Katherine said.

"We can monitor for that with MRIs every two or three years," he assured her.

"But you can't guarantee she will never need dialysis or a transplant?" Maddy asked. "Or have an aneurysm?"

"No. I can't do that," he replied. "I'm sorry I can't offer you more. I suggest we deal with what is in front of us right now."

"Does the infection and shock—all of this have anything to do with this polycystic kidney disease?" Maddy asked.

"No. PKD is an entirely separate entity. I won't say it has nothing to do with her problem, but I don't believe so. We are allowing her kidneys some time to restore function while treating the infection. However, if that doesn't occur soon enough, we will have to put her on dialysis temporarily.

"Our main goal is stabilizing her and then looking at what is causing the blockage of the left kidney," the doctor said. "As I said, I'm going to consult with the urologist. Are there any other questions, because I do want to check on her and finish my rounds?"

Astrid couldn't believe how much the two older women's questions reflected her own fears and concerns. She heard Katherine release her breath before she spoke, "No. Not now."

No one else said anything. Astrid didn't know any of this, but how could she? Thanks to them, she knew nothing at all.

"If it is all right, I'd like to speak with Doctor Castle and Astrid," Doctor Stanley said.

Sam moved to leave and held the door open for Elsa and Maddy. Katherine hesitated then followed them out. Julia moved to leave.

"You may stay, Doctor Comedy," he said. "Please sit down. Doctor Castle, I have reviewed the urinalysis and blood work you faxed in. Her kidney function was irregular but overall, fine. And now it isn't. I strongly believe it is an infection. Unless something changes, we'll continue our treatment for that."

"With the possibility of surgery, I understand," Lincoln said. "I don't know if it matters, but you should know Kate was nine weeks pregnant at the time of her accident."

"I see. Yes, possible surgery, and while we are on the subject, I believe in taking the proactive approach. I don't believe in waiting until the last minute. However, I didn't want to upset the rest of your family. I would like to run some discreet blood tests on Kate's family members for a possible donor, just in case we have to go that route." He looked at Astrid. "Are you and Kate full sisters? Blood sisters?"

"Y—yes," she said. She was still stunned by it all. The past accident and now all of this. Kate could have died two years before and Astrid wouldn't have ever known about it, or anything else, without her. Pregnant? And she lost the baby? How very sad for her. Kate's life hadn't been charmed at all.

"They're fraternal twins," Lincoln said. "Twelve minutes apart. I apologize, but I delivered them."

"Then you would be the best candidate," the doctor told her. "Would you be willing to be tested as a possible donor? We'd have to run tests to ensure you're compatible."

"You mean donate a kidney—my kidney?" Astrid said. Through the entire discussion she just heard, she never considered that possibility.

"Of course, it is a big decision. Plus, we can check to see whether you have PKD too," Stanley said.

"You mean, I can have this kidney disease too?" She'd heard it, but the probability never dawned on her until he said it.

He nodded. "Statistically, because PKD is autosomal, which is non-sex dominant, one of you would have inherited PKD. Fortunately, only one of you has shown symptoms so far. Statistically, fifty percent of children in a family will inherit it. I highly recommend being tested while you are here to be sure. Of course, the decision is yours."

"If I have this disease too, can I still be a donor for her?" Astrid asked.

"I wouldn't recommend it. However, you may never get it," he said. "Odds are if you have it, it would have shown up by now. That is why we call it adult-onset polycystic kidney disease."

"And dialysis?" Astrid asked.

"I won't lie to you about it. It has its disadvantages, as you already surmised, and it does take its toll on the body. Of course, not all transplant patients live an event-free life either. It is a big decision. Either way, if it is more than acute kidney failure, we will have to start her on dialysis, but that is just temporary. What she would really need is a transplant. A close family member is best, such as a sister. As I said, there is no need to go there yet, but we should be prepared."

"I'll have to think about it." Astrid stood up. This was way too much for her. All of this.

"Astrid—" Julia said.

The doctor stood as well. "Of course. Let me know what you decide. I do strongly suggest we check your kidneys while you are here. We can run a simple blood test and urinalysis to check for kidney function and do an ultrasound to check for cysts. It really isn't all that involved. It's been my experience that those that are under the care of a nephrologist fare better than those who aren't."

"Thank you, doctor," Astrid said and stormed from the office.

Lincoln shook his head. "I'm just an old country doctor, but I get the gist of all of this. What can I do to help?"

"Be there for the family. Get her sister tested, if not as a donor, to ensure she doesn't have the kidney disease herself," the doctor told him. "Any questions you or they may have, don't hesitate to contact me."

Lincoln nodded. The two men shook hands and Lincoln departed. He couldn't get it out of his head that this could have been avoided if he had been more insistent with Kate heading to a specialist. Now, he wondered if anyone could do anything at all.

Chapter 22

Astrid stormed from the doctor's office and down the hall, stopping just outside Kate's room. She avoided looking at her through the glass.

Julia grabbed her elbow. "Think about it? What's to think about? If you do have this disease, you'll need proper medical care and, that, I insist on. And if she does need a kidney—she is your sister."

Astrid avoided looking at Julia. "I don't know. Maybe I don't want to know if I have this disease. They say ignorance is bliss. Maybe it is. Look at the last twenty-four hours. I was happy. I was me, until she came here to tell me who I really was. I don't know her. I know nothing about her. I don't know what kind of person she is, her character."

"What kind of person? She traveled here to see you as soon as she knew about you."

"To get a kidney from me."

"I don't believe that," Julia said. "And neither do you. She never mentioned it."

"She was waiting," Astrid said.

"Waiting for what?" Julia asked.

"For me to let down my guard."

"You don't believe that, do you?"

Astrid turned away, stared at Kate momentarily, and looked down. "I don't know what to believe." What else could she say? Nothing.

Julia reached out and took Astrid's hand in hers. "You need to do this test. If not for Kate, for yourself, to see if you have cystic kidneys."

"I can't," Astrid said.

"Why not? What are you afraid of?"

"What if I have this disease too? I'm scared. Maybe it's better if I don't know."

"No," Julia said. "Ignorance may be bliss, love, but it isn't realistic. You need to do this test. All it involves is a urine sample and some blood work. An ultrasound. You have to do it. I insist."

"You heard what that doctor said, even if I do have it, there is no treatment. So why bother?"

"I also know you heard him say that patients under proper care fare better than those who aren't do." Julia released her. "All right—let's look at it another way. If the shoe was on the other foot and I could have this disease, what would you tell me?"

Astrid sighed and shook her head. "You know what I'd say."

"Tell me."

"You'd better get the test done or I'd whip your butt," Astrid said. "It's better to be safe than sorry."

Julia glared and folded her arms across her chest.

"All right. I'll do it," Astrid said. She led the way to the nurses' station, but first she stepped back outside Kate's room and looked in through the glass.

"Do you think the kidney cysts are why she's ill?" Astrid asked.

Julia brought a hand up and rested it on her shoulder. "I don't know, but there's no real way to tell unless they go in there and examine the kidney. Right now, they're doing what they can to avoid surgery."

"Let's go do these tests and get it done," Astrid said.

"My thoughts exactly."

Astrid threw one quick glance over her shoulder at Kate and went to the nurses' station to speak with the doctor.

"Yes, Miss Thomas," the nurse said. "I see that Doctor Stanley already wrote up some orders for you. If you come with me, I'll get you all set up."

"Can she come with me?" Astrid asked, indicating Julia.

The nurse smiled. "I see no reason why not. This way please."

eɔeɔ

Katherine marched from the specialist's office and took a seat alone in the corner of the waiting room, as far apart from Maddy as she could get without leaving Kate.

Lincoln wasn't far behind her. He took a breath, walked over to join her, and sat down next to her. "I'm sorry. I should have stopped her. She is very much your granddaughter," he said.

Katherine looked up at him. She wanted to cry, but she wouldn't. She wouldn't be weak now, not when Kate needed her. "Tell me the truth. Is she going to die?"

"No, of course not."

She studied him. "I said don't lie to me." She couldn't handle any more lies. No more lies!

He pursed his lips. "She's young and strong but, yes, that's always a possibility with kidneys, Katherine. I ran tests back home but, except for you and Kate, I do not practice medicine anymore. Oh God, Katherine, I told you two to get a new doctor." He sighed. "I'm not a specialist. I should have made the appointment for her. I should have made sure she went. I only told her a few days ago."

"It's not your fault," she conceded. "She's stubborn. Nothing you or I said would have prevented her from coming out here." She sighed deeply and turned away from him. "I told you to get rid of the Black one. You lied to me."

"I did get rid of her," he said. "I sent her up north to an orphanage. You didn't really mean to get rid of her, to harm her?"

"I did—back then." Now, she wasn't sure of anything. It was all surreal. She looked across the room at the girl she'd discarded thirty years before. Her son's other daughter. She was alive and here for Kate. Katherine couldn't deny that.

"I'm sorry, Katherine. I couldn't do that. She's my granddaughter too, just like Kate is."

She shifted in her seat to face him. "Oh God, Lincoln, whatever are you talking about? Kate said you told her that. Why on earth would you tell her such a lie?"

"Because it's true. Jax was my son. We both know that."

She shook her head. "Jax was not your son."

"What do you mean? Of course, he was."

"No, he wasn't."

"But you and I—Jackson was away so often. We—I have to be. "

She saw the shock in his eyes, but the truth was the truth. She brought a hand to her chest. "Jackson was Jax's father. Kate is not your granddaughter. Jax was not your son. I should know."

"But you said—you led me to believe." He stared at her. His

mouth dropped open. "You let me believe Jax was my son and that Kate was my granddaughter."

"I'm sorry. I never told you Jax was your son. I can't help it if you believed it."

His words were a forced whisper. "You let me believe. How could you?"

She sighed and felt the tears fighting their way through her icy reserve. "Oh, Lincoln, I'm sorry, but he wasn't your son and Kate's not your granddaughter." She had to tell him. Too much time had passed already, but he deserved it. "I'm very sorry."

He shot to his feet, his eyes glaring. She'd never seen him so angry. She never saw him angry at all.

His words were still a forced whisper. "Sorry? You lied to me? I loved you! All these years while you were married to Jackson, I waited. When he died, I waited again. How could you?"

"I'm sorry, Lincoln." This was all getting to be too much to bear. "This isn't the place or time to discuss this."

"No, it isn't." He sat down, leaned toward her, and continued in a whisper. "Was this a game to you? With the twins? With everyone else? Was it?"

She sighed. "No. It was necessary to protect me, Kate, and my family."

"And the other men, Giles Edmonton, Gary, were those rumors true?"

Her eyes turned icy. "I won't explain myself to you or anyone else, Lincoln."

"And what about Kate?"

"What about her?"

"She worships you."

She turned away from him with her head held high.

"And the other pregnancy," he continued, "the child you lost from your riding accident. Was it mine?"

She shook her head.

"I loved you. I was in love with you. Did you ever love me?"

"Linc—"

"Did you? The truth?" He wouldn't back down. "Answer me."

"No. I've always loved Jackson. He was my life. Even when—" She took a calming breath. "I needed you to be there. I cared for you, but I wasn't in love with you. I'm sorry."

"Sorry? Jackson was a bastard!" His voice rose this time. He couldn't believe what she said. He refused to believe. It wasn't possible. He couldn't remember the exact date their affair began. All he recalled was that he was in love with her from the moment Jackson introduced her to him at their engagement party. He didn't mean to fall in love with his friend's wife.

She hadn't been married to Jackson very long and it just happened. He stayed for dinner with her one night when Jackson was away, traveling to build up the horse farm and its reputation. Jackson's parents, Dixie and Jack, were away…somewhere. Lincoln couldn't recall. He and his sister Betsy—the three of them played cards afterward, as it later became their weekly habit with or without Jackson home, and then he took his sister home. He never knew what drew him back to Katherine that night. He returned to the house to be with her and he was with her in the morning. The affair continued for years. It never really ended.

He interned with his father, another country general practitioner and Thayer family physician and close family friend. When Lincoln saw the lab work his father ran on her, he knew the child had to be his. Katherine wanted a child so badly. Of course, when Katherine became pregnant, he couldn't help but assume he was the father and she never said different. How could he believe anything different? Now, to learn the truth fifty years later like this. How could that be? It wasn't possible. He couldn't contain his fury. For a moment, he was blinded with it. He forgot where he was.

"Damn you, Katherine! Damn you to hell!" He couldn't look at her, but when he heard her sob, heard her sniffle, he couldn't just walk away. He couldn't just turn his back on her. Not when she needed him more than ever. Not after all this time. This woman was in his blood.

She turned away. "I am already there and so is Kate. I am there. First, my boy, Jax, and now Kate, again. All the lies, all my sins, they're coming back at me now through Kate. If she dies, it's all my fault." She buried her face in her hands. "I'm sorry, Lincoln. I'm so sorry."

He had no choice. He was drawn to her as a moth was drawn to a light and certain death. He couldn't resist her. If he had to die for her, so be it. He had no life without her, anyway. He still loved her and nothing would ever change that. He had waited fifty years for her and never married.

He placed his hands on her shoulders. She was trembling and

he knew why. She was scared about Kate, but wouldn't admit it. "You foolish, stubborn woman,"

"I'm no fool, Lincoln," she said. She sniffled.

"Of course you're not," he said and held onto her shoulders, discreetly. "You're the bravest woman I've ever known. The bravest person I've ever known. I'm not going anywhere. I still love you and I always will. I still love Kate, too. I'll be here for both of you."

She stopped crying after a few moments. She would not let anyone see her cry. Never, not even him. He couldn't recall ever seeing her cry, not even when Kate was hospitalized before.

"Excuse me, Lincoln." She stood up. "I should be with Kate," she said and left him alone.

ৼৈৼ

At the other end of the waiting room, Maddy sat alone. She was stunned by it all. How could everything go so wrong so fast? First, Kate discovered the truth, and with it, a chance, though slim, for them all to become a family. And now this. What happened? And she could only imagine what Katherine and Lincoln were discussing across the room. She couldn't hear a word, but Doctor Lincoln didn't seem at all his usual, calm self. And neither did Katherine.

Maddy knew they had a history that went beyond being just friends.

For a moment, she heard Lincoln raise his voice and then it was quiet again.

She didn't even hear her son sit alongside her.

"Mama, are you all right?" Sam asked.

"Livie's other girl, you found her? How?"

"I'm sorry, Mama," he said. His mouth was rigid. "I should have told you, but Kate wanted to see her first and talk to her. I owed it to her to honor her request.

"Of course, you did, son. I just never expected to see her here. To ever see her at all again. She's beautiful, like her mama." She reached out to him and touched his cheek. "Like your sister."

He took her hand into his. "She is, Mama. They both are."

Maddy was at her breaking point, too. "We may lose Kate after all," she said.

"No, we won't, Mama. She's young and strong and stubborn

like you and, I hate to admit this, like Katherine. Those are good odds."

"No. It's all gone so terribly wrong."

He took her hand. "Mama, she'll be fine. She's a lot stronger than her mother was, than Livie was."

"Your sister shouldn't have gotten pregnant. The doctors said it was risky. Lincoln warned her, but she loved Jax so much. We should have supported her. We shouldn't have been against her marriage. We shouldn't have gone along with Katherine and Jackson and your father, and we shouldn't have kept it all from Kate."

"Mama, we did what we thought was right."

"But we didn't do what was right. And now Kate is paying for it. All of it. Our wrongs, our sins. May God help us." She leaned against his shoulder. "We were wrong, Sam. We need to be there for Kate now and her sister. For both of them. We need to do right by them. We need to do right for our family. We were so wrong, son, so wrong."

"We will, Mama. We will." He took her hands in his. "I promise."

She glanced over at Katherine and wondered how two such good friends could grow so far apart? They shared a granddaughter, two now. And yet…

ᴇ/ɔᴇ/ɔ

She remembered the day of their first big fight, the one that put a crack in the wall and started the downfall. They were in Katherine's room at her house, since back then in 1962, the two young women, one White and one Black had to hide their friendship. Katherine had told her the happy news and all she could say was, "Katy."

Katherine was staring in the mirror and fussing with her hair. "Katherine, Maddy. I told you that. I'm going by Katherine now. Katy is for children and so yesterday."

Maddy was seated at the window seat. "Katherine," she said. "I'm happy for you, except…"

Katherine was putting her hair up and turned to face her. "Except what?"

Maddy just spit it out while she had the courage. "I don't think you should marry him."

Katherine stopped what she was doing and placed her hands on both hips. "Why not? He's handsome. He's rich. He comes from a good family. And I love him."

Maddy had to say what she felt. Katherine was her best friend. She loved her. "He's too handsome, and showy. He's not good enough for you."

Pursing her lips, Katherine studied her. "Oh, I get it now, Maddy. You're jealous."

"I'm not jealous."

"Of course, you are. Why else would you say that?"

"I care about you."

"You're jealous because I'm getting married and you're not."

"That's not true, Katy—Katherine, and you know it."

"If that's the way you feel, Maddy, then you don't have to come to my wedding, and you don't have to be my maid of honor." Katherine spun away from her and went back to fussing with her hair. "I wouldn't want you to do anything you don't want to do."

Katy always was stronger. She always had a fierce temper and Maddy was always the first to give in. She didn't want to hurt Katy. She didn't want anyone else to hurt her. "I'm sorry. You're right. I'm jealous."

Katherine faced her with a huge grin. "Now, doesn't it feel better to just come out and say it?"

Maddy nodded. Of course, she wasn't jealous at all. She just didn't want to argue. She just didn't trust Jackson Thayer IV. And, as later experience showed her, she was absolutely right about him. Too right about him.

Of course, her husband George didn't help their friendship either. George was the blacksmith who worked for Jackson Thayer III. And on one of her visits to see Katherine to try and maintain their crumbling friendship, she had met him. They dated and married a year later. He was king of his castle and made sure Maddy knew it.

"I'm not letting my wife be friends with no White woman, so you can get that idea out of your head now, woman. Do you hear me, Maddy?"

"Yes, George." Giving in was so simple, so much easier than arguing with him, especially since Katherine had new friends now with her marriage to Jackson, and Maddy was no longer one of them. The last time she saw Katherine was a week before her

wedding to George. Maddy asked Katherine to be her maid of honor. Of course, it never happened. George wouldn't have a White woman, his boss, at his wedding, and Jackson wouldn't allow it either.

Maddy missed her deeply, but time passed, though its passing did not heal the wounds that shattered her. And when she caught Jackson's eye several years later, it was all so easy. She and Katherine weren't friends anymore and Jackson was so handsome, so charming, so strong, and so virile. He swept her off her feet immediately. Of course, the fairy tale romance didn't last long and didn't end well.

കൈകൈ

Astrid eyed them both from across the room with bitterness and resentment. The White grandmother and the Black grandmother. She didn't get them and didn't care to. They obviously didn't like each other, but here they were, together. That puzzled her. She watched them each interact with the person that sat with them. Katherine seemed to be in a deep discussion with the elderly doctor and then she got up and left to go in and see Kate. Astrid watched as she disappeared into the glass room.

"I wish we had more time. I wish…" Astrid looked up at Julia. "Do you think I should go back and see her now, or should I wait a little longer?"

"Is that what you want, or what you think is the right thing to do?"

"Are you analyzing me now? Please don't. I can't handle it."

Julia shook her head and placed her hand on Astrid's. "No, love. I just want you to be sure."

"I'm not sure of anything anymore. I'd be lying if I said I was. Would you think I was crazy if I told you that I feel close to Kate and need to be there for her?"

"No. Not at all," Julia said. "I knew that, since we came here. If you didn't feel that way, we wouldn't be here now."

Astrid stood up. "I'm going to see her."

"Good call. I'll be here."

Astrid squeezed her hand then released it. She went back to the ICU room. A nurse came out with a tray of tubes of blood and met her. Obviously, she'd just taken blood samples from Kate.

"Is it all right for me to go in?" Astrid asked.

The nurse nodded and moved away, back to the nurse's station.

Katherine was seated by the bed, her back toward the door and Astrid's entrance.

Astrid took a deep breath, slowly walked to the bed, and sat down in a nearby chair, across from the other woman on the other side of Kate's bed.

Katherine eyed her then stood up and walked out of the room.

Can't even sit in the same room with me, huh, Grandmother? Guilt got you by the throat, or is it my blackness that turns you off? It certainly didn't repulse my daddy, my mother being Black, or I wouldn't be here now. She glanced at Kate. She wouldn't be here now either.

"I wish we had more time to talk," she said to Kate. "It's times like this I'm reminded of how very short life is. This wasn't supposed to happen. You're only thirty. I thought I've have more time to hate you, to resent you. Were you angry when you found out the truth? Were you scared? I am scared to death." She leaned in closer so that her mouth was closer to Kate's ear. "They say you may need a new kidney. Maybe, maybe not. And that I'm the best candidate because we're sisters. Even though we're twins, my kidneys are fine. Of course, they can't guarantee they'll stay that way. Do I do it or not, if you need it? We don't even know each other. What would you do? Would you donate your kidney to me? A total stranger? Of course, we're not really total strangers, are we?"

She glanced over Kate from toe to head and at the tubes feeding into her veins, nose, and hand. Slowly, cautiously, she reached out a hand and laid it on top of Kate's. They certainly didn't look alike. Light brown skin against the white. They both had long, slender fingers, but Kate obviously didn't bite her nails. Bet she didn't have a reason to do so. Astrid's warm touch met very hot skin. "You're so hot, but you're clammy, too." She stood up, pulled the covers up, and tucked the edge under Kate's neck as best she could without disturbing the tubes. She felt wetness on her cheek. A tear had fallen. She wiped it away with the back of her hand.

"Thank you for coming, for bringing the journal." She ran her hand along the cold metal bed rail. "I don't know if you can hear me. Some people say when a person is unconscious or in a coma you can hear, and others say you can't. Julia believes you can, so

I'm going to talk. I really don't know what to say. I always thought I was an only child. I guess you believed the same thing. I have no memory of you. No memory of our mom and dad, of anything, but I guess we couldn't, seeing how we were just born when I was sent away." Tears fell from her eyes and backed into her throat. "I'm trying not to cry here. Why am I crying? I don't know you. And you don't know me." She reached out a hand and touched Kate's cheek then pulled back. "I'm sorry. I can't do this. Not now." She stood up and wiped her eyes with the back of her hands. "I'll be back," she said. "I promise. I won't leave you."

She ran to the door, pushed it open, dashed through it, and stopped in her tracks. Outside, she took a soothing breath to calm herself. She couldn't even look back.

"She was very angry when she found out the truth," Katherine said. "She left home without a word to anyone to come and see you. She wouldn't be deterred by anyone."

Astrid had no words. The anger within her was overwhelming. If she didn't step away, she couldn't be held responsible for her actions toward this...person.

Katherine took a step toward her. "You owe me nothing, but if you could save her life, whatever you can do for her, I'd be eternally grateful to you."

Astrid spun to face her. This woman had gall. "Do you really think I care what you say? *If* I help her, it wouldn't be for you, any of you." She rushed off in a huff.

Katherine placed a hand on the cold wooden door but couldn't go back in, at least not right now. As much as she hated to admit it, Astrid was right. But it was the green eyes glaring at her that unnerved her more than anything. Those were her son's eyes and Kate's. They were her eyes looking back at her, deep into voids she hadn't gone into in a very long time. They were areas of her soul that she had given over to darkness a long time ago, that began with her first affair, continued onward through her husband's adulteries, and suffocated her with her son's death. If Kate died, Katherine didn't want to live anymore. Kate had been her only reason for living. Kate was her savior in an otherwise evil world.

Chapter 23

Lincoln sat in the waiting room. A quick glance at his silver watch showed that it was nearing ten o'clock and he couldn't stifle his yawn. If he was tired, he could just imagine how tired the two women must be by now. With the exception of speaking with the nephrologist earlier, neither one of them ever left Kate's bedside. That concerned him deeply. Neither woman was getting any younger. He knew the added stress of fear and worry about Kate added its toll on them, especially since neither showed any interest in eating. Something had to be done. He decided to take the direct approach and try to reason with them.

He stood up, stretched out his arms, and went inside the room. There they sat. Maddy was in a chair on one side of Kate's bed. She held onto Kate's left hand. Katherine was on the other side holding Kate's other hand. They looked like bookends.

He would have laughed, if not for the seriousness of it all. And there was Kate's sister seated in the back of the room on the sofa with her friend. It was good to see her safe. Sam and Elsa sat on the other end of the sofa and held hands.

Lincoln walked to the end of the bed. "It's getting late. You've both been up all day. You need to get some sleep. You both don't need to be here."

They ignored him, both of them.

"There's nothing you can do for Kate. You should get some rest," he repeated.

Katherine ignored him. Maddy spoke. "Thank you, Doctor Lincoln, for your concern, but I'm staying."

He sighed. He knew he'd get better results if he hit his head against the wall, but he tried again. Their welfare concerned him. He didn't want either one of them to worry themselves sick. He still blamed himself for Kate being in that bed and for not being able to save her mother. "You both know I'm right. You both need to rest. With the three of you, you don't all have to be here. You can take turns," he suggested.

"Forget it, Lincoln," Katherine said. "I'm not leaving her."

"Neither am I," Maddy said.

"Ladies—"

Maddy cut him off. "Thank you, Doctor Lincoln, but I'm staying."

Lincoln brought a hand to his neck and rubbed it. He turned around and caught Sam's eye. He went outside and Sam followed him.

"You're right, Doctor Linc. Mama needs to rest. They both do," Sam began. Julia stepped outside to meet them just as Sam spoke. "Those are two stubborn women, Doctor Linc," he continued.

"Son," Lincoln said, "you have no idea." He sighed. "And her sister?"

"Believe me, she's stubborn too, just like Kate is."

"Terrific. They all need to rest, Sam. You know I'm right. They need to eat too."

"You'll get no argument from me," Sam said.

"May I say something?" Julia asked.

"Please do," Lincoln said.

"I see they both care about Kate, but maybe it is also something more. The two women don't like each other, that's obvious. Perhaps, neither wants to leave before the other does."

"Is that a professional opinion, Doctor?" Lincoln asked her, impressed by her observation.

"No, just an observation."

"You're correct there. And Maddy might leave, but Katherine won't. She raised Kate." He appreciated her insight, professional and otherwise. At least, he was still of sound mind and body. He wondered sometimes. Katherine drove him to distraction.

"After her son Jax killed himself?" Julia said.

"Y—yes," Lincoln said, eyeing her.

"We know," Julia said. "Kate came and told Astrid everything."

Of course, she did. *Oh, Kate.* "I'm going to get some assistance here. I'll be right back," Lincoln said and walked away.

"How long has he known them?" Julia asked

"Longer than he's known me—fifty-two years."

"Incredible," Julia said. "Have they always hated each other?"

"As long as I've known them," Sam said.

"There's no need for both of them to be here. Astrid and I are staying."

"Thanks. That could make a difference, with Mama, at least." He extended his hand. "Sam Johnson. We didn't get a chance to meet."

She took it and grinned. "Julia Comedy, I'm Astrid's...best friend."

"I'm glad to see Astrid here. Really glad," he said. Mere words couldn't express his true feelings about it. "It was important for Kate to see her and explain everything. Not for her, but it was important that Astrid knew. She felt she owed it to her."

"I understand," she said. "And as much as it hurt Astrid, she needed to know."

Just then, Lincoln returned with the nephrologist in tow. "Okay, let's go and see what we can do," Lincoln said and led the way back to Kate's room.

൚൙൚

"Ladies, there is really no need for both of you to be here all night. Kate is unconscious and may remain that way until we get her stabilized," the nephrologist said.

"Can you guarantee she won't wake up while we're gone?" Katherine asked.

"Or that she'll be alive in the morning?" Maddy added.

The doctor eyed Lincoln. "No, I can't guarantee either scenario."

"Then we know all we need to," Maddy said. "Thank you for your time, Doctor."

Doctor Stanley tried again. "Ladies, there's no real reason for you to stay when you could be resting."

"Thank you, Doctor," Katherine said and turned her attention back to Kate.

The nephrologist exchanged glances with Julia and Lincoln, shrugged his shoulders, and left. Lincoln walked over to the end of Kate's bed and tried another tactic. "Ladies, what do you think Kate would say to you if she knew you weren't taking care of yourselves? She'd be furious and neither one of you want that, do you?" Silence met him. "You both need to take care of your-selves if you want to help Kate. You know I'm right."

Julia stepped forward. "I know you don't know me or trust me, but I liked Kate, right from the moment I met her. There's no need for both of you to be here when Astrid and I will be."

Sam went to Maddy. "Mama, you need to rest. You made a long flight. You haven't eaten. Kate needs you to be strong for her. Both of you women need to take care of yourselves for her."

Maddy studied Kate and Katherine and sighed. The last thing she wanted to do was abandon her granddaughter, but the fact was, she was exhausted. She had no choice but to give in. Sam was right. She hated to do this, but—

"Katherine, you'll be here for her. I know you won't let any-thing happen to her."

Katherine glanced up at her. Their eyes met for the first time in so long a time. Katherine nodded and went back to staring at Kate. That eased Maddy.

"You'll let us know if anything changes, if she wakes up?" she asked.

"Of course we will," Lincoln said.

Maddy stood up. "All right, son. Just for a few hours, but we come right back." She led the way out of the room. Out in the waiting room, she stopped and looked back. "I don't want to leave her. What if—"

Sam placed his hand on shoulder. "Mama, the hotel is ten minutes away by taxi. Katherine is here. Astrid is here. Kate will be fine."

"I know Katherine won't let any harm come to her. She'd fight the Devil himself to protect her, but this Astrid. I don't know her."

"She's Kate's sister. She's Livie's daughter. Isn't that enough?"

It should be, but the fact was, she didn't know the girl. "Sam—"

"Mama, trust me. She's a stubborn woman, as stubborn as the rest of the women in this family. She took on you and Katherine and is here for Kate. Doesn't that count for something?"

"Of course, it does. Of course." Anyone who took on Kathe-rine and lived to tell the tale was a hero in Maddy's book.

"Mama," Sam said. "Kate and Astrid just met yesterday and that girl is here now. I trust her."

That was good enough for her. She brought up her hand and patted his chin. "This goatee beard of yours, son, I'm not so sure of it."

"I like it," Elsa said from behind as she joined them.

"Then it stays," Maddy said. "I am hungry."

She led the way to the elevator.

"Sam," Lincoln called from behind them. They stopped and turned. Sam took a few steps back to meet with him.

"What hotel—where are you staying?" Lincoln asked and removed his cell phone from inside his sport jacket.

"Hotel Mark, Seventy-Seventh and Madison. We have two rooms. We haven't checked out." Sam gave him the phone number and room numbers. "Would you like me to get two more rooms for you and Miss Katherine?"

"Yes, Sam, thank you. That would be wise, though I don't think she's going to use them."

Sam reached out a hand to touch Lincoln's shoulder. "I don't know. You were pretty convincing in there. Thank you."

"You take care of your mama and wife and we'll all look after Kate," Lincoln said and forced a weary grin.

Sam extended his hand. "Sounds good. We'll be back first thing in the morning, or when Mama says to, whichever comes first. Please, call us if anything changes."

Lincoln shook it. "You know I will."

Sam released him and went to meet up with his mama and wife.

Lincoln watched them leave. At least he was able to get one of the two women to get some rest. Maddy was always the more sensible one. Of course, he didn't know her really well, certainly not as well as he knew Katherine. It was a shame their friendship didn't endure time. Of course, he knew Jackson and his parents didn't make it easy for Katherine to maintain it.

He turned back and eyed the ICU room Kate was in. Now only if he could get the other stubborn woman to listen. Now that Maddy was gone, he knew that getting Katherine to rest wouldn't happen tonight. Of course, that didn't mean he wouldn't try. He returned inside. He glanced at Julia and she nodded. Astrid sat next to her and leaned her head against her shoulder and dozed in and out. The girl needed to sleep too, and he tried to remember if he even saw her leave to get something to eat. He was glad she wasn't alone and had a doctor friend with her. At least she was in good hands. She was obviously as stubborn as her grandmothers and sister and that was no surprise to him. No surprise at all.

He went to Katherine's side, but before he had a chance to speak, Katherine did. "I'm not leaving her." She didn't even look at him.

He sat down in a chair next to her and whispered, "You're not getting any younger, Katherine. You need your rest. It's been a long day—"

"I beg your pardon. I'm perfectly fine."

"Katherine—"

She raised a hand at him. "Go if you want. I'm staying."

യായ

Daylight broke over New York City quickly the next day. Maddy paced in the living area of Kate's hotel room where she spent the night. Kate's belongings remained behind in the closet and her toiletries on the bathroom sink. Maddy didn't want to remove anything. It comforted her to be at least a little bit close to Kate. Right now, after everything that had happened with all of it coming to a head, she'd take anything she could get. Of course, she took most comfort from the small plastic card Kate left standing up along the sink. She very much needed to hear the words on it. *God grant me the serenity to accept the things I cannot change. Courage to change the things I can, and Wisdom to know the difference. But God, grant me the Courage not to give up on what I think is right even though I think it is hopeless.* The words comforted her. Maddy needed all of God's help now. The words were familiar. She knew the prayer well. It had helped her over the years to get through some rough times. It endeared Kate to her even more that the younger woman held this prayer close to her.

Maddy walked across the room back and forth a few times to ease the anxiety stirring in her. It did nothing to soothe her nerves. There was only one thing on her mind, the only thing she wanted to do now. She didn't want to wake them, but she didn't want to run out on them either. They didn't need to worry about her also. She stepped outside across the hall and knocked on the door to their room.

After a few minutes, she heard Sam unlock the door. "Mama, what's wrong?" He was wearing pajama bottoms.

She stepped inside and he closed the door. "I'm going back to the hospital."

He glanced at the window and then faced her with a perplexed look. "Mama, what time is it?"

"I don't know. I left my watch at home and I didn't check before I came over here."

He went up to her. "Did you even sleep last night?"

She touched his chin. "I dozed off a few times. I just came over to let you know I was going back."

"Give me a few minutes and we'll go together," he said and headed toward the bed.

"No. You don't have to. I'll take a taxi."

"Not a chance, Mama."

"I can take care of myself, son. Thank you."

"I know that, but I don't want to have to worry about you too."

His concern for her welfare always touched her. Even when he was a little boy, she and Livie were always his concern. "All right, son, but don't wake Elsa."

"Wake her? She's already up and in the shower. She couldn't sleep last night either."

Maddy shook her head. "None of us can afford to get sick, son."

"I know. Look, let me get dressed and we'll come get you. We'll get something to eat at the cafeteria. At least we'll be nearby in the hospital."

"Fine. I'll wait for you," she said. She opened the door and left.

Elsa came out of the shower in a fluffy robe. Her hair was wrapped up in a towel. "Was that Mama? Is she all right?"

"Says she is, but she has that funny feeling of hers," he said. "And she didn't sleep either."

Elsa went to him, wrapped her arms about his waist from behind, and kissed him on the shoulder. "Did she say she had her feeling?"

"No. Didn't have to. I saw it in her eyes." He took her face into his hands. "God, baby, I'm so scared for Kate."

She reached up and took his hands in hers. "I know, Sam, but she's going to be fine. I have a feeling too." She leaned forward, kissed him on the lips, and then stepped back. "Remember, I'm a health care professional."

"You better get dressed, or I won't be able to control myself, and Mama will leave without us."

She patted his face. "All right."

"We'll get breakfast at the hospital. It'll make Mama feel better," he said as he watched her walk away and back into the bathroom. "I never get tired of looking at you, Mrs. Johnson."

She turned around and blew him a kiss. "I love you too, Mister Johnson, and when Kate is all better, I will show you how much."

He caught the kiss in his hand and stared after her. He couldn't imagine his life without her. He knew exactly how his sister felt for Jax. *Oh, Livie. I'm so sorry, sis. When you love someone, nothing else matters. Nothing. I wish I knew that then.*

Twenty years of marriage with Elsa and he still loved her as much as he did the first day he fell in love with her. It was the day he lost his best friend to a major infection. She sat with him afterward, though her shift at the hospital ended hours earlier. She listened while he expressed his fears about life, death, and war. She evidently knew he shouldn't be alone. She invited him to her apartment for dinner. One thing led to another as they often did. On that cheerful note, he moved to get dressed.

☙❧

Astrid stepped outside the ICU room to get a drink of water from the nearby water fountain. The cool water felt good going down her dry, irritated throat. Even when she didn't cry, she managed to swallow tears.

That was when she heard the voice from behind her. "I'm sorry, child. I'd like to apologize to you."

Astrid stood up from drinking. "I'd rather not speak with you."

"I know. I just wanted to explain. I need to say—"

Astrid spun around to face her. This woman had gall too. This was too unbelievable. "I don't care what you need. Where were you when I needed you? Kate came to tell me about my parents, and all of you. She obviously cared and wanted to do right by me. Where were you? Why didn't you come and tell me?"

Maddy just stared and shook her head.

"You can't answer that, can you?" Astrid moved to walk away from her, but then stopped. "You know, I can get that other grandmother's reasoning. I'm Black, she's White. She didn't want me. But you're Black and I'm Black, what's your excuse?"

Maddy moved to open her mouth, stopped, and then said, "I'm sorry. I was wrong, so wrong."

"Just leave me alone. You weren't there when I needed you, and I don't need you now. Just stay away. You have nothing to say that I want to hear and I have nothing to say to you."

❧❧

Maddy watched her go. Why didn't she answer her? She couldn't. What could she say? The truth? Maybe she should have said that. Easier said than done. She was still so shaken up with everything. How on earth did Katherine remain so strong and unyielding with all of this unraveling around them?

"Mama," Elsa said from behind her. "Are you all right? Did you get a chance to speak with Kate's sister?"

"That child hates my guts. She won't talk to me. How do I make it up to her and Kate?" Maddy sensed the void expanding out between her and the girls and it saddened her deeply.

Elsa placed her hands on Maddy's shoulders from behind. "Oh, Mama, all you can do is the best you can and leave the rest in God's hands. Just tell her the truth."

Maddy leaned against her. "You're right, child. I believe in the almighty and, with him, all things are possible, but will he forgive me? Will they?"

"Come on, Mama." Elsa took her hand. "We'll go sit down and say a prayer for Kate before we go back into see her."

❧❧

Back in Kate's room, Astrid walked in with Julia and found the two women sitting near the bed on opposite sides. Katherine kept up her bedside vigil at Kate's side, as did Maddy. Neither paid any attention to the other, except to hear anything the nurse or doctor may have said to the other. As much as Astrid hated to admit it, the sight touched her deeply. These two women were rotten to the core, as far as she was concerned, but here they were in the same room for Kate.

Kate? Her sister? That feeling of connection was strange and overwhelming, yet comforting at the same time. How could that possibly be?

She walked over to the bed on the side Maddy was sitting, took a chair by the wall, and sat down near the head of the hospital bed. Should Kate open her eyes, even for just an instant, Astrid wanted her to know that she was here in the room with her. Why she needed to let her know that, Astrid couldn't explain, not even to herself.

Kate was breathing shallow. The silence in the room made everything sound louder than it really should be. Astrid reached out and took Kate's hand in hers. Kate was hot to the touch. She didn't stir and, if not for the machines showing her heartbeat, pulse, and blood pressure, Astrid wouldn't know she was alive.

Suddenly, she noticed Kate's eyelids flutter. She had to blink a few times to ensure she wasn't dreaming. She wasn't.

Kate opened her eyes and looked right at her. "As—Astrid?"

Kate's voice was barely audible, but Astrid had heard it. She wasn't dreaming. She leaned over her. "I'm here, Kate. I'm here with you."

Katherine jumped to her feet at the same time Sam entered. "Get a doctor now!" both grandmothers hollered at almost the same moment.

Sam rushed back out of the room.

Katherine rushed to Kate's side and took her other hand in hers. "I'm here. Grandmother is here."

Maddy was on her feet next to Astrid. "We're here, Kate. All of us."

Astrid noticed that Kate couldn't keep her eyes open.

"Grandmother?" Kate whispered.

"I'm here, darling," Katherine said. "I'm here and I'm not going anywhere."

"We're all her for you, child," Maddy said. "You need to rest and build up your strength."

Astrid held onto her hand. "They're right. You need to rest. We're here."

"Astrid, I—I'm—so sorry," Kate stammered.

"Don't you worry about anything. None of it was your fault," Astrid said.

The machines started to beep louder and quicker.

"You're here?" Kate said. "Astrid, you're really here?"

"I'm here and I'm not going anywhere. You get better and

we'll get to know each other. We'll talk and do the town." She leaned closer to her ear. "Julia gave me our mother's journal."

Kate blinked and forced a smile. "She—loved you. They—both—did."

Astrid felt tears forcing their way through. "They loved both of us."

"They—wanted—you, both—of…" Kate's eyes closed. The machines lowered in volume and rhythm.

Astrid felt the tears fall and didn't care. She found the words falling from her lips. "Kate, hang in there. Please. Please, don't leave."

The nephrologist hurried in with another man beside him. Sam and Lincoln were close behind.

"She woke up," Katherine said. "She spoke to us. That's a good sign, right?"

"She did speak," Astrid said. "Then she went back to sleep."

The two men rushed to Kate's side, ignoring the women. The kidney doctor scanned her machines while the other man viewed her chart. Both men looked at Lincoln.

Lincoln turned to Katherine. "Let's go outside."

Katherine resisted. "Wh—what? Why? What for?"

"Just for a few minutes," he said.

"No. I'm not leaving her," Katherine said.

Julia went to Astrid. "Let's go outside."

Astrid eyed Julia and the two men. "Why? What's going on? She woke up. She spoke. That has to be good, right?"

"Let the doctors do their job," Julia said.

"No. I want to know what's wrong," Astrid said.

Two nurses walked in wearing surgical garb, pushed in a gurney before them, and set it directly next to Kate's bed. They wore green hospital scrubs and scarves on their heads and moved toward Kate. White masks were about their necks.

"They're taking her into surgery," Doctor Stanley said.

"Surgery?" Maddy said. "What surgery? You said she needed to be stabilized first. She was getting better. She spoke to us."

"Her condition has changed. We have to remove the bad kidney," the unknown man said.

"And who the hell are you?" Katherine demanded.

"I'm sorry," Doctor Stanley said. "There wasn't time. This is Craig Thorne. He's the urologist who will do the surgery."

The nurses were busy, removing the tubes from the wall, unplugging cords, and putting them onto vertical posts attached to the gurney.

"You said she was getting better," Katherine said. "You lied to us?"

"Take her out," the urologist said to the nurses. He faced the family. "We'll do what we can. She's young and strong. You have to let us do our job."

"Wait a minute! Who are you? We don't know who you are," Katherine shot out.

Lincoln came up beside her. "Let them do their job."

"She was getting better," Katherine declared. "She was getting better. She woke up."

Astrid didn't know what to do. She looked at Julia. Julia took her hand. "They need to take her."

The nurses were joined by two men who entered the room. Together the four of them lifted Kate's motionless body from the bed onto the gurney and began wheeling her toward the door.

"I want to know what's going on and I want to know now!" Katherine demanded. "Or you're not taking her anywhere!"

Lincoln grabbed her from behind and moved her aside.

"Get your hands off of me, Lincoln!" she yelled and shifted in his grip, trying to break free. "What are you doing? Let go of me!"

"Stand there and shut up. Now!" he said. "She's going into surgery and there's nothing we can do for her now, except pray!"

She stopped fighting and lowered her head.

Astrid was stunned into silence by his actions. Since she'd been at the hospital, this white-haired white man seemed to cower to Katherine. Astrid guessed he had either had enough, or he was trying to help Kate. Either way, she appreciated his presence. Lincoln was the man who was nice to her mother and took care of her. He was also the man who couldn't save her life.

From behind, she heard Maddy, Sam, and Elsa begin reciting the Lord's Prayer. Astrid didn't pray. Prayers were for other people.

Chapter 24

Katherine stormed out of the ICU room and into the waiting room. Lincoln was right behind her.

She whirled on him. "Exactly what is going on, Lincoln?" she yelled. "How dare you hold me back? I don't know who those men are—"

"Damn it, Katherine," he said softly. "You could test the patience of a saint. They're doctors and we need to let them do their job. You already met the kidney specialist."

"What kind of place is this? At home, the doctors come out and at least introduce themselves before they take someone away and cut them up," she said.

"This isn't home. Now relax."

"Relax?" she shot back. "We're in a hospital surrounded by Yankees."

"You need to calm down. I understand you're frightened," Lincoln said.

"I'm not frightened!"

"You always become hostile when you're frightened," he said. "We have to let the doctors do their job."

She relented and pulled away from him. "You know nothing about me, Lincoln."

"I know enough."

"Can you tell us what is going on?" Maddy asked him as she made her way into the waiting room, with Sam and Elsa close behind.

"Sit down, all of you." He waited until they all sat. Katherine was the last one and then he sat down next to her. "I spoke with both the urologist and the nephrologist, the urinary and kidney doctors. Kate isn't responding as they hoped she would. They fear it's something in the kidney."

"Like they said earlier," Sam recalled. "The kidney doctor had said something about it when he met with us."

"Yes," Lincoln said. "They're going to do a test to see what could be causing the blockage and see if they can repair it. If not, they may have to remove the kidney. They're also going to start her on dialysis, temporarily."

Katherine brought her hands to her chest and clasped them together. "Dialysis? Oh God, they said she wouldn't need that. They lied?"

Maddy brought her hands to her mouth. "Is it that bad?"

"They didn't lie," Lincoln said. "Things are not going as they should. Kate is not responding to standard treatment. The infection has developed into acute kidney failure. They're going to do a test to check the kidney and possibly do surgery. They'll probably need to get her started on dialysis too in order to filter her system until her kidneys heal and restore their normal function."

"If they heal?" Astrid said. "That is the question, right?"

"Yes," Lincoln confirmed.

"But that was what they were trying for and it hasn't worked," Astrid said.

"This is why they're doing this test and, if necessary, going to remove the kidney."

"What kind of test are we talking about?" Maddy asked. "Is it dangerous?"

"From what I've been told, it is relatively simple," Lincoln said.

"For them, you mean," Katherine remarked, folding her arms across her chest.

Lincoln ignored her. "They're going to anesthetize her and inject a dye into the ureter, the tube leading from the kidney down to the bladder. They want to see what is causing the blockage of urine. If it is a stone, they can remove it. If they need to remove the kidney, they can do that too. I've asked around, and she's in excellent hands."

"She is in a top notch facility here," Julia said. "She will get the best care. I assure you."

"And exactly what do you know about it?" Katherine asked.

"She's a medical doctor," Astrid said. "A psychiatrist. She knows a lot of the doctors here."

"Not all, but some. They're very good here. I wouldn't worry if I were you," Julia said.

"But you're not us," Maddy said. "You're not her family."

"No, but she's mine and I trust her, and I think Kate would too." Astrid knew she had said more than she meant to but, right now, she could care less. These were the last people on earth she cared about, or what they thought. "You can all do what you want. I'm supporting whatever helps Kate and, if this is what it takes, then we do it."

"Seeing we have no choice, anyway," Lincoln said. "It is a moot point now."

Katherine got up in a huff and stalked from the room and down the hall.

"Excuse me y'all," Lincoln said and followed her.

Maddy got up and left quickly too with Sam and Elsa on her heels.

⚘

When Lincoln found her, Katherine was out in the hall near the operating rooms. Her arms were folded against her chest, in defiance against the world, no doubt.

This woman was going to be the death of him. He knew it, but he couldn't stop loving her and worrying about her. He stepped toward her, stopped just behind her, placed his hands on her upper back along her neck, and rested them on her shoulders. She was tense all over.

"I know you didn't want to hear any of this, but you all had to be told," he said.

She didn't face him. "Tell me the truth, Lincoln, how bad is it? Really? I must know. Will she die?"

"Katherine, we should wait to see results—"

She looked up at him. The years of guilt were etched deeply in her face along with worry. "I want to know," she said. "Please, Lincoln. Tell me."

"If she continues going downhill, her other organs will shut down as well. Yes," he said. "Many times other organs fail before the kidneys do. It's a good sign that they haven't, which leads them to believe hers is an abnormality within her kidneys."

"Good sign?" She sighed, brought her hands up, and buried her face in them. "Oh God. I can't lose her. I just can't."

"Come with me," he said.

"No. I'm not leaving her."

He took her hands in his. "We're not leaving her. Just come with me, please."

Back in the waiting room, Astrid watched the other half of her family. Sam held his mother against him and held Elsa's hand. The man and woman appeared to be very much in love. They never left each other's side, except to run an errand. Was that what her parents looked like? They remained with the older woman—her grandmother. Her mother's mother. *Blacker than I am and she gave me up? Hypocrite!*

Julia turned to Astrid. "We should get something to eat."

"I'm not hungry." Her stomach was tossing about and food was the last thing she was thinking about.

Julia stood up and waited. "Nevertheless, we're getting something, anyway."

"You're getting really bossy lately, you know that?" Astrid said.

"I thought that was the reason you fell in love with me. The fact that I don't back down from you when you get in a huff," Julia said with her hands on her hips. "Now let's go to the cafeteria."

"I am not in a huff." Astrid got to her feet. "But if I must." She took a quick glance at the three people across from her, then took the lead, headed off down the hall to the stairway entrance, swung open the door, and began the descent downstairs. All the way down, all she heard was the footsteps of her and Julia.

Astrid entered the cafeteria, gathered a tray from the stack along the wall, and stood in line. Julia stepped up behind her. Astrid took a burger and fries plate from the shelf of hot foods and almost threw it onto the tray. Julia copied the choice, but instead placed her plate of food gently down. Astrid grabbed two cups off the shelf and, at the soda machine, filled each cup with iced tea, placed a cover on top of each, and grabbed two straws from the dispenser. At the register, Julia paid and they moved away to find a seat. The cafeteria was a good size and could seat a large number of people, but not so large that you couldn't see other customers at their tables. Most of the tables were now empty.

Astrid noticed Katherine and Lincoln seated at a table in the back. She was going to sit across the room when Julia stepped past her and walked to a table a few steps away from the older couple. She sat down and motioned for Astrid to follow.

Astrid held her tray and approached. "Why did you sit here when there are so many other places to sit?"

"What's the difference?" Julia said.

She lifted the bun from her burger, took off the tomato slices, and placed them beside it on the plate.

Astrid motioned with her head at the older couple. "Them."

Julia glanced around. "Oh, for heaven's sake, sit down, love. You're bound to run into them while you're here. Don't let them get to you."

"I'm not. I just don't want to sit near them," Astrid said.

Julia opened a packet of ketchup, spread it on the burger, and replaced the bun. "You're free to sit somewhere else."

Astrid waited, expecting Julia to get up. She sighed in frustration, knowing Julia wouldn't. She sat down next to her, side by side. "This won't work."

"What won't?" Julia bit into the burger and chewed.

"Don't give me that innocent look of 'I don't know what you're talking about.' That person threw me away. I'm not talking to her."

Julia swallowed and wiped her mouth with the paper napkin. "I *don't* know what you're talking about. Who says you have to talk to her?"

"Just so we're clear," Astrid declared. "I don't want you playing psychiatrist with me and them. You hear me, Julia?"

"I don't play at being a psychiatrist, love. I am one, and a very good one at that." Julia took a fry and dipped it into the glob of ketchup she'd put on the side of her plate.

"Too good, if you ask me. Just don't do it. Besides, it won't work," Astrid said as she took the sliced tomatoes off of Julia's plate and put them on her own burger. "Those people didn't want me. They proved that."

Julia eyed her while taking bites from her burger and eating a few fries. Astrid could sense someone else looking at her too. She glanced sideways and saw Katherine staring at her. Astrid turned away and tried to ignore it.

She pushed the tray away to the side of the table. "It's no use. I'm not hungry."

"Try and eat something," Julia said. "A couple of fries. Drink the tea. I don't want you getting sick." She picked up the cup and offered it to her.

Astrid took it, tried a few quick sips, and set the cup back down. "I can't. I'm not hungry. Besides," she replied. "She's staring at me."

"Who is?" Julia lifted her cup of iced tea from the tray and sipped from the straw.

"*Who* is? That woman, my so-called grandmother."

"Oh, ignore her." Julia set the cup down. "She probably thinks you're beautiful. I do."

"I'm serious, Julia," Astrid snapped. Most times, she appreciated her lover's good humor, but this wasn't one of those times.

"So am I." Julia took her hand in hers. "She's probably realizing what she gave up."

Astrid looked back and stared at Katherine, but instead of turning away from her, Katherine didn't flinch. Not only did that rattle Astrid, it irritated her.

Astrid stood up. "Well, I've had enough."

"Let it be. She's not hurting anyone," Julia said.

"I don't want to be stared at. She hasn't the right." Astrid stormed away from the table, marched right up to theirs, and stopped. Julia was on her heels.

Katherine looked up at her. There they were, green eyes staring at green eyes. One set mature and one younger set examining the other one.

"What are you looking at?" Astrid demanded.

"You. You're a beautiful girl," Katherine said matter-of-factly and her stare didn't waver.

"Take a photo, *Grandmother*. It'll last longer."

"I would like to."

Astrid backed up a step. The woman's reply unnerved her. How many times had she told someone that remark? On a subway ride when someone had stared at her, on a bus, in line at a supermarket. No one ever replied in the affirmative, if they replied at all. People had acted as if they had never seen a Black woman with green eyes before and who knew? Maybe they hadn't.

Katherine stood up. Her voice had a melancholy tone. "I'm sorry, so sorry."

"Sorry? Sorry about what, Grandmother? Sorry Kate is ill and may die? Sorry that my parents are dead? Sorry that you threw me away, or sorry that you have to confront my Black face here and now?"

Julia grabbed Astrid's arm from behind. "Astrid, calm down.

This is not the place or time. It really isn't." She faced Katherine. "I'm sorry. I'm Julia Comedy."

"Don't you stand there and be civil to her!" Astrid snapped.

"You need to calm down," Julia said softly. "This won't do anyone any good."

"It will do me lots of good!" Astrid spun on her heel, turning back to Katherine, to just catch sight of the older woman as she reached out a hand to her and then recoiled.

"I'm sorry," Katherine repeated. "You're a very beautiful girl. Your father was my son."

"And he was my father!" Astrid advanced on her. "And he'd be alive if all you had just been there for him. But no, you were all a bunch of bigots. Stay away from me!" She held up her hands in defense. "Just stay away!"

Astrid stormed away.

"I'm sorry, but you all hurt her very deeply," Julia said. "I don't know what you all were thinking, if you were thinking at all, but what you did was very wrong."

"I know," Katherine said simply. "I know that now. I'm so very sorry. Please, tell her that."

Julia looked at this woman. She was not the same tower of strength, or pillar of bigotry that Julia had first encountered. This woman was softening. The point was becoming dulled and lifeless and, evidently, the fight was taken out of her, or would soon be.

Julia couldn't guess the woman's age the first time she had seen her in the waiting room because of her vitality and the heavy makeup she wore, but now the makeup was gone and Julia saw up close the wrinkles and crow's feet of time's passing.

"I really think you need to tell her that yourself," Julia said.

"How? How do I do that?" Katherine asked almost pleadingly.

"That, Mrs. Thayer, I can't answer. Excuse me." Julia nodded at Lincoln and left.

"She's a beautiful girl, isn't she?" Katherine said.

"Yes, she is," Lincoln agreed.

"She looks so much like her father."

"I noticed that too."

"Kate looks more like her mother."

"We should sit back down," Lincoln said. "You need to eat something."

"No. I'm going back and wait to hear about Kate. I shouldn't have left."

He placed his hand on her wrist. "You haven't eaten anything today."

"I said—" She swallowed hard and removed his grip from her. She didn't want to argue, especially with him, especially now. "No." She marched away.

ℰↄℰↄ

Astrid didn't see or hear them approach her back in the waiting room. She wasn't listening much to anything or anyone except Julia and news about Kate. She didn't much care about anything else at this junction.

"May I join you?" Maddy asked. Sam was with her by her side and Elsa in tow.

Astrid looked at her. This woman was no better than the other one. She wondered if the two women knew just how very much alike, they were. "No," she replied. "I don't think so."

"She just wants to talk to you," Sam said.

"Sam," Maddy rebuked. She nodded to him and he left, reluctantly, with Elsa.

"I would like very much to speak with you," Maddy said.

"Why? What could you possibly say that I would want to hear?" Astrid said.

"I'm sorry for what happened, for what we did?" Maddy said. "It was wrong, terribly wrong. I was wrong, so horribly—"

Astrid sprang to her feet. "You're as bad as the other one, aren't you? Do you really think words thirty years later could make up for what you did? What you all did? Do you really think I care about what you want to say? Get away from me!"

Astrid had moved so quickly that Julia wasn't prepared. When she did stand up next to her and tried to calm her down, Maddy was moving on her way out. Julia placed her arms on Astrid's shoulders from behind. "Easy, love. Easy."

Astrid didn't turn to face her. She was too angry to move. "Do you believe these people? Who do they think they are?"

"Like it or not, they're your family," Julia said.

Astrid spun around. "Family! Are you insane?" She stopped when she saw Julia's expression. Astrid took her hands in hers. "I love you. I didn't mean that."

"It doesn't matter. You're upset. Perhaps I am for loving you." Julia grinned. "One doesn't choose their family. You know that. You met mine."

"Yours are normal," Astrid said.

"Mine? Normal? Define normal," Julia said. "My father was a stereotypical Black man. He had eight children by six different women and bragged about it, but didn't marry one. My mother was a crack head and spent five years in prison. But you know all that."

"But they love you. They're there for you. They didn't discard you with the trash."

Julia reached out and cupped Astrid's chin in her hands. "Astrid, appearances are so deceiving. Now, they're here for me. Not back then, not when I needed them. Sometimes, I wish they had given me away. You know that. In high school, things were so bad for me, I tried to kill myself, twice. But you know all that."

"I'm sorry, I forgot. I'm being so selfish. I don't know what's happening to me—"

"No, you're being normal," Julia said. "Right now, what is happening here is happening to you and that is all you can think about. Right now, all you can think about is yourself, and that is all right. It is."

Astrid shook her head. "How did I ever wind up with someone as good as you? I love you."

"Just lucky I guess. I love you too."

Julia took her into her arms. Astrid felt her lover's fingers brushing her hair. "Everything is going to be fine. One way or the other. I promise. The worst will soon be over. You'll see."

"I don't want Kate to die, Julia. I really don't."

"I know. I know."

* espes*

Maddy and Sam sat in the chapel downstairs on the main floor in the back of the hospital. It was the smallest chapel she'd ever been in. It didn't matter where she was, she knew God was by her side. Except for the two of them, they were alone.

"We're going to lose her," Maddy said. "Oh God. It's my fault, my sins, my pride." She brought her hands up to her chest and clenched them into fists.

Sam put his arms around her. "No, Mama. We won't."

Her handsome grown son with the acorn-colored skin and warm brown eyes. He was her tower of strength.

"This is happening because of my sins, son. Our Sins. We were so wrong, so very wrong. All of us."

"Mama, you did what you thought was right. We all did," he said.

She pulled back. "But we weren't right. We sent away that child, that baby girl, your sister's baby." She turned away. She couldn't bear to look at him. She was so ashamed. "I lied to you, son."

"It doesn't matter now. That's all in the past."

"No. Not all of it. Kate is going to die and I never got to know her, really know her." She buried her face in her hands. "And her sister, my baby's babies, my granddaughters. What have I done?"

"Mama, you're being too hard on yourself. You weren't in this alone."

"No, I wasn't. We'd discussed it, the four of us, right up to that night when those babies were born. We swore, your daddy and me, along with Katherine and Jackson," Maddy confessed. "Katherine was always the stronger one."

"Mama, what are you talking about?" he asked. Elsa came in. He nodded for her to sit near them, and she complied. "Mama, you don't have to talk about that night," he said.

"But I do, son, don't you see. I have to tell you the truth. I have to while I have the courage." She looked him in the eyes. "We were so blind the four of us. I hated them, Katherine and Jackson, so much. I hated their son. That boy never did a thing wrong to me. Never. We swore that whatever the baby was, it would be sent away. The four of us agreed. Lincoln and Betsy would help us. He'd say the baby was stillborn. It'd all be so easy. We didn't want any part of it, the baby." She felt the tears begin to wet her cheek but didn't wipe them away. "It was easy too, then. As soon as that little girl was born, Betsy took her away, out of the room, didn't even let your sister see her, just as we agreed. We didn't know there was another."

"You didn't expect a twin?" Sam asked.

Maddy shook her head. "No. Twins didn't run in our family."

"What about tests?"

Maddy went on. "Your sister—Livie wanted it to be a surprise. She was so happy. I never saw her so happy. I should have been happy for her. We, your father and I, should have been happy. When that second baby came out, we were all surprised and when Katherine and Jackson saw her, they kept her. They wouldn't send her away. She was lily white. Beautiful. My heart sank," Maddy said. She swallowed hard, but the tears in the back of her throat wouldn't go down. "When your sister died, I lost my will to live. I didn't care about anything. I was so glad you were away. Then Jax, he shot himself that same night, and Katherine became another person, harder than she already was. She and Jackson made us, all of us in that room, swear never to speak of it again. And I didn't. Jax—he loved her. He really loved your sister. He didn't care she was Black. He was smarter than all of us. She didn't care he was White. Oh, my God, Jesus, hear me now."

"Mama, what about the baby, Astrid? Why didn't you keep her?"

"We had agreed. She was gone. It was too late. Lincoln and Betsy had sent her away."

"Didn't you ever try to find her?"

"No. It was too late. And your daddy didn't want a mulatto baby in his house. Later on I asked. Doctor Lincoln wouldn't say a word. He wouldn't betray Katherine, not for anyone. And now, I'm going to lose my baby's girl and the other won't have anything to do with us. Kate is paying for my sins, your father's and mine."

"No, Mama. I should have been there that night. I could've taken the baby and raised her," Sam said.

"You were a boy. You were in school."

"I wasn't a boy, Mama. I was eighteen. I was at West Point. I could've quit."

"No. You couldn't. We wouldn't have let you. We were so proud of you. Your daddy was so proud. This is my mistake, my sin. Not yours. I never left that house or that land because I wouldn't abandon my other granddaughter. I just couldn't. Katherine had offered to buy me out so many times after Jackson died. I wouldn't. I couldn't. I wouldn't leave Kate and now she's going to leave us." She lowered her head into her hands again. "Oh God, please, please don't take my baby's girl from me. Please, Jesus. I'll spend the rest of my life making it up to them, to you. I swear. Please spare her. Let her come back home to us, all of us, both of them. I'll do anything, anything you want. I'll make peace with Katherine. Please, Jesus, don't take my other baby away. Please."

She felt the strong hands of her son surround her and she let go. Elsa wrapped her arms around them both. Maddy was surrounded by the love of her children, but she'd never felt more alone. As far as she could remember, for a long time, there was only one time in her life that she ever felt really safe and that was years ago, sixty-two years ago to be exact. She sat up, wiped her eyes, and told them the story of how she and Katherine came to know one another, of how it all began…

⌇⌇⌇

It was just another night that her father had hit her mama, but it was the first time he had beat her up. It was nineteen hundred and fifty-three, and the world was a different place then. Colored people and White people couldn't be friends, at least not out in the open. Many weren't friends at all. But Katherine was always different and Maddy had treasured that.

She needed a place to run to, and there was only one place she knew to go. One place that she always heard her mama say she too had felt safe. Maddy wondered if she would too.

It was dark outside that night, except for the full moon, and she hoped no one saw her. She had to hide. She was too scared to go anywhere else. At least she knew this place.

"Hello?" she heard the voice say. "Who's in here? I saw you."

Maddy hoped the person would go away.

"Hi," the little White girl said as she looked around the corner at her. She had seen the little girl before, but never spoken to her.

Maddy tried to hide deeper under the potting table but couldn't. With nowhere to go, she said, "Hi," and bit her lower lip.

"I'm Katherine, but they call me Katy," the other girl said. "Who are you?"

"Maddy." She looked at the ground. "Please don't tell anyone I'm here. Please don't."

"I won't." Katy stepped forward. "What are you doing here in our garden?"

"Hiding," Maddy said.

Katy kneeled down next to her. "Why are you hiding?"

"I'm scared."

Katy reached out to touch her and Maddy pulled back. Under the moonlight shining through the glass, she noticed the other girl saw her cheek. "You're hurt. Who did that?"

"No one. I fell," Maddy said.

"You want to come in my house with me?" Katy asked.

She wanted to, but… "I can't."

"Why not?"

"Because."

"Because why?"

"I'm Colored," Maddy said.

Katy laughed. "So? It's my house. Are you hungry? Are you thirsty?"

Maddy was starving. "Uh-huh."

Katy stood up. "Then come with me."

"Uh-uh. I can't. My mama works for your mama and if they knew I was here, I'd be in trouble and mama too."

"I won't tell. I promise," Katy said. "I have lots of food inside and chocolate milk. Do you like chocolate milk?"

"Uh-huh."

"Then come inside. I promise it will be okay, and I won't let anyone hurt you," Katy said.

"Okay," Maddy said and followed Katy across the lawn to the house.

Katy tiptoed up the front stairs and opened the wooden screen door. "Come on," she whispered.

Maddy stopped on the stairs. She shook her head.

Katy whispered. "What's wrong?"

"I can't go in the front door. I'm Colored," Maddy said.

Kate opened the screen door wide. "I'm White, so what? This is my house, and I say it's okay."

Maddy hesitated then went in and waited for her.

Katy closed it slowly behind her and then led the way into the kitchen. "Shh," she whispered.

Maddy nodded and followed her. Inside, Katy took out some bread and jars of peanut butter and jelly out of the refrigerator. At the sink, she stood on a chair and reached into the cabinet for two glasses. She set the glasses and two small plates on the table. She went to the refrigerator, took out a big bottle of chocolate milk, and set it next to the glasses.

"Sit down," she told Maddy. "It's okay. My parents are up-stairs sleeping."

Maddy pulled out a chair and sat down. Katy went to the drawer, pulled out a teaspoon, and brought it to the table. Once there, she began making two sandwiches using the spoon. "My mama and daddy don't let me use a knife yet," she said. "You can pour the chocolate milk, if you want."

Maddy took the two glasses and the big jug and moved to pour it. The jug slipped and spilled, fell onto its side and choco-late milk began to fall out onto the floor. Maddy jumped back.

"It's okay," Katy said, as she grabbed the jug and stood it up. "Don't be scared. I can clean it up. Good thing it didn't break." She went over to the sink, pulled out a couple of big rags from underneath, and wiped it up. She took the two towels, went out of the room into another, put them into a bin, and closed the door. She went back to the table. "Maybe we should do this together." She lifted the jug. "You hold the glasses, okay? And I'll pour."

Maddy nodded and did so and they successfully filled two glasses with chocolate milk. Katy sat down at the table. Maddy copied her. Katy took a bite from her sandwich. Maddy copied her.

"Good?" Katy asked.

"Uh-huh?" Maddy said, chewing, and then swallowing each bite and following it with a sip of the milk.

"What happened tonight?" Katy asked. "Why were you hid-ing? It's okay to tell me. I won't tell anyone. I promise."

Maddy set down her sandwich. "My daddy beat my mama. He hit me too."

"Your daddy beat your mama? Why?" Kate asked.

Maddy shrugged her shoulders. "Don't know. He does it a lot. He's scary. I don't want to go home tonight."

Katy reached out a hand and placed it on the other girl's hand. "It's okay. You can stay here."

Maddy shook her head.

"Because you're Colored?"

"Uh-huh."

"I don't care about that. We can be friends if you want. I don't have any Colored friends."

"You'd be friends with me?" Maddy asked.

"Sure. Why not? I don't care you're Colored. Do you care that I'm White?"

"Uh-uh," Maddy said.

"That settles it. We're friends now. You can stay here tonight in my room. It'll be our secret."

"Okay."

"When I go to school tomorrow—do you go to school?" Katy asked.

"Uh-huh."

"We'll sneak out of the house tomorrow and we'll go to school, okay?" Katy asked.

"Okay."

Katy stood up. "We better do the dishes so they don't know we were down here." Katy brought some stuff to the sink and Maddy helped. Together they washed the dishes, dried them, and then put everything back.

Kate tiptoed out of the kitchen, toward the hallway, and to the staircase. Maddy copied her. Neither said a word. At the large wooden staircase, Katy spoke. "We have to be quiet because we'll be passing my parents' room." She brought a finger to her lips. "Sh." They'd started the ascent when Katy stopped and pointed to a step ahead of them. "See that step. Don't step on it. It squeaks really loud."

Katy stepped over it holding the handrail for support. Maddy copied her. On the landing, they tiptoed again. As they passed a door, Katy held up a finger to her lips and said, "Shh, my parents' room."

Farther down the hall, Katy opened the door and motioned for Maddy to go in first. Maddy went in and Katy closed the door.

"This is my room," she whispered. "You'll be safe here tonight." She went over to her white dresser, pulled out two pairs of pajamas, and handed one set to Maddy.

Maddy shook her head.

"It's okay. I say so," Katy said.

Maddy took them and admired them. "They're pretty."

"Thank you. My daddy gave them to me. I love horses," Katy said.

"Me, too." Maddy took off her clothes and replaced them with the pajamas. She took her clothes, folded them neatly into a pile, and set them on the chair next to the bed.

"We can go riding on our real ones, if you'd like," Katy said.

"I'd like that."

Katy changed too then walked over to her bed. "Here's where we sleep. I'll sleep on this side near the door so you don't have to be afraid, okay?" Kate got into bed.

Maddy nodded and followed her.

"Don't be afraid, Maddy. It's nice here. My daddy doesn't beat my mama and we're friends now. Friends forever."

Maddy laid back her head onto the soft pillow. It smelled of flowers. "Friends forever?"

"Uh-huh," Katy said, turning on her side to face her. "How old are you? I'm eight."

"Me too," Maddy said, turning to face her, her new friend with bright green eyes. Her new friend with long red hair.

"See. We were meant to be friends," Katy said. "Good night, Maddy. I'm glad you're here. See you in the morning."

"Good night, Katy. Thank you."

"That's what friends are for, huh?"

"Uh-huh," Maddy said.

 భావా

That was the best night sleep she'd ever had in her life. Ever. No matter what else happened in her life since then—her graduation from high school, her marriage to George, her graduation from college, the birth of her children—she never slept so peacefully, so safe again.

Sam and Elsa stared at her and then Elsa reached out and took her hand. "Mama, I had no idea."

"It was a long time ago," Maddy said.

"I understand now, Mama," Sam said. He clasped one hand on his mama's and the other hand on his wife's. "I had no idea you were friends. What happened?"

She took a deep and slow breath. "A great deal." And she began to tell them exactly what went wrong. She'd never told another soul before.

Chapter 25

Astrid paced in the doctor's office. Doctor Stanley entered to meet with them.

"The good news is that you are definitely sisters." He caught himself. "I'm sorry. I didn't mean to insinuate—"

"Better than a birth certificate, I guess," Astrid said. "Go ahead, Doctor. I know what you mean."

"The good news is that you are a perfect donor match for your sister. You show no signs of cysts in your kidneys. However…"

"Go on," Astrid said.

"As Doctor Comedy can tell you, there is no guarantee that something can't change later on. We still don't know a great deal about polycystic kidneys."

"What are the odds?"

"I don't like to give odds, but it is possible you may not show any signs, as you haven't yet. The good thing is that no one in your family has shown signs of the disease and if no one in your family has needed dialysis, odds are you may not either. Of course, no doctor can guarantee you never will. All I can say is that the disease is in your genes. Why it developed so quickly in your sister, we can't answer."

Astrid had to make a choice. "So I could donate one of my kidneys and we both could live with only one kidney, but chances are likely I may need a kidney later on?"

He looked at Julia. Julia placed a hand on Astrid's shoulder and squeezed.

He nodded. "That is a lot to think about, I know. It is a difficult decision. No one can make it for you."

"I'll do it," Astrid said. "If need be, if she does need a kidney, I'll do it."

He nodded and left them alone.

"I'm doing the right thing, right?" Astrid asked.

"Only you know the answer to that," Julia said.

"She came here to tell me she was sorry. To tell me the truth about who I was." Astrid chewed on her thumbnail. "I owe her something, don't I? No one else came to tell me anything?"

"Do you owe her a kidney that you may need later?"

"I thought you supported my decision, no matter what it was?" Astrid snapped.

"I do. I just want you to make the right decisions for you."

"Are you telling me I shouldn't?"

"That's not what I said."

"Here you go analyzing me again. I really hate when you do that. Okay, you want to be a doctor now, tell me what I should do. No. Tell me in layman's terms, statistically and realistically, as a medical doctor, is it wise to donate one of my kidneys?"

"I looked over your all your tests. Your kidneys are fine and healthy. The fact that no one in your family has kidney problems is a good sign. The fact that Kate does isn't. She is your twin. How it affected her so soon, and not you, I can't answer. I'm not a specialist. In my opinion…"

"Go on," Astrid said.

"No one can tell you the future, love. Not me. Not the specialists. No one. Clinically though, I foresee no problems. You and Kate have a fifty-fifty chance of having the disease. Fifty percent of a parent's affected children will inherit the disease. Kate, it seems is that fifty percent." Julia reached out a hand and cupped Astrid's chin. "That doesn't necessarily mean you won't get it. I love you. I wouldn't let you do anything that might endanger your life. I think you're safe."

"I love you too." Astrid squeezed Julia's hand. "If she does need a kidney, I'm doing it. I couldn't live with myself if I didn't and I could have saved her."

"That's one of the reasons I love you. Your selfless nature."

"You'll be here, if I have to do it?"

"Just try and get rid of me."

❧❧❧

Katherine paced back and forth in the waiting room. Lincoln got up to be with her. "You should sit down," he said.

"Why? Will it make things move any quicker than it isn't already?" she snarled. "They've had her in surgery for two hours.

How long is this supposed to take? How come they haven't come out and given us a status report? What is going on?"

"Katherine," he hushed firmly. "You're not helping yourself any or anyone else."

"Do you really think I care about anyone else now? All I care about is Kate. She's the only one I care about. The only one worth caring about." She spun on her heel and stomped away from him and out of the waiting room.

"She's right," Maddy said. "It's been so long since Kate's been in there." She looked at Lincoln. "Doctor Linc, is it supposed to take this long?"

He walked over to them and sat down in the vacant seat next to Maddy. Sam and Elsa were seated on the other side of her. "They said it would take about an hour for the dye test plus prep and another hour or so for surgery. That is, if they can do it laparoscopically. If not, it may be longer."

"How much longer?" Astrid asked.

"They will come out and tell us when they are done," Julia said. "And let us know what they found out and how she is.

"Maybe," Maddy asked, "you can find out something for us, anything."

Julia nodded. "I'll be glad to." She stood up. "I'll be right back."

Astrid made a face at her. Julia grinned and disappeared out of sight.

"She's a lovely girl," Maddy told Astrid. "Your friend."

Astrid eyed her and turned away, not very interested in what this woman had to say.

Katherine went to loiter by the doors to surgery. An orderly noticed and went over to her. "You shouldn't stand here, ma'am. The waiting room is over there."

Katherine raised a hand at him. "Don't. My granddaughter is in there and I'm not leaving this spot until she comes out. Is that clear?"

The young man of twenty-something didn't know what to say. He nodded and went through the doors.

Katherine paced back and forth in the hallway outside the surgery.

℃℈℈

Everyone was seated in the waiting room waiting for some

word on Kate. By time the surgeon came out three hours later, everyone was on edge. "Is Kate Thayer's family here?" he asked.

Astrid was the first one to her feet. "Here, Doctor. How is she?"

Everyone copied Astrid's actions.

"I'm sorry we didn't get a chance to meet earlier," he said. "But there was no time. I'm Doctor Thorne, the urologist and surgeon. Kate is out of surgery and stabilized at this time." He was still dressed in green surgical garb with his mask down around his neck.

"I'm her grandmother," Katherine said. "Is she really all right?"

"Your granddaughter is a very strong young woman. She has a strength of will that I think will get her through this," he told her.

"Will she be all right?" Maddy jumped in. "Did you fix the problem? Did you find it?"

"Yes, but we did have to remove her left kidney."

"Oh, God," Katherine exclaimed. "Oh God."

Lincoln placed his arm around her shoulders.

Maddy was speechless.

"Just tell us, Doctor, please," Lincoln said.

"There was an injury to her left kidney and scar tissue that replaced normal kidney tissue. We also did find several stones in the ureter—the vessel leading from the kidney to the bladder. That is what caused the infection. The left kidney could not be saved. I'm sorry."

"And dialysis?" Sam asked. "Is she still going to need that?"

"No. Not yet. Her right kidney seems to be handling the load just fine. It is functioning within normal limits for now."

"Will she recover?" Katherine asked. "Will she be all right, or is there a chance we can still lose her?"

He raised his hands in the air. "We don't want to go there right now. She is holding her own. She is young and strong and that is what is important."

"But you can't guarantee she'll remain that way, can you?" Katherine demanded.

"No. I can't do that. We're going to send her back into intensive care and monitor her. As she is sedated and resting comfortably through the night, I suggest you all go home and try to get a good night's sleep. And get something to eat. Tomorrow, we'll see what it brings us," he said. "I'll be here for the rest of the evening and here tomorrow to monitor her. Doctor Stanley will be here also. Are there any questions I can answer for you now?"

"Is there any chance she'll wake up tonight?" Katherine asked.

"Doubtful. As I said, she is heavily sedated. Go home. Get some rest," he replied. "Any more questions?"

When no one answered, Lincoln spoke for all of them. "No, Doctor, not now. Thank you."

The urologist nodded and headed back the way he came.

Lincoln turned to Katherine. "We should head back to the hotel and try and get some rest."

"Rest? Are you kidding? How can I rest?" Katherine shouted.

"We can't do anything for her tonight. I strongly suggest it," Lincoln said. "You heard what the doctor said."

"I heard he's not sure she'll make it. That is what I heard, Lincoln!" Katherine said.

"He said she may," Astrid interjected. "And that she is strong and we need to wait until tomorrow."

Katherine eyed her and then turned back to the elderly doctor. "All right, but I'm not leaving until I see Kate."

"All right," Lincoln said.

"And I need to stop somewhere first."

"Fine," Lincoln agreed.

Sam turned to Maddy. She sat back down in her chair. "We should go to the hotel too."

"No. I'm not leaving."

"Mama, you really should try and get some sleep," he said. "You didn't sleep much last night."

Elsa sat on the other side of Maddy. "Sam's right, Mama. You haven't been eating or sleeping much since we got here."

"I'm fine. And I'm not staying another night in an overpriced New York City hotel on Kate's dollar," Maddy said.

"Mama, we're not. It's on my tab, but we can stay somewhere else, if that is what you want," Sam said. "Elsa checked and found a few you'd be happy in and made reservations in one."

"Please, Mama," Elsa pleaded. "We're only two blocks away, five minutes there and back. Kate would want you to."

Kate? My baby's girl. Maddy closed her eyes for a moment and opened them to find her son and daughter-in-law waiting expectantly. "No. Not tonight. I'm staying with Kate tonight."

That is if Katherine let her. "But I do have to do something first."

She left and, a few minutes later, a female nurse appeared in surgical garb pushing a gurney ahead of her. She pushed the gurney toward the room and punched the large round button just outside the door. The large wooden door opened as the gurney neared it. Astrid stood up, followed her to the doors, and waited outside. Through the glass, she watched the nurse push the gurney into the room and shove the headboard up against the wall. Another nurse in purple scrubs joined her and they both went to work tending to Kate. When they were done, the first nurse exited.

"Can I go in now?" Astrid asked her.

"Yes, she is sleeping."

"I know. Thank you."

The nurse departed and Astrid walked in. Slowly, she made her way to the end of Kate's bed and watched her. Kate was motionless. The other nurse checked over all the cords that ran from machines and into Kate's arms and nose. There was also a cord running from her torso and into a small clear bag. Obviously, it was a catheter.

"Is she in any pain?" Astrid asked.

"No. None." The nurse smiled. "She's resting soundly. You should try and get some sleep too."

"I will. Thank you."

The nurse nodded and exited. Maybe she would do just that, except that she had to do something first. Something she hadn't done in a very, very long time.

e/se/s

Maddy entered the small chapel. She stepped to the front row and sat down. Sam and Elsa followed her and took a seat next to her. Maddy kneeled down and started to pray silently. She needed God to hear her. She needed his help more than ever now. More than she ever needed him before. Kate had to be okay. She just had to be.

From beside her, Sam and Elsa did the same. Without asking them, Maddy knew what they prayed for. It was almost the exact thing she prayed for. Kate to get better and go home safe and sound.

A few minutes later, Maddy heard footsteps but didn't turn to look. When she did glance up, she noticed it was Katherine and Lincoln walking toward the front. They sat down in a pew across from them. Katherine met her gaze and nodded. Maddy nodded back. It was the first time, in almost forever, Katherine had ever acknowledged her presence, except for last night. Katherine leaned forward and went down on her knees. She brought her hands together, placed them on the bar before her, and lowered her head. Lincoln did the same.

Shortly thereafter, Astrid and Julia entered the simply decorated chapel. Astrid glanced around and saw the others sitting up front. Her first instinct was to run away, but she wouldn't give them the satisfaction. She had as much right to be here as they did. It was ironic, though, as she hadn't stepped foot into any kind of church in many years. And here they all were in the same place for obviously the same reason, to pray for Kate. At least they had that much in common. At least those two women cared about someone else other than themselves. She had to admit that and didn't want to, but she couldn't deny it because there they were.

The two women were unalike as two people could be. The White lady Katherine was tall yet voluptuous, and practically towered over Maddy. Katherine was outspoken, emotional, and seemed to bully everyone around her. The Black grandmother Maddy was soft spoken and rational, yet far from being a mouse, and her son and daughter-in-law evidently loved and respected her, as evidenced by their deference to her. Her Black son and White daughter-in-law. Now that was irony. But what Astrid noticed most was the common concern these two very different women showed for Kate, when they obviously couldn't stand to be in the same room with each other, and their spirit of independence. In the midst of the chaos and worry before them, they both possessed a confidence and the attitude of not deferring to a man because he was there. That too, she had to admit, she admired.

Astrid stepped into the last pew and sat down. "I hate churches."

"I know. We don't have to be here. We can go," Julia said.

"No. I need to. Just in case. But I don't know what to say. Kate shouldn't be alone."

"You came here for a reason. She'll be fine for ten to fifteen minutes," Julia said. "She will. Kate will understand."

Astrid debated and decided to do what she came to do.

"Just say what's in your heart," Julia said.

"Do you think there really is a God?" Astrid asked.

"Your guess is as good as mine," Julia said. "But it wouldn't hurt to tell him your feelings, would it?

"That's why I have you," Astrid said.

"My feelings won't be hurt. I promise."

"Just say what I feel, huh?" Astrid asked.

"That's what they say."

"Who are they?" Astrid asked.

"The clergy. The experts," Julia said.

Astrid leaned forward in her seat and lowered her head. She saw Julia copy her and was glad for her presence.

Hello there, God. This is Astrid, Astrid Thomas. Once known, I guess, as Black and White baby Thayer. You'd know better than I would who I was before. I haven't spoken to you in a long time because, frankly, I stopped believing in you. I still don't believe. You were never there when I needed you. You certainly weren't there when my parents needed you. When I was a baby and really needed you. When my sister and I needed you, where were you? I didn't know my parents, but you know that because you let them die. My sister, Kate, I never knew, she's in bad shape. I'd like to get to know her. If you're really there and you care, will you please do that for me? I mean, look, I don't believe in you, but Kate might. I don't know. Please make her live. I didn't even get to know her yet. Astrid wiped her cheeks with the back of one hand. *I don't know what kind of person she is, good or bad, but she did right by me, in the very short time we met, she was good to me.*

Julia must have heard her begin to cry because she reached out, grasped her hand, and held on tightly.

Katherine was the first to lift her head and glance behind her. When she saw that everyone was down in the chapel she rushed out, without a second thought, to return to Kate.

დოდ

It was two years ago, Katherine held Kate's hand as she slept. Five days had passed and still Kate lay unconscious from the riding accident. Kate underwent so much as a result of being thrown from the horse and Katherine wouldn't leave her, no matter how long it took. Kate had to wake up soon. She just had to.

Doctor Curtis had no idea when she would, if she would. It could be today, tomorrow, or next week. Katherine couldn't help dozing on and off. She was surprised when Kate began to stir.

Her eyes fluttered open, she looked up, and spoke in a weak voice. "Grandmother?"

Katherine stood up and placed a kiss on Kate's hand. "I'm here, darling. Don't you worry about anything. Everything will be just fine."

"Wh—where am I?"

"You're in the hospital, darling. Don't you remember?" Katherine said. Hammond had said there might be some memory loss from being thrown.

Kate laid her head back. "Adam? Where's Adam? Is he all right? Where is he, Gran? Is he somewhere else? I remember, we were riding."

Katherine ran her hand along the side of Kate's face. "No, darling. I'm so sorry. He had a broken neck. I'm so sorry, he's dead, darling." She choked out the words.

Kate stared at her then began to fidget in her bed and tried to sit up. "No. Not true. It isn't. It can't be."

She tried to get up but Katherine caught her hands and held her still. Katherine sent for the nurse via the call bell. "Darling, it will be all right. I promise," she said. "Hold on, darling. Please calm down. You mustn't exert yourself."

The nurse came over and administered a sedative, as prescribed, through the IV tube.

"Darling, you need to calm down," Katherine pleaded.

"My abdomen hurts. Why? Why does my stomach hurt? What's wrong with me, Gran?"

"Oh, darling." Katherine took her hand in hers. She knew exactly how Kate felt. "You were pregnant. They couldn't save the baby. You were bleeding so heavily, they had to take out your uterus. I'm sorry, darling."

Kate fell back on to the bed. Katherine placed her hand against Kate's head and brushed her hair with her fingers. "I'm sorry. We'll get through this. I promise you. I won't leave you. I'll see you through this. I promise, darling."

"Oh Adam. I'm sorry. I'm so sorry. It isn't possible. We used protection. We didn't want children." Kate barely got out all the words, but Katherine heard every one. Kate's eyes fluttered and then they finally closed.

Katherine sprang to her feet and yelled, "Kate?"

The nurse was there immediately. "It's fine, Mrs. Thayer. She's resting. The sedative is taking effect. That is all."

Katherine nodded and sighed in relief. "Thank God. Oh God, darling, I'm so sorry. I'm not leaving you. I don't want you to worry. I'm not going anywhere."

৩৩৩

"I promise," Katherine mumbled in her sleep. "I promise." She woke up when Lincoln shook her and found him staring at her.

"You were dreaming, Katherine," he told her.

"Yes, I was. Of the last time I almost lost her," she admitted.

"But you didn't," he said.

"No. And I won't lose her this time. I won't let it happen. I don't care what it takes."

"You need to calm down. You can't help her if you go off on everyone here. I understand how you feel—"

"Understand? How could you possibly understand? You have no children, no grandchildren." She stopped, appalled. "I'm sorry, Lincoln. I didn't mean to hurt you."

He took her hand and placed a kiss on her knuckles. "It's okay. Really. But you really need to get some rest. Tonight, at least, listen to me. Please. Maddy is here. Astrid is here, let them help and sit with her. You can't do it all."

৩৩৩

After saying her peace in the chapel downstairs, Astrid hurried back to ICU to ensure Kate wasn't alone. There, through the glass, she saw Katherine inside the room sitting by Kate's bedside, her back to the window. It was obvious that the older woman cared deeply for Kate. Her sister? How many times had she wanted to say that over the years? How many times had she hoped it was true? From the years spent inside group homes and foster homes, Astrid had longed to have a sister to share with, the good and the bad times. Now here she was, her sister, and before Astrid even could get to know her, before she could say she was sorry for rejecting her, she might lose her.

"We should return to the hotel and get some rest," Julia said from behind her.

"No. Those women said they'd be going to their hotels to rest. Someone should remain here with Kate."

"You mean your grandmothers?"

"The other women."

"It looks like this one changed her mind," Julia said.

"We'll see."

Katherine stood up and raised her hand to touch Kate's lips and then Kate's hair. She brushed the younger woman's face with her fingers and placed a gentle kiss on her forehead. Astrid couldn't make out what she said to her.

Lincoln approached her from behind and spoke to her.

She couldn't hear them but obviously the old woman didn't agree with him.

Astrid stepped in, "If you're going to argue, you can both leave."

"No one tells me what to do or where to go, young lady," Katherine said.

"Astrid. My name is Astrid, and I just did. You can stay as long as you don't cause Kate any problems."

Katherine eyed her. Lincoln moved to say something but Katherine waved his concern away with her right hand. "As we both share the same concern over Kate, I anticipate no problems with that—Astrid."

Astrid had to turn away. She couldn't hold the gaze. Katherine moved to leave, but stopped at the door.

"You'll be here with her, Astrid?" Katherine asked. "You won't leave her alone?"

"I'm not leaving her," Astrid said.

Katherine studied her. "You care for her?"

"Yes."

"Why?"

"She's my sister," Astrid said. "Why do you care about her?"

"She's my granddaughter," Katherine said.

"Ditto." Astrid said. "It seems we have something in common, Grandmother."

Astrid thought Katherine was about to reach out to her, but then she pulled back. "I'm sorry, Astrid. I wish—I hope you never have to experience the loss of a child. I hope—"

Astrid cut her off. "Good night."

She went back to Kate's bedside.

Katherine led the way to the elevator, but stopped in her tracks. Lincoln went to her side.

"What's wrong?"

"I can't leave."

"Katherine, you need your rest."

"Later. Not yet." She turned around and went back to Kate's room just as Maddy took a chair next to Kate's bed.

Chapter 26

Katherine stared at Kate's motionless body. This was eating away at her. She wouldn't dare admit that all of it was breaking her down.

I should have told you truth, darling. I always told you the truth. You always asked questions and I always answered them. I never hid anything from you, except about that night, your parents, my dislike of your mother, Maddy. She sighed deeply and took Kate's limp hand in hers. *I'm so very sorry, darling. If I had just answered you, told you everything you wanted to know when you asked me that night, that night before you left home, you wouldn't be here now, battling for your life.*

She brought Kate's hand up to her lips and kissed it. *I always took pride in the fact that you never just did what I wanted you to do, simply because I told you to. You weren't a robot. You never did anything you didn't want to do. You're smarter than I ever was.*

It was up to Katherine to try and repair the damage. She knew it. After all, it was she and Jackson who began it. She must be the one to end it.

She stood up, leaned over, and placed a kiss on Kate's forehead. The child was still so very warm. She hoped and she prayed, but she knew that whatever the doctors were doing for her just wasn't working and she fervently hoped she was wrong.

Katherine looked at Maddy. The other woman was staring at Kate and had placed a hand over Kate's. Katherine couldn't deny anymore that Maddy had as much right to be here now as she did. More so even, since it had been her daughter who lost her life to give this child hers and the other one. She looked at the back of the room. There she was sitting on the guest sofa with her friend. The other one, Jax's other child, her son's other daughter, her other granddaughter. Astrid stared out the window. There was nothing to see but a parking lot, but Katherine understood. The girl—young woman—was here for Kate, her sister, and Katherine couldn't deny that either, no matter how hard she tried. Skin color no longer mattered. Blood did. That was the way it should have been from the start, when Jax announced his intentions for Olivia. They should have supported their children's marriage. All of them.

Seventy years old and she felt no smarter than when she was seventeen and foolishly married Jackson. Where was the wisdom that came with getting older? She didn't feel any smarter than she was at thirty-nine when she forbade her son to see Olivia. Or any smarter almost a year later when they sent the other baby away and almost did the same with Kate. If she hadn't looked at Kate, Kate wouldn't have been in her life for the last thirty years. If she hadn't messed with fate, if she hadn't interfered in her son's life, she wouldn't be here now in this hospital room with an ill Kate either. Katherine was so tired. She could no longer think clearly and she had to face it. Tonight, she had to do something she hadn't done in a very long time. Tonight, she had to do something she thought she'd never do again. She had to trust someone else. She had to trust Maddy to be with Kate.

Cautiously, she stood up on unsteady feet. She walked around the bed toward Maddy, placed her hand on the other woman's shoulder, leaned down, and whispered, "I'm sorry, Maddy."

Maddy felt the grip and was stunned to see the speaker. She turned, but Katherine was already on the way out of the room. Maddy stood up and moved to follow when Sam met her.

"Are you all right, Mama? Did Katherine upset you?" he asked.

"No, son. Nothing like that. Stay with Kate for me." Maddy moved out of the room and looked for Katherine, but there was no sign of her. Where did she go? She wouldn't just leave Kate now. This was so unlike her. In reflex, she brought a hand to her chest and held it there. She grabbed for the gold crucifix that hung about her neck and held it. Fear gripped her throat. If Katherine broke, what chance would she have? Maddy always believed that she endured so much and lived as long as she had because she refused to die before Katherine did.

She felt a light touch on her shoulder.

"Mama, are you all right?" Elsa said. "Can I get you something? Mama?"

Maddy shook her head. "I'm fine, child."

"What's wrong? You look scared. More so now."

She wouldn't tell her children her fears. They had enough to deal with now. They all did. Lincoln was with Katherine. She'd be fine. At least she hoped so. Katherine was always the stronger one. She was that one tough, proud stubborn tree that stood tall in the forest under the heaviest of winds yet, didn't break or yield to anyone. Maddy was the smaller tree growing alongside in the shadow and protected by the other's presence. For ten years of her life, Maddy had been proud to call Katherine her friend. When Whites and Coloreds weren't supposed to be friends, they were. And it all had changed so quickly too. Almost in the blink of an eye and she never saw it coming. For a while, she wondered if Katherine ever saw it. For a while, she wondered if Katherine even cared. Of course, none of that mattered now. Kate mattered and the other one mattered, Astrid. And strangely, Katherine still mattered to her even now. Still, after all these years Maddy couldn't give up on the other woman, despite their differences and years of hostility.

Was Katherine's strength running out? Was that possible? She and Katherine had been through so much over the course of their lives, but they had endured. They always survived. Of course, Kate was the reason both women had endured the last thirty years. If Kate didn't survive, Maddy knew that she couldn't go on. If Kate died—no, she couldn't consider that. Of course, she never considered Olivia dying in childbirth either. Not once, for the fear of considering it might make it true. No one had expected that, not in reality.

Maddy didn't even feel the tears fall.

Elsa took her hand. "Mama, why are you crying? Kate is going to be just fine."

Maddy touched her cheeks and sighed. Lost years, she wanted to say, lost time, regrets, but she didn't. "Let's go back with Kate," she said, instead, but not without a last glance at the elevators, willing for a moment with Katherine.

❧❧❧

Lincoln found Katherine seated at the desk near the window when he came in in with a glass of water in one hand and a pill bottle in the other. He set them down on the edge of the desk just in time to see her close her wallet and return it to her purse. She set her purse to the side of her desk and stood up.

"Did you reserve these suites for us?" she asked but didn't turn to face him.

"No. Sam did. This is where he and Kate were staying. They had Kate's and his room on the eighth floor." He knew she didn't really care and that she was trying to distract herself with something else. It was her way of dealing with things.

She sighed.

"You need to rest," he said and moved alongside her.

She shook her head. "I should never have left her. I should be there with her now. I should go back."

"There's no need to. Maddy and Astrid are there. They'll call if anything changes. You know they will."

She looked up at him. "Astrid. She's my other granddaughter. How could I have been so wrong?"

He'd never seen her so worn and beaten. "You're human, Katherine. We all make mistakes."

She glared at him. "No. Not as many as I have. I didn't want that girl. I wished her gone. I wished her harm." She turned away from him and began to pace. "This is my fault. All of it. If only I had told Kate, she wouldn't have taken off. She would have been home safe, eating properly. Instead, she makes herself sick with worry and grief and doesn't take care of herself." She brought her arms up to her chest and wrung her hands. "It's all my fault, all of it. I should have supported Jax. He was my son. All he wanted was for me to accept Olivia, the baby, but I couldn't. I just couldn't. I wouldn't. And Maddy and George didn't want him with Livie. I should have supported him. And then the baby, none of us wanted the baby. It's all my fault." She continued wringing her hands as she paced. "But when I saw Kate, I couldn't send her away too. I just couldn't. Not after I held her. But the other one—my God, Lincoln, she's my blood, too."

He couldn't stand to see her this way. "It wasn't your fault," he said.

"But it was, don't you see? If I had accepted Livie, maybe she'd be alive. Jax would be alive. I was so wrong, Lincoln! How could I have been so wrong?"

Lincoln went to her side and seized her by the shoulders. "Enough, Katherine!"

Her eyes widened at him. "What? How dare you? Let go of me!"

"No," he said calmly.

She tried to break free and roared, "Are you insane? I said let go of me!"

"And I said no," he repeated. He wouldn't match her. It wasn't his way.

She fought to pull away from him. He held her and pushed her up against the wall. "Enough, Katy! Enough! I won't stand here and listen to this horse shit anymore! You want to hit me, yell at me? Go ahead, but I won't allow you to take the blame for all of it. Olivia bled to death in childbirth. There was nothing we could have done differently. You didn't kill her. Jax killed himself. You didn't kill him."

She turned her face away. "No," she whispered.

"Yes. He killed himself out of grief. He couldn't live without Livie. He loved her. We were all there that night. We all know what happened. We all saw. We all sent that baby away, your granddaughter. Maddy, George, Jackson, Betsy, and I all swore never to speak of it again. We all knew what we were doing. We're all adults. I won't have you taking all the blame for something we all did that night. I won't have it. Do you hear me? Enough, Katy! Enough!"

She stared at him. Her mouth dropped open. Her eyes widened. He knew he appeared crazed, but he didn't care. If that is what he had to do to calm her, then so be it. He just didn't care. Not tonight. Everything else seemed miniscule tonight.

"I've loved you forever, Katy, and I won't have you do this to yourself. I just won't. Do you hear me, woman?" he said.

She stopped fidgeting and fell against him. She crushed her body into his and he wrapped his arms around her. "Enough, Katy," he whispered. "Enough. It's all in the past, over and done with. We move on from here." The smell of her hair, her skin, awakened the recesses of his soul. Her need for him rejuvenated him.

She broke down crying. "I want my boy back. I want Kate back. I want…" She buried her face in his chest.

All he wanted to do was make the pain and nightmare go away for her. He was just as guilty as she was, they all were, except the only ones left to pay and make things right were now reduced to three. Katherine, Maddy, and him.

"Oh God, Lincoln, I miss my boy. I'm going to lose Kate and I've lost the other one too."

"You won't lose Kate. The surgery went as planned. You won't. There's still hope and time to keep them both." He held her against him. "There's always hope and time. Always." After she cried for a few moments and he heard her sniffle, he took her hand in his. "Come with me." He led her over to the bed, though he already knew her response. He sat down on the bed next to her. "I'm going to give you a sedative."

She held up a hand. "No. No sedative. No drugs."

"You need to get some sleep," he said.

"No. Kate needs me," she said. "And you know how I feel about drugs."

"If you want to help Kate, you need to get some rest," he said.

"No."

"Yes," he insisted. "I know you don't like to relinquish control to anyone, but this time you are going to listen to me. You trusted me for fifty years as your physician. You trusted me with Kate. You have to trust me now." He took the bottle, opened it, and shook out a pill into his hand. He offered her the glass of water and the pill. "You want to help Kate? You need to get some rest. Now, I insist."

She stared at it as if it were poison. "All right." She reluctantly reached out, took the pill, swallowed it with the glass of water, and handed the glass back to him.

He eyed her. At least now, she'd get some well-deserved rest whether she wanted it or not. He stood up and walked to the doorway. "I'll be in the living room if you need me."

She watched him leave. He was a good man and a good friend, to her anyway. She never meant to hurt him. He was collateral damage in her quest to protect herself, her family, and their secrets. She couldn't help what he'd believed.

Only now did she see the harm it caused. Only now did she see how she should have set him straight back then, but she couldn't—she wouldn't have. She needed no man, least of all her husband, Jackson, but her carnal desires were strong and she would not deny herself the pleasures of that. Lincoln, as with the rest of her paramours, was nothing more than escape from the tedium, loneliness, and stress she endured in her faithless marriage. Her son Jax was her world, but taking care of him wasn't enough. Being a mere housewife, mother, wife, and horse farm owner and breeder wasn't enough for her. She needed more. She wanted more and the men were so readily available. Jackson wasn't faithful to her. Why should she be faithful to him? It was just like her mother said, there was no reason a woman couldn't take care of herself first.

⚬⚬⚬

Back at the hospital, Astrid sat next to Kate's bedside with her hand over Kate's. Kate wasn't as hot as before, just warm under Astrid's touch.

"I'm so sorry, child," Maddy said from across Kate's sleeping form. "We were wrong."

Astrid glanced at her. "I have nothing to say to you."

"But there is so much I have to say to you."

"No," Astrid said. "I'm here for Kate." She turned back to her sister. "She is all I care about. Just leave me alone. Please." She couldn't bear to hear their apologies and lies and their regrets. She should leave. Part of her wanted to just get up, walk out, and put all of this behind her. The other part, the stronger, wiser part of her said that this is where she should be, where she needed to be, and nothing or no one was going to make her leave. She'd endure their presence if that is what it took.

"Kate, you have to wake up, come morning. Okay?" Astrid said. "They say you're better now, so please wake up when you're supposed to."

She felt Julia's hand on her shoulder and leaned against her for strength. Julia knew her so well. She knew when Astrid needed her and when she just needed to be alone. Astrid knew just how lucky she was to have someone good to love and be loved back.

"She's going to be fine. Her temperature is close to normal. Her blood pressure is back up. She'll be fine," Julia said. "Her blood work shows significant improvement."

Astrid knew that, but she also knew—"But there's always a chance things can still go bad, isn't there? They just don't know. You doctors just don't know everything, do you?" And that was what frightened her.

"You're right on that." Julia squeezed her shoulder. "But I have no reason to anticipate otherwise. If she is just half as stubborn as you are, she isn't going anywhere."

Julia's words did as they always did. They reassured her. Astrid stared at Kate, sensed Maddy's gaze, and when she looked up, she saw the older woman watching her, almost pleading with her. Their eyes met for a moment and then Astrid turned away. She couldn't look at her. She was breaking down, softening the more she stayed with Kate and worried about her, but the anger still remained. The anger at what could have been, what should have been for her, for them as sisters and friends. There was no way she could forgive them, at least not now, maybe never.

Chapter 27

*I*t was that night again in 1985—the night that changed everything and shattered the lives of all those concerned. It was the middle of a still, dark night. A new moon began and blackness swallowed everything around it, yet Katherine saw it clear as a bell as a viewer rather than as a participant.

Livie felt a pain and poked Jax. Jax stirred awake and sat up. "What's wrong? Is it the baby?"

"I think so. It hurts."

"Stay here." He was out of the bed and out of the room before she could stop him.

Jax banged on the guest room door. "Uncle Linc, open the door! She's not feeling well."

"What's wrong?" Lincoln answered.

"It's the baby. You have to come quick."

Back in their bedroom, Jax slipped into a pair of jeans and a T-shirt and rushed to her side. "It's okay," he told Livie and took her hand. "I'm here."

"I'm fine. It's just a baby," she said.

He sat on the bed with her.

Lincoln and his sister Betsy rushed in and Lincoln opened his medical bag. "Tell me what you're feeling, Olivia," he said. He listened to her heartbeat, and the heartbeat of the baby.

Katherine and Jackson entered the room in their pajamas and robes and watched from the background. "What's happening?" she asked. "Is she all right?"

"She's going into labor," Lincoln said. "Betsy, get me some clean towels and boiling water. We're going to start this baby off right. Better let Maddy and George know, too."

Betsy left the room.

"Now, Livie," Lincoln said. "I don't want you to worry. Do as I say and you'll be okay. All right?"

"All right. Ugh! Ouch! Arrgh! It hurts," Livie yelled. "Is it supposed to hurt like this?"

"I'm here, baby," Jax said. "I won't let anything happen to you."

"I know. I love you, Jax," she said.

"I love you too, baby." He kissed her hand. "Don't be afraid."

"I'm not. Our baby is being born tonight," she said and forced a smile. "Our baby— She screamed again.

"I can give you something for the pain," Lincoln said.

"No. No drugs," she said. "Don't hurt the baby." She screamed again. "Arrgh!"

Betsy returned and joined Lincoln.

"Her water has broken," he told Betsy. He turned to Olivia. "I want you to breathe normally. I know it's difficult."

"Easy, baby," Jax told her. "I'm here. I'm not going anywhere."

Olivia screamed again. "Oh God, it hurts. It hurts," she moaned.

"When I say push, Livie, I want you to push. Do you understand?" Lincoln said.

"Y—yes. Oh God. Is it supposed to hurt this much? Oh God, it hurts so much."

"Push, Livie. Push," Lincoln said.

She did and moaned along with it.

"Get the towels ready, Betsy. The baby is coming. Okay, Livie, push again," he said.

Jax held onto her hand, kissed her cheek, and wiped her brow with the corner of his T-shirt. "You're doing great, baby. It's coming."

"Our baby. Oh God, Jax," she moaned.

"I love you, baby. You're doing fine. I love you," Jax said again.

"I love—you," she said.

"Here it comes now," Lincoln said.

Katherine and Jackson stepped forward to view the birth. She noticed how pale Olivia was. Katherine placed a hand on her son's shoulder. She reached out to touch Olivia's forehead. The girl was so cold. Katherine didn't need to be a doctor to know this wasn't good. She stepped back and out of the way, but remained just behind Lincoln.

"Here's the head," Lincoln said. "Here we go. It's a girl."

Maddy and George entered the bedroom and waited at the end of the bed. The four grandparents glanced at each other knowingly.

"A girl? Let me—see her. Please—" Olivia said.

Lincoln turned and handed the baby to Betsy and she left.

"Let me see my baby," Livie said again.

"I'm sorry, Livie. She was stillborn," Lincoln said.

She turned away and cried. "No—my baby—"

Jax leaned against her and wiped her tears. "It's all right, baby. We'll just try again when you're stronger, if that is what you want."

"I want to see her, Jax."

"That's not wise," Lincoln said. "It's best to let her go."

Livie turned away and shook her head. After several minutes, she moaned again. "Oh it hurts—again. It hurts more." She began breathing rapidly again.

Lincoln moved back between her legs. "Push, Livie, there is another one. You're having twins. Push, Livie. You can do it, honey."

Betsy was back beside him with a towel ready to take the baby from him.

"Twins," Livie asked. "Are you sure?"

"Here it comes. Keep pushing, Livie," Lincoln ordered and focused on his task before him.

"I love you, baby. You're doing fine," Jax told her. He wiped the sweat from her forehead with his hand.

She forced a grin. She pushed and Lincoln caught the child and guided it out.

"It's another girl," he said. "It's a beautiful, healthy little girl."

"I want to see her," Olivia said. "Let me see. Jax, please."

Lincoln gave the child to her. She took the baby into her arms and rested the child on her chest.

"Jax, look she's beautiful. Look, a girl."

"She's beautiful just like you," he said. He placed his lips on Olivia's and wiped her brow with his hand.

She pulled away from him and moaned again. "Oh God, Jax it hurts. Ouch!"

Lincoln's expression was not hopeful. Jax leaned over to him. "What's wrong?"

"Hold her hand, son. Talk to her." He turned to his sister and whispered, "Betsy, take the baby. She's bleeding and I don't know if I can stop it."

He turned to hand his sister the baby, but Katherine stepped forward and took the child into her arms for a long moment. Katherine said a few words to Lincoln and then handed the baby to Betsy and she left the room.

"Livie, I want you to try and relax," Lincoln said. "Try to control your breathing. It's very important."

Katherine leaned forward. "What's wrong?"

"She's hemorrhaging and I can't stop it. I'm losing her," Lincoln said.

"You have to help her. Do something, Lincoln. This is not supposed to happen," Katherine said. This was not what she wanted. Breaking up her son's marriage was one thing. This was something she wouldn't allow.

Maddy stepped forward but said nothing. Instead, she brought her hands to her mouth and mumbled a prayer. George remained rigid by her side.

Jax took Olivia's hands in his. "Hold on, baby. Hold on. I love you."

She struggled to breathe. "Something is wrong, isn't it, Jax? Something—is wrong. I know it."

"No. Of course not. You're going to be fine," he said, kissing each of her hands one at a time.

"I feel it, Jax. I'm so tired. I love you, Jax. I—love you with my whole—heart."

"I love you too, baby. I love you too. I love you more than my own life," he said. "Hold on, baby. Hold on." She reached out to touch his face. He caught her hand and brushed it against his lips. "I love you, baby. Don't you leave me. Stay with me. I need you."

"I'm so—tired. I'm—cold, Jax," she said weakly.

He pulled the covers over her shoulders, stood up, and went to the foot of the bed. "Help her!" he said. "Help her, Uncle Linc! Do something!"

"I can't, son. She's bleeding too much. I'm sorry."

"No!" Jax rushed back to her side. "Baby, you hang in there. Don't you leave me, baby. I need you. I love you, baby. Do you hear me? I love you, baby."

Her words became an effort but she tried to smile, for him.

"I—love—you—Jax. You—made—me—so—happy. I love you, Jax. Kiss me..."

He leaned over, placed his lips on hers, and took her into his arms. She kissed him with her last breath. He released the kiss and stared at her. "I love you, baby. I love you. Livie, you wake up and answer me." He held onto her lifeless body. "Livie, answer me, baby, I can't live without you. Livie! Livie!"

Lincoln stood up and placed his hand on Jax's shoulder. "She's gone, son. Let her go."

Maddy nearly collapsed, but George caught her. "Get hold of yourself, Maddy," he told her.

"No! No!" Jax was crazed and wouldn't let any of them near her. "She's not gone! She wouldn't leave me. We love each other! She wouldn't leave our child! Get out!" Jax ordered, "Get away from her! All of you! Get out of our room!" He faced his parents, her parents, the doctor and his sister. "This is what you all want! You don't like her! You don't like me! You didn't want us to get married and you didn't want our baby! You got what you wanted, didn't you? Damn you! Damn you to hell, all of you! Now get out!"

"Pull yourself together, son!" Jackson ordered. "Let her go."

"I said get out! Get out! We don't want you here!"

Jax was blind with fury. Katherine saw it in his eyes. He shoved his father against the wall.

"Oh, darling. Let her go, son," Katherine said and took a step toward him. "She's gone. You can move on from here."

"Move on? Move on!" He advanced on her. She found herself backing up. "Move on where, Mother? Livie is my wife! My wife and my life! You never understood that! I'm not going anywhere without her!" Jax shook his fist. "Get out of here, all of you! Get out!"

Katherine backed up. She'd never seen her son so angry! Never. It was then that she realized just how very much her son loved Olivia. Why hadn't she seen it before? The look in his eyes—it tore a hole in her heart that would never heal.

The four grandparents walked to the door. He followed them, slammed it shut, and locked it behind them. As a last ditch effort, Katherine tried to talk sense to him through the door, but he wouldn't listen. A divorce he could recover from, but this. Of course, she'd be there to see him through it all, if he let her. She could make it all right, if he let her.

She didn't want him to wallow in grief, but he ignored her pleas.

Jax spun on his feet and walked back to Livie. There she lay on the king sized bed, their bed. Blood covered the linens between her legs, beneath her. Her blood. He lay down on top of her and cried. "I told you that I can't live without you. I won't live without you. You're my life, baby. I love you, Livie. Why did you leave me? I would have taken us away from here, anywhere you wanted to go. Anywhere. We could have taken our child with us. Paris—we could still go there if you want. We can leave anytime you say." He sat up, ran his fingers over her lips, and kissed her. "You're cold, baby." He brought the covers up. "Why did you leave me?"

He pushed himself back from her and stared at her. "You're so beautiful. You're my everything, baby. I told you that. I can't raise a child without you. What do I know about raising a child? I couldn't protect you from dying. How can I protect a child?" He brushed her long hair away from her face. For a long moment, he just stared at her lifeless body. There was only one thing left to do for him, for her.

He walked across the room to the bedroom closet, opened the door, and took a shotgun from the back wall. From the shelf, he retrieved a box of shells. He dropped the box and the extra shells he didn't need, walked to the bar, and took off a bottle of whiskey. He brought the items back with him to the bed. There, he removed two shells from his hand and loaded the shotgun then set the gun down on the floor with the stock between his feet. He opened the whiskey bottle and began to drink from it. He leaned over to the bedside table, pulled off a sheet of paper, grabbed a pen, scribbled a note, and put it on the foot of the bed.

He lifted the gun up and lay back next to her. "I love you, baby and I won't live without you. I can't do it. I won't do it." He put the stock down between his feet. "I can't live without you, Livie. I told you that." He placed the barrel in his mouth and held the gun by the trigger. He extended his other hand over Olivia. "Wait for me, baby. I'll be there soon and we'll be together again." With one quick movement, he pulled the trigger.

Katherine heard it first and sat up in bed. She clenched her hand into a fist. "Jackson," she yelled.

From his expression, he'd heard it too and she knew he feared the same thing she did. He looked at her then ran from their room with her close on his heels. They rushed to Jax's room but couldn't get in.

"He's locked it," Jackson said.

"Open it, quickly," Katherine said. She feared the worst. She shouldn't have left him alone. She went to the door. "Jax, son, open this door, please." But there was no answer. There was no sound at all.

George and Maddy ran up the stairs and joined them. They hadn't even left yet. Lincoln and Betsy rushed out into the hall and to the bedroom door to join them.

"Give me a hand," Jackson said to George and Lincoln. "He's locked the door."

The three large men turned sideways and struck the solid oak door with their shoulders—once, twice, three times. The fourth time, it began to give way. The fifth time the heavy door swung open. The two sets of parents and doctor and sister rushed in to find Jax lying on his back across Livie's body. Blood and bloody fragments were splattered across the linens and wall behind the bed.

Katherine nearly fainted when she saw that the top of her son's head was gone from the shotgun blast. Jackson caught her from behind. "Lincoln, get her out of here."

Lincoln moved to escort Katherine out of the room, but she pulled away from him and went back. She noticed the piece of paper on the bed. Blood was on it. She didn't need to pick it up to read it. She recognized her son's handwriting immediately. She read it. I can't live without her. She was my life. You never understood. You can all go to hell now!

She stepped away from the bed and the bodies it contained. The body of her beloved son and his wife. But she wouldn't cry. She couldn't cry. She refused to be weak and let her emotions get the best of her. All she could do was move on. Pretend this entire horrible mess hadn't happened.

Maddy stepped forward and nearly collapsed at the sight before her. George caught her.

"We don't talk about anything that happened here tonight," Katherine said. "Never. To anyone."

Jackson nodded. "Swear it," he said looking at Maddy, George, Lincoln, and Betsy.

"I swear," George said and looked at his wife.

Maddy nodded through her tears. Lincoln and Betsy copied her.

"The day you do, I'll have that house torn down around you and the land burned," Jackson said to George and Maddy.

"We won't say anything. We agree. The children shouldn't have married. The babies shouldn't have been born," George said. "The damage is done. It's over."

"Swear it," Katherine repeated. "Swear it. Swear it," she repeated again.

დადი

"Swear it!" she yelled. "Swear it! Swear it! Swear it! Swear it!"

"Katherine, wake up!" Lincoln ordered. "Katherine, wake up! You're dreaming! What's wrong?"

She opened her eyes to find him watching her, his face awash with concern. He was by her side, sitting on the edge of the bed. He held her by her shoulders.

"Oh God, Lincoln. Oh God," She fought to catch her breath. "I was there all over again. I was there. I saw it all again!"

His eyes studied her. "Where were you? Saw what again?"

"That night—that horrible, horrible night when I lost Jax."

"It was just a dream."

"No. I saw it. It was real, so damned real," she said. "I saw it all over again. Jax shot himself."

"Katherine, it was a dream. You never saw Jax shoot himself," he told her. "No one did."

"Oh God, Lincoln, it was horrible."

"It was just a dream," he repeated.

"No, it wasn't. You were there that night. You know that. Oh God, what have we done?" She fell against him. "Oh God, my Jax. I'm so sorry, darling. I'm so sorry. I should have been there for you. I should have supported you. I should have accepted Olivia. I never wanted any harm to come to her."

"Katherine, think sense. It wasn't real."

"I know it was a dream, but I saw it—the whole thing. It was like watching a film. I saw it all over again. Oh my God, oh my God."

"Katherine, it was a nightmare. That is all, and it's over. It's been over for a long time."

"No. It isn't over. It's just begun. Don't you see? This is the fallout from it all—the lies, the secrets, my vanity, my pride, and my bigotry. I always knew there would be a price to pay for our deception. I just never knew it would come so soon or that it would harm Kate. This is what has come out of it. Oh God, if she dies, I don't want to live anymore. It's all our fault, don't you see? Mine and Jackson's. All of it. She wouldn't be in that hospital if we had done right by them. Oh my God..." She began to sob. "Jax, forgive me, son. I was wrong. I was so very wrong. I'm sorry, Livie. I'm so sorry."

He wrapped his arms around her. She snuggled close.

"It's all right now, Katherine," he said. "I'm here and I'm not going anywhere."

She burrowed into his embrace and the tears fell, breaking through the icy fort she'd built around her for so long. She felt his hands rest on her shoulders and then her back. She cried years of tears for those lost. They were tears she'd held back when her husband died. Good riddance. He didn't deserve a tear. They were the tears she had held back when her son killed himself. They were tears for the baby she lost when her horse threw her and the loss of never having another child after Jax. The tears she held back when she almost lost Kate two years before and lost the great grandchild Kate carried. The steel armor she had worn for so long was beginning to show its age. It wasn't as shiny or new or virtually impenetrable as it once had been.

Years ago, Katherine cried when she discovered Jackson had cheated on her just a month after they were married. In turn, she began her own affairs and she never again cried when she discovered Jackson cheated. The last few times she ever cried was when her mother died, when Maddy's mother Olivia died, and when she lost her baby brother Jefferson in the Vietnam War. Tears never came again for her. She wouldn't let them. Let Jackson travel, the more the better. Let him cheat. She could care less anymore. She merely remembered her mother's admonishment about how best to survive in a man's world by utilizing her assets. A woman need not settle if she took control, using what she had. And it proved true, for no matter where Jackson was or who he was with, he always returned to her bed to be with her. That is, when she let him. When she presented Jackson with a son nine months to the day after Jackson had first cheated, her father-in-law, better known as Jack Thayer, gave his son full control of

Magnolia Lane Farm in trust for his grandson, Jackson Thayer the V, quickly nicknamed Jax by his maternal grandmother, Caroline.

Katherine thought back to the day she discovered Jackson caught in a heated embrace with an old girlfriend only a month into their marriage…

𝒞𝒟𝒞𝒟

She ran home to find solace in the only place she ever felt safe, back to her mother's embrace and wisdom. After she spent the day and evening crying, Katherine heard her mother Caroline enter Katherine's childhood room.

"Do you know what you're going to do, darling?" her mother asked and shut the door behind her.

"No, Mama. I haven't thought about that. At first, I wanted to kill them both."

"That's an option," Caroline said.

Katherine eyed her. "Mama, be serious."

Caroline reached out and took her daughter's hand as she sat down on the bed next to her. "I am. Darling, the options for a woman are limited even in 1962. The way I see it is that you have just three options."

Katherine wiped her eyes with the back of her hand and sat up straight to listen.

"One, you can leave Jackson. Divorce him and most likely get nothing in the settlement. Two, you can stay with him and make your own terms by using what God gave you, or three, you can kill him."

"Mama, you can't be serious."

"Yes, darling, I am."

"But, Mama, I love Jackson. I don't want to leave him. I just don't want him to cheat on me again and I don't want to kill him."

"That leaves you with just one option, go home and make your own terms."

"Really, Mama. How? How do I do that? He doesn't even miss me." Katherine turned away.

"Nonsense. He's been calling here all day. I told him I don't know where you are."

"Mama," Katherine scolded. "Why?"

Caroline reached out and put a hand on her daughter's shoulder. "Darling, I know men. As much as they hate to admit it, they can't live without us and that's why they so often cheat. He'll want you more if he can't have you, if he doesn't know where you are, and thinks you left him for good. Don't make it easy for him. Challenge him. They're fools, so many of them, not all."

"Like Daddy."

Caroline was silent for a moment. "Your daddy was a fool, too."

"Like when he tried to beat you that night when I was little and you had to shoot him?" She'd never forget the night her daddy died. For some reason he became angry with her mama and tried to hurt her. Katherine only got through it because of the love of her mama and Maddy's mama, Olivia.

"Yes, darling. Now tell me this. You are a beautiful and intelligent young woman. What does Jackson most desire from you? Your brains? Your beauty?"

"Sex and a son."

"Exactly." Caroline cupped her daughter's chin in her hand. "Give him what he wants, darling, and then take what you want. He'll deny you nothing."

"I thought it was me. Will he still cheat?"

"Yes, most likely," her mother said. "Only you'll know that. A leopard doesn't change its spots, but I'll be here for you whenever you need me."

Katherine lowered her head. "I think I may be pregnant, but it's only been a month."

Caroline grinned and placed her arm around her waist. "Oh, darling, you know that all it takes is just one time. Think about this. What do you want? Dixie and Jack won't be around forever. One day, that property, that house, and all on and in it will belong to Jackson and you, if you want it. What do you want most of all for you and your child? What do you see in your future? Make it legal. Put it in writing. And never, ever let Jackson know your intentions."

Katherine leaned into her, for the comfort and warmth, and sighed. Her future was a life with Jackson and their children. That was her future when she married him. Now, she had to think about it. But it wasn't difficult. "I want Jackson. I want his children, but I won't be cheated on and I won't be used. I won't."

"Then you need to decide what you want from him and exactly how to get it. There's nothing saying a wife can't have an affair if her husband cheats on her. There's nothing saying you can't take care of yourself first and always, darling."

"D—did you ever cheat on Daddy?"

"No. Never. But your daddy never gave me a reason to do so." Caroline kissed her daughter's cheek. *"Women need to make their way in this world in a way they are happy with."*

Katherine took her hand. *"Thank you, Mama. You speak a great deal of sense. I love you."* She knew exactly what she was going to do, if she had to.

ಲ೨ಲ೨

Her mother was a great source of support until she died ten years later and, with that, Katherine lost the greatest ally she ever had. Her mother was only forty-eight when cancer consumed her body, first her breasts and, later, all of her. She never got to see Jax grow to the handsome, young, caring, man he was or her beautiful namesake, Kate, but she left behind a legacy even so.

Of course, Katherine couldn't speak to her mother-in-law about anything. Katherine had very little use for her. First, Dixie Canfield Thayer didn't like her daughter-in-law. She even went as far as telling Katherine so one evening after she had a bit too much to drink after dinner.

"I don't think you're good enough for my boy, but you're his choice, so I'll have to learn to live with it."

That was before she presented "Madame Dixie" with a grandson. From that day on, life revolved around Jax. It didn't take long to figure out why Dixie disliked her. Dixie was a weak and foolish woman and resented her daughter-in-law's strength, intelligence, and independence. Dixie had no strength of will. When Jack slipped up and cheated on Dixie from time to time, the older woman either buried her head in the sand, or in a bottle. Katherine wouldn't become like her. Her mother, Caroline was a woman to emulate, not Dixie.

When Jack Thayer died two years after Jax's birth, Katherine made the threat of taking Jax away and sealed the deal with her husband that put her in charge of everything. It was a fruitful deal for both of them, though it proved in the end to be a far better one for Katherine. She never had to answer to anyone, any man, ever again. Truth be told, she would never take her son away from what rightfully belonged to him. She stayed with Jackson to ensure her son's future.

But there was also something missing in her life. After Jackson first cheated on her and broke her heart, she swore never to open her heart to anyone again. Her heart was closed to everyone around her. Everyone but her son Jax. When Jax broke her heart with his marriage to Olivia and then killed himself, she swore never to love anyone again. Never again was she going to be vulnerable to her emotions. That was how men survived and took charge. They didn't get emotional and, when they did, it was their downfall. That was until that fateful night she held Kate in her arms. From that moment on, her life was changed. Kate saved her from a life of gloom and doom. Kate saved her from the bitterness and resentment that consumed her. Kate rejuvenated her soul. Kate gave her a reason for living again and living life her way. And she lived to pass that wisdom onto Kate.

છ૭છ૭

The next day before the sun even came up, Katherine rushed back to the hospital. She sat down near the head of her bed in order for Kate to see her when she woke up. Her only concern was that Kate would not wake up as the doctors expected she would.

A couple of hours later found the two specialists, who were responsible for Kate's health, in the nephrologist's office. They conferred over the laboratory data they viewed on the computer screen before them.

Doctor Stanley sat behind his desk and pointed out the results to his colleague. "This can't be right."

"I had them run the tests twice to be sure," the nurse told them as she stood in front of the desk.

He looked again. "Run it a third time," the urologist said. "Just to be sure."

"Yes, Doctor," the nurse said and departed.

It was a couple of hours later that day when Kate slowly opened her eyes and had difficulty focusing. At first, everything was a bit blurry, as if she was looking at things through a glass of water. She blinked a few times, trying to see properly. It was as if sand lined her eyelids. She willed her arms to move and they seemed like pieces of stone. Her throat was dry. She was thirsty. Why was she so thirsty? Her eyes were heavy, but she was determined to keep them open.

Her head was heavy, but she exerted all her strength to turn it and looked to her right. The first thing she saw was a head of short black hair on her bed.

"Astrid?" Kate's voice was weak. She could hardly hear her own voice as she repeated. "Astrid?" She swallowed and tried again, this time stronger. "Astrid!" She couldn't move her hand to reach out. Someone was holding it. "Astrid?"

Astrid lifted her head and their eyes met.

Kate tried to smile. "Astrid. Is that really you?" she said weakly.

Astrid squeezed her hand and forced a weary smile. "It's me. I'm here, Kate."

Katherine was on her feet immediately from alongside the bed. "Kate, darling, oh thank God. She's awake. Someone get the doctor. Thank God. Darling, we're here for you. All of us."

"Astrid?" Kate repeated and couldn't help but smile at her. "How? Where am I? W—What happened?"

"You're in a hospital," Astrid said. "You almost died,"

"But you're going to be fine," Katherine said. "Just fine."

Kate faced Astrid. Unlike the others, she knew she could trust her. She closed her eyes momentarily. The memories were slow to return. "I—I remember. Sam? Where's Sam?"

"I'm here, kiddo," he said from the back of the room. She saw him back there, standing with Elsa, their hands in each other's. She was seated and he was standing by her. "I told them to check your kidneys, Katy, and they did."

Katherine took Kate's left hand and held it up against her mouth, placing a gentle kiss on her knuckles. "You're going to be all right, darling. You will, Katherine."

There it was again. Her grandmother addressing her by her full name.

"Grandmother—you look—terrible," Kate said. "I didn't mean—I'm sorry."

Her grandmother had lost her vibrant glow. There were circles under her eyes and her skin was pale. Her normally immaculate hair was hanging down loosely around her shoulders. Kate had never seen the other woman look so worn, so old, so beaten down. She hadn't meant to worry anyone.

Katherine laughed. "Oh God, darling, you said nothing wrong. You look beautiful. I'm so sorry. I'm so sorry. I'm so ashamed. Please, forgive me."

"Oh child," Maddy said. "We did a terrible thing to the both of you. We love you, both of you. I'm sorry."

"I love you, Gran, Maddy. I forgive you—all of you. Life is too short to be angry." She turned to Astrid. "Have you met my sister, Astrid? My sister—Astrid."

"Yes, and she's beautiful," Katherine admitted. "You're both so beautiful."

"Just like your mama," It was Maddy. She was by the top of Kate's headboard, her fingers brushing Kate's hair. "You're going to be just fine, child."

"How long—how long have you been here?" she asked Astrid.

"As long as the rest of us, longer," Katherine said. "She never left."

"None of us did," Maddy said. "Where would we go without you?"

The urologist entered the room, with Lincoln in tow, and moved to her bedside. She watched him as he checked the machines that monitored her life signs. They told them whether she was alive or dead, breathing or not.

He turned to her. "Good afternoon, young lady. Can you tell me your name?"

She smiled at the silly question. "Kate...Katherine Thayer. Kate."

He was handsome. He was tall, though everyone, at the moment, was tall to her from her point of view. He had a head of thick black hair, piercing blue eyes, a pleasant voice, and an air about him that made her feel safe.

"Fine," he said.

His eyes studied her, making an independent human assessment no machine could ever replace. As far as she was concerned, computers and machines could never replace the human touch in human or animal medicine.

"Do you know where you are?" he asked.

"Hospital," she said matter-of-factly. "I'm in a hospital in New York City."

"Fine." He took out a penlight from the breast pocket of his white smock. "Look at a spot on the ceiling for me."

She did. She saw the tiles of a drop-in ceiling, squares of Swiss cheese and perfectly white, as if they were brand-new. He examined her eyes, checking her pupils for reactions.

"Are you in any pain? Headaches? Abdominal cramping? Anything irregular?" he asked as he put his penlight back into his pocket. "Tell me how you feel."

"My back hurts," she said.

He nodded. "We'll get into more of the details later, when you're stronger. We had to remove your left kidney. It was no longer functioning. You had a bad infection. You were in shock, but everything is functioning normally now. "

"I'm hungry and thirsty," she said. "Tired."

"Normal and good. I have you on a liquid diet to begin with. I'll have them bring in a tray."

"Jell-O?"

"Yes, Jell-O is on the menu," he said with a smile.

"I want to go home," she said.

Suddenly, she missed the small town of Thayersville, the friendliness of the people, and that happy-go-lucky attitude that didn't seem to exist up North. The relaxed, easy-going attitude of taking it all in stride. Tomorrow would soon be here—no need to rush it.

"I'm sure you do. I'll have a nurse come in and remove the catheter. As long as you relieve yourself normally and your blood work is normal, I see no reason why we can't send you home tomorrow," he said. "Sound good?"

"Yes. Very." Her throat was so dry. "Can I have something to drink?"

"I don't see why not."

Katherine moved in reflex, but Astrid beat her to it. She stood up, took the plastic pitcher of water from the bedside tray, poured water into the pink plastic cup, and held it for her. Kate struggled to sit up, but she wasn't alone. The doctor pressed the buttons on the bed to raise it. Maddy and Katherine each placed a hand on Kate's back and supported her from behind. Kate put her hands around the cup. Astrid placed her hands on top of hers.

Kate sipped slowly. Their eyes met—Astrid's green eyes to hers. "No contact lenses today?" Kate said.

Astrid forced a smile. "No, no lenses. I don't need them anymore."

"You never did," Kate said. "You have our father's eyes."

"So do you," Astrid said.

"They loved you—our mama and daddy," Kate said.

"They loved both of us," Astrid said.

Kate couldn't stay awake. "I'm tired."

She released the cup. Astrid took it and set it down.

"Lay back now, darling, and rest," Katherine said.

"We're all here, child," Maddy said. "And we're not going anywhere."

Kate let her head fall back and held onto Astrid as her eyelids closed on the other set of green eyes watching her.

Katherine brought her hands to her mouth. Maddy brushed Kate's hair.

The doctor stepped forward and eyed the machines. "Don't worry. She's just tired. It's been a long couple of days for her. For all of you. She may go in and out like this all day. There's nothing to worry about."

Katherine was the first to speak, "You said she can go home tomorrow. Isn't that too soon? She's had major surgery? She was so sick?"

"We were able to do what is called Band-Aid surgery to remove the bad kidney. We removed the kidney through a small incision. You'll hardly notice the wound. And she's doing fine. Exceptionally well. The nephrologist and I are very impressed, even astonished, with her recovery. As long as she progresses this way, there is no need to keep her here. She'd actually do better with recovery at home."

"Thank you, Jesus!" Maddy exclaimed.

"Yes, I wouldn't deny a divine hand intervened on her behalf. Whatever you did or said, I'd keep at it for her sake." He took a last look over her monitors. "I will be here the rest of the evening. So any questions or concerns, please have a nurse find me."

"Thank you, Doctor," Astrid said.

She sat back down next to the bed and held onto Kate's hand. She considered what Kate said. Kate forgave them all, just like that. How could she after all they did to them, to their parents? Astrid couldn't do that.

Chapter 28

Maddy went outside to take a breather and thank God. Katherine went outside too and sat down next to her. Maddy faced her. This was the opportunity she wanted. "We should talk—" she began.

But Katherine cut her off. "We should. We need to, but not now. I just can't. Not until we know Kate is really going home. All I can do is focus on her first and foremost."

Maddy more than understood that. "I agree."

Katherine reached into her purse, pulled out a weathered white envelope, and handed it to her. "This belongs to you. Jackson wouldn't let me give it to you at the beginning and, later, I didn't want you to have it. It belongs to you. Kate wouldn't have it any other way now. I am sorry, Maddy." She got up and walked away back into Kate's room.

Maddy looked at the legal sized envelope. It was worn, dog-eared, and tattered in the corners. It was obviously a very old letter. She lifted her purse from her shoulder, dug inside for her brightly flowered case, and put her eyeglasses on.

Carefully, she opened the unsealed enveloped and took out the two-page document. The staple at the top left corner was rusty and almost worn through the fragile sheets of paper. They were yellowed from age and, when she read it, she knew why. It was the deed to her home and the property it sat on. The house and property that sealed the deal when they all swore their silence from that fateful night.

Katherine had given her the house and property when she had married Jackson all those years ago, but Maddy never received the deed and had forgotten all about it. Katherine had said that she wanted to keep her best friend, Maddy, close to her. Of course, after that, things had changed between them considerably. Once Katherine married Jackson, Maddy didn't see much of her at all. Once Maddy married George—well, she rarely saw Katherine again. And yet, here it was all these years later, a promise made good in writing. A promise that was stored away. Did Katherine forget about it, too?

Maddy read it over. Katherine Eleanor Beauregard Thayer sold the three-thousand-five-hundred square-foot house and the one hundred fifty acres of prime land it sat on to one Miss Madeline Olivia Williams Johnson for the full price of one dollar, paid in full.

It wasn't sold to George. It didn't belong to him. It was her house and hers alone, just as Katherine promised.

It was dated and signed by Katherine, on the first of May in nineteen hundred and sixty two, one day after she married Jackson.

Maddy stared at it. She didn't hear her son come and sit down next to her until he spoke. "Mama, everything all right? What's that?" She was still a bit too astonished to speak and simply handed it to him. He eyed it. He eyed her. "Mama, where did you get this?"

"Katherine."

"She gave this to you, now?"

All Maddy could do was nod.

"Mama—why? What happened? Where was this all this time?"

"Katherine gave me the house a long time ago. I gave her a dollar as a joke and she did this. Jackson and his family—they would never have given me this. But she kept it all this time. I thought she would have destroyed it after what happened, but she didn't."

"But, Mama, why? What does this mean?"

Maddy placed her hand on her son's hand that held the deed. "It means—" She felt tears build up. "Katherine and I are no longer enemies and Kate is going to be just fine." She just knew it. She'd made a promise to God to make peace with Katherine if Kate was all right. Had Katherine made the same promise, or was Katherine merely softening from what happened to Kate? Katherine didn't soften two years ago, but Kate didn't know the truth then. Or was Katherine simply doing the right thing? "Thank God, Sam."

Sam hugged her and nodded. "Yes, Mama. Thank God."

Of course, she agreed with her son. Where was it all this time and why didn't Katherine destroy it, especially after she found out about Maddy and Jackson?

✐✐✐

Kate woke two hours later and tried to sit up in bed. From the way she felt, she knew they'd removed the catheter, and all she wanted to do was to go home.

"Whoa!" Astrid said and was at her side. "What are you doing?"

"I have to go to the bathroom," Kate answered.

"Let me help you," Katherine said. She pressed the button on the bed to a higher sitting position. Astrid lowered the bed rail.

"Lean on me," Astrid said.

Kate sat up with Katherine and Maddy's help. Their hands eased her upward. She made a move to stand and almost fell backward.

"We have you, child," Maddy said as Kate felt hands holding her up.

"I feel like a newborn foal," Kate said.

Astrid grabbed her hands to help her up. "You mean a baby horse?"

"Yes, a baby horse. Exactly." Kate suddenly remembered and turned toward Katherine. "The foals, Gran? Are they all right? Delta?"

"Carl called a little while ago to let me know that the foals and mama are doing just fine, just like you are now," Katherine said. "Just fine."

Kate nodded. She heard the exhaustion in her grandmother's voice, saw it etched on all their faces. Kate turned around and tried again to get out of bed and, with Astrid's help, got to her feet. She moved toward the bathroom, leaning on Astrid for support. Julia pulled the IV stand on wheels along for her. At the bathroom, Julia opened the door and Kate stepped in with Astrid close behind.

Kate stopped. "I think I can manage the rest myself."

"You sure?"

Astrid was concerned. Kate heard it her voice and saw it on her face in her widened eyes and arched eyebrows. How many times had she seen that same expression on her grandmother's face?

"Yes. Thanks." Kate stepped inside, pulling the IV stand inside with her. "You can close the door, though."

Julia closed it and Astrid stood by outside. She released a breath she hadn't even know she was holding.

"She's going to be just fine," Julia said.

Astrid nodded. She looked up and saw everyone in the room looking her way. The minutes in there seemed like hours until Astrid heard the sound of the toilet flushing and the sound of water turning on and then off.

The door opened and Kate staggered out. "I think I can go home tomorrow," she said.

Kate glanced at the people in the room. All eyes were on her and all she could think of was home. Home seemed so far away from where she was now, and it was. Though, not everyone would agree with her, Mississippi was the best place in the world to live. She knew from experience that most visitors to Mississippi, and the South in general, couldn't tolerate the carefree and laid back, no hurry, no worry pace attitude that she loved. It was home. A visiting friend from up North once commented that there was no fast food in Mississippi. It was a joke about how slow the service was at fast food restaurants, but came to stand for everything the state did in Kate's friend's eyes. Everything and everyone moved too slowly for her and she had to go home. Kate tried to explain more than once that things moved at a slower pace and people liked it that way. They cherished it. Things would get done. Tomorrow would soon be here whether we wanted it or not. Live in today and enjoy it. Life was way too short to rush things. Tomorrow would come and go. There is no need to rush.

Mississippi had a bad reputation because lots of people based it on what they'd heard without even visiting, which wasn't fair. Visiting sometimes just wasn't enough time to really get to know the Magnolia state. A classmate once remarked that Mississippi was backward and way behind in things, compared to the rest of the United States. Kate didn't take it personally. People didn't understand unless they lived in Mississippi, and as she tried to explain again. Mississippi might be slow to adapt and catch up with things because there was no rush. Adapt, it would. Eventually. Adam understood and came to love it. It was one of the reasons he stayed and made it his home. Of course, the other reason he stayed was Kate.

Katherine glanced at Maddy and raised a hand at her. Maddy noticed and followed her out of the ICU room. The two women passed the nurses' station and entered the waiting room. "I think we need to talk now," Katherine said.

"We do, but not here," Maddy said and led the way to the elevators.

Katherine followed. It was the first time she'd followed Maddy anywhere in a long time. Maddy pressed the button to go down. They stepped out of the elevator and headed to the chapel. Inside, Maddy faced her. "I think that, under the circumstances, this is the more appropriate place for us to talk."

"I agree," Katherine said.

The chapel was empty. They sat down side by side. Katherine began, "I think for the sake of our granddaughters, we need to settle things between us."

Maddy nodded. "*Our* granddaughters?"

"Yes, *our* granddaughters," Katherine repeated.

"It is what our children would have wanted," Maddy said.

Katherine nodded. "We owe it to them. I'd like for us to be amiable toward each other when they come home."

"I agree—*if* they come home," Maddy said. "If you can swallow your pride, I can swallow mine."

"We can try. Both being stubborn and proud as we are."

Maddy nodded. "Any idea how should we start?" she asked. "Being civil? It's been so long—the hatred between the two of us?"

"I always found that meeting things head on is the best approach," Katherine said.

"I agree."

Katherine glared. "I hated you for so long. I hated you for not liking Jackson. I hated you for having an affair with him. I hated you for being Black. I hated you for your daughter taking away my son, for him committing suicide over her. I just hated you, Maddy. I blamed you for everything. But to Kate and Astrid, to our granddaughters, we lied so much. We hurt them so much. We must act civil toward each other."

Maddy nodded. "I hated you because your son took away my baby girl. I hated you because you were White. I hated you because you took my granddaughters and sent one away, but I didn't say anything. Do anything. So I'm just as guilty. Most of all, I hated you for making Jackson end his affair with me."

"I never made him end the affair," Katherine said. "I never knew until afterward. That's when I found out."

"He told me—he said you were going to leave him. You mean he lied to me?"

"It seems he lied to both of us, Maddy."

"Were you ever planning to leave him and take Jax?"

"No. The farm belonged to Jax," Katherine said. "I would have never let Jackson take away my son's inheritance. Never. The sad thing is that I loved Jackson, but I never trusted him again. I hated him. At times, I wanted to kill him. When he died it was a blessing. "

Maddy extended a hand and laid it on top of her old friend's. "He said—another lie. What about Lincoln and Giles?"

"They were diversions. I never loved them. Jackson was rarely home, and busy when he was, and now I know where he was when he wasn't in the house." Katherine eyed her. "You never told Jackson, anyone else? Why?"

"I hated both you and Jackson so much by then, I decided you deserved each other." Maddy placed a hand on Katherine's arm. Katherine didn't even flinch. "I'm sorry, Katherine. Very sorry. Jackson made fools of both of us. And we let him do it."

"I'm sorry too, Maddy. You were right about him. I guess it's just like Kate tried to tell me. In the end, you and I, Black and White, we're really no different, are we?"

"No, Katherine, I guess we're not. Not at all." Maddy looked away. It was a long moment before she spoke again. "He raped me, Katherine."

"Wh—what? Who did?" Katherine asked.

"Jackson. He raped me—the day he ended it. I was so angry, I attacked him. I wanted to kill him. He raped me and I became pregnant. I didn't want his baby. I got an abortion—an illegal one. You know how things were in those days. I couldn't just walk into an abortion clinic back then. I couldn't have any more children after that, even if I had wanted to. I never told George. He would have killed Jackson. I know it. In those days, they would have hanged George, for sure. I just couldn't chance that."

Katherine reached out and laid her hand on Maddy's. "Oh my God, Maddy, I'm so sorry. I didn't know."

"I'm sorry, too. I hurt you badly," Maddy said. "And for what? A stupid man like Jackson."

"You were right about not liking Jackson. He was too handsome for his own good, for any other woman's good, too. I shouldn't have gotten angry with you. I thought you were just jealous and being mean because you were jealous."

"I was, but I didn't trust him. He wasn't good enough for you."

"Or you." Katherine sighed. "There were others you know, other women. I shouldn't have hated you so much. You were my friend, my best friend. We grew up together when we couldn't be friends and we were. What happened to us?"

"We grew up. We grew apart." Maddy extended her other hand and placed it on top of Katherine's. "I betrayed you with him. I was a fool. I'm sorry, Katherine. I guess I just wanted a little something of what you had."

"But you had George. George was a good man. He loved you. He never cheated on you."

"No, he didn't, but we had our problems. He couldn't stand Livie—our girl—being so white," Maddy admitted. "He was a bigot. He didn't like us being friends. I just let things happen. It was easier than fighting with him. He would never have accepted Elsa. Never."

"And I became a bigot. Me. I'm such a fool, too. I should have never abandoned our friendship," Katherine said. "I hope he's burning in hell—Jackson. I hope he's the devil's whipping boy."

"I definitely agree with that. That two-timing son of a bitch," Maddy said. "Forgive me, Jesus, but I do, too."

For the first time in a very long time, Katherine got a strange feeling in the pit of her stomach, a feeling she lost when her son died. It was the feeling she hadn't let through in so long—a laugh. And she let it out and laughed. Freely. Wholly. Without reserve.

Maddy stared but couldn't help it either. For a few minutes, the laughter came until it just stopped.

"Remember when we were young and talked about getting married?" Katherine said. "When we thought our husbands would be like gods."

"Oh God, yes. Was that a big disappointment or what? George was no god," Maddy said.

"Neither was Jackson, though I'm quite sure he thought he was," Katherine said. "That's why I was so glad when Kate met Adam, even though he was a Yankee. They were good together and for each other. Oh, they fought, argued quite a lot, but Adam respected her. I don't think Jackson knew the meaning of respect, not when it came to women."

"Amen. Nor George."

"Jax did," Katherine said. "He was so unlike his father in that way."

"So is Sam," Maddy added.

"Sam is a gentleman. I see that," Katherine said. "Jax and Sam were raised right."

"We raised them," Maddy said. "Katherine, the deed you gave me—How? Why? All this time—"

"It's yours, legally yours, always has been. I had it written up, but Jackson, his parents wouldn't sign it. Not back then. Jackson outright refused. He took it, tore it up, and burned it that night." She sighed and lifted her chin into the air. "I figured he would after he refused to let you come to my wedding, which is why I had two copies drawn up. I put my copy away for safekeeping. When Kate left and I found myself alone and bored. I went through some of my old stuff in my old jewelry box, the one my father gave me, and I found it. Something, told me to bring it with me. Last night I went into the chapel and prayed for Kate and for peace of mind. I prayed for the strength to make things right. So much time was lost. We lost so much time, Maddy, you and I. Our children and our grandchildren. I was wrong, so very wrong."

"We were all wrong," Maddy said.

"I didn't know it. I wouldn't admit it until now how very wrong I was, for all of it. You and I—the girls—those girls are our blood. Our children's children and they need us. They need us not to hate each other. I need to not hate you anymore. I'm very sorry, Maddy. I missed you." Katherine extended a hand out to her. "Please forgive me."

Maddy took it. "I'm sorry, too, Katherine and I forgive you. I missed you too. I never gave up on you. We need to do right by the girls."

"We have to make it up to them. Somehow. I don't know how, but we have to," Katherine said.

"We hurt them terribly," Maddy said. "Our granddaughters are beautiful, though, aren't they?"

"Like their mother and grandmothers before them," Katherine admitted. "Olivia was a beautiful girl, inside and out. I wish I had taken the time to know her. I wish I hadn't been so blinded by anger—"

"I wish I had gotten to know Jax better when he was a grown man," Maddy said. "He was a fine young man. You should be proud. My baby loved him so much. When we told her she couldn't see him anymore, she told us to go to hell."

"He did, too. And they showed us when they got married," Katherine said. "They were fine children. Both of them."

"They had fine children, too," Maddy said.

"Our grandchildren," Katherine said.

"Our grandchildren," Maddy echoed.

"It's going to be a hard, long road," Katherine said.

"One we both deserve to be on," Maddy said.

Katherine reached out to her with her other hand. "You're right. For as long as it takes," she agreed. "I'm so sorry, Maddy."

Maddy grasped Katherine's hand. "I'm so sorry, Katy."

They pulled themselves into each other's arms and hugged for all the time lost between them, as friends, their children, and their grandchildren.

☙❧❧

Astrid stared at Kate and heard the two older women return. Astrid remained in her spot in her chair near the middle of the bed. Maddy took a spot within a few inches from Astrid near the headboard. Katherine went to the other side of the bed and sat down next to it.

Kate began moaning in her sleep. She began to flinch too, which caused Astrid to jump to her feet. "What's wrong with her? Should I get the doctor?" she asked.

Katherine got to her feet. "No, that's not necessary, Astrid." She leaned over Kate, ran her hand over her granddaughter's forehead, down along her cheek, and spoke to her. "It's all right, darling. Grandmother is here. Sleep now, Kate. Easy, darling." She rested her hand on Kate's shoulder.

Kate calmed down almost immediately under Katherine's touch. Astrid moved back to Kate's side, sat down, and rested her hand on her sister's right shoulder. "Was she dreaming?" Astrid asked and couldn't help staring at the older woman.

Katherine was amazing. If this was anywhere else, if she was anyone else, Astrid would admire her. As circumstances stood, the bitterness and resentment remained.

"Yes, she gets nightmares," Katherine said and looked right into Astrid's eyes.

Astrid swallowed and eyed Kate. "About losing her husband?" she asked and sympathized with Kate.

"Yes, sometimes."

Astrid looked directly at Katherine. "And you touch her and speak to her and that's all it takes to make her feel safe?"

Katherine met her gaze again. "Of course, I'm her grandmother. I raised her. I love her."

Astrid turned back to Kate. "It must have been very difficult for her, losing her husband."

"Yes. It was."

"I wish—" Astrid swallowed hard. It was out of her mouth before she could stop it. "I wish I had been there for her."

Katherine reached out a hand across Kate's body and cautiously rested it atop Astrid's. "I'm sorry, Astrid. I'm so sorry."

"We're both sorry, Astrid," Maddy added.

Astrid stared at Katherine, at her hand on top of hers, and then she had to turn away and pull her hand free. She couldn't look at Maddy either. She couldn't do this. She was too full of anger just to push it aside. She shook her head and moved her gaze back to Kate. Kate did right by her and she was the only one that mattered right now.

From a quick glance behind her out of the corner of her eye, she saw Sam and Elsa come back in, followed by the old doctor and Julia. This was her family, if she wanted it. But she couldn't do this. She'd remain for Kate, but that was all.

Katherine took back her hand. "It's all right. I understand." She sat back down and placed her hand back over Kate's.

That touched Astrid deeply and brought tears to the surface. The older woman was capable of so much. She obviously loved Kate. Why couldn't she have loved Astrid when she needed her to? She tasted the bitterness of bile rise to the back of her throat. Why didn't anyone keep her?

❧❧❧

Katherine stepped out of Kate's room and took a deep, slow breath. She meant to take just a moment to collect her thoughts, but there was something she had to do first. She had to clear some unfinished business.

Sam and Elsa sat in the corner of the waiting room. She walked up to them. "If I may have a moment of your time?"

They looked at her. She brought her hands up to her chest. This wasn't easy for her to do. "I wish to apologize for the other night. I shouldn't have struck you, Sam. I had no right. I am not in the habit of apologizing. I apologize to you, both of you. I was afraid of losing Kate."

Sam stood up to meet her. "Because of the truth. I understand. We were all afraid of losing her because of the truth. No problem, Miss Katherine. I bear you no grudge. I love Kate very much. I would do anything to keep her safe. "

"Thank you, Sam. I know. You're a fine young man." She moved to walk away.

"Miss Katherine," Sam said.

She stopped and faced him.

"I miss Jax, too," he said. "He was a good friend to me, just like a big brother. The big brother I never had."

She swallowed hard. He touched her deeply, as if he read her mind. "Thank you, Sam." She reached out to touch him and then pulled back. "You're a good person, both of you. You're lucky to have each other. Be good to one another. Love one another. Never let anyone come between you." She moved away, determined not to fall to pieces in front of anyone.

Sam watched her leave. Elsa came to his side and took his hand. "What was that all about? Did she mean all of that?"

"Yeah. She did," he said without a doubt and grasped her hand with his. "Two years working for her and you haven't learned anything? That woman says nothing she doesn't mean." *Just like Kate*.

♡♡♡

Back at the hotel, Katherine tossed and turned over and over until she'd had enough. She couldn't sleep, even though it was nearing two in the morning. She got up from the bed and made her way to the window, staring out onto the neighborhood below. It was late but the crowded city was still awake. The hotel was surrounded by homes. There wasn't a business building within sight. Lights were on in homes below, cars and taxis were on the streets. There were even some people walking the sidewalks. Streetlights shone above them all. It was so different from home. Home? She closed her eyes for a moment to the outside world. She had to do that frequently to maintain control. Katherine never looked back over her life. Not once. There was no reason for it. Nothing good ever came out of looking back. It was way too painful. But she couldn't help it now. The way things were going now, she just couldn't help looking back. Back to where her world started to crumble, where things began deteriorating, and she didn't even see it then. She'd been so much in love with Jackson. What a fool she was then, at the beginning of it all. Her marriage to Jackson all started out with bad karma.

Katherine remembered the exact moment with her friendship with Maddy had gone wrong. First, there was the argument they had over her marrying Jackson a week before. She thought Maddy was just jealous of her.

Then there was the argument she had with Jackson about allowing Maddy and her mother to attend her wedding…

e∽e∽∂

Maddy was to be her maid of honor and she wouldn't back down. Maddy had overheard Jackson and his parents talking about no Colored people being allowed. Maddy told Katherine. Now Katherine had to convince him to support her. They were in the big house at Magnolia Lane Farm inside the parlor.

She stood her ground. "Jackson, you have to talk to your parents about letting Maddy be my maid of honor."

"Not a chance," he said and took a sip of brandy. "You know how they feel. It's no secret."

"Wh—what?"

"She's Colored. There is no way my parents are going to let a Colored girl be in our wedding party, in this house or in our church. No way. Whites don't mix with Coloreds, Katherine. Never."

"She's my best friend, Jackson."

"She's Colored. She's no friend of yours, not anymore. I'm going to be your husband. I'm your best friend."

She turned away from him. She was so angry.

In a moment, he was behind her. She felt his warm breath down along her neck. "Katherine, you're going to have to choose. Me or that Colored girl. You can't have both." He was behind her and took her into his strong arms. He placed his burning lips on her neck. "You love me?"

She felt him from behind, his strong desire against her. He was so virile. She was under his spell. She faced him. "You know I do."

"Then there is no problem." He placed his lips on hers and that was the end of it.

❧❧❧

She didn't need to remember any more. That should have been a clue, a warning that their marriage was a mistake, but she'd ignored it. Things just continued to go downhill from there. *Never let a man run your life or you'll soon regret it. Stand on your own two feet. Make your own decisions and your own mistakes.* She had instilled that into Kate from day one. *Kate, my darling, little girl.*

That was then. This was now.

She moved over to the bed, sat down, and picked up her purse. She pulled out her wallet, laid it open, and placed her hand on the photo. "My dear son, Jax. What did I do to you? Your little girls? I should have supported you, but why oh, why did you have to fall in love with Maddy's girl when there were so many others who adored you?"

He smiled back at her from the photo. He was a handsome young man. It was easy to understand why Olivia Johnson had fallen for him. He was kind and gentle, yet strong and sure of himself. He was loyal and faithful. Olivia was lucky to have had him. He would never have cheated on his wife the way his father had cheated on Katherine. She just knew it. Jax wasn't that way. Yes, he was Jackson's son, but he was so unlike his father.

"Your little girls are all grown up and you didn't even get to see them. They're beautiful, both of them. They have your beautiful eyes." She ran her fingers over his eyes. "My darling, son, I miss you so very much. I was wrong. I wish you could hear me. I was so very wrong. I'll never be able to make this right. Never. What do I do now? Where do I go from here? When God took you away from me, I swore never to go to church or pray again and I didn't. I went into the chapel yesterday to pray. What did I teach you? If you make a mistake, you must own up to it and then try to make it right. I don't know if I can."

She didn't hear Lincoln enter the room. She didn't know he was there until he sat behind her and she felt his large hands on her shoulders. His warm breath was on the curve of her neck. She leaned into him. "I was so, so wrong," she told him. "And now I could lose Kate. Her sister doesn't want to know me, and I can't blame her."

The sound of his steady breathing comforted her. The sex she had with Gary was pleasurable and distracting, but there was no substance to it. It was simply concupiscence and nothing more. "You were always there for me," she told Lincoln.

"And I always will be. I love you," he said.

She sat up. Even at seventy-four, he retained his youthful glow. "Why? I've been a horrible person," she said.

He cupped her chin in his warm hand. "You have a good soul. You just don't let it out often enough to let others see it."

She turned away from him. She couldn't bear to look at him or be looked at by him. Not now. All these years he had been there for her, at her beck and call, steady as a tall ship in a calm sea. He had never wavered. He was simply there.

He placed a hand on her shoulder. "You need to sleep," he said. "You need your rest. Do I need to give you something to sleep again?"

She waved her hand at him. "No. No more pills." She took a deep breath. "He cheated on me. I loved him so much and Jackson cheated on me. With Maddy, with his secretary, with others. I swore I'd never again be used by any man. I had affairs but they meant nothing. He traveled so much, probably was with other women then too. I'm sure. I gave up caring."

"I know, Katy."

She turned to face him. His expression agreed with his words. But still... "You knew? Of course, you did. Did everyone? Was I a figure of laughter?" Of course. It was the price of living in a small city. Even with care, secrets didn't remain that way.

"No, but I knew Jackson. And I loved you. That is why I was always there for you—hoping, waiting."

"Oh, Lincoln. I'm sorry. I'm such a fool. I never meant to hurt you."

He took her hand and kissed it. "I know why you stayed. He

gave you power, comfort, wealth. I was a country GP. I could never have given you all those things."

He was right, somewhat. After she learned about her husband's brief affair with his old girlfriend, she'd threatened to leave him. She knew that losing his son and heir was something he wouldn't allow. Of course, she wouldn't have actually left. She proposed a deal: He could do as he pleased from then onward, as long as he was discreet and careful. She would not allow him to father an illegitimate child, or bring home a disease. In turn, she could do as she pleased and he couldn't say a word about it. Cornered, he agreed. The farm, house, everything and anything connected to it belonged to her from that day forward. Totally and freely without any strings. She even made it legal by hiring her own attorney. She wouldn't dare chance running it through Giles or anyone in his firm.

She raised a hand to Lincoln's face. She'd never seen him not shave before. The stubble gave him a rustic roguish look. He was even more handsome.

"I love you, Katy. What can I say?" he said.

"You're the only one that ever calls me that since—the only one I ever let call me that in a long, long time."

"I know."

"I can't lose Kate," Katherine said. "Until she comes home, anything can still happen to her."

"You won't. We won't let anything happen to her."

"Don't say things we can't control." She moved to turn away but he caught her arms and held her.

"I don't lie, Katy. I never have, except—"

She brought her hands to his face. "Except for that awful night when I asked you to and afterward."

"You didn't twist my arm. I knew what I was doing. I'd do anything for you, Katy. Anything." He took her hand and brought it to his lips. "Anything."

She pulled him to her and pressed herself against him. He wrapped his arms around her. She could smell the lingering scent of aftershave on him. "Hold me, Linc."

"Always, Katy. And Kate will be just fine. You'll see. We'll see her first thing tomorrow." He laid her back on the bed and leaned over her. "I'm no spring chicken, Katherine."

He ran his warm slender fingers against the side of her neck and she pressed into his touch. She raised her hand to his face and a finger to his lips. She had no desires tonight. She had only re-grets.

"Just hold me."

Chapter 29

Bright and early the next morning, Katherine woke up without the assistance of any alarm clock or hotel wake up call, remnants from her life running the farm. She showered and dressed quickly, ready for Lincoln to pick her up so that they could ride to the hospital together. She wanted to be there first thing when Kate woke up and she wouldn't be delayed. The only concern she had now was getting Kate safely back home as soon as she was able to.

Life had been on automatic over the last few days. Doing things she had to do to get through each day became a reflex action. Spending day and night at Kate's bedside, and then trying to eat, except for the last two nights when against her natural inclination to be with Kate, she returned to the hotel to try and get some sleep.

First thing she did on each day was to get up, take a quick shower, and fill herself with coffee, lots of it, to get her through each day.

And then she rushed back to the hospital in order to be there for when Kate needed her. For when Kate woke up.

She was ready ahead of time and sent for lots of coffee. She'd already drunk one pot, and was at work on her second pot, when there was a knock at the door. It was thirty minutes too early for Lincoln to arrive. When she opened the door, she nearly fainted.

"What on earth—Gary, what are you doing here? How did you find me?" Katherine demanded and slammed the door behind him. She didn't appreciate this invasion into her privacy.

He sauntered in, and she didn't like the way he took in the view of the sun-filled suite and high-end furnishings. He threw his briefcase onto the sofa. "It wasn't difficult," he said. "The private investigator I hired for you called me to tell me where Kate was, and he also told me where you were. He thought the whole thing was some kind of joke since I hired him for you. He wasn't amused. Neither was I."

"Send me a bill," she told him as she stormed past him to the table across the room. She grabbed the pot and the cup and proceeded to drink her coffee.

She felt him behind her as he placed a kiss on her neck and his hands on her waist. "I thought you might need me when he told me where Kate was."

She sipped the cup and set it down with saucer on the table. "You thought wrong. You can go home now."

"You're kidding, right?"

She removed his hands from off of her and faced him. "Do I look as if I'm kidding, Gary?"

"No. You look...different. Tired. I can understand that."

"Can you, darling?" she said, annoyed with his intrusion. "How?" There was very little he could understand.

"Wh—what?"

"Tell me how you understand. Like your father before you, you were never married. You have no children, no grandchildren. How do you understand how I'm feeling?" Katherine said.

"Look, you're upset. I get that. But I just wanted you to know I care. That I'm here. We'll leave it at that, okay?"

"No, Gary. I'd really like to know."

"I care for her. All right? Kate is a nice young lady."

She stared at him. "Yes. She is. What is this all about, Gary? You didn't travel all this way to tell me that, or for sex? I know better than that. I'm no school girl besotted by your boyish charms."

"Fine. Let's talk business." He went to his brief case, picked it up, and placed it on the glass coffee table that separated them. He sat down on the sofa and removed some papers. "If you want to retain the sole property rights to the farm, you will have to have Kate incapacitated and now is a good time."

"I don't understand," she said. "The farm is hers. It has always been and always will be. Those are her father's wishes and mine. And she isn't going to stay ill. She's out of surgery. We'll get her on her feet again soon."

"And what about you?" he asked.

"What about me?" What was he getting at? She had to know.

"Are you willing to give it all up?" he said. "The farm is worth millions, plus the crop and the horses. In the meantime, while she is incapacitated, I can get a court order for you to gain control."

"Gain control? If I wanted control, I wouldn't have given *her* control. My granddaughter is worth more to me than all the money in the world," she said. "You need to go home."

"Don't be a fool, Katherine. This is business. It's not like Jackson was really Kate's grandfather. You can do what you want with the farm."

Katherine laughed, so that was it. "What on God's green earth are you talking about?"

"You and my dad. He was Jax's father, not Jackson. That makes Jax and me brothers, half anyway."

"Who told you that nonsense? Giles?"

"Yes, he did. And I guessed. Jackson wasn't up to the task. Why else be with my father?"

"You are a fool, Gary. Your father would be so proud. Two fools."

"Be nice now. There's no need to be nasty, Katherine. It's not nice to speak ill of the dead."

"Your father, Giles, was not Jax's father. Jackson was. There is no question about that. I know. Jackson knew, too."

"You're lying."

"No doubt I've told a great many lies in my lifetime, but Jackson being the father to my son is not one of them. Do you really think I would sink so low as to have someone such as Giles father my child? Who else knew?"

"No one. Dad never talked to anyone. You know that. But he really thought Jax was his son. He would have made it public, except Jax didn't need anything from him. I really thought—so he wasn't my older half-brother at all? Wow. Color me stupid."

"No. Jax wasn't, and Giles obviously said enough. Your father was a diversion when Jackson was away on business. That is all. Just like you were, darling, a diversion and nothing more."

"I know my father was a shit. He didn't acknowledge me as his son until I was in high school, but you don't have to be hurtful to me, too when I'm merely trying to look out for you," he said.

"Look out for me? When did you ever do that? You looked out for my interests as long as they interested you. Both you and your father."

"Now that isn't true."

"Isn't it? Gary, I knew your father wasn't the marrying kind. Neither of you were interested in a long-time commitment, which was perfect, as I could never love anyone but Jackson. Why do you think I never pressured you or your father for something more?"

"Fine. Believe what you will. But I care about you," he said. "I always have and always will."

"Dear Gary, darling, the only ones you ever cared about was you, yourself, and you. Not me. Not Kate. Certainly not even your father."

"You know my father could have told Jackson about you and him, back then, later on, before he died, but he didn't. That should count for something. I could have told Kate, too."

"Why didn't he—you?"

"Because dad knew Jackson would divorce you, keep Jax, and leave you with nothing. Kate probably wouldn't have believed me."

"No. You father was afraid that Jackson would have killed him, and he would have too, and he was afraid I'd lose everything," Katherine argued. "But you're right, Kate wouldn't have believed you."

"Maybe. Maybe not. We'll never know, but if you don't do something, you'll lose the farm to Kate. Forever. Now, that, I'm certain of. Do you really want to lose it to her? God! Katherine think sense. She's half-Black."

That caught her off guard. "W—What did you say?"

"You heard me. It's no secret. Everyone remembers Livie being Maddy's daughter. Her going off to college didn't erase people's memories. Oh, some people thought she was adopted by a good hearted Black woman, but most knew that Livie was passing. But people in Thayersville liked you and Jackson. You were pillars of our town. They weren't going to insult you. Hell, your families go back centuries. You're our people. But Livie passing makes Kate half-Black. Do you really want to have your farm run by a coon?"

Katherine hadn't been filled with such a fury since she had beaten up upon Sam. With one hand, she reached out and slapped him hard across the face. The anger was two-fold. Anger at her own ignorance, her bigotry, and the blatant display of his. "Get out!"

He reeled from the blow, bringing a hand to his jaw. "Let's discuss this rationally—"

"Do you really think I would betray my granddaughter? You underestimate me, Gary. I would die for Kate. Get out before I kill you myself! I swear! Get out!"

He hesitated a moment, then walked over to the table, picked up his briefcase, and walked back to her.

"You're making a mistake, Katherine."

"You have no idea how many I have made already!" she said. "Get out. Send me a bill. You're fired."

"Wh—what? You're kidding," Gary said.

"Do I look as if I am kidding?"

"My family's firm has been your family attorney for nearly fifty years—"

"Fifty years too long," she said. "Time to make a change. Good bye, Gary." She walked to the door and opened it.

"I'd rather things didn't end this way between us," Gary said. "We've had some good times."

"Sex, Gary, is what we had. Nothing or no one harms my granddaughter. Now, get out."

"You'll miss me, Katherine," he said.

"I think not. You're good, darling, just not that good to make me lose control of my senses. Good bye."

"Look, I can drop the idea of taking the farm from Kate, if that's what you want?"

"Good bye, Gary," she said again.

"God, Katherine, I'm trying here. Give me a break."

"I'll count to three, then I will pick up the phone, call hotel security and the police. I won't repeat myself a third time."

He stepped through the door.

"Gary," she called. He turned and his eyes brightened with hope. "If you say anything to anyone about any of this," she said. "I'll see to it that your disbarred and never ever again practice law in Mississippi, or any of our Southern states, if need be."

He sighed, turned around, and walked out. She slammed the door after him, leaned against it with her back, and took a deep, slow breath.

It did nothing to soothe her nerves. What if Kate didn't fully recover? What if she died? There was still time left for something to go wrong.

A parent should not outlive their child. A grandparent

shouldn't outlive their grandchild. This was all so wrong. She was definitely being punished for the past. There was no other reason.

Chapter 30

Later on that day, at around ten in the morning, Doctor Stanley entered Kate's hospital room and sat down in a chair next to her bed. "Now I know you already discussed your surgery with Doctor Thorne. I won't go over that again, unless you want me to."

"No, that's not necessary. He said my left kidney was no longer functioning and caused an infection, which necessitated removal. Please go on."

"You have what we call polycystic disease. Are you familiar with it?"

"I've heard of it. Animals get it, too."

"Yes, I suppose they do. That isn't my specialty."

"It is mine," she said.

"Yes, of course. I see no reason why you can't lead a normal life even with PKD and one kidney. You just have to be more careful with your activities. No extreme activities now such as sky diving."

"Horse show jumping, too. I understand," she said.

"I strongly suggest you find a nephrologist when you get home. Statistically, patients do better under the care of a nephrologist than without one."

"I'll do that. I will." This time she meant it.

"Do you have any questions for me?"

"Actually, yes." If it was anything like animal medicine, she already knew the answer but had to ask. "Tell me what my options are should my remaining kidney fail."

"I don't think you have to worry about that. As I told you earlier, with your grandfather and his father, their kidneys didn't fail. The odds are good yours won't, either."

"No. I know how they died—aneurysms, but it is possible." She leaned forward. "Doctor, let's be up front. I'm not a human doctor, but I know a little bit about medicine and kidneys. What are my options should my kidneys fail? Dialysis or a transplant, correct?"

He nodded. "Dialysis is very effective, and you have your sister, which is a good candidate for a living donor—"

"But she could still develop cystic kidneys too, can't she?"

"Statistically, half of the children born to parents will get it. You have it. She shouldn't."

"We both know statistics are no guarantee of anything," Kate said. "She could. There is no guarantee that she still won't."

He shifted in his chair. "No. There are no guarantees. But there are organ donors."

"Doctor, I know enough to know that there are not enough organ donors to fill the need for every person needing an organ donation. Tell me, how many people die waiting for a kidney?"

"Doctor Thayer, every case is evaluated different—"

She cut him off. "But you and I know, whether it is animals or people, we really know very little, and what we do know, we tend to place them into different groups by standards. How many die on dialysis waiting for a kidney?"

He coughed and averted his gaze. "Five thousand people die each year." He looked up at her. "But there's no need for that to happen to you. Your sister is compatible donor."

"Only if she doesn't get PKD herself."

"The odds are slim. If she was going to develop it, she would be showing signs by now."

"Thank you, Doctor. I think I know all I need to know. Tomorrow, next month, next year, my remaining kidney could fail."

"I wouldn't exaggerate that much."

"But it is possible. I've seen it happen in small and large animals. I know. But that's fine. I'll just deal with it when I come to it." Just like everything else, she did in life. She'd deal with it head on when she had to.

"Well, I guess you know enough about PKD. Any other questions?" he asked.

"No. Not now, though I think I can do the research, if need be," she said.

"I'm sure you can, Doctor. I do have some literature here that I give to all my patients. There is only one organization out there that promotes information about PKD—the Polycystic Kidney Foundation. I suggest you make contact with them. You might find answers or support, should you feel you need it later down the line," he said as he handed her a booklet.

She took it. "Thank you. I'll do that, too."

"May I say something to you non-related to your kidneys?" he asked.

"Yes, please," she answered, curious as to what was on his mind.

"You have a unique family, Doctor Thayer."

She knew what he was going to say—Black and White—interracial etc. She was prepared for that. "Oh, in what way?" she asked.

"They didn't seem to get along when I first met them, but from what I saw while they were here, they put aside their differences and came together to put your well-being first. Not many families are able to do that."

She smiled to herself, pleased to be wrong about her initial thought. She only wished they had done it sooner, as in years ago, when her parents had needed them too. But better late than never. "They did. I'm glad."

"You're a lucky young woman."

"Thank you, Doctor, but I don't believe in luck," she said.

"I'll have a nurse come in and check you out and you can be on your way." He extended his hand. "Good luck, Doctor."

She shook it. "Thank you, Doctor."

He stood up and took his leave.

Have no regrets. Be kind to one another. Life is short. She couldn't hate her grandparents, no matter how hard she tried. Everything happened for a reason. Maybe this was her wakeup call not to hold their mistakes, their secrets, and their lies against them. She couldn't do that. She loved them, but it didn't mean she had to like it.

Had this happened to her to remind her of how precious life was, again? Had she forgotten from two years before? No, she hadn't, though her brief stint with drug addiction had taken away that lesson.

Astrid and Julia came back in when the doctor left and they nodded in passing.

"So," Astrid asked, first staring at the ground then at her. "Do you get to go home now?"

"Yes, I do. Just waiting for the nurse to let me go," Kate said.

"Good. So back to Mississippi then?" Astrid asked.

"Yes. I'd like you to come back with me. See where our parents were born and grew up."

Astrid waved a hand. "See where they died? No thanks."

"That's okay," Kate said. "You don't have to do anything you don't want to. I understand." She hoped Astrid believed her. "You don't have to go back. I know how you feel. When I first found out, my first instinct was to run away. I was so angry. I hated them all and didn't want to see any of them again. But I pushed on to find out all I could, and all I could do next was go look for you. I'm sorry, Astrid. I didn't think about the consequences until I hurt you. That was never my intention. I never meant to turn your life upside down."

Astrid reached out. "My life had been upside down for thirty years. Only when you showed up, when you told me the truth and left me our mother's journal did it set itself right side up. You made everything clear for me. I wasn't an orphan anymore, just a woman who lost her parents, and her family." Astrid stared at the floor. "Y—you could stay here awhile," she said and glanced up with a hopeful look.

"It's been awhile since I've been here and so much I haven't seen yet. I'd like that, if you're willing to put up with me," Kate answered.

"We'd love to have you," Julia said. "You can stay with us. We have a spare bedroom."

"I wouldn't want to intrude. I can stay in a hotel," Kate said.

"Not a chance. We've been through life and death together. We're family now," Julia said. "Astrid and I won't take no for an answer."

"Thank you," Kate replied. "For everything and for being there for my sister."

"You don't have to thank me for that," Julia said.

"I know, but I want to." Kate glanced from one to the other then back at Julia. Homosexuality, gays. She wasn't sure about the whole lifestyle thing. It was foreign to her and that was fine. She had no ambition to learn about it, but she would accept it for Astrid. And she would try to understand it for her, too. The two women evidently cared a great deal for each other, loved each other, and that was enough for her. "Thank you," she told Julia.

Julia nodded and grinned.

Kate extended her hand out to Astrid. "Friends? Sisters?"

Astrid took one of Kate's hands in her right one and the other hand into her left one. "Both. And since you're packing—" She looked at Julia and the other woman pulled her hand out from behind her back and handed Kate the journal. "This belongs to you," Astrid said.

Kate eyed it and then Astrid. "It belongs to both of us."

"You found it. You keep it," Astrid said. "At least I'll know where it is if I ever want to see it again. At least I'll know it'll be safe."

Kate took it. Astrid held onto it.

"I would like to get a copy of the photo, though, if that's okay," Astrid said.

Kate gripped her hand. "Consider it done. That belongs to both of us too."

Astrid gripped back and then released the book. Kate turned around and placed it in the plastic shopping bag on the bed that the hospital gave her for her belongings.

There was a knock at the door. "May we come in?" It was Katherine's voice.

Kate heard the anxiety.

"We'd like to speak with you, both of you," Maddy added.

Kate looked at them. There they stood, side by side. Before they had been totally different. Tall and voluptuous Katherine with lily-white skin and fire red hair and with usually perfectly manicured nails, both hair and nails professionally done. Maddy was short and slender with thick black hair that she brushed away from her face. Now, the two women were similar in appearance. They were still each Black and White, tall and short, but both had signs of worry and fatigue etched on their faces. Circles were under their eyes and they were both pale and haggard. Neither was concerned about putting their hair up. Did they know how very similar they appeared, or was it merely her perception of them that had changed?

She heard the uncertainty and fear in their voices. She wished she had a camera. Seeing them standing there, side by side, together, was a first for her, especially knowing about their animosity toward each other. She nodded. Had their worry for her made them make peace with one another? Was it possible or was it merely wishful thinking on her part? To get them in the same room together was an extraordinary feat. To have them standing here together, now was amazing. She wouldn't look a gift horse in the mouth. She'd accept it and be glad for it.

"We know we can never make it up to you. Our actions were deplorable." Katherine stepped into the room slowly and spoke first to Kate and then to Astrid. "But we'd like to try."

"If you'd let us," Maddy said to Kate and Astrid, copying Katherine. "We'd like to get to know you and you know us. Tell you about your parents."

Katherine stepped toward them. "A grandparent's love is supposed to be unconditional, just as a parent's love is. I forgot that."

Maddy stepped alongside her. "We both did. You should know—" She glanced at Katherine, who nodded. "We've been friends, good friends, and best friends since we were eight years old, since 1953. We're so sorry."

"Please forgive us and give us a chance to make it up to you both. Skin color should never have mattered. Blood does, our blood, your blood," Katherine added.

Kate stared at them. Friends? Best friends? She'd had no idea. Wow! Her eyes were opened all the way now. Friends since 1953? It had to be in secret, just like the elderly ladies she met on the train. She smiled inside. But what happened? Why did it end? How did a friendship that endured and crossed racial lines turn so bitter? Was it Maddy's affair with Jackson, or was it more than that? She had to know, but not now. She looked up at Astrid. Her sister watched her. Astrid needed her more than they did and Kate needed to be with her too. They lost a great deal of time together. The grandmothers had to be put on the backburners for now. They would have to wait.

Katherine spoke again, "I'm a stubborn, old, proud Southern woman and I've never asked anyone for anything. Until now. I'd like to start new with you and your sister, if you'd both let me. I'd like to get to know both of you again. Just the way you are."

"We're both stubborn and proud, but we both want to do whatever we can to know Astrid and you again, if you'd let us do so," Maddy added. "We were wrong."

"Horribly wrong," Katherine echoed. "Inexcusable."

Kate examined their faces, their eyes. They both appeared older than she remembered. She had forgiven them already, but she had to know. "Do you mean that? No lies, Grandmother? Maddy? I won't put up with them anymore. Not a one. You took away a part of me, of my life. You took away Astrid's life. Another lie from either of you and you'll never see me again."

"No more lies," Maddy said.

"None," Katherine said. "I think we've told enough lies and hurt you both enough." She took a step toward them. "I want you—we want you—Maddy and I want, both of you to come home," Katherine said.

Astrid glanced at Kate and Julia then back at Kate. "Is that what you want, Kate?"

"Right now, I want what you want, Astrid. No one can make you do anything. The choice is yours. I'll back whatever you decide," Kate said. "Perhaps, in time, you'll want to."

"We'll see," Astrid said, not even looking at them, her gaze on Kate.

"That's fine," Maddy said.

"That's more than we expected," Katherine said. "Of course, whatever it takes, no matter how long."

"Whatever it takes," Maddy added.

"Fine then. I'll stay for a while and we'll get to know each other," Kate told Astrid. She saw the two grandmothers share a look. She owed them nothing and they didn't need her. Astrid did.

"You're—not coming home then?" Katherine said.

"No, Gran, not yet. Astrid and I need to spend some time together."

"Of course you do," Maddy said.

"Of course," Katherine echoed.

Kate eyed the women, her family, and Julia. "Do ya'll mind leaving Katherine and I alone for a few minutes?" She noticed her grandmother flinch at the use of her Christian name over the title of Grandmother.

"No, of course not," Maddy said. She and Katherine exchanged a glance.

Astrid nodded and led the way outside with Julia. Maddy was the last to exit and gave a last glance over her shoulder at Kate.

Kate placed clasped hands on her lap and faced her. "Grandmother—"

Katherine held up her hands as if to calm Kate. "Now, darling, I know what you're going to say. I'm sorry, darling. I should have told you everything. I shouldn't have hidden anything from you. I should have been there for your parents. I'm so sorry, darling. I will do anything to make it right for you and your sister."

Kate heard the trepidation in her grandmother's voice. "No lies, Gran. That's all I want now."

"No lies. I swear."

"Tell me something, Gran. I have two questions for you and I want the truth."

"Of course, darling. Anything."

"Is it true?" Kate swallowed hard. "Is it true that the four of you—Jackson, you, Maddy, and George—conspired together? That none of you wanted me or my sister because our mother was Black, our father was White, and we were of mixed race?"

Katherine shook her head. "Oh, darling, that was a long time ago—"

"The truth, Grandmother," Kate demanded and left no room for doubt.

Katherine brought up her hands and clasped them across her chest. Kate saw her green eyes darken. Katherine looked away and down and, when she finally spoke, Kate heard sorrow. "Yes. It was. I'm so sorry, my darling, but we were wrong, so very wrong—"

Kate cut her off. "Lincoln—is he—" She coughed to clear her throat. "Is he my grandfather?"

"No, darling. He isn't. He thought he was. I let him believe so. But no, he isn't. I swear it."

"But you did have an affair with him?"

Katherine averted her glance for a moment and then their eyes met. "Yes. I did. Darling, I want to explain—"

"No, Grandmother. It isn't necessary. If he isn't my grandfather, it doesn't matter. It isn't any of my business. I have no fond memories of Jackson, so I can understand. We both know he didn't love me and we both know why." Kate heard her sigh and looked for a reaction.

Katherine reached out for her hand. "Oh, darling, I'm so sorry. I never wanted you to know any of that."

"It doesn't matter anymore. It's fine." Kate took her hand and held it. "I never doubted your love and I'll always treasure that. In the end, I just can't remain angry with you. I love you, Gran. Maybe later on, I'll want to hear the rest, all of it, but not now. Right now, I want to move on. I forgive you, but I can't forget, but I don't want to hear anymore right now."

"I understand. Jackson was a fool. We all were so foolish. I will make this right for the both of you. I promise."

Kate studied her. The admission gave her a sense of relief, more than she thought it would. She couldn't do anything but believe her. "I love you very much, Grandmother, but if you ever lie to me again, I will leave home and never return. I mean it."

"I understand, Kate. No more lies. I swear it, but you will come home? Soon?"

"Yes, after, but my sister and I need time to get to know one another."

"Of course you do. Do you know when?"

"I don't know."

Kate watched her. She'd never seen her grandmother this amiable, so giving with anyone else. True, her grandmother always gave her anything she wanted. This was more. She knew it. Katherine was ripped apart by all that had happened, as Kate was. She could feel her grandmother's anxiety as it filled the room around her. She could almost smell the fear that filled the older woman because it filled her as well. Her grandmother was frightened, truly frightened that Kate would leave her. And Kate might, if there was another lie, but for now she wouldn't, couldn't, do that. Katherine meant home and stability. Only time would tell. Only God knew the future.

Suddenly the tension at hand was seared through by an unfamiliar voice.

"Who is ready to go home?" the nurse asked as she entered the room. She held a clipboard in one hand.

Astrid, Julia and Maddy came in just behind her.

Kate faced her. The lady had beautiful light skin, was rounded, and could have passed for being White. Kate studied her and noticed Astrid did the same. Kate wondered if Astrid thought the same thing. Had their mother lived today, would she look anything like this woman did?

The woman was about fifty, with short cropped black hair that framed her gentle olive face. She had high cheekbones, a full mouth, and a cheerful disposition.

"I am," Kate said and released her grip on her grandmother.

"Fine. We'll go over some things and get you on your way," the nurse said.

"That'll be fine," Kate said. She couldn't wait to get out of the hospital.

The woman held the clipboard in her hand and went over instructions and questions. Ten minutes later, she handed Kate the clipboard, to review and sign, and gave her a copy of the paperwork.

"You must be her grandmothers," the nurse said. "You've been here the entire time. Ya'll have a safe trip back home now."

"Ma'am, excuse me, but you're not from NYC, are you?" Kate asked her.

"Oh, lord no, honey. Mississippi born and bred. Moved here to be near my children. And where might you be from? Not from here either, from what I hear."

"No, ma'am. Mississippi too. Thayersville."

"Thayersville, of course. Honey, I'm from Grenada." The woman's eyes brightened. "I love Thayersville. I stop there and in Yazoo every time I drive into Jackson or Madison. I love the barbeque and little shops."

"Yes, ma'am. Me, too," Kate said.

"Well, it just goes to show what a small world we have. Ya'll have a safe trip home and give my regards to old Mississippi. God Bless you, honey."

"Yes, ma'am. Thank you, ma'am."

"I'll be back in a jiff with a wheel chair and we'll get you on your way." The woman disappeared as quickly as she had appeared.

ഏന്ദ

Outside in the hall, Astrid turned away.

"You can go back with Kate, if you want. I don't mind," Julia said.

"To Mississippi? Not a chance. Why would I want to do that?" Astrid said.

"This is what you wanted. To find your family."

"Yes, a family that wants me."

"From what it sounded like, both your grandmothers want you both to come home," Julia reminded her.

"For Kate." Astrid said.

"No, for you," Julia said.

Astrid turned away. "No. Not now. I can't."

"Then we'll wait," Julia, said.

"For as long as it takes," Kate said as she joined them. The nurse wheeled her out of the room in time for her to overhear the last part of their conversation. "I'm staying. For a while, anyway, just like I said. I'd like you to go back with me someday, but it is up to you when and if you want."

She reached out to Astrid and they took each other's hand. Never before had Kate felt so free and happy with her life. Now that she knew exactly who she was, she could only hope that her sister felt the same, at least a little.

THE END.

About the Author

S. J. Francis is a freelance writer with over three hundred publication credits, a University Lecturer with Doctorates in English literature, Mass Communications, and Law, and most recently, a novelist. Francis writes for many publications, as well as regularly contributing to the local newspaper. Francis' background also encompasses working as a television producer. A frequent traveler, Francis has resided in thirteen states and three countries. A confirmed bibliophile, when not writing Francis can be found reading a good book, or spending time in the outdoors. Francis currently lives in Mississippi, where a major part of *Shattered Lies* takes place, but grew up in New York City where the latter portion occurs. Francis has a great respect and fondness for both places and considers the world a notebook full of endless ideas. The family dynamic is a never ending source of ideas and *Shattered Lies* is no exception. As in all the stories Francis writes, in the end, it's all about family. Future projects include a sequel to *Shattered Lies* and a novel about the dynamic relationships in Hollywood.

Connect with Francis at http://sjfranciswriter.com
or at one of four blogs:
http://sjfranciswriter.blogspot.com
http://onefortheanimals.blogspot.com
http://aconsumersview.blogspot.com
http://abookreview4u.blogspot.com
Look for S. J. Francis all over the internet.

48168383R00224

Made in the USA
San Bernardino, CA
18 April 2017